"Walt Becker has written one of the finest first novels I've read in years. *Link* starts with a fascinating premise and moves on to a gripping plot, intriguing characters, and very good writing. The opening scenes actually gave me goose bumps."
Nelson DeMille

"Simply superlative . . . fascinating and exciting . . . frighteningly realistic . . . the best thriller of the year."
*Palo Alto Daily News*

"Exciting . . . Recommended reading for anybody who enjoys intellectual calisthenics."
Paul Harvey, WGN-AM Chicago

"An outstanding adventure novel."
Tony Hillerman

"A read that blends romance, violence, technology, and history into a fast-paced odyssey that never lets up."
Clive Cussler

"Irresistible . . . an amazing tale that brings new life to an old science fiction speculation."
*Tuscaloosa News*

"A Michael Crichton-style adventure tale . . . that evokes suspense and moments of gee-whiz wonder."
*Kirkus Reviews*

# WALT BECKER

# LINK

AVON BOOKS NEW YORK

AVON BOOKS, INC.
*An Imprint of* HarperCollins*Publishers*
10 East 53rd Street
New York, New York 10022-5299

Copyright © 1998 by Walt William Becker
Published by arrangement with the author
Library of Congress Catalog Card Number: 98-24615
ISBN: 0-380-73161-4
**www.harpercollins.com**

Published in hardcover by William Morrow and Company, Inc.; for information address Permissions Department, William Morrow and Company, Inc., 10 East 53rd Street, New York, New York 10022-5299.

First Avon Books Printing: February 2000

AVON TRADEMARK REG. U.S. PAT. OFF. AND IN OTHER COUNTRIES, MARCA REGISTRADA, HECHO EN U.S.A.

Printed in the U.S.A.

WCD  10  9  8  7  6  5  4  3  2  1

To Mom, Dad,
Marcel, and Jennifer

# ACKNOWLEDGMENTS

There are so many people deserving of thanks who have not only championed this story but have gracefully sustained the author with their love, wisdom, and tireless encouragement.

I am grateful to my parents, who have been extraordinarily helpful. Dad, who read and reread the manuscript more times than I care to remember and who always did so with the same enthusiasm. Mom, for all her helpful suggestions and—more important—for the daily prayers that have never failed me for thirty years. My brother, Marcel, who continues to be an inspiration for me. And Jennifer, who has made life so special during this time. I couldn't have done it without you. A big thanks to all my friends, who provided me with a rich source of characters to draw from, who put up with my long absence, and whose repeated phone calls to get me out reassured me that life did exist beyond this novel.

To Gregg Davis, who not only believed in *Link* from day one but has always believed in a storyteller who promised so many big things. Your support and friendship after grad school have made all this possible. To my literary agents, David Vigliano and Alex Smithline, who shepherded the novel through its initial stages, and my Los Angeles agents, Philip Raskind, Ari Greenburg, and everyone at Endeavor.

Thanks to the talented people at William Morrow. Specifically, Paul Fedorko, who has given me this wonderful opportunity; Betty Kelly, whose editing insights and encouragement were so appreciated; and Maria Antifonario, who fielded my questions and concerns. You have all made the rigorous journey of a first-time novelist enjoyable.

Others who have helped shape this manuscript are Ed Stackler, whose supportive nature and intelligent suggestions were invaluable; Dick Marek, whose wisdom made *Link* much stronger; and my friend Bill in the desert.

Lastly, though *Link* is a work of fiction and the views in it are mine, I'm indebted to the men and women whose research provided the scientific matrix for this book. Among them are Arthur Posnansky, Charles Hapgood, Jane B. Sellers, Giorgio de Santillana, Graham Hancock, Robert Bauval, John Anthony West, Maurice Chatelain, Richard Milton, Robert Temple, Malcolm Godwin, and all the others who weren't afraid to ask the tough questions. Their courageous spirit provided the inspiration for the book's main characters, and in seeking the truth, regardless of its implications, they have initiated a paradigm shift that will forever change the way we human beings see our past—and our future.

Truth has usually been found to be a lonely business and has seldom followed the majority.

——MALCOLM GODWIN

The Nephilim were on the earth in those days——
and also afterward——
when the sons of God went to the daughters of men
and had children by them.
They were the heroes of old, men of renown.

——GENESIS 6:4

# PART ONE

# MALI

Samantha Colby paused on her way back to the tent.

Strange, she thought. She'd hardly slowed down since her team landed on the remote airstrip outside of Mopti five days before. In the rush to set up camp and plot the excavation site, Samantha had run herself ragged.

Now, she could barely get her feet to move. Maybe it was the way the setting sun bathed the rugged plains of southern Mali in golden light. Or maybe it was the smell. She took a deep breath. It had to be the smell. There wasn't anything like it in the crowded metropolis she called home for much of the year. This was distinct to central Africa—a mixture of scrub grass and lowland trees, of animals that ate, gave birth, and ran free on the open land.

She let down her hair and shook out the accumulation of fine dust that coated everything, from the expedition's sonar sensing equipment and laptop computers to her lace bra. Samantha let water from her canteen wash through her hair, then pulled the long strands from her face, revealing the blue eyes that had enraptured many a fellow Princeton scholar. She had become acutely aware of the effect her eyes could have when a few of the native Dogon men she hired for this dig also stopped to catch a glance. For the Dogons, Samantha's dominant social position among her peers heightened her allure. To them, a woman who could command such a presence among her white male counterparts had to possess some "good magic."

She called out to them. Her limited knowledge of the Dogon language made for rough going at times, but she had developed a vocabulary of important words that enabled her to carry out her work fast and efficiently. The men picked up their baskets of dry dirt and continued down from the site.

Samantha knew the Dogons thought her a considerate and honest employer, but they still seemed to fear her. The Dogons called her *Awa Zantu*. With a little prodding she learned that *Awa* loosely translates as "fiery" and *Zantu* was the Dogon name for a small, ferocious badger that lived in the African dirt. While the name wasn't exactly flattering, Samantha didn't really mind. In fact, she liked it.

"Sam!"

Ricardo Olivarez ran up the grassy hill, nearly tripping on a sifter used to comb for fine bones and bits of pottery. Samantha held back a grin. She'd known the portly, clumsy, lovable Ricardo for eight years, first through the Internet, then personally, when he joined her at Princeton after earning his most recent doctorate at MIT.

At forty-four, he was one of those degree hoppers Samantha always envied. A certifiable genius, Ricardo would study something, master it, and move on to the next discipline, making life miserable for classmates who found just one doctorate an overwhelming challenge. A physicist, a medical doctor, and a respected paleoanthropologist—it amazed her that a man with such a great mind could still find so many ways to fry it on late nights with friends. Still, she knew if there was anyone she trusted in this world it was Ricardo.

"I think we found something," Ricardo said, eyes gleaming. He got his breath back. "A small opening."

"Leading to another system?"

Goose bumps stippled her forearms. Samantha had

thought—hoped—they might find another chamber in the excavated cave, one that would allow them to go deeper without having to blast through the volcanic stone permeating its lower strata. She felt a new surge of energy and turned back toward the site.

"I think so."

"It would save us a helluva lot of work."

"Maybe get us out of here faster, huh?"

Samantha smiled. Ricardo had already been struck with a bad case of safari gut, just like on their last trip to Mali. No matter how much of the pink stuff he packed, or how many shots he got, he always seemed to fall victim.

"I see the irony of my situation isn't wasted on you," Ricardo said. "A refugee from the country that invented Montezuma's revenge, I know—"

"Has anyone been through?" Samantha asked, cutting him off. She loved being first.

"Doesn't look like it."

Butterflies tickled her abdomen. "Let's do it."

The back of the cavern was dim and foreboding. The cave's natural humidity seemed to be enhanced by the perspiring workers who were clearing the excavated dirt and rock. A crowd of Dogons spoke excitedly about the hole. Samantha brushed past them. She clicked on her helmet light without even pausing to let her eyes adjust to the cavern's darker reaches.

Show time, she thought.

Ever since deciding on paleoanthropology as a career, her favorite part of "playing in the dirt," as her father dubbed her job, was when she stepped into the unknown.

A picture of the late Mary Leakey on a dig on the shore of Lake Turkana had started it all. The image of that independent woman, caked with dust and standing by her great discovery of the Turkana Boy fossil, had inspired Samantha to pursue a discipline where the great names were just being made. Paleoanthropology—the young science, the open science—was inhabited by die-hard souls who searched for the keys to human history. They sought bones, ancient prehuman bones. And Samantha had always dreamed of finding something that would be a milestone in her field, guaranteeing her a place in the world of science—in the world of men.

The fissure was even tighter than she imagined.

"Don't touch anything," she yelled at Ricardo, who followed her.

Samantha shimmied through the tight space headfirst. Ricardo followed shortly with more lamps and a small vinyl bag full of picks and brushes—but only after widening the hole several more inches.

"So I'm retaining a little water," he told her sheepishly.

She didn't answer. Samantha shook her head before turning her attention to the cavern wall. "What do we have here?" She widened her headlamp's beam to illuminate more of the chamber. The cavern ceiling hung twelve feet above them and continued for twenty yards before the rumpled rock surface tapered toward the floor at a steep angle. Samantha could just see the back of the cave, where it terminated in an impassable fissure only a few inches wide.

"Did you bring my recorder?" she asked.

Ricardo handed her a small micro-cassette recorder.

"*Gracias.*" Samantha pressed record. "March eighth, 1998. Day six. Have discovered opening to another chamber in the cave system."

Dust particles flowed through the beam of her headlamp. The yellow light bobbed first on the floor, then up toward the back wall.

"Looks like the smaller cave's the result of a sinking water table. Signs of volcanic activity. Similar to larger cavern. Looks like a completely undisturbed environment."

"This is good. This is real good," Ricardo muttered.

Samantha knew this smaller cavern might mean better

preserved fossils. A dig site untouched by the human
and animal inhabitants of the last thousand years—not
to mention the picks of other paleoanthropologists.

"Should we start gridding?" Ricardo asked.

"Yeah," Samantha said. "But I don't want more than
a half-dozen people down here at any one time. Ask
Twana to pick two of his best."

"You got it."

Ricardo left to get the stakes and rope they needed to
systematically map the chamber.

Twana was a high-ranking Dogon whom Samantha
appointed as her foreman. Some of the Dogons, especially the younger ones, were careless with the delicate
pieces of bone and flint tools they had found. They
didn't seem to understand why any of it was important.
But Twana was absolutely meticulous.

Samantha brushed away the volcanic ash of a small
area in front of her. She knew they'd have to dig at least
a few inches through the accumulated dust of thousands
of years, but she couldn't hold herself back. Beneath her
might lie the prize she sought—ancient hominid remains
that could answer the question of humankind's origins.
She wanted that treasure desperately. Her career couldn't
support any more failures.

She tried to convince herself that her overbearing family could all go to hell, but in the deeper reaches of her
soul she wanted more than anything to make them proud
of her. She couldn't help it if she wasn't the star quar-
terback, or the canny politician, or even the famous
opera singer her hard-line father wanted her to be. There
had been a few problems with those vocations: One, she
was born a girl. Two, she hated politics. Three, she
couldn't sing. Not even in the shower. As an only child,
it upset her that her mother was unable to have more
children after her complicated birth. She'd never really
forgiven herself for that. She knew her father hadn't.

*     *     *

They were halfway through laying the thirty-eight grid sections that would make up the floor of the cave when a thundering rumble took them by surprise. Dust engulfed the crew. The back wall of the newly opened cavern gave way, and a ton of dried mud and stone came crashing down.

One of the terrified Dogons tried frantically to squeeze back through the entrance. Samantha grabbed his arm, forcing him to stay. "It's all right," she told him. "Happens all the time." She took a verbal head count and heard all five voices call out from various parts of the cave.

She crawled toward the crumbled slope, squinting as more of the dust settled. She brushed the hair from her brow, then spoke into her recorder:

"Collapse of the back northwest corner of cavern two. Uncovering newer volcanic sediments beneath substratum five."

Her headlamp lit the back wall, and she gasped. A lump formed in her throat. In the pale yellow light she noticed a reflection. A few feet above the floor, imbedded in the volcanic ash that made up the cavern face, she thought she saw what might be a group of bones.

"I need some wedges," she said. "Now!"

Ricardo carefully brushed away the loose ash to make sure they placed the wedges correctly. They had to clear a two-inch shelf of packed soil before the cave wall could fully reveal its secret. Ricardo tapped gently at the steel wedges, and the last shelf of compacted ash slipped from the wall, creating another small wave of dust. Six headlamps lit the area, and the excited murmuring began.

*Bones*. Samantha felt like she could faint. Her breathing got shallow.

"Looks like a rib cage! The whole skeleton could be intact," she said into the micro-cassette recorder.

Ricardo moved closer. "Can you see a skull?!"

Samantha began to make out something that just

couldn't be. She waved a cloud of dust away with her trembling hand before everything became clear. She froze.

The crew's excited chatter suddenly ceased. The sound of Samantha's recorder hitting the ground echoed through the chamber.

"Oh my god," she whispered.

# ECUADOR

Dr. Jack Austin paced back and forth, avoiding a muddy portion of the clearing where he had trampled the grass during his last lecture. He enjoyed teaching outside, despite the fervid humidity that darkened patches of his khaki shirt. A paleoanthropologist belonged outside, in the dirt, he always told his classes. If one had a proclivity for cleanliness, they had chosen the wrong career. You couldn't gather clues about the origins of man inside a sterile laboratory.

A dozen sweaty grad students were perched on blankets or backpacks in the thick jungle grass. He could always tell who was with him at a particular point in the lecture, and for the most part, this class was eager and attentive. Many of the students had flown thousands of miles to study the ancient ruins outside of Cuenca. Jack was glad they had. The small fees he received from the Universidad de Ecuador for his summer field sessions managed to keep him going for the rest of the year. It fell far short of his previous salary, but it kept him teaching.

Today's lecture dealt with the possible existence of a long-forgotten piece of technology—a device that harbored an endless source of energy—a machine the ancients said harnessed the power of the sun. The notion persisted in a variety of myths and legends. But Jack believed *The Source* to be more than just myth. He believed that somewhere along the line, the human race had lost a wonderful technology—a treasure technically superior to anything in contemporary science.

"C'mon, Dr. Austin. Don't you think that's a bit absurd?" asked Gary, a bespectacled NYU doctoral candidate in a tie-dyed shirt and Birkenstocks.

Jack didn't like Gary, but at least the young man had the *cojones* to contradict what he was saying. Jack recalled how annoyed he used to get after an hour and a half of lecturing at the University of California. Not because his students were disruptive, or even uninterested, but because the class often passed without one question. Not one question! They must be afraid to speak out, he'd initially thought, although they certainly found their voices after grades were posted. Jack was saddened by those who refused to question science—to challenge it. Which is why he appreciated Gary's assertion, even though it contested his own ideas.

"I do think it's a bit absurd," Jack said. "But not more absurd than the current school of thought. In fact, the sheer absurdity of the current view forced me to posit my 'slightly less absurd' hypothesis."

A few of the other students chuckled. They didn't seem to care much for Gary's personality either.

"We've been taught that humankind is at the apex of civilization at the present time," Jack continued. "That we've been evolving from the ignorance of our ancestors and their humble roots as hunters and gatherers. But to me, that's an arrogant view. Many clues challenge us to accept the idea that at one time civilization was as advanced as ours today. At the very least, these anomalies suggest that our predecessors could have had access to technology and knowledge with no parallels in what we know today."

Jack took the aluminum pointer out of his pocket and extended it to full length. "Let's get a little cozier, shall we?"

The students stood. Jack led them toward a group of immense, smooth stones that rose abruptly from the jungle floor, starkly out of place amid the lush vegetation. The sheer size of the temple and the precision with which it was built gave it a disturbingly modern feel. Time had worn down most of the stones, and nature was busy breaking up the blocks, vegetation growing wherever a small crack allowed a seed to germinate.

This was always the most dynamic part of class, and Jack loved it. Studying things in detail, touching the stones, feeling them, made the past come alive. If you sat and listened long enough the ruins would sing answers.

"How much do you think this block weighs?" Jack asked, pointing to the immense cornerstone.

"A hundred tons?" Gary, as usual, was the first to answer.

"Ah, you've read the text. That's great. But does anyone have any ideas on how the people who built the Cuencan temples moved these? Or, for that matter, how the builders of Baalbek in Lebanon managed to lay foundation stones that are as tall as five-story buildings and weigh over *six* hundred tons?"

The class remained silent. Jack paced again, enjoying the students' bafflement.

"How about the Abu Simbel statues in Egypt? When an international task force of the world's finest engineers was commissioned to save them before the completion of the Aswan High Dam, they decided the only possible way to move them was to cut them into small sections and reassemble them on higher ground. Yet the original builders quarried the rock from a source miles away and moved it in one piece. . . ."

Jack twirled the pointer in his hand. He could see a few desperately search for answers before giving up.

"Well, don't worry. You're not alone," Jack said. "No engineer on the face of the earth has been able to answer those questions. And thousands have tried."

"Are you saying that it's physically impossible to move these blocks as whole pieces?" The pretty brunette from Amsterdam spoke in a thick accent.

"Impossible with today's technology. Perhaps not impossible in the future."

Gary again: "Dr. Austin. With all due respect. It has to be possible. I mean someone cut and placed these stones thousands of years ago. The people who built these temples sure knew it was plausible, right?"

Jack smiled. *Like lambs to the slaughter . . .*

"Absolutely right. Thousands of years ago, ancient man did build these temples. And moved these megalithic stones. So, yes, it must be possible. Which led me to deduce one of two things—that our ancient forefathers, who supposedly hadn't discovered the combustion engine, or hydraulics, or nuclear fusion, or even how to work heavy metals, prayed for—and got—a bloody miracle . . ." He paused to take a deep breath. The class was silent, waiting for his finishing words.

". . . Or they had help."

# RICARDO

Ricardo hated helicopters. Two of his colleagues had perished in the ungainly steel contraptions, and this particular one didn't look like the poster craft for aviation safety. He guessed it was an early model Huey. He could smell the engine's inefficient burning of fuel, and the whump of the rotors seemed especially loud. It didn't help that the machine lacked anything resembling a door. Still, on such short notice he couldn't be picky. In his long journey from Mali, Ricardo had fearfully boarded two small planes and an aging 767 before landing at the national airport in Ecuador. Only the adrenaline rush of the last forty-eight hours had gotten him this far. He was then informed that taking a helicopter was the only means of quickly reaching the highlands where Dr. Jack Austin was teaching at the ancient ruins of Cuenca. The roads were nearly impassable after the recent rains.

He wondered what Jack would say when they met. They hadn't seen each other in nearly six years, not since Jack was summarily fired from the University of California at Berkeley. Jack never seemed to get along well with authority. And the authority, in this case, were the Regents of California. Most of his colleagues regretted Jack's firing, but even Ricardo and Samantha had had doubts about his absurd theories. But Jack was never one to back down. And he was willing to make an ass of himself—a rare trait for a person of science.

The emphasis at today's universities was to do extremely careful research, then more of the same. A scientist's worst nightmare was to publish, then be subsequently snuffed by the critics—often close colleagues who eagerly pounced on new ideas. Jack had gone through hell after publishing his ideas about *The Source*, and how such an advanced piece of technology could have been present before the beginning of recorded history.

Even in the world of paleoanthropology, which had its share of hasty claims about a new missing link, or wild theories of a new species of hominid, the climate encouraged caution at every step. But Jack just didn't seem to care.

One person who did was Samantha. She, along with the rest of her colleagues in anthropology, had renounced Jack's bizarre paper and his methods. Ricardo shuddered, remembering Jack and Samantha's painful split. The lovers had been inseparable at one point. In walking a tightwire of support for both friends, Ricardo found only hurt and regret. Even after all the years, he had no doubts that the mere mention of Samantha's name would be enough to keep Jack from returning to Mali. But they needed him. He would keep quiet for now. Jack was the one man who could make sense of their unimaginable discovery.

"Señor." The pilot pointed toward the lush mountain growing larger before them, shrouded in mist. Through a break in the clouds, Ricardo got his first glimpse of the temples of Cuenca.

Jack watched the chopper descend, its rotors creating ripples in the puddles on the ground. A few students chased lecture notes that started blowing away from the site. Some balled their fists and extended their middle fingers.

Jack held on to his Cal baseball cap and marched angrily up the worn stone stairs leading toward the chopper, whose skids were now bouncing on the stone. What idiot would attempt a landing here? Jack's eyes watered in the rotor wash. He cleared the last step and jogged toward the dilapidated vehicle. What a piece of crap, he thought. *Who the hell . . .*

The plump Latino face in front of him was smiling above open arms.

"Ricardo Olivarez," Jack finally managed to say.

It had been a long time.


The students watched from the bottom of the stairs as the man grabbed Dr. Austin in a bear hug. A few of them contemplated rushing to his aid before it became clear that the two men knew each other. The men shouted back and forth, but it was impossible to hear over the din of the chopper. The entire class watched as Dr. Austin became infected with the same frantic vibe his large friend emoted. Then Dr. Austin stood completely still. His arms dropped to his sides. He didn't seem to notice as his Cal baseball hat flew off his head and down the stairs into a pool of mud at the base of the temple. Whatever was being said must be important, they thought. Dr. Austin loved that cap.


In seconds, Jack digested what his friend had come to say. His legs felt weak as he stumbled down the stairs back to his astonished class. Jack simply picked up his backpack. He realized that he had blanked on everybody's name, his mind now conjecturing wildly about Mali. He checked his pack. It held his eyeglasses, a plastic Evian bottle, his field notebook, and various paleoanthropologic tools. He lacked toiletries, but he did have his wallet and passport. He cinched up the bag and turned toward the helicopter.

The class looked on in shock.

Gary marshaled some courage. "Hey, where are you going? It's only two-thirty!"

Jack started up the temple stairs. He yelled over his shoulder without breaking stride: "Class dismissed!"

# REUNION

"You hanging in there?"

Ricardo managed a nod before leaning his head into a small plastic bag. Poor guy, Jack thought. Ricardo had been evolving through shades of green ever since they boarded the worn Cessna in Bamako. The small plane ricocheted like a pachinko ball in the turbulent uprisings of warm savanna air.

"I always thought it was helicopters you hated," Jack said after Ricardo blew his nose.

"It was . . . until I hopped inside this sorry shitcan."

Jack silently agreed. The plane was making the rickety chopper ride in Ecuador seem like a pleasure cruise. Compared to the 747 wide-body that had whisked them over the Atlantic, the diminutive aircraft felt like a spastic gnat. The North African pilot at the controls didn't help matters. The Cessna wasn't flying, it was at war. Jack decided that the man was either not certified, or certifiably crazy.

It had been thirty-two hours since Ricardo had shown up at Cuenca. Jack reviewed his notes on Mali and his two previous expeditions there—trying not to heed the growing anticipation that welled within him. His first trip, a dig in the south, yielded nothing of scientific worth, other than adding to the fossil record a buffalo species of the last glacial period. While those bones would have made many a paleontologist happy, they weren't the bones Jack was interested in.

His second trip to Mali bore much more directly on his true passion, searching for clues to the origins of man. As a paleoanthropologist, only one genus held his interest: *Homo*. The study of human beings included that of our most distant direct ancestors, *Australopithecus afarensis*—admittedly an ape, but one that walked on two legs—and *Homo habilis*, toolmakers and the earliest species to earn the genus *Homo*.

Then came the great *Homo erectus*, shockingly human-looking, but clearly not human in the modern sense of the word. They emerged about 1.7 million years ago and showed evolutionary progress until 300,000 years ago, when they disappeared. They had used much more sophisticated tools than *H. habilis*, and their brain capacity grew to a maximum of about half that of modern humans. The best known erectine was probably "Turkana Boy," a ten-year-old found by the Leakeys hundreds of miles east of Mali in Kenya in 1971. This discovery had initially prompted Jack, like many other scholars of his generation, to take up paleoanthropology.

Ricardo heaved, unleashing a splatter of unintelligible grunts and groans into the barf bag. Jack couldn't help thinking this must have been what *Homo sapiens neanderthalensis*—the quite recent species with the thick brow ridges and short muscular frame—sounded like. The Neanderthals had a larger brain case than most modern humans, but they did not appear to have full language skills. In fact, *Homo sapiens* bore a closer genetic resemblance to chimpanzees than to the distinct, dead-end Neanderthal species. Modern humankind may have been to blame for the Neanderthals disappearance, as the latest evidence suggested that the two species actually coexisted for thousands of years. No one was certain, however, because even when hard facts were unearthed, interpretation of those facts differed widely. Hard science this was not, and that's exactly why Jack savored it. He loved the uncertainty. For him, the last great frontier wasn't space. It wasn't even the ocean. *The last great frontier was understanding our past.*

At the heart of paleoanthropology lay the most profound question of our time: How did our species come to dominate Earth? Most anthropologists believed that one or two million years ago, tribes of thick-skulled *Homo erectus* started to migrate from Africa, eventually settling in the Middle East, Europe, and Asia. Most also agreed that by about 30,000 B.C. the only hominids left on the planet were fully modern humans known as *Homo sapiens*. The as yet unanswerable question is what happened in the mysterious millennia in between.

For Jack, the specific mystery was how our species appeared overnight—without any decisive link. *Homo sapiens* didn't grow smoothly from *Homo erectus*. Something radical had to have happened—and all in the blink of an evolutionary eye. *Homo sapiens* was almost a foot taller and had a pronounced chin. The cranium rose to its greatest height above the ears, unlike that of *erectus*, and lacked massive ridges on the forehead. *Sapiens'* teeth were amazingly delicate, as was the entire bone structure for its height. We were born bigheaded and for a long period of time were helpless, with a skull barely five millimeters thin—not at all like our thick-skulled ancestors. And then there were the defining characteristics of intelligence, self-awareness, culture, and spirituality—traits *Homo sapiens* embodied unlike any other predecessor. Plainly put, an enormous remodeling job had taken place—a fairy tale transition from pumpkin to golden coach—in the equivalent of an evolutionary millisecond.

Why? Jack wondered. And more important, how?

He hoped his knowledge of human myth and his understanding of the technological accomplishments of the ancients might help answer those questions and the others that haunted him. How had super humans emerged from slow-witted ancestors to forever change the world? Why the literal explosion of civilization in such an infinitesimally small period of time? To what did the human race owe its superior intellect? Jack had vowed to make a life finding out.

# THE DOGONS

The small plane began to climb and passed through a few scattered clouds. Jack saw a substantial mountain range beneath them and knew they must be close. Nestled among the rolling Mali plains just beyond the divide was the homeland of the Dogon people. Jack had taken his second trip to Mali solely to study the warrior tribe. He believed a clue to his newly emerging theories lay within this strange culture.

He had spent the better part of a year with the tribe and become a close friend of Xwabatu, the tribe's spiritual leader, who taught Jack the myths that remained unchanged since the birth of the great clan thousands of years ago. Part of those myths contained scientific information about the stars that baffled today's researchers. For instance, they knew that a dense star—what Western astronomers call a white dwarf—circled Sirius every 49.9 years. They named this star Po Tolo, and even knew its exact density. But how? How could the primitive Dogons have known this, when Alvan Clark only discovered Po Tolo in 1862 with a high-powered telescope? Furthermore, Western science hadn't learned of the star's extreme density until 1915. This tribe also knew about the satellites of Jupiter and even that Saturn had rings. But where did they get all this data?

The Dogons had gathered this information without any advanced scientific equipment. They had never possessed a simple telescope, yet the clan had passed the knowledge down from generation to generation over the millennia. Most researchers chose to relegate this fact to the bin of "unaccountable" anomalies. Jack could not— so he studied the tribe at length. Most considered him an expert on Dogon culture.

Spying the terrain beneath them, Jack leaned forward and tapped the pilot on the shoulder. "Where's the landing strip?"

The man laughed and pointed below to what appeared to be a small dirt road in between two steep ridges.

"No. He asked where the landing strip is," Ricardo added.

This time the pilot responded by banking the small Cessna into a steep dive. Jack grabbed the frame to keep from sliding into the Plexiglas window. He shot a quick look at Ricardo, who was ghost white.

"Good-bye, my friend," Ricardo managed between Hail Marys. He put his head between his arms and continued to pray. Jack struggled through the descent, convincing himself he wasn't afraid. A few moments later, however, Jack found himself mouthing the Lord's Prayer in Spanish, trying to keep up with his frantic Mexican colleague.

It took a few seconds before Jack realized the plane was still intact. The dust slowly cleared. The pilot chuckled to himself and taxied the Cessna back toward a small dirt clearing. Jack felt a glimmer of respect for the deranged maniac sitting in front of him.

The engine finally shut down in a cloud of smoke. The plane had stopped next to a thatch hut that served as fuel depot, baggage claim, and air traffic control.

The door didn't want to open, but Jack finally kicked it free and gradually got his feet back onto the blessed ground. He helped Ricardo, limp and trembling, spill out of the plane. A dozen scrawny chickens clucked around their ankles. Jack watched as a few ebony women collected water from a deep well. Some carried a bundle of sleeping infant tucked in the crook of their smooth black arms. He recognized a few words—the women spoke in their native Dogon, not French. Jack rolled up his sleeves, a quick concession to the intense dry heat. Where the hell was his baseball cap, he wondered?

"Sorry," Ricardo said.

"For what?"

Jack followed Ricardo's eyes to his own boots, which were covered with a thin orange slime. An inquisitive chicken pecked at the goo.

"Oh great."

Ricardo took a handkerchief out of his back pocket and dropped it on Jack's left foot. Jack shook his head. Ricardo could only muster a shrug. As he started cleaning Ricardo's breakfast off his boots, the strong grassy aroma of the nearby plains overpowered the sour smell of stomach. Jack paused. He inhaled deeply and closed his eyes. Only the sweet scent of Africa now.

He was back.

Jack took a few seconds to look over the shoddy excuse for an airstrip. The blatant poverty of Mali always shocked him. Once a colonial territory of the French, the small republic was one of the poorest nations in the world. Barely fifteen percent of its population was literate, and the life expectancy at birth for most of these people was only forty-four. Jack shook his head. These noble people struggled endlessly, always keeping their dignity. And for what? To live a half life. It didn't seem fair.

He and Ricardo paused under the forgiving shade of the hut for only a moment before Jack noticed two beat-up Land Rovers being filled with petrol from a large forty-gallon barrel. Propped on the dashboard of the Rover facing them, a large placard showed the name: DR. AUSTIN. Jack started across the dirt field to the two vehicles, followed by Ricardo. A figure stood behind the sign.

"I'm Dr. Austin," he said.

The figure stepped forward. Jack stopped cold.

"No way. Not a chance!" He pivoted and started back toward the plane.

Samantha shut the Rover door and started after him. "Jack, please! Just listen to me for one second!"

Jack heard her but didn't slow. He closed quickly on the Cessna, ready to make its return trip to Bamako. He passed a doubled-over Ricardo, who had just finished getting sick again.

"You're dead," Jack told him.

"Wait . . . Jack . . . I can explain. . . ."

"*Your* dig?" he grunted.

She broke into a half-jog. "Jack, you lived with the Dogon. They trust you. I can't tell you how much you're needed here. For godsake, please don't make me beg."

Jack threw his bag onto the plane, then grabbed the wing strut and pulled himself up.

"Damnit, Jack," Samantha screamed. "We just measured the cranium at twenty-one hundred cubic centimeters!"

Jack froze. A chill ran through his spine. His grasp loosened, and his leg slowly felt for the earth beneath him.

# THE FIND

The two-hour ride to the site was mostly silent, only the hum of the engine and the grinding of a worn clutch. Jack had thrown his gear back in the Rover and remained silent. Samantha tried to talk to him for a few minutes as the Rovers left the airstrip, but Jack made it clear that he needed some time to himself. After they passed a few Songhai herdsmen driving their goats to a water hole, she also fell silent. For that Jack was thankful. The past was threatening to overwhelm him.

Jack had fallen for her, right from the beginning. She was only twenty-three, young for most of the graduate students at Princeton, where he was enrolled. He first noticed her studying beside the magnolia bushes in the Humanities square, and whether it was the sweet scent of the blooming magnolias or the way the morning sun caught her light brown hair, he felt instantly drawn to her. He undid his watch and slipped it into his pocket as he approached her . . . so he could ask her for the time. It was in one of those magic first moments—when she looked up from the book with her blue eyes—Jack knew he was finished.

It didn't matter that she couldn't answer his question. She didn't wear a watch. Nor did the awkward silence that followed matter, as Jack simply stared at her. He couldn't recall what he said next, but it must have been stupidly charming because she laughed. He *did* remember the important lab session he skipped so he could get something to eat with her. By the time they had made their way to the coffeehouse and Jack had found out that she was also planning on getting her doctorate in anthropology, he knew he had to have her. Or at least make a complete fool of himself trying.

Jack never considered himself a ladies' man; he found his work much more enjoyable and stimulating than skirt chasing. And he knew from past experience that he tired quickly in relationships. But with Samantha he found something he'd never known before or since. Their union possessed a rare blend of passion and friendship. The two had a special bond, forged from common spiritual beliefs and a love of science. In the second year of their doctoral program together he had proposed. Their engagement was going to last until sometime after they completed their studies. But a year after graduation, things started to sour.

Jack found himself getting angry again and decided not to think about it. Mercifully, after the Rovers crossed the gently flowing Niger River by means of a rope-and-wood bridge, Ricardo sat up from his snooze and pointed to some distant ridges. They were almost there.

Scattered at the base of one of the ridges, just beyond an expanse of Mali prairie, an elaborate system of tents surrounded the site. The number surprised Jack. This was a huge dig by any standards, surely the biggest one Samantha had ever led. The Rover weaved through the maze of canvas and pulled up alongside a large field tent.

In contrast with the primordial African terrain, seven high-tech solar panels collected the sun's energy and transferred it through black cables into the tent. The panels could power quite a few specialized machines, and judging by the setup, Samantha probably had them all— DNA analysis, carbon dating. A few laptops sat outside the tent on an aluminum fold-out table. Jack noted a satellite uplink dish set up behind the tent.

Whoever was bankrolling this thing was definitely not messing around.

"This is big, Samantha. You must be in heaven," Jack intended to think, not say.

"You want a quick tour?"

"I want to see *it*."

Samantha's showing off would have to wait. Jack had done a good job concealing his enthusiasm, but now it was impossible. A cranium that measured over 2100 cc's was larger than anything in the fossil record—even larger than the brain case of the Neanderthals. As he followed her up the gentle slope, all other matters disappeared from his consciousness. She had found in a cavern something that might finally vindicate him.

They approached a rocky overhang, the entrance to a

system of caves on the northeast ridge. Samantha walked Jack and Ricardo by various Dogon workers who paused only briefly to check out the newcomer before dumping their basketfuls of earth. Two white men armed with AK-47 automatic weapons stood up as Samantha approached the roped-off entrance.

"He's fine. Thanks," Samantha said to the taller man.

She lifted the rope and held it for Jack and Ricardo. It took a few moments for Jack's eyes to adjust to the darkness, but by then Samantha had handed him a lighted helmet.

They followed the three bouncing streams of light toward the back of the cave, where Jack noticed a smaller opening. A jagged crevasse tucked behind an outcropping of rock.

"One of our workers uncovered a new cave system while we were excavating the back grids," Samantha said. She went down to her belly and slid through the hole, headfirst.

Ricardo was smiling. He knew what this would mean for Jack and pointed toward the hole. "After you, *amigo*."

"Thanks."

It took Jack only seconds to adjust his broad shoulders to the dimensions of the hole. He squeezed past the tight seam and pulled himself through to the next chamber. It was darker, more confined. Jack adjusted the beam on his headlamp, widening it to fill the black void. Only a trickle of light from the entrance filtered through the small hole behind him. Diffused by dust, the yellow beam illuminated various sections of the walls. A canvas tarp covered the far side, supported by a framework of wood planks.

Jack noticed huge folds of volcanic rock. He studied the darker seams for a few moments. Mount Sikasso, the dormant volcano fifteen miles west of the site, might have been the source, though he couldn't be sure. The volcanic activity in the lower reaches of the cave system could have also resulted from a simple fissure. A molten spring. Probably fairly recent, geologically speaking.

"We dated the volcanic strata between thirty thousand and fifty thousand years ago. It was a baby flow."

Jack shook his head. He and Samantha had always had an uncanny ability to read each other's thoughts.

"We uncovered it in a layer of the same volcanic sediment," Samantha said, helping the rotund Ricardo off the hard, gravel-strewn floor. "It was a gift, Jack. It's totally intact."

She led the two men toward the tarp, just beyond a roped-off section of the cave.

"There's no need to rush to any conclusions, Sam. It's easy to get overexcited."

Jack hadn't meant to sound quite so condescending, but Samantha had that look in her eyes. He knew she was annoyed. His comment dredged up an embarrassment Samantha had suffered during her first field session after becoming "Dr." Colby. In her haste to make a name for herself she had reported the discovery of a well-preserved *Australopithicus afarensis* skull, the bipedal hominid. But Samantha had also found an intact femur, one that contradicted the species' bipedal motion. It was an amazing find, and Samantha basked in the glory of it for almost eighteen months—until another colleague proved that it wasn't a bone of *Australopithicus* at all. It belonged to an unrelated earlier species of ape, of which many remains were subsequently found at the same site. Samantha was stung by her mistake.

"I'm sorry," Jack said, although without much sincerity. "It's just . . . do you have any idea of the implications you're raising?"

Samantha reached for the long canvas tarp and gathered it in her dirty fingers.

"That's just it, Jack. I'm not raising them," she said, "*he* is . . ."

She ripped back the tarp and let it fall to the floor.

Jack had to choke back his response. He felt flushed, and his mouth seemed to dry instantly.

"My God."

All he could do was stare at the perfectly preserved fossil resting in the volcanic ash in front of him. Between the three headlamps the entire form was visible, enough to floor even the most staunch skeptic. Its form was distinctly humanoid, yet not so crude . . . almost angelic.

Jack stared at the skull. "The head," he whispered.

"Larger than *Homo sapiens*," Samantha said. "Too delicate for Neanderthal."

The skull was too big to be human, and judging by the ocular recessions the eyes were larger as well. Jack's fingers gently traced the fully intact bones from the hip, up over the spine. It probably stood somewhere near six and a half feet.

"It's taller than any hominid," Samantha said.

Jack looked on, speechless. He traced one of the curled-up arms and followed it to the hand, where he counted only four digits. Four digits! For a second he thought he would faint.

"The bones are anatomically correct," she said. "This species had only four fingers. No thumb!"

Ricardo put his hand on Jack's shoulder. "I told you, my friend."

"Four digits . . ." Jack whispered.

His mind pored over past research, keeping time with his thumping heart. Suddenly, the cynic and rebel had become a little child again. He asked what seemed like a hundred questions. Have you run DNA? What were the carbon dates? Have you cross-checked them against the sediments? Jack barely gave Samantha enough time to answer before he blurted another question. But still, part of him wouldn't allow him to believe.

He took in the finer intricacies of the figure in front of him and asked the next logical question, "How do you know it's not an undiscovered hominid species?"

The question wasn't belittling at all. Finding another hominid species was an unbelievable dream for any paleoanthropologist. But it would scale back the enormity of the discovery.

"Because we just got the test results back from something else we found. A large object—lying just underneath the left femur."

"An object?" Jack moved closer, immensely intrigued.

"It's made entirely of one element that doesn't exist here."

"In Africa?"

Samantha paused before she slowly said, "On Earth."

# THE OBJECT

Jack's head was spinning. The three bummed cigarettes he had inhaled on the way to the large field tent hadn't helped matters. He must have seemed schizophrenic as he babbled to Samantha the whole way down. What else had they found? Half his brain was occupied in a heated conversation on the ramifications of the find. The other half was engaged in an endless loop—fixed on one word that echoed throughout his mind. Confusing him. Exciting him . . .

*Extraterrestrial.*

He had expected the shock. What he didn't expect were the emotions he now felt, so entirely different from the ones he had imagined himself feeling. Jack had seen this scene in his mind a thousand times—he had always dared to believe. He had based much of his work on the idea that extraterrestrials had visited the planet long ages ago, perhaps sharing technological wonders with the early humans. It was the only theory that could explain so many of the scientific mysteries. One of the only things that made the legends of a *Source* plausible. Strangely, he felt none of the satisfaction he thought he might upon discovering hard evidence of extraterrestrial life. He had no urge to hop on the phone and smugly break the news to the same colleagues who had mocked him. He didn't even feel relief at having been right. All he felt was sheer wonder, a wonder for a world he now felt strangely more connected to.

We weren't alone.

Ricardo looked equally amazed. "When did you get the results back?"

"A day before you returned," Samantha said.

The three scientists passed more heavily armed men at the field lab entrance. One was white, with a scruffy beard of about a week. Samantha had called him Baines. The other two Jack instantly recognized as Zulu from the great Bantu tribe in South Africa. Now all the security made sense. Samantha had always been paranoid about someone disturbing any of her digs. But he couldn't blame her now. Not with something of such incredible magnitude, such sweeping implications.

In fact, he thanked her.

Samantha stopped and looked into his eyes.

"For bringing me in on this one," he said after a few more moments.

His sudden graciousness seemed to take her aback. "Well, I can't say it was completely selfless. I really need you here."

They entered the tent. "You're not going to believe this," she said, unhooking a padlock to a large steel case. The few seconds it took for Samantha to fiddle with the lock felt like hours. Finally the lock slid off. Samantha popped two clasps and slowly raised the lid.

Radiant light danced about a metallic object inside.

Jack's pupils contracted, trying to compensate for the extreme reflection. After a moment, he could see again.

But he didn't trust his eyes.

"Two of the fossil's fingers were still clutching it," Samantha said.

Jack inspected the metallic artifact, but he'd never seen anything that could shine like this. "Have you handled it?" he asked as his hands felt the cold smoothness of it.

"Go ahead, my friend. It's durable"—Ricardo chimed in as Jack pulled the object out of the case—"and heavy!" Ricardo shouted, lunging for the object. Jack had nearly dropped it on the dirt floor.

"I'll say."

They both got control of the piece, and Jack rested the artifact on the table.

The object was an isosceles triangle, about the size of a large platter. It reminded Jack of the pope's miter and was almost the same size. It was about two inches thick. Across the two sides that extended down from the apex of the triangle shone precisely engraved inscriptions that resembled Egyptian hieroglyphs. Jack had no clue what they meant. He didn't inspect them for long though because he found something at the base of the triangle much more interesting. In the exact middle of the triangle's base a dark, semicircular inset radiated from the bottom edge like half of a black sun rising over the horizon. The inset was covered by a thin opaque shield.

"We've analyzed the semicircular casing," said Samantha. "Underneath that crystalline plate, it's pure beryllium." Jack knew there were rich deposits of beryllium in the lowland hills of Mali. It was one of the country's few natural resources.

"The rest is made up entirely of an unknown element. Here. Look at this."

Samantha handed Jack a spectrum analysis of the object. It was a graph. Spikes of various size shot up from the bottom of the chart. These spikes measured various properties such as density and molecular structure. One in particular was circled in red wax pencil.

"It's probably closest to titanium. But we're pretty sure nothing like it exists on this planet," Samantha said.

Jack took this all in. The paper shook gently in his hands as he looked over the unearthly characteristics of the metal.

"Do . . . do you know what this means?" Jack asked, removing his glasses.

"Yeah."

Samantha paused. A smile crept across her face. She knew exactly what it would mean.

"We've just proven the existence of extraterrestrial life," Ricardo said. "Extraterrestrial life . . . *on Earth*."

Jack put his arms around Ricardo, slapping his back. This went beyond words. He held his friend tight. It was apparent to everyone in the room—with the exception of the large Zulu guarding the entrance to the lab—what this meant to Jack.

Jack let go of Ricardo. "The ancient Dogons *must* have gotten their astronomical data from the extraterrestrial," he said, excitedly. "It could prove actual contact!"

"We still can't say for certain if concrete interaction took place," Samantha said. "But if it did—well, there's no telling what influence the extraterrestrial could have had on early humans."

Jack's eyes looked glazed.

"I told you, *amigo*," Ricardo said. "Nothing else could have gotten me into that flying coffin."

Jack couldn't understand why Samantha would be so bothered that he was staying in the field tent. He knew it was a control thing again, or possibly paranoia that somehow he'd run off with the artifact and claim it as his own. Whatever the reason, it made him remember how tense much of their relationship had been. It took about fifteen minutes to convince her he didn't need as much rest as she thought he did. A chronic insomniac,

Jack knew he'd be unable to grab anything but catnaps, and the field tent was the place for them. He found it nearly impossible to shut his mind down—especially when darkness removed most sensory stimulation.

After everything that had flooded his brain during the last forty-eight hours, one thing about the artifact particularly troubled him.

It looked somehow . . . familiar.

Jack opened his frayed, leather-bound notebook. It had accompanied him around the globe. He flipped toward the end of the book and jotted down a new entry, writing in the date and the coordinates according to the last GPS readings he took before retiring. Then he wrote Samantha's name and paused, grabbed a few colored pencils from his worn travel bag, and began sketching the artifact in detail.

He had become quite skilled in his renderings, and some even fancied him an artist. Even in childhood he'd loved drawing, particularly skeletons at Halloween. Jack wondered if these were the first signs of the man he'd become. A little boy's fascination with Halloween and skeletons—were they the budding signs of his future career in paleoanthropology? Jack had recently finished a book on morphic resonancy that affected him deeply. It was written by Dr. Rupert Sheldrake and challenged the fundamental assumptions of modern science . . . which was why Jack found it so intriguing.

Sheldrake proposed that all natural systems, from crystals to human society, inherit a collective memory that influences their form and behavior. What scientists call "instinct" in animals was not chemically or biologically wired into an animal, Sheldrake wrote. It was the presence of the past—a morphic field—a memory of all the other animals of the same species that this particular being drew from.

Morphic resonance does not involve a transfer of energy from one system or another but rather a nonenergetic transfer of information, which is why it is so difficult to confirm through conventional physics. All the predecessors of a species form a collective memory that is inherited by the individual in the present. It helps shape behavior, and even physical form.

Sheldrake had support from some unlikely sources. Wilder Penfield, the great neurologist and one of the leaders in research on memory, had once convinced the world that human memory could be found as "memory traces" somewhere inside the brain. Ten years after his famous proposal in 1951, he recanted all, saying he now thought the idea of memory being physically present in what he coined "the memory cortex" was a mistake.

Could it be, Jack wondered, that memory wasn't stored in the mind at all? Might memory exist in a parallel dimension—one that lacks known physical properties, making it difficult for scientists to analyze? Through morphic resonance, could the past exert a direct influence on the present? He thought so. While the notion was hard to get hold of conceptually, it explained how certain patterns of behavior evolve in animals. It explained why people seem to come up with the same ideas at the same time. How his childhood fascinations with skeletons influenced his career choice in paleoanthropology. No wonder it was so hard to move on from the past, Jack thought.

Psychologists have long known how emotional wounds in childhood can have lasting effects through adulthood. But morphic resonance would explain why it was so difficult to heal those wounds. The past wasn't something stored deep in the brain as a "memory trace." It existed, fresh and powerful, as part of our own individual morphic field.

As he sketched the artifact and inspected the strange icons that ran along its sides, he began to get an eerie sense of déjà vu. He flipped back to his research on the Dogons four years ago, but he couldn't place any of the symbols. After half an hour of puzzlement, Jack resigned himself to simply finishing the sketch of the object and recording the data from Samantha's analysis.

Jack had been more exhausted than he thought. When he next groped for his book, the sun was already casting an orange glow against the east side of the tent. Jack rubbed his eyes. He must have fallen asleep, he thought. And for several hours, by the looks of it.

He got up and looked around. Two shadows outside sipped coffee. As one turned, he could make out a large automatic rifle. But these men were smaller than the three who had watched the field lab earlier. There must have been a change of shift during the night. The steam rising from their cups made him want a cup for himself. He had fallen in love with the strong West African coffees, which were his solace on many a morning during his last expedition here.

"You still talk in your sleep."

Samantha was sitting behind the carbon dating machine, holding two cups of coffee. It felt great to see her. Her presence in the dawn transported Jack back to grad school. She always looked sexiest in the mornings.

Jack walked over to her. "Hope I didn't incriminate myself."

"Oh, but you did."

Samantha used to regale him in the morning with a recap of his night's commentary. Sometimes it was absurd dream talk. Other times she would surprise even him—recounting a theory that was obviously just forming in his head.

Still other times she'd wake him in a huff. An apparent night of passion with a partner of a different name didn't sit well with her.

He had quickly learned to milk the most out of this nocturnal habit, though. Often he'd wake before her, nudge her slightly, and then begin mumbling. When he knew she was alert and listening, he'd whisper sweet nothings until the sun rose. He knew it made her feel

good. She would begin gently caressing his hair while
he feigned sleep.

He missed that.

He missed her.

"Nothing like it back home, is there?" she said, handing him his cup.

"No. There isn't."

Jack wasn't sure whether his answer referred to the
coffee or to her.

Jack finished his breakfast of hard bread and yams inside
the cavern while sketching the fossil. Samantha agreed
to let him draw it in its present state, before she imple-
mented her carefully detailed plans to unearth the precious prize and move it to the field lab. Samantha looked
over his shoulder excitedly.

"It's almost too good to be true," he said.

"I know. I know," she said. "Seems like the whole
thing was preordained or something. The volcanic ash
preserved it perfectly. Just like Pompeii."

In front of Jack lay a fossil preserved in the same way.
He thought about how easily nature could have robbed
them of this discovery. Had the extraterrestrial died in
the open, or had it been geologically displaced by the
earth's constant folding—exposed to air or even different elements—the molecules that made up the bones in
front of them would have long ago ceased to exist in
their present form.

The preservation of the fossil might have been preordained, he reflected.

"What are we looking at geologically?" He was talking about the eruption that sealed the extraterrestrial's
fate.

"We dated the volcanic activity at thirty-two thousand
years ago. Give or take a few thousand."

"Thirty-two thousand years ago," Jack mumbled to
himself. He jotted something in his book, then inspected
the fossil more closely with his hand loupe. "Looks like

our friend went out in one hell of a barbecue. Did you check these carbon resins?"

Samantha felt a twinge of defensiveness. She hated to be patronized and made it known in her tone. "Of course we did. He definitely died during the volcanic activity. Probably instantly, judging by the positioning of the spine."

Jack inspected an outline of wax pencil that traced a triangular shape beneath the fossil's right hand.

"Inside the semicircular casing on the object. You said it housed beryllium."

"99.8 percent pure."

Again Jack wrote. Samantha hated how he could keep things to himself and that damn book. "What are you thinking?"

"That whatever the heck that artifact is, it can refine elements. There's a lot of concentrated beryllium ore in Mali, but nothing like that."

"It doesn't necessarily mean he used the device for refining. Just as likely, it's only a receptacle. There could have been another object used for the refinery process."

"Good point," Jack said. "They might have needed the beryllium as a fuel for this thing . . . whatever it is."

"However they refined the ore, it's a good bet our fossil-friend was probably here collecting the stuff. You'd have to go to South Africa to find anything close to the concentrations in Mali," Samantha added.

The "he" she used to describe the fossil was probably accurate—assuming a few things about animal species on earth could be applied to this one. The fossil had distinct humanoid characteristics. The pelvic bone spacing indicated a male of the species. A female pelvis would be much shallower and wider, with a pubic symphysis joint shaped to allow childbirth.

"I don't know if we'll ever be sure what the object was used for," Jack said. "But I'll tell you one thing. That artifact is absolutely—"

"Priceless."

Someone else had finished Jack's sentence, and it sure wasn't Ricardo. Jack turned. A man with piercing blue eyes stared down at him through expensive eyeglasses. The silver frames accented the streaks of gray in his flowing hair. Though dressed for the field, the man obviously had money. He could pass for an older male model, aristocrat, or gentleman if one didn't know him.

But Jack knew who the man was. And the knowledge made him ill.


# DORN

Jack had hoped he would never hear Benjamin Dorn's South African accent again. He had no idea Samantha was still seeing him, but he should have suspected. Samantha's digs were never self-financed, and this costly operation could be no exception.

Jack had learned about Dorn from reading *Earth*, a popular science magazine, three years after he and Samantha had split. There was a photo of Dorn, arm around Samantha, in front of an excavation site in southeast China. He remembered the pangs of jealousy he had felt when he read about their working relationship, which soon blossomed into a romance. His jealousy surprised him—given how much pain and anger he still connected with her. Jack couldn't help feeling insecure about her new love. Dorn was intelligent and rich.

It wasn't until a few months later that Jack happily discovered the ugliness beneath the man's polished veneer. A journalist friend had written a *Newsweek* piece

on Saddam Hussein's brash arms buildup, which set the
stage for the Persian Gulf War. And there, in a related
article, was an exposé of the men who had made for-
tunes selling implements of war to the highest bidder.

Dorn was one of those men. Jack had followed up his
reading with a Nexis search. Dorn had made a fortune
in the international arms trade. He was an astute businessman who parlayed the wealth from weapons sales
into the acquisition of more legitimate and socially ac-
ceptable companies. He owned a large mining conglom-
erate in Africa, and even a pharmaceutical company,
Helix Corp., the third largest biotech firm in the United
States.

Dorn had funded two of Samantha's digs. Jack knew
Dorn saw it as a shot at legitimacy and a classy way to
spend time. Besides, who could fault him for becoming
the sugar daddy for a brilliant knockout like Samantha?
Dorn sought the prestige of new scientific finds in circles
that wouldn't have otherwise admitted him. In this way,
Jack knew he and Dorn had something in common. They
were both outcasts in the world of science.

It could have been his shady past as an arms dealer,
or his arrogance, but Jack loathed this man. The fact that
Dorn was making love to a woman he'd once planned
to marry only compounded the resentment.

"It's a pleasure to have you here," Dorn said. "I only
just got back myself." He turned to Samantha. "I heard
the great news about the test results."

Jack stood silent.

"Ben is funding the operation," Samantha said. "He's
been very helpful in dealing with the Mali government."

Jack forced a smile. "Can I go over a few things with
you back at the lab?"

"Sure," she said. "Would you excuse us for a bit?"

"Certainly," Dorn said. His grin, Jack thought, was
evil.

\*        \*        \*

Jack and Samantha marched angrily back through the camp, briefly noticing a dispute among a group of Dogons. The workers seemed as agitated as Jack was. He remained silent until they walked through the entrance flaps of the tent.

"I can't believe you didn't tell me who was bankrolling this," Jack said. "The man's an arms smuggler."

"*Trader*. And there's nothing illegal about that," she said. "Besides. He hasn't been in that business for years. You know that."

"You're a sellout, Samantha. Always have been."

His words hurt. There was some truth to that, and Samantha knew it.

"Are you saying you don't want to be a part of this?"

"I'm saying either he goes or I go."

Jack stared at Samantha until Dorn unexpectedly entered the tent.

"It's okay. If you want me to leave for a while, I will," Dorn said, making it plain that he'd overheard their conversation. "I have some unfinished business in Cape Town anyway. I could return in a week and check in."

"I'm not having any of it. This is completely insane," Samantha said.

Both of them were fighting for the Alpha wolf position, Jack thought. And for Samantha's loyalty.

"Jack, If I may . . ." Dorn took a seat at the fold-out table. "I'm a huge fan of your work. In fact, I'm delighted Samantha called you in on this."

Samantha looked like she might say something, but Dorn spoke again.

"It was a mutual agreement. We felt it would benefit the whole operation. The important thing is that you're here. That you're part of the greatest natural discovery the world has ever known."

The thought worked on Jack, but not enough to rid him of his resentment. Still, he knew he couldn't leave, even if it meant dealing with Samantha, her lover, and the tumult of emotions he now felt. "I'm not sure I want to be a part of anything that's funded with your money."

The insult stung Dorn; Jack could tell. But before Dorn could respond, Ricardo burst into the tent. It was clear that he'd been running, and clearer still that he was close to panic.

"Jack! Come quick!" he said. "It's the Dogons!"

# ZAMUNDA

The two scientists and Dorn rushed out of the tent and followed Ricardo up the embankment toward the dig site.

Close to two hundred Dogons moved about and chanted in unison, building themselves into a fury. Some waved digging implements, others large steel machetes. A few carried hunting lances or old rifles. It scared Samantha. In actuality, it scared them all. The weapons had appeared from nowhere.

Dorn's right-hand man, Baines, jogged up to them carrying an M-5 assault rifle.

"They started with all this about an hour ago," Baines said. "And it's getting worse."

"What the hell are they doing?" Dorn asked.

"From what I can tell, word somehow leaked back about the object. The whole village knows now."

"I thought we sequestered the two who found it."

"We did. It leaked all the same," Baines answered.

Samantha stared into the small valley at the glistening bodies and the lances reflecting the rays of the sun in brilliant flashes.

"Why would they be so passionate about the artifact?" Ricardo asked. "I don't even think they realize that the artifact or fossil is extraterrestrial."

"It could be anything. Perhaps they're just complaining about the working conditions. Maybe some damn native got them in a huff about a wage increase," Dorn replied. "I'm sure it's not too serious."

Jack's eyes scanned the crowd. "This is bad," he said. "The Dogons are normally a reserved tribe. I've only seen them chant like this a few times."

"During some sort of ritual?" Ricardo asked.

"No." Jack started down the hill. "When they're mad as hell."

The group followed on his heels. Samantha's nervousness was beginning to show. Dorn leaned over to her. "Don't worry, darling. Nothing's going to happen to your find. I'll sort this all out. I promise you." Dorn's voice was sure and confident. "This is nothing. Trust me."

"I know . . . I know." Samantha took a few deep breaths.

She doubled her pace to catch Jack.

Dorn turned to Baines and grabbed his arm hard, pulling him close. The truth was Dorn was very concerned. More than anybody. "Get Anthony and François up here, too. With the heavy stuff," Dorn whispered.

Baines got on a walkie-talkie. When his men responded, Baines cupped his hand over the transceiver. He told them to bring the AK-47's—and plenty of ammo.

During the first few minutes Jack could accomplish nothing. Four of the Dogon spiritual leaders yelled over one another. It was hard enough translating Dogon in a controlled conversation with one, much less five. The men were shouting expletives, Jack was sure, because he didn't understand half the words. He simply kept repeating the Dogon word for calm.

Dorn's men arrived just as Jack had begun making headway. They were carrying heavy artillery, and as soon as the Dogons noticed, it only made matters more tense. A few Dogons holding antiquated rifles loaded their weapons. Jack glared at Dorn, then turned to keep Anthony and François at some distance; the Dogons were antsy enough already.

One of the leaders, Mimbasha, spoke for the group. Jack knew him to be a fair leader. He also knew him to have a terrific sense of humor, but there were no traces of comic timing now. Jack translated Mimbasha's tirade. At times during the diatribe, the crowd erupted in discussion, showing their agreement.

"He's basically saying that the artifact belongs to them," Jack explained. "He wants to know what it will cost them to get it back."

"Tell them I'm not sure what I'm going to do with it right now," replied Dorn.

"They aren't really asking," Jack said. "It's a rhetorical question. They haven't given us any other options."

"Then you explain to him that we're sorry, but it's not for sale."

Jack paused. He was about to tell Dorn what an ass he was, and that there was no way he was going to translate that to them—but then the youngest of the spiritual leaders, who evidently understood tidbits of English, began translating for his people.

"Oh shit," Ricardo said. It was plain to everyone what had just happened.

Soon the news spread through the whole crowd. Deep bellowing voices shouted their disdain. Mimbasha scowled. He wouldn't take his eyes off Dorn.

A few young warriors started hopping again in unison. Soon the whole crowd was bouncing. Chanting. Building fury. One of Dorn's men clicked off the safety of his submachine gun.

Jack yelled for Samantha to slip away to the field tent. But before she could protest, the shouting and jumping began to cease—in a wave from the back of the crowd.

The throng hushed and began to part.

The Dogons began staring at the ground, averting their eyes from a group of elaborately dressed men. They wore a distinctive ceremonial garb of animal skins and crimson cloth.

"What's going on?" Samantha asked.

Jack breathed in relief. "It's Zamunda. Their chief."

"Do you know him?" Dorn asked.

"I've met him only twice. Briefly. He doesn't hold court with foreigners often."

The Dogons were respectful of their tribe's leader, Jack knew. Only a few in the higher social ranks were permitted to look at him directly. Soon, he could see the high-feathered headpiece of the Dogon chief behind his private guard of tall warriors.

It was then that both Jack and Dorn realized why the tribe was up in arms.

Hung around the chief's neck was an ornate, feathered breastplate. Though tarnished with a black residue, and obscured by the feathers and bones that outlined its sharp edges, there was no mistaking its brilliant metallic properties.

"Good god . . ." Dorn whispered.

It was identical to the artifact they had found with the fossil.

# BREASTPLATE

The chief was a tall, slender man who carried himself with the nobility of a lion. His stride was long and smooth, and he seemed calm compared to his frenetic kinsmen. He had at least two inches on Jack, who stood six one in his boots. Zamunda himself wore only thin leather sandals. He must have been in his sixties, but his sinewy body didn't show the wear of those years. The only real hints to his age were the short silver curls on his head and his tired, yellowed eyes.

"It was right here," Jack mumbled to himself. "It was here all along . . ."

He couldn't take his eyes off the chief's breastplate. Though tarnished and embellished, it had to be an exact twin of the artifact.

"Do you see what I see?" Samantha asked anxiously.

He nodded, still dumbfounded, memories rushing back into his head. "I knew I'd seen the symbols of the artifact somewhere before. They were engraved on the chief's staff. I noticed them in my last trip," Jack whispered to Samantha. "But I've never seen the breastplate."

Zamunda walked up to Jack and gazed intently at him. His voice was deep, rich, and he spoke slowly, so Jack would have no problems interpreting him.

"He says they need it," Jack said after Zamunda finished. "They need it to talk to the gods. He says the artifact was a gift from the Fathers of Knowledge. He brought out this sacred piece to prove it to us."

44

"Who are the Fathers of Knowledge?" Dorn asked.

Jack would have to explain later. Zamunda began speaking again, his tone more grave.

"He says that we will not be allowed to leave with it," Jack told the group. "It belongs to his people." Jack's mind raced. He courteously stepped away from the chief to confer with the others.

"I understand why this means so much to them, but that artifact is ours. Everything about the dig is legit," Dorn said.

"We've got all the paperwork," Samantha added.

"This goes beyond permits. The Dogons have incorporated the artifact into their religion. You're asking them to do the impossible. Think about what this means to them. This is beyond scientific discovery. It's like—"

"—finding the Shroud of Turin. Or the cross itself," Ricardo said.

"I can respect that." Dorn was getting angry. "But it seems we've reached a stalemate. Because we're *not* giving it up. EVER. You tell your friend that."

Jack paused, turned to Zamunda, and began patching sentences together in Dogon. The chief listened intently, then conferred with two of the elders at his side. After a few more moments, Zamunda nodded, then waved his entourage back. The group watched as the crowd parted again for him.

"What did you just say?" asked an amazed Samantha.

Jack had only bought the group some time, telling the chief they would hand over the piece in the morning. The arguments about that lasted well into the night.

"Well, you lied, Jack," an angry Dorn said, repeating that he would never hand over the artifact.

Ricardo struggled through the discussion, generally agreeing with Jack. Options were hashed and rehashed. Every possible avenue was explored: Dorn had thought about offering the tribe money, but Jack quickly snuffed that idea. The Dogons, while poor by world standards, were definitely rich in spirit—their spirituality deeply ingrained and not easily bought.

"Besides," Jack said, "the artifact occupies a revered place in their belief system. This wasn't one of the lesser objects. It came from the inner world. It's sacred."

"It came from space," Dorn said. "Has it occurred to you that an extraterrestrial artifact is also sacred to the world?"

"That's not the point."

"Then what is?" Dorn asked.

"The point is, the Dogons are adamant about not letting us leave. Regardless of who or what the artifact could benefit. Regardless of where it came from."

Dorn stood up. "Let them try and stop us."

Jack took a deep breath. "Don't you understand? These people are willing to die for this. And if they're willing to die for it, they are certainly willing to kill for it."

Dorn sat back in his chair, rocking himself gently, thinking.

"How about contacting the Mali government?" Ricardo suggested. "They could probably arbitrate the dispute. We've got all the necessary paperwork."

"They could get here by late morning," Dorn added.

"No good," Samantha said.

"Why not? Those permits cost me a fortune. It gave us right of ownership. I made sure of it."

"And whom did you bribe to get right of ownership?" Jack asked.

Dorn hesitated. "Maybe my attorney smoothed over a few people in the Ministry of Land Management."

"The Mali government couldn't give two shits about us digging up old bones," Jack said. "But if they got word that we found the artifact, they'd settle the dispute immediately." Jack lit another cigarette. "They'd take it for themselves."

"Without question," Samantha reiterated. "I've dealt

with these guys for years. If they smell any kind of
money, there'd be a feeding frenzy."

"Then, there's only one option." Dorn chewed on his
pipe, which remained unlit. "We get out of here before
morning."

"My friends," Ricardo said, sighing, "that's the best
damn idea I've heard yet." He got up and gingerly made
his way toward the green Porta Potti outside the tent.
Again.

"We take the fossil and the artifact and get to the
airstrip," Dorn said. "Before dawn. We can deal with the
Mali government and the Dogons through international
channels. Once we're in a neutral country we'll talk.
That way this can all be settled peacefully and we'd be
assured that everyone's views are represented."

Dorn paused and let everyone chew on this before
adding, "Of course, there's not a doubt in my mind we'll
win in court."

Samantha looked at Jack. Her raised eyebrows conveyed her agreement.

Jack knew Dorn didn't care about the Dogons or the
Mali government. He simply wanted the artifact. But on
this one point, Jack couldn't entirely disagree. He knew
by the emotion in the tribal elders' voices, there'd be no
chance the group could openly leave with it. A few of
the choleric warriors had been shouting about spilling
blood. The Dogons weren't going to negotiate. And if
there was one thing Jack feared more than the Dogons
right now, it was losing the find of the millennium.
Though it upset him that he and Dorn shared some of
the same selfish motives, he had no choice—for in the
darkest reaches of Jack's heart, he wasn't prepared to
hand the artifact over either.

Twenty minutes later, the group decided that Baines,
Anthony, and François would help load the Rovers with
the most essential equipment under the cover of dark.

Dorn also decided to double the watch with his remaining six men.

The men were Zulus whom Baines had brought from his native South Africa. Jack was glad they were on his side. A Zulu warrior was an intimidating spectacle. The average man stood six feet two. And in contrast to the slight build of the Dogons, the Zulus were strongly muscled. There was also something about their eyes. Jack noticed it every time he'd been in South Africa. It wasn't exactly noble . . . it was fearless. Maybe it was hereditary, or part of the socialization of the Zulu people, who even in this modern age were still aware of their great warrior roots. But wherever they got it from, to a man, they beamed it from those eyes. They were even more intimidating holding semiautomatic rifles instead of steel-tipped spears.

The plan was set: Just before daybreak, the group would leave in the three Land Rovers and Dorn's Humvee. The tents and other supplies would be left behind. Jack knew the Dogons were probably watching them, and completely breaking down the camp without notice would be impossible. After putting distance between themselves and the Dogons, they'd be able to deal with the tribe on a more equal basis.

Logistically, the plan could succeed, but they would have to work fast. Ricardo made sure that Baines and his crew treated the expensive machines with due caution. Samantha, Jack, and Dorn carefully packed the fossil in a plaster cast before putting it in an aluminum case for transportation.

Because the Dogons had no interest in the bones, the fossil sat with some of the other supplies on the Rovers. Dorn didn't want to take any chances with the artifact, though. Instead of packing it in the trucks, he kept it in the large field tent under the close watch of Baines and François.

*     *     *

By a quarter to one that morning the work was done.
An exhausted Ricardo retired to his tent leaving Samantha, Dorn, and Jack by one of the fold-out tables outside.
They took turns drinking from a large plastic water container.

"I think we better turn in," Dorn finally said. "A little
sleep is better than none."

"You're probably right," replied Samantha. She stood
up.

Dorn joined her and put his arm around her. Though
Jack had guessed they were sharing the same tent, he
stared at the ground, ambushed by emotions that short-
ened his breathing.

Samantha was embarrassed by the situation. "We'll
see you at five?" she asked.

"Five o'clock." Jack wondered if the jealousy showed.

"Night, Jack," Dorn said, smiling.

Jack didn't look up at them as they left.

In his peripheral vision Jack saw them enter their tent
and draw the flaps. He sat for about fifteen minutes,
thinking and sipping water. In the distance, he could
make out the faint beating of Dogon drums. He listened
to them and the crackling fire on the edge of the encampment before he too retired for the evening.

# AWA

Samantha sat on the edge of her cot and undid her boots,
staring at the ground.

"He's still smitten with you, isn't he?" Dorn asked.
He was preparing his own cot across the tent.

"Not after what we've been through," she said.

"He's a prickly fellow," Dorn said, walking to her. "I'd say he was jealous."

Samantha slipped into her cot, but said nothing.

He kissed her on the forehead, then turned for his own bed. "Although I wish he had more reason to be."

The night was humid even for Mali. Jack could feel beads of perspiration collect on the nape of his neck before trickling down his back. He stared at the top of his tent and watched as a horned dung beetle, silhouetted by the moonlight, crawled across the canvas. It was a disgusting creature, more than three inches long, with horns that branched from a heavily armored head. The weight of its fist-size body created a moving depression on the top of the tent as it trudged along, probably drinking condensation from the cooling fabric. Dung beetles lived on the excrement of the various animals that grazed the Mali plains. Not exactly a glamorous job, but a necessary one nonetheless. Jack thought about some of the men he knew who were like this. Vile creatures whose jobs were arguably necessary in their particular environment. Men like arms dealers. Men like Dorn.

Jack anguished over the situation he now found himself in. Seeing Samantha again had been traumatic enough. To learn Dorn was the man funding the expedition only made things worse. Still, he knew, no one could get him to leave now.

Jack stood and slipped on his worn leather boots. He knew sleep would be impossible. The rhythmic drums of the Dogon continued from over the next ridge. It was a standard Dogon rhythm that had no real significance. But still, the sound was haunting in the thick air. The fact that any ceremony at all was going on this late at night concerned him.

He fastened the utility belt on his dirty khakis, unzipped the tent, then slipped into the night.

*     *     *

Jack hiked the mile or so to the Dogon encampment at a good clip. The drumming was louder as he approached the rocky ridge. The deep thumping echoed off the canyon walls, amplifying the effect. He could make out the orange glow from the Dogon fires. It bathed the opposite side of the ridge with light. Occasionally, a flurry of sparks rushed toward the bright stars, carried by strong winds. Jack began his ascent of the ridge, loose rocks making for slow going.

He chose a path through the larger boulders and tried, whenever possible, to keep close to the lowland bushes. Before reaching the apex of the ridge, Jack heard a noise behind him and paused. Quietly, he stepped back into the bushes.

The sounds of heavy breathing, closing from behind, seemed headed straight at the bush that concealed him. The heavy footsteps crunched along the pebbled slopes. Finally, Jack could make out the dark figure of a large man. He wondered if the man could see him. The person was coming straight at him.

Quietly, Jack groped at his waist and felt the cold bone handle of his field knife. His fingers pressed gently against the aluminum snap. Finally, with a pop he feared must be audible to the figure, his blade was free. He gently pulled it from its leather sheath.

Still, the figure came.

In an instant, Jack's large hand clamped the figure's mouth—the other pressed the blade to the man's larynx. The man struggled until the blade creased a thin red line across his neck. Then he capitulated and went limp, as if begging for mercy. Jack was finally able to take a good look at the man in the moonlight.

Dorn.

When the shocked South African realized it was Jack, he began struggling again—until Jack made it clear he wouldn't let go until he calmed down.

"What the bloody hell are you doing?" Dorn whispered, his fear displaced by anger. "You could have killed me."

Jack slapped his thick palm back across Dorn's mouth and squeezed. Then he bent over and whispered into his ear, "Another fifty yards, and *he* would have."

Jack twisted Dorn's head and pointed it up the slope, then motioned to a group of rocks. Gradually, Dorn's eyes found the Dogon sentry sitting on a boulder. He was holding a long lance. Jack removed his hand.

"You can't think he would have done anything," Dorn whispered.

"Why don't you go find out?"

Dorn slid closer to Jack so he could speak in a whisper. "Your distaste for me is barely concealable. But I want you to understand that I wanted you here as much as Samantha. We both need you. For the sake of all this could mean to the world, I'd like to put away our differences and try to forge a working relationship."

"I'm sorry you thought my distaste for you was even slightly concealed," Jack said. "Because it wasn't meant to be."

Dorn's face darkened, but he let Jack finish.

"To be honest, I don't care for you at all. In fact, I think men like you should be tried for war crimes. But this find transcends my dislike."

The beating drums continued over their silence.

"Well, then," Dorn said, "it'll be a working relationship."

"But I'm not working for you. You understand?"

"Of course."

"I'm not going to answer to you. On anything."

Jack knew Dorn's blood was percolating. Jack had been testing him, pushing him, but he knew Dorn hadn't gotten rich by giving in to brash impulses.

"I would have never expected you to," he said calmly.

Suddenly the drumming stopped. The symphony of insect life took over while the men remained completely motionless. In unison, low howls pierced the silence.

What seemed like a thousand deep voices boomed over the terrain. In a half-chant, half-song, the men bellowed. Then the drumming began again. This time louder. Fuller.

Dorn could tell Jack had become more apprehensive. "What's going on?" he asked.

"This is not a standard ceremony. They're using sacred drums now," Jack whispered.

"What kind of ceremony is it?"

Jack looked up through the thick undergrowth. A walkable path, concealed by tall shrubs, led to the top of the ridge—away from the sentry's position.

"We're about to find out," he said.


Samantha awoke suddenly and looked over at the cot next to hers. Ben had disappeared. She hadn't even heard him get up. She wondered where he'd gone, but she was used to his idiosyncrasies. She had quickly learned not to worry about his comings and goings, telling herself that it was precisely his independent spirit that attracted her. At least he never interfered with her work and wasn't put off by the time she devoted to it.

She had met him at a gallery opening in the Museum of Modern Art. As soon as she noticed his rich South African accent, Samantha knew things might get complicated. He was very smart. Samantha liked that. But it became apparent after time that something was missing. She couldn't put her finger on it, but she was painfully aware of it at their one year anniversary dinner. The handsome man seated across from her had everything a woman could ask for. But still, there was something wrong.

A year and a half later found them planning this expedition to Mali. It was obvious to them both that things weren't exactly perfect. But the relationship was cordial and convenient. He gave Samantha things she didn't have—like support for her fieldwork, both emotionally and financially. But seeing Jack again had gotten her thinking.

She slipped on her thick wool socks, then turned over her field boots and shook them violently. A couple of fire ants fell from one of them, and she squashed the insects with no remorse; she'd been bitten before. Then she put on a white cotton tank top over her bare chest. Jack had loved them on her, especially without a bra, she thought. But her soiled tank top wasn't worn for him or any man now; it was just hot as hell.

Both men were out of breath by the time they reached the top of the ridge. Below them, five large bonfires cast an eerie glow on hundreds of Dogons. They danced rhythmically, in sync with one another. Their feet raised small puffs of dust from the hard earth. Some of the Dogons had lances, but most circled the fire unarmed. A few men on the outskirts of the circle leaned on the large machetes they used to cut the rough savanna.

The dancing culminated with a melodic chant from a group of Dogon women. Then, to a cacophony of howls and shouts, the dancers ceased. One of the tribal elders slowly entered the illuminated circle and began a solo chant.

"One of their spiritual leaders," Jack whispered.

The man wore a large headpiece consisting of a vertical slat of wood, intersected by two horizontal slats near either end. It looked like a crudely built model airplane with a larger-than-average tail. In a few moments a smaller group of dancers came out and joined him in a hypnotic ballet around one of the glowing fires.

This dance seemed different. More elaborate.

"What does it mean?" Dorn asked.

Jack didn't answer at first. He had just figured out who these people were, and it made the pit of his stomach knot up.

"Those people dancing are the *AWA*."

"The *AWA*?"

"A masked Dogon society . . . funeral dancers."

"Whose funeral?"

Jack was already scrambling back down the slope. "Ours!"

# ATTACK

Baines had posted his Zulus along the perimeter of the camp. Wandile, the tallest and youngest of them, was to watch the east flank, which bordered a high stand of grass. The night had been uneventful for Wandile, and he saw nothing through the darkness since Dorn passed him a half hour earlier. He fingered the AK-47 and took a drink from the cowhide waterbag around his neck. Wandile came from a long line of warriors. His great-grandfather was made a prince by Chaka Zulu himself before the Zulu-British war of 1879. The name of Chaka's people meant "the Heavens," and for a time "the People of the Heavens" had ruled much of South Africa with ultimate authority. It all changed when the British finally crushed his people. On the Fourth of July in 1879, at the battle of Ulundi on the Mahlabatini Plain, Wandile's forefathers saw the last of their pride and power stripped away forever.

Wandile would never forget the way his own father died. It was fifteen years ago. He was only thirteen, not quite a man. He watched with pride, then horror, as his father led a group of Zulus into a line of South African police. The police had shields of Plexiglas and helmets, and they carried big guns. His father carried only a machete. He remembered running to his fallen father after the police had opened fire. Wandile wasn't supposed to cry, but he recalled the tears dropping onto his father's chest anyway.

Wandile could have stayed with his people, but that type of life wasn't for him. He was a warrior. A Zulu. How proud his mother would be as he told her tales of his adventures. He would buy her a proper house, and she would finally be treated with the respect she deserved. Yes, he thought, that will be a great day when I come back. He felt like belting out a warrior's howl. But in that same moment, a strong hand clasped his mouth. Instinctively, Wandile bit down and tasted blood. In an instant, the hand was gone. Wandile noticed a dark figure scurry into the night.

It was a Dogon warrior.

Wandile tried to scream for his comrades, but he could only hear a gurgling, hissing sound. That's when he felt his warm blood splashing in gushes upon his feet. He realized his throat had been cut. As his blood continued to pour from both arteries, Wandile tried to finger his weapon. If he could just get a few shots off, he could alert the camp. But his fingers didn't seem to respond. His head was getting light and he could no longer see. Then his body fell into the pool of blood, and his spirit departed.

Samantha had laced and tied her left boot when she heard a sound at the back of her tent. She listened intently, but all was silent once again. She sensed something was wrong. Something was definitely wrong. She looked at her watch. It was a quarter to two in the morning.

What the hell was Ben doing? She struggled slightly with the right boot and finally got it to slide over her ankle. Then she heard automatic weapon fire from the east side of camp.

\*     \*     \*

Jack had half tumbled down the backside of the ridge, barely aware of the gash the volcanic rock cut in his shin. His heart thumped, and he could hear Dorn's panting grow fainter in the distance as he outpaced him.

As Jack rounded a small knoll he could see tracers light the night sky. He was too late. The attack had begun. The cracking of automatic weapons sent the sleeping prairie into an uproar. Jack asked even more from his burning legs.

He fought and slashed through a stand of eight-foot prairie grass, and the tents suddenly became visible. Black forms scurried about in the darkness, and every few seconds a flash of fire from one of the AK-47s would give the position of Dorn's men away. Soon though, Jack's eyes blocked out the surrounding melee.

He sought Samantha's tent.

A kerosene lantern inside swung madly back and forth from one of the support beams, creating three silhouettes. One of them, the smallest, had to be Samantha. He clutched the knife in his hand even harder.

"Jack!" The shout from behind him caused Jack to turn just in time to parry a Dogon warrior's spear thrust. Any later and he would have been dead.

The lanky warrior had overextended himself, and he fell into the ground in front of him. Jack's leg cocked and his boot landed squarely on the man's skull. He heard a pop as the warrior's skull fractured. The man didn't move.

It was only then Jack realized Dorn had shouted his name, warning him about the approaching Dogon. But there was no time for thank-yous. Jack ran toward Samantha's tent.

Dorn watched him go, then headed for the largest field tent. Through the darkness, he saw his men defending the area—and his artifact. Ricardo heard the first shots from inside the Porta Potti, the dank, plastic container that had become his home away from home. He wasn't exactly sure what the popping sounds were at first until three .45 caliber shells ripped through the side of the container.

"Oh shit!"

Ricardo fell out of the toilet still pulling up his pants. He slipped quietly behind the mess area and made his way toward the center of the compound, where the Zulus were firing at anything that moved. Ricardo kept low. He didn't want to be a casualty of friendly fire—though that oxymoron never made any sense to him. He crawled behind some of the equipment trucks.

Then he heard Samantha . . .

Her scream was muffled, but the voice was unmistakable. He was only twenty yards from her tent but would have to cover each inch of it over open ground. He grabbed a small shovel from one of the Rovers, took a deep breath, and sprinted into the open.

Samantha swung the kettle again. And for a second time, the Dogon warrior at her feet collapsed, unconscious. Her addiction to coffee was paying off. The cast-iron pot was her only defense when the first tribesman entered her tent.

Her attempt to talk to the Dogons was futile. In the terror of the situation, she was mutilating the language. It might have been what kept her alive for the last fifty seconds. At first, the two warriors didn't know what to make of the raging maniac in front of them.

"BEN!"

Samantha screamed as loud as she could but had a sick feeling she was on her own.

"Stay back!" she warned her other attacker in Dogon. But the man lunged at her with a stained machete. Samantha felt the steel tip graze her thick cotton khakis. The kettle dropped and she backed into a small workbench.

She could feel the heat of his breath as he got closer and raised the machete above his head.

"Samantha!" Ricardo stood at the tent opening.

The Dogon turned. Ricardo hurled the shovel. It glanced off the man's forearm and slammed into the kerosene lamp dangling from the cross wires.

The lamp fell and burst into flames, creating enough diversion for Samantha to slide toward Ricardo, who was attempting to make his way to her. The fire bloomed.

"The opening!" Samantha saw another Dogon enter behind Ricardo, cutting off their escape.

"Get down!" yelled Ricardo, forcing her to the floor.

Dorn found François and Baines steadfastly covering the main field tent, firing at anything that moved. Two men lay dead in front of them, their blood soaking in the dirt.

"Where's the artifact?" asked Dorn, wheezing heavily.

"In the case. We tried to get it to a Rover but our friends outside intercepted us," Baines said.

François checked the ammunition on his belt. "We've each got three clips left."

"Give me a weapon."

Baines tossed Dorn an Israeli-made Uzi from the table, which he loaded like a seasoned infantryman. He released the safety and threw back the bolt.

"You two grab the case. We're getting it out of here."

Baines and François slung their weapons over their shoulders, and each grabbed one side of the aluminum box. They heaved it off the table, surprised at how heavy it was. But when they turned back toward Dorn, Baines dropped his end of the case.

Three of the most powerful-looking Dogons he had ever seen rushed in behind Dorn.

One of them was the chief himself.

The flames quickly spread toward the top of the tent, and the canvas caught fire almost immediately. Thick smoke bellowed ever closer to the floor, where Samantha and Ricardo rolled to escape a series of blind machete slashes from the Dogon.

Ricardo tackled the man and wrestled him to the ground.

"Ricardo!" Samantha screamed. Ricardo lay under the ebony warrior, and she could tell, even amid the chaos, that he was being strangled.

Ricardo managed to wedge an arm through the man's grasp and gulped a few seconds of air. "Get . . . out," he managed to say before his breath cut short again.

But Samantha wouldn't listen. She leaped on the Dogon, digging her nails into his neck and drawing blood. He screamed. In one quick motion he flung her hard against a burning table. She quickly rolled off.

But for Ricardo, the fight was finished. He lay unconscious. The warrior now turned his attention to her. Samantha noticed the red streaks of blood on his neck, then the huge machete in his hand. Two long strides and he was nearly upon her. For whatever reason, she closed her eyes. She didn't want the last thing she saw in this world to be the angry man in front of her.

She kept them closed, waiting for the steel of his blade to kill her. She didn't open them until she felt a strong hand grab her arm.

Jack was standing in front of her, holding a shovel. The Dogon lay dead at his feet.

# ROVERS

Jack and Samantha pulled Ricardo from the inferno seconds before the tent collapsed behind them. Ricardo came to, coughing.

"Jack," he said. "Where's Samantha?"

Samantha stroked his hair from his eyes. "I'm here. I'm here. Everything's okay."

He coughed, smiled. "Thank God."

Jack looked toward the trucks. Four Zulus had kept the area clear. They fired sporadically into the darkness. Only a few Dogons had rifles, and machetes and lances were no match for the Zulus' automatic weapons now that the element of surprise was gone. Their attackers had disappeared into the terrain.

Jack pulled Ricardo to his feet. Samantha helped support him as they ran toward the Rovers.

"*Yithi! Yithi!*" Jack was shouting, "It's us—it's us," in the Bantu language of the Zulu.

Two men rushed to their aid, hustling them to the safety of the packed trucks.

"Where is everybody?" Samantha yelled.

Before anyone could answer, the Hummer slid to a stop before them. Baines was driving Dorn and François. Dorn hopped out.

"Are you okay, darling?" he asked, throwing his arms around Samantha.

"I'm fine. I'm fine," she mumbled into his chest.

"As soon as Anthony brings the last truck around, we go," Dorn said. "It looks like the Dogons are retreating."

"Regrouping," Jack said.

"Do we have everything?" Samantha rushed to one of the trucks and flipped up the canvas skirt that covered the back. She breathed a sigh of relief. The aluminum case containing the fossil was nestled tightly inside. "Do you have the artifact?" she asked Dorn.

"It's in the truck."

"You sure?"

Dorn yelled for Baines to lift the tarpaulin. Inside she saw the case that held the artifact.

Baines started to re-cover the truck, but Samantha stopped him.

"I'm sorry. This is so neurotic." She adjusted the case so she could get at the latches, then flipped them open.

The artifact shone brilliantly, even in the moonlight.

Jack noticed something on the floorboard of one of the backseats.

"Oh my God," he said. "What have you done?"

Before Baines could stop him, Jack swung the rear door open and pulled out an object that made his skin crawl.

It was the chief's tarnished breastplate.

"There was no way out. Trust me. It was us or them," Dorn said.

"I believe you." Jack had also killed in self-defense that night. But knowing it didn't make him feel any better.

"Would you rather I'd left it to burn?"

The answer was no. But still, the thought of Dorn taking it off the dead chief was unsettling. It was stealing—looting at best. Still, how often had he "looted" tombs in the past, in the name of science? Should he have left the artifacts he found in Ecuador? Should he have thought twice before taking the gold burial chains of the young maiden he uncovered in Machu Picchu to a California museum?

"The artifact wasn't Dogon, Jack. Let's not forget that. If it belongs to anyone, it belongs to the world."

"Does it?" Jack asked. "I think that's the million-dollar question right now—who *does* it belong to?" He wished he knew.

When Anthony approached in the last truck, the conversation turned to logistics. Baines and his men issued sporadic cover fire as the crew boarded the Humvee and three Land Rovers, Samantha making sure she rode in the truck that contained the fossil. Jack drove and led the caravan. He knew the landscape better than anyone.

They were tensely alert over the next half mile, but the group detected no signs of the marauding Dogons. The only noises came from the roaring of the engines and the sound of gravel kicking into the mudguards. The chaos of the camp began to feel surreal. Distant. But something about the quiet made Jack nervous.

As the trucks sped through a narrow depression between two ridges, Jack's sense of unease became palpable. This was the perfect place for an—

"Ambush!" Jack yelled as a fist-size stone came crashing through the windshield.

On either ridge two dozen or more men stood out against the starry backdrop. A storm of stone assailed the Rovers. The height of the ridge combined with the trucks' velocity would make a direct hit a fatal one. A few gunshots echoed from the hills.

"Get down!" Jack yelled.

Samantha burrowed as far into the truck as she could. Automatic weapons fire popped back from the trucks, but the speed and terrain over which the vehicles were traveling made an effective shot almost hopeless. The warriors got within yards of the trucks. Jack heard the Zulu behind him shriek as a three-foot spear found his thigh, lodging itself in bone.

The trucks slowed only slightly through the barrage. It wasn't until they cleared the valley that some of the group noticed the gruesome scene behind them. The screaming mob had descended on a lone figure who was rolling on the ground.

"Holy Mother of God . . ."

Sizwe, the eldest of the Zulus, was no longer sitting beside Baines in the trailing Hummer. He had been knocked from the rear of the truck by a heavy stone.

"Sizwe!" shouted a Zulu in another truck. The desperation and intensity of the scream brought the entire caravan's attention back toward the ravine.

"Jack! We lost somebody!" Samantha watched as the mob descended on Sizwe, who made a valiant effort, if only for a moment, to keep them at bay. The screams of the mob drowned out his own while machetes hacked into his form.

The caravan kept going. No one said a word. What

they had just seen was beyond that. Jack's ankle ached as he kept the accelerator pedal pressed to the floor. Then he got a glimpse of the moonlit waters of the Niger River. Samantha finally spoke.

"The bridge."

Jack could see it also, and turned slightly east to make for it.

In the Humvee, the tension left Dorn's face. In less than six seconds they'd be on the bridge and over the Niger, safely on their way toward the airstrip. But in the next moment, he saw Jack's truck swerve madly to the right, brakes jammed. Jack had realized something— almost too late.

The bridge had been cut.

"What now?" Samantha shouted.

Jack threw the Land Rover in reverse. "The shallows. A few miles downstream!"

The others followed as the lead truck fishtailed along the riverbank. Jack navigated the mudflats on the river's edge like a seasoned road racer. He kept a careful eye on the odometer, and at three miles, he began searching for the shallows. At last he saw the white caps of a fordable section of river. He pointed the large truck toward it.

"You sure it's shallow enough?" Samantha cried. She was a poor swimmer—and if Jack hadn't already known that, her eyes would have told him.

"I think so."

"You think?" she screamed. "You *think*?"

"I hope . . ."

Samantha grabbed the door handle and squeezed as a huge wall of water slammed into the front of the truck.

The impact was jarring, but once the initial wave sloshed over them, they could see that the water was only three feet deep, making it fordable, though barely. The Hummer had an easier time of it and slowed only slightly as Baines and Dorn entered the swiftly moving water.

Jack knew from experience that the Land Rover was king on the safari and could traverse water well up its engine block. So it was strange that the Rover started to sputter—just as the large tires gripped the opposite bank and pulled the truck out of the current.

He coaxed the rpm's a bit, but the engine abruptly seized. A moment later, the second Rover sputtered to a stop. The third shortly followed.

Jack got a sick feeling in his gut. "I need a flashlight!"

"Here," Ricardo said after fumbling through one of the glove boxes. Jack flicked it on. The beam penetrated the darkness. He quickly pulled himself underneath the chassis.

"Dammit," he said from underneath the vehicle. "I knew it."

He reappeared an instant later rubbing black oily grit between his thumb and forefingers, "The Dogons put sand in the crankcases."

"This one too," Baines said from underneath the Humvee.

The vehicles were hopelessly stalled.

"No plane could get anywhere near here," Jack said. "Are there any choppers at the airstrip?"

Dorn's sardonic smile answered that question. They were in remote Mali. Even Ben Dorn would need a few hours to procure one. "Baines. Tell the men at the airstrip we're not going to be making it. Give them our GPS and get a chopper out here from Kabuti," he ordered. "Have them try and get here from the strip as well."

"Even if they could pull together a few trucks, it would take them at least two hours by car," Samantha said.

"Then I suggest we get these things into the brush." Jack was already moving.

The group was out of options. They would have to wait for either the chopper from Kabuti or Dorn's men from the airstrip. Baines took out a small Global Positioning Satellite unit from a leather case. There was a slight delay as the signal pinpointed their location and beamed the signal back. Baines's receiver converted the SV signals into position, velocity, and time estimates, giving him a precise reading of their location.

They radioed the position to Dorn's men at the airstrip. The plane was waiting but it would be some time before they got vehicles to the group by land. They'd try locating a chopper in Kabuti simultaneously. Either scenario meant a few hours.

"We have less than forty rounds between us," Baines said. "Some of those are probably wet." The tenseness in his voice rippled through the group.

"If we're lucky, the Dogons won't make it this far downriver," Jack said. "If we're even luckier, they've given up the pursuit altogether."

"They didn't look like they were going to let up," Samantha said.

"If word filters down their chief is dead, they will," Jack answered.

"They'll have to bury their chief immediately. It's their custom. It might buy us some time."

At any rate, all they could do now was wait.

# SWEATING IT OUT

Baines directed the group in how to cover the trucks. Using the land's natural contours and the foliage dotting the riverbank, Baines hid them almost perfectly. The trucks could pass for a dark berm or large bush at night.

But in less than three hours it would be light and concealment would be an impossibility. There was nothing
left to do but recount the happenings of the evening, or
worry. Most did both.

A nervous Samantha checked on the fossil, and re-
packed it more carefully in the Rover.

Jack joined Dorn and Baines at the Humvee.

"I'd say five for sure," Baines said, referring to the
number of Dogons killed. The group had lost Sizwe and
Wandile. Dorn told Baines to draft up letters to the next
of kin, although he wasn't sure the men had any. Most
of the men Baines hired were loners, and a mercenary
was rarely missed.

"Send it to the post office in their hometowns, care
of any family member," Dorn said.

"It will accomplish nothing."

"I know."

Baines nodded and headed off to get the relevant information from the Zulus.

"I wanted to thank you," Jack said. "For the warning."

Dorn looked up and smiled, obviously pleased with
Jack's humility. "Think nothing of it. You would have
done the same."

Jack wasn't sure. He pondered the moral quandary for
a few moments.

"Will the Dogons report any of this?" Dorn asked.

"No."

Jack's voice reflected certainty. The Dogons dealt
with death in a different way. Though death was sacred—especially for the royals—it was as expected as
the summer rains. There was never a right or wrong way
to die. For the Dogons, *all* death was natural. They
would bury their dead and move on, regardless of
whether those deaths were at the hands of others. Which
wasn't to say they would forget.

"I didn't think so," Dorn said. "I'm glad no one from
the science team was hurt." Jack knew Dorn's relief
went deeper than superficial concern for his scientists.

Losing an American national would have made things complicated. It could have made it practically impossible to reveal the find on his own terms.

Samantha and Ricardo approached.

"You know, I was thinking," Ricardo asked, "is it really necessary to call for the choppers?"

"Yes," Dorn said. "I'm not even sure if my men can get to us from the airstrip."

Ricardo grimaced, recalling his last helicopter flight.

Samantha started, "You'll be fine, Ric—"

But Jack's hand motion stopped her. He was looking upstream. "Everybody down," he whispered.

Heads slid behind the Rovers, peering out through small cracks in the camouflage.

On the water, slipping slowly toward them was a canoe.

"There're at least five," Dorn said so softly he practically mouthed it.

The canoe looked large, perhaps twenty feet long. As it drew closer, the unmistakable forms of the Dogon coalesced, five figures in all. Two paddled gently in the front of the canoe. One paddled in the rear, while another used his diamond-shaped oar as a rudder. But it was the figure in the middle who was of the most interest. He continually glanced at the floor of the canoe, and from time to time he shook a gourd full of beads. The sound reflected off the water and amplified upon reaching the bank, making an angry noise, like a rattlesnake.

Baines fingered his revolver. "They must have seen us," he said. "Must have . . ."

The canoe was so close Jack could make out the deep grooves in the side, where craftsmen had carved out an intricate design. The breathing of the group seemed to stop.

Then, as suddenly as it came, the canoe slipped past them, hugging the bank and continuing downriver. No one said a word for nearly a minute.

Finally Dorn whispered, "It's a bloody miracle. They missed us."

Baines put the safety back on his revolver.

"No way," Jack said. "If they were looking for us they would have found us. The Dogons have roamed this land for thousands of years. They weren't after us." Jack grabbed a flashlight, which he used to find his field book.

"What the hell do you mean?" Dorn asked.

"They were medicine men. Going to bury their dead chief before sunrise. He must be placed in the royal burial site."

"That's preposterous."

"The Dogons believe in burying their dead before the next rising of the sun—just like the Egyptians."

"And what if these nomads had been miles away from this burial site when the chief passed on?"

"He'd be placed in a makeshift burial site before sunrise each day."

"It's true, Ben. There've been documented cases of people being buried and reburied over a distance of eight hundred miles," Samantha said.

She turned to Jack to acknowledge some agreement, but he had already stuffed his field book into his shirt and was heading down along the water's edge.

"Where are you going?" Samantha asked.

"In the two years I lived with the tribe, they never revealed the royal burial place," Jack said. "It was strictly forbidden. But Xwabatu told me there were great secrets in that place. It probably has something to do with the breastplate. There have to be some answers there. He said it's where they talk to the Fathers of Knowledge."

"My men are on the way, Jack."

"Look. I'll be back in plenty of time. But I'll be damned if I miss this opportunity. It's the only chance we'll ever get."

There was a long pause.

Samantha's mind must have made the decision unconsciously, because before she knew it she blurted out, "I'm coming too!"

"You'll never find them," Dorn said. "And you might get hurt."

"Shamsasa Falls is only three miles downstream," Jack said. "The burial plot has to be somewhere before the falls or they would have put in downriver."

Jack started off.

"Samantha. We have what we need. Your whole future is in these two boxes. This other stuff is irrelevant. Petty, in scientific terms," Dorn said. "You could get yourself killed. Besides. Both of you don't need to go."

Dorn wondered what made her so impulsive. Was it the simple urge for discovery? Perhaps she didn't want to be one-upped by Jack. Whatever her reasons, he could tell by Samantha's glare that he'd overstepped the lines.

"This is my decision, Ben. And I'm going."

# THE FALLS

Jack and Samantha made slow progress, slogging through mud and thorny vines. The roar of Shamsasa Falls grew louder, gradually drowning the sound of the large beetles that crackled in the night air. The vegetation grew thicker, almost tropical. A cool mist from the falls settled on their faces and hair, the moisture creating a microclimate vastly different from the drier plains to the west.

"They've got to be close," Jack whispered from

twenty feet ahead. His flashlight illuminated the large dugout canoe of the Dogons beached at a calm eddy.

Samantha knelt in the moist mud and examined the footprints. The tracks headed inland for a few yards before hugging the shore again, disappearing in the direction of the falls.

Jack tapped her on the shoulder, then signed something to her in ASL. She understood immediately—her favorite aunt was deaf. Samantha had taught him American Sign Language back in school. It had been their private language, one they continued to share. Jack wanted her to stay right behind him so they wouldn't get split up.

She signed back, You got it.

Jack untucked his shirt and spread the cotton fabric across the face of the flashlight. Sufficiently muted, the beam allowed them to follow the footsteps through the wet mud without being too visible.

They walked for five minutes, each yard becoming more treacherous. Mud gave way to long slabs of wet sandstone. The constant misting from the falls provided a perfect habitat for moss and lichen, which made the rocks as slick as an oily garage floor. Twice Samantha stumbled, scraping her knees against the rough rock. More disconcerting, they could no longer follow any tracks.

As they neared the top of the falls, both realized a slip now would be disastrous. The rocks in front of them dropped off to the valley floor. While it was nothing compared to the magnificent waterway at Victoria Falls, Jack thought, the hundred or so feet the water cascading before smashing into the swirling pool below required extreme caution.

He stopped abruptly and surveyed the scene. The falls were so loud Jack felt confident speaking again. "We're not going any farther."

"They've gotta be close," Samantha pressed.

"It's too risky. A slip here isn't a bruised knee or cut shin."

"But I just dragged my ass over two miles."

"You always hated exercise."

"I always hated an exercise in futility. There's a difference."

Samantha shrugged in frustration. He'd gotten her inspired by another of his wild goose chases only to disappoint her again. But as they began their walk back, she remembered her fossil and artifact. She imagined the honors she'd receive for finding it. Nothing would ever be able to get her down again, she thought.

Jack followed another path back. It was drier than the route they had taken because it was slightly upwind. The din of the falls seemed to be receding when Jack's hand shot out and stopped her.

"Look." He pointed toward a smaller set of falls upstream. The cascading sheet of smooth water was backlit . . . by torchlight!

Jack smiled in amazement. "No wonder I never found it."

As if in a trance, he followed the light, Samantha trying to trace his steps exactly. From the side of the small falls, Jack could see it must conceal a cave system. He stuck his hand through. A thin sheet of water was all that separated them from the cavity behind it. He grabbed Samantha's hand. "Are you ready?"

Samantha nodded. They turned and plunged through.

Jack didn't use the flashlight for fear of discovery. Moonlight filtered in through the veil of water, meeting the amber glow coming from farther inside the cave system.

Jack helped Samantha slide down a smooth crevasse into another tunnel before a large cavern opened up in front of them. Here they could hear the deep chants of the Dogon spiritual leaders echoing up to them. They worked their way around a large stalagmite. The cavern just beneath them was filled with the oily smoke of torches. Samantha could detect the smell of herbs and incense. As they cleared the mineral spire, they got their first unobscured glimpse of the cavern below.

"Amazing," Samantha finally said.

"I know. I know." Jack had already begun sketching the elaborate ritual being played out below them.

The cave was large—about the size of a small opera house—and the acoustics were no less dazzling. Along both sides of the chamber stood six stone figurines. Crudely cut, nearly life size, they marked the tombs of past Dogon chiefs, each topped with a different head-dress carved into the stone. The shape was angular and crude, strangely reminiscent of the Easter Island statues, Jack thought. The stone figures brooded over the dead chief, who lay at the foot of a recently carved statue, which was lighter in color than the others.

Strings of gold chains and colorful feathers decorated the chief's chest. Around his waist wound the skin of a cheetah—the symbol of Dogon nobility. Five medicine men performed an elaborate dance around a large stone obelisk centered between the two rows of figures.

The obelisk was stunning.

It stood close to ten feet tall and must have weighed upwards of two tons. It looked as if it were carved directly from the stone of the cave, rising up from the rocky floor. Intricate engravings covered the whole of it.

At the top of the obelisk were carved various constellations—Jack could make out Orion, Sirius, Gamma Canis Minor and the Pleiades—that hung above stellar configurations Jack didn't recognize.

"See those strange star systems?" Jack said, hushed. "Maybe they're a clue as to where our extraterrestrial came from."

Below the stellar imprints ran large Dogon script, which Jack copied down furiously.

"What does it say?" Samantha asked in a whisper.

Jack translated roughly as he sketched into his book.

"It talks about the Shining Ones. And the gift . . . of communication. It mentions something about the chiefs of the great Dogon people . . . who will always have the ear of the ancient Wise Ones." Jack paused, trying to make out more. "That's the basics. But there are a lot of words I've never seen. It looks like an earlier version of Dogon."

"How old?"

"I'm not sure. It's probably the equivalent of eleventh-century Old English. Some of the syntax and grammar are the same, but the spelling is almost unrecognizable."

At the bottom of the obelisk, directly under the Dogon inscriptions, shone what looked like a crude angular eye. Jack could tell Samantha recognized it.

The Eye Goddess was worshipped by a number of ancient cultures, including the Egyptians. But statuettes of the Eye Goddess had also been found in Europe, dating from about the seventh to the fifth millennium B.C. These early peoples of southeastern Europe developed a unique civilization that owed nothing to the cultures of the Near East, and in fact predated them. Yet like the Egyptians, they worshipped a crude, angular eye.

What anthropologists found so fascinating about these seemingly independent peoples is that their extensive worship of the Eye Goddess suggested similar experiences. The idea of autonomous cultures partaking in the same rituals was a troubling enigma. Was it simply serendipity—or did something connect them?

Jack had seen the angular eye on rudimentary carvings and statuettes from various parts of the globe. But there was something troubling about seeing it on the obelisk.

Something unsettling.

Maybe it was the unusual depiction—out of the angular eye appeared crude rays, as if the eye was sending beams into heaven. Jack thought it might represent the rays of the sun; he wasn't certain. He just knew that seeing the angular eye here—in this place—seemed wrong.

"I didn't know the Dogons worshipped the Eye Goddess," Samantha whispered.

But at that precise moment, everything clicked.

The truth came to Jack in a flood.

"They don't." Jack leaped to his feet. "That's not an eye. C'mon!"

# REVELATION

Jack and Samantha reentered the encampment. He had hustled her back along the riverbank without pausing, telling her he'd explain when they got back to camp.

"What's happening?" Dorn said. He had drawn a pistol at the first sounds of footsteps.

"Where are the two artifacts?" Jack asked, out of breath.

"Jack!" Samantha yelled. "Tell me what the hell's going on . . ."

"I knew the pieces looked familiar, but something just didn't jibe." Jack ripped off his jacket and spread it out on the hood of one of the Rovers.

"Careful, now," advised Dorn as Baines and François took out the breastplate and laid it on Jack's coat.

Jack was flipping through his sketchbook.

"What is this all about?" Ricardo asked.

At last the other piece lay next to the first on the hood of the Rover.

Jack sighed in triumph. "It's simple, really."

Both triangles sat side by side, their apex pointed away from the group. Jack laid his open book above the two. Samantha, Ricardo, and Dorn crowded in—pushing the larger Baines out of the way like three hungry chicks.

"I knew these pieces looked familiar," Jack said. "But I didn't understand why until we saw the angular eye on the obelisk."

"What obelisk?" Ricardo asked.

Samantha shushed him.

"There's a very good reason I couldn't place them." Jack paused. The air hung thick with anticipation. He swallowed, his throat was dry.

"I couldn't place them. Because they're not two pieces . . ." Jack pulled the points away from each other—bringing the bases together until they nearly touched. "They're one!"

There was a brief moment of silence.

"Bloody hell," Baines said.

The triangles turned sideways looked like an angular eye.

The drawings in Jack's book documenting the Eye Goddess worship looked like a carbon copy of the two pieces before them on the hood. Dorn didn't take his gaze off them. Neither did Samantha. "Jack!" she screamed.

She was the first to notice that the objects had begun to rattle. They became . . .

Alive.

No one moved. Nothing did except the two pieces, which closed the half inch of space that separated them and joined with a snap.

"Holy shit . . ." Ricardo mumbled.

The seams between the two melded together, and in an instant, any sign of a joint or seal was gone.

"What the hell just happened?" asked Dorn.

Before Jack could tell him he had absolutely no idea, the radio of the Land Rover suddenly blared on, scaring everyone—including the Zulus, who had come to investigate.

The object rose slowly off the hood of the car by some three inches.

It *rose* off the hood!

The morphed triangles began to spin. The headlights of the Rover clicked on and off. The Zulus backed away with the rest of the group. Jack started to lose the definition of the points of the triangles as the object spun faster and faster. As the edges disappeared in a blur, a single stream of light protruded upward out of the center of the piece—from the beryllium circle that formed the pupil! The beam was a bright blue, so bright it lit the plains like a stadium, bathing everything in its deep hue.

Many of the Zulus had retreated toward the other end of the encampment. While they were afraid of nothing on this earth, this obviously wasn't of it.

"Jack . . . what is—" Samantha stuttered.

The blue beam suddenly spread outward like a cone—breaking into a hologram of Earth. It was three-dimensional. The landmasses appeared in red hues. Precise squares crisscrossed the planet, forming lines of longitude and latitude. Beneath the planet, a series of panels took shape. The panels looked like touch pads.

The hologram began to widen, forming some sort of galactic grid above the earth. The grid depicted unknown stellar constellations—various equations appeared beside the different clusters. An intense beam of light originated from one of the clusters and landed on the planet.

"It looks," Baines said, "like some sort of a map."

Samantha followed the thinner, more intense line that originated from space. "This beam's marking something on the earth's surface."

Ricardo leaned over her shoulder. "Perhaps it's a homing device . . ."

"But for what?" she said.

Jack remained silent the whole time. He hadn't taken his eyes off the intense beam, which terminated in South

America, at the northwest tip of the continent.

Dorn noticed this. "Could this be a homing device for *The Source*?" He clearly knew about Jack's research into the ancient myth.

"I don't know . . ." Jack mumbled almost imperceptibly. "But I am sure about one thing." His finger tapped the air on top of the beam's termination point. "I know exactly what place this is marking." His expression was grave and his voice trembled. "I've been there."

# EQUINOX

"You've been there?" Dorn's voice overpowered the crackle of night bugs that swarmed toward the hologram's glare.

Jack nodded, still deep in thought.

Samantha moved closer to the 3-D matrix. The beam terminated somewhere in the northwest of the continent—near the ruins of Machu Picchu. But that would have been farther north. She traced the outline of an immense lake. "Tiahuanaco . . ."

"Tiahuanaco?" Dorn asked. "Is that a town?"

"A place," Jack answered.

"They're abandoned ruins," Samantha said. "In Bolivia. Jack studied near there . . ."

Samantha's voice trailed away, as if the painful undercurrents of Jack's departure still resided somewhere deep within her. Jack had left for almost a year—in the midst of his doctoral studies. Samantha told him how badly it would set him back in the program, but Jack didn't listen. Maybe she should have told him the real reason she thought he should stay: She needed him and would miss him terribly if he left. That trip had started the inevitable demise of their union. It was where he first formulated his bizarre theories. Jack had studied the Inca ruins at Cuzco, but he wrote to her many times about his side excursions to Tiahuanaco just a few hundred miles away. She recalled his intense excitement about the anomalies at the site—the megalithic stone blocks cut with laser precision. The alloy staples that held these huge blocks together were made from metals that joined only under intense temperatures. Incredibly, the builders would have needed the equivalent of a portable smelter to pour these staples—something ancient man couldn't have possessed. Those anomalies stared at the human race, he had said—daring us to believe.

"Magnetics," Ricardo said. He bent sideways, staring through the inch of space that separated the bottom of the artifact from the steel hood of the Rover.

His voice broke Samantha's introspection. She paced around the hologram. The artifact had stopped spinning—seemingly "booted up." The instrument rested, perfectly motionless, on a cushion of air.

"It's generating an electromagnetic charge?" she asked.

Ricardo nodded. "That's how it stays suspended. Probably what caused it to join."

"But why would something like this be marking abandoned ruins?" Dorn asked.

"Maybe the hologram *does* work like a homing device for something," Jack said.

The group pondered the hypothesis in silence. A gust of wind sang through the reeds by the river.

Samantha shivered. "You can't think the ship—a spacecraft—is still here?"

"It just might be," Jack said, his blood chilling. "Think about it. The extraterrestrial was killed suddenly in a volcanic eruption. Probably collecting beryllium. He obviously never finished—or made it back to where he came from."

"Or maybe he was dropped off here first," Samantha said. "Which means our extraterrestrial wasn't alone . . ."

"In either case, the ship could *still* be in South America," Dorn said.

Jack wanted to read Dorn's eyes, perhaps confirm the hunger he thought he heard in the man's voice, but Dorn's spectacles reflected only the image of the radiant three-dimensional matrix. "If the beam is marking an object," Jack said, "a ship—maybe another piece of technology—it has to be well hidden. Archaeologists have combed that site for years. And in all my visits I've never noticed anything other than ancient architecture."

"Could whatever the hologram is pointing to be buried?" Samantha asked.

"Has to be," Jack said.

"Where would one look?" Dorn asked.

Jack paused. "I'd start at the Temple of *Kalasasaya*. It's the centerpiece of Tiahuanaco."

"I suppose you have a theory," Dorn said.

"Theory's too strong a word. I've got thoughts."

"Thoughts?"

"I'm getting close to an educated guess after seeing the obelisk."

"*What* obelisk?" Ricardo asked, exasperated.

"I'll tell you all about it later," Samantha whispered.

A sense of urgency creased thin lines in Jack's forehead. He looked around, as if trying to find someone with a watch. "What's the date?"

Dorn tilted the face of his Rolex. "The sixteenth. Why?"

"We only have four days."

"For what?"

"The temple at Tiahuanaco was built to keep track of the spring equinox—"

"Of course," Ricardo interrupted, suddenly understanding.

Samantha looked puzzled. "Why is it so important to get there before the equinox?"

"Because of the obliquity of the ecliptic."

"Say bloody what?" Baines said.

"It's a bit difficult to understand."

"Try me," Samantha said.

"The earth is hurtling through its orbit around the sun at over sixty-six thousand miles per hour, right? We all know it takes a year for the earth to complete this orbit. We're aware of this, as ancient man was, because of the continual change of seasons."

Dorn waved him along. "This I understand. What about this obliquity business?"

"The earth rests at a tilt—approximately 23.5 degrees to the vertical. This points the north pole away from the sun for six months a year while the southern hemisphere gets the solar rays of summer, and vice versa. This tilt, in technical jargon, is known as 'obliquity.'

"The seasons are marked by four crucial moments, which were extremely important to ancient cultures," Jack continued, satisfied everyone was following him. "The winter and summer solstice and the spring and fall equinoxes. In the northern hemisphere the shortest day of the year is the winter solstice, which falls on December twenty-first, marking the first day of winter. That same day marks the summer solstice for the southern hemisphere. The equinoxes, on the other hand, are the two times of the year on which day and night are of equal length."

The group eagerly recalled each fact in silence. Only the Zulus at the edge of the gathering continued to mumble among themselves.

"Now it's not hard to believe that ancient cultures could pinpoint these 'cardinal points' of the year—the equinoxes and solstices. The unbelievable thing is that certain ancient people recognized a strange phenomenon

of celestial mechanics called the 'precession of the equinoxes.' "

"Precession . . ." Samantha repeated. "You've written
about it, but I don't remember—"

"Precession is extremely difficult to observe and even
harder to measure accurately without sophisticated in-
strumentation. The earth's position relative to the sun
changes almost imperceptibly over the course of
thousands of years. It's due to a wobble of the axis that's
caused by forces you don't need to understand. This
wobble causes the constellations you observe during the
equinox to seem to move, ever so slightly, rotating
through each zodiac sign. This tells us earthlings that
our position in space has changed. This changing of constellations is known as precession."

"And ancient people knew about this precession?"
Dorn asked.

"Yes. Many cultures did, including the first people
who built Tiahuanaco. They believed that the most significant of all the constellations in a given era was the
one under which the sun was observed to rise on the
morning of the spring equinox," Jack said. "For the last
two thousand years the sun has risen in the constellation
of Pisces. We will soon pass out of that, and the sun
will rise against the backdrop of Aquarius. This rotation
happens constantly, but very, *very* slowly."

"How slow are we talking?" Samantha asked.

"Each constellation 'carries the sun' for 2,200 years.
So the earth completes a full precessional cycle once
every 25,776 years, what the ancients called a Great
Year," Jack said. "That means civilized human beings,
according to the current view, haven't even been around
to witness one fifth of a Great Year—yet they knew
about this precession."

"And this temple of yours was built to measure the
phenomenon?" Dorn asked.

"No doubt about it. The Temple of *Kalasasaya* serves
as a clock—an enormous stellar timepiece. Whoever

built the temple wanted a precise calendar that could tell them the earth's exact position in space. The observation platform and the obelisks around the temple were built to record the exact moment of the spring equinox. In that way—by looking into the sky at the changing constellations—they could keep an accurate calendar into infinity. But, you know what? I don't think it was the only reason the temple was built."

Dorn leaned in. "What do you mean?"

"I think the temple was also built as a shadow marker."

"A shadow marker?" Ricardo said. "Like at Teotihuacán?"

Jack nodded. The ruined Aztec city Ricardo spoke of lay fifty kilometers northeast of Mexico City. "During midday of the equinox at Teotihuacán, a sharp shadow is cast on the lower facade. It appears for exactly sixty-six seconds—precisely at midday—then vanishes instantly. I think the same thing occurs at Tiahuanaco."

"But there haven't been any noticeable shadow markers reported," Ricardo said.

"That's because the edifice that created the shadow has been moved."

"Moved?" Samantha asked.

"You remember me writing to you about the Gateway of the Sun?"

Samantha nodded.

"A series of as yet undeciphered inscriptions appear on an immense basalt monument called the Gateway of the Sun," Jack explained to the others. "Whoever built the Gateway repeated the engravings on many of the structures in the area—as if the builders had foreseen a great catastrophe and wanted to make sure the information wasn't lost."

"What sort of information?" Baines asked.

"Scientific equations. An unknown algorithm. The symbols seem like instructions."

"Instructions for what?"

Again, the sounds of the African night filled the silence.

"I don't know," Jack said.

"And the inscriptions have never been deciphered?" Samantha asked.

"No. They've never been deciphered—they're not even finished. Halfway through, the markings stop—as if in the midst of all this painstaking and important work, the builders suddenly vanished."

"So the catastrophe they feared did happen," Ricardo said.

"It looks that way. The Gateway was found over a hundred yards from the rest of the temple, lying face-down in a bed of clay. Miraculously the clay preserved the engravings from the elements. The problem," Jack added, "is that we don't know where the Gateway was originally positioned."

"Why would that be important?" Dorn asked.

"Because if we don't know where it stood, we won't know where to look for the shadow marker—a marker that might have revealed the same thing this hologram appears to be noting."

"Incredible," Dorn said softly. "Do you think you know the original position?"

"If I can figure the exact age of the temple by comparing the stellar constellations I saw on the Dogon obelisk to my data from Tiahuanaco, I should be able to figure out where the Gateway would have been placed back then so as to be aligned to the equinox of that era."

"And then?" Samantha wondered.

"We fabricate a facade of the monument in its original position." Jack stared at the artifact and hologram; the entire scene was so contrary to the bucolic savanna. "As long as we get to Bolivia in time, we can build a mock-up out of tarps in a few hours. We just have to simulate the dimensions of the monument."

"And if we can't get there by the equinox to test your theory?" Dorn asked.

"Then we'd have to wait another year."

As Jack spoke, they heard a commotion in the tall reeds by the river.

One of the Zulus ran up to Baines and said something in Swahili.

Baines's face grew taut. "The Dogons have resumed the search. This man saw torches two miles upriver."

Jack took a few steps back. "The light," he said. "They must be able to see the light."

In their wonderment, no one had thought about the bright blue effulgence that bathed the surrounding prairie and lit the sky. The calls of river bullfrogs couldn't mask the rhythmic sounds that began echoing along the river—the distant thumps of Dogon drums.

# SWITCH

The intense blue glow seemed less wondrous now.

"We've gotta turn that damn thing off," Baines said.

"He's right." Dorn's eyes scanned the river in consternation.

Jack surveyed the artifact closely. He had no idea where to begin. "This can't be any more difficult than a household appliance," he said.

"Careful," Samantha said. "You couldn't even program our VCR, remember?"

Jack turned to Ricardo. "Why don't you put that physics degree to work?"

Apprehensive, Ricardo shuffled around the hologram. His shirt glowed in its ebullient output. Ricardo touched the cold artifact, each time gently—with hesitation. "Talk about losing the instruction manual."

"We don't have much time," Dorn warned.

Tiny rivulets of sweat hiding beneath Ricardo's sideburns made a run for it down his cheek. "I'm thinking. I'm thinking."

"Try hitting the thing," Baines said.

"*You* hit it," Ricardo answered. "Just let me get a few hundred yards away, okay?"

Ricardo wiped the perspiration from his eyes, then turned his attention to the series of panels along the bottom of the hologram itself. Each one had an icon overlay in the top right corner. It looked promising. Perhaps they acted as function keys.

"It just feels right, doesn't it?" Ricardo asked, pointing at the brightest panel.

Jack hadn't a clue. "Whatever you say."

Ricardo took a deep breath and put his hand out toward the hologram. The others took a few steps backward. "I can feel the energy . . . like static elect—"

Ricardo's finger broke the plane of the hologram. The three-dimensional grid vanished, leaving in its wake a complete and utter blackness. The effect momentarily blinded everyone. Then dim moonlight gradually filled the void.

"I guess we found the off switch," Jack said.

The moon's rays soon became distinct enough to cast sharp shadows. The artifact rested on the hood of the truck just like before.

Ricardo trembled. "I suggest someone write that down for future reference."

Jack concentrated on the glow of oncoming torches. The Dogons were only a mile away he figured; beyond the large bend in the river. The group spoke only in whispers, crowding around the relative safety of the vehicles, whose steel shells provided a welcome shield from unseen dangers.

Dorn and Baines were struggling to convince the Zulu that the amazing spectacle played out earlier was just a high-tech piece of American equipment and they needn't be afraid.

The Zulu weren't buying it.

"Samantha," Dorn whispered.

"Yeah."

He crouched beside her. "You okay?"

She nodded.

"Take this." Dorn handed her a 9mm Browning pistol. "It's loaded. Safety's on."

"No thanks. I'm not big on guns."

"It's just a precaution."

"I can't even hold a BB gun without getting ill."

"You don't have to hold it," Dorn said. "But let me show you how to use it. Just in case." Dorn rested the weapon in his palm. "Here's the safety. Push this in and the gun will fire. Keep the safety on until you know you're going to need it." He locked the safety back.

Samantha was careful not to touch the weapon. "Then what?" she asked.

"Then you just point and shoot."

"Point and shoot," she repeated softly.

He left the gun on a flat rock beside her.

Upriver, the Dogons rounded the bend, their torches flickering in the distance like tiny stars. Conversation ended. Baines placed armed men at perimeter points. Jack wove through the group, telling them to remain silent. He knew Dogon scouts were ahead of the main contingent; any noise would give their position away. Then Jack settled down behind the Land Rover, fingering the AK-47 Baines had given him.

*If my students could see me now.*

It grew so quiet, the swirling river could be heard passing through the reed banks. Occasionally, chunks of earth slipped into the water with a splash.

A loud screech pierced the silence.

Something close enough to panic welled in Baines's eyes. It was the truck radio. An African voice announced call signs to the entire prairie. Baines sprinted to the truck and turned down the volume. Jack listened to him as he answered in a whisper and described the clearing.

Jack heard the faint sound of oncoming vehicles.

Dorn cracked a smile. "We've made it."

The sound signaled their salvation. It was Dorn's team from the airstrip.

The three safari vans felt even more uncomfortable than the Rovers. Dorn's men had "borrowed" them from a local tour operation in the middle of the night; they'd been the only vehicles large enough to extract the crew with all their equipment. Whether the increased reinforcements frightened the pursuing Dogons, Jack wasn't sure, but Dorn's men had evacuated the expedition without incident. The torches had remained just a faint glow in the distance.

Though the jostling vans sent reverberations through the aluminum benches and their human cargo, no one seemed to mind. The group was enraptured. They talked about the extraterrestrial device, and what the hologram might be leading them toward. The mere speculation caused Jack to shudder. He could sense the same anticipation in Dorn. The man looked obsessed.

"Four days," Dorn said. "That doesn't give us a lot of time."

"I know," Jack said.

"If we miss it, we'd have to wait until next spring?"

"Yes," Jack said. "But I'm not missing this chance."

Ricardo slid across the front bench to get a little closer. "I don't know about you. But I don't think there's any need to go rushing off to Bolivia. I say we take our time. Wait till next year."

"You know we can't do that," Jack said.

Samantha agreed. "That hologram is leading us to something remarkable."

"Perhaps more remarkable than anything we've found here," Dorn added.

"We're going now," Samantha said.

"But we don't have time to apply for scientific permits," Ricardo said. "Much less visas. We'd have to enter the country illegally—as fugitives, for godsakes. Not to mention the hassles and delays we'll face securing and transporting all the equipment on such short notice. Besides, commercial flights and their inevitable connections and payload restrictions wouldn't give us enough time to set up for the equinox anyway."

Out of breath, Ricardo seemed to have convinced himself the journey was impossible.

Dorn responded by shooting down every one of Ricardo's objections. "I should be able to pull a few strings and buy us some leeway with the permits and visas," Dorn said. "We'll be illegal for a short while, but I can get all the paperwork in order. My team is also expert in dealing with the logistics of moving tons of supplies quickly and discreetly."

Jack knew those tons of supplies Dorn's team moved had usually been weapons.

"Anyway," Dorn said, "we're not flying commercial."

"What exactly does *that* mean?" Ricardo asked nervously.

# PART TWO

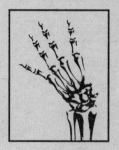

# CARGO

The cavernous hull of the C-130 reverberated with the whine of the Allison T-56 turboprops that powered it. Built to transport goods, the plane wasn't passenger-friendly. Dorn and Baines sat just behind the cockpit, where they placed various calls from the heavy satellite field phone. Anthony and François smoked cigarettes, skimmed *Penthouse*, and argued about everything and nothing.

The one Zulu Dorn had decided to bring with him sat silent but awake. Jack couldn't fathom what was going on in his mind. Bongane was the man's name. He had to be in his late fifties, Jack thought. The other Zulu had stayed behind. Dorn had assured Samantha that none of his men would speak about the incident. Jack believed him, though how the man commanded such obedience made Jack uneasy.

The only one in the whole plane who didn't notice the unpleasant surroundings was Ricardo, who lay unconscious in a pile of cargo netting. As soon as he set foot in the metal monster he had rifled through the first-aid box in the cockpit, then persuaded Samantha to inject him with a Demerol-filled syringe. Mixing that with a cocktail of Vicodin, Ricardo slept like a baby. Jack hadn't seen him move in over an hour.

Jack readjusted the sleeping bag that served as his pillow and looked outside one of the few small windows in the plane. A frost coated the glass around the edges.

Through the misted porthole shone the first rays of dawn. They were flying west and would race the sun for most of the trip. Jack stared out over the Atlantic. They had left all land behind thirty minutes ago. The sun cast a few gleaming rays over the unending blue surface of the sea. Jack thought it a strange contradiction that our planet was named Earth. A more appropriate name would have been Water.

Samantha weaved among the cargo in the tail section. Jack had seen her get up twice before to check on the traveling cases that protected the artifact and the fossil. After every bout with turbulence, she stumbled back to make sure the cases sat tightly secured to the plane's side. Jack didn't blame her. The cargo was beyond precious for both of them.

Samantha made her way back from the rear of the aircraft and plopped down beside him, resting her back against his rolled sleeping bag. Jack continued staring through the frosty window.

"It's a lot to take in," she said.

Jack nodded. "Yeah."

"You know it actually makes me sick. My stomach aches."

Jack knew she didn't mean the flight. She meant the fossil. The artifact. The idea that our planet wasn't alone in the infinity of space. "I know exactly how you feel."

"Do you know what this will mean to the world? To science? To history? What we discovered back there will change everything." She paused. "The funny thing is"— her tone grew introspective—"sometimes I catch myself wishing I hadn't found any of it."

"But you did."

"Yeah."

Samantha fidgeted in the silence that followed. Jack could sense her discomfort.

"You saved my life back there," she said, moving closer. "I don't even know what to say. But . . . I've never come that close, you know?"

"I know."

"Well," she said, choosing her words carefully, "thank you. I know it's probably par for the course for you—rescuing damsels in distress. But I was scared. Really scared."

"So was I." Jack put his hand on top of Samantha's. She didn't move it.

Jack wondered if she felt the same thing he did—butterflies emerging from cocoons within deep reaches of his stomach. The tactile connection sparked kinetic energy that had always flowed between them. He could feel his heart quicken, though he sat perfectly still. Jack looked back out the window, slightly embarrassed.

"I have no idea when we'll end up publishing," she said. "Or *what* we'll end up publishing."

Jack found her eyes. The fiery colors of dawn brought out the small specks of gold that dotted her pupils. "The *what* doesn't matter as long as it's the truth."

"I want you to author with Ricardo and me."

"It's your find."

"Yeah, but most of the find wouldn't make sense if it weren't for your previous work."

Jack let his hand slide off hers. "Work?" he said. "Is *that* what you're calling my research now?"

Samantha looked confused. "What are you talking about?"

"I remember 'rubbish' being one of the more gentle descriptions you used for the same ideas."

"That's not fair."

"What do you know about fair?" Anger welled within him.

"I disagreed with your theories. How could I have backed them?"

"You could have backed *me*. That's all I asked for."

Some extended turbulence caused Samantha to grab hold of one of the long ropes that ran the length of the plane's side. She looked stung. Moisture formed in the corners of her eyes. "You know it went beyond supporting your speculations. You were testing me. Pushing me," she said. "*That* wasn't fair."

Samantha got up and went to check on the gear again.

Jack massaged the back of his neck, which felt like a coiled spring. He had done it again. That powerful warrior called pride had over-powered his ego, finding its way out of his subconscious. It had been the source of many arguments with Samantha. Pride. Honor. The haughty emotions teetered on a razor's edge, embracing a self-respecting dignity on one side; an often fatal self-importance on the other.

Jack rested against the tarp that covered most of the instruments and equipment they brought, and let the two halves of his soul play out their continuing struggle. One combatant was fueled by pride, bitterness, anger. The other was, in a word . . . peaceful. This rational half always calmed Jack. It was forgetful—forgiving. It was the part that kept trying to heal wounds that the other half could rip wide open in an instant.

Jack's thoughts drifted back to Princeton. He'd never met a more competitive person. Samantha wasn't just a woman in a man's world, it went way beyond that. She graduated ahead of him in the anthropology program—Jack's disconvergent views didn't go over well with the faculty. But Jack didn't mind, he fell easily into the role of the rebel.

At first Samantha seemed to enjoy watching him expound on bizarre theories. In fact, Jack remembered that the first year after graduation went swimmingly well. They shared the same dreams and fantasies, and together they found fun in even the most mundane errands. Then there'd been the sex. The physical passion between them was unrivaled and was made stronger by their shared passion for learning. Gradually, though, the rebelliousness in Jack's work became usurped by something more acute for Samantha. Some of his theories ripped apart whole bastions of science—like Darwinism.

He remembered the late-night lectures Samantha gave

him about using his research to make fools of tenured professors. It wasn't good business she always told him.

She might have been right.

In the two years that followed, Jack found it amazing how quickly he became an outcast. He'd become known as a carpetbagger, an insurgent, and that's when Samantha shut down. She so wanted to succeed, and the only way to do that was to support the currently accepted thoughts of the establishment. Their relationship hadn't ended instantaneously—that would have been easier. As time dragged by, Jack felt each gradient of withdrawal. She became cold. Distant.

The inevitable soon followed when Jack mustered enough courage to ask her about three possible dates for the wedding. He knew what was coming, but it didn't dull the pain. Her eyes got teary, and Jack remembered feeling a tinge of nausea as her words echoed off the concrete walls of the lab: "I can't go through with this."

*Well, screw that. Screw her,* Jack thought. He readjusted the sleeping bag beneath his head. Jack's heart thumped loudly now. It reminded Jack which half of his soul felt stronger. Perhaps because he *allowed* it to be stronger.

Jack noticed small specks of land edged by rings of white—water on reef; probably the Canaries.

*Why was he still so angry?*

Though it happened years ago, he could never forget the way that small diamond solitaire glistened in the light as she twisted it off her finger. He could never forget how condescending the *I'm sorry* sounded to him as she placed it in his palm.

Jack crawled over to where Ricardo had nestled himself in the cargo net and rifled through his bag, pulling out the bottle of Glenfiddich, the single malt scotch he and Ricardo were fond of. The alcohol burned his throat. Single malts tasted much better sipped—and on the rocks. He closed his eyes, feeling a gradual numbness on his skull. Jack sank farther into his resting place and

his stomach got warm. He knew now he'd be able to
forget.

At least for a while.

The C-130 had been in flight for more than eleven hours.
The light cargo meant they wouldn't have to put down
to refuel. After a while, Samantha stopped checking on
the artifact and the fossil after every bit of turbulence.
She knew it would take an 8-point temblor to dislodge
the carefully packed cases securely fastened to the plane.
Besides, the insulation inside the durable steel containers
kept them cradled like eggs.

She tried to get back into the book she picked up in
Heathrow Airport on her way to Mali. Sixty pages in,
however, she put it down. This was the sixth legal
thriller from the same author, but she could have sworn
she was reading the first. *Or was it the fourth?* The
courtrooms all seemed to blend together.

She reached into her pocket and fished out a small
piece of North African gum. It tasted awful, but at least
it gave her mouth something to do. She tried waking
Ricardo but with no success, and after noticing the half-
grin cemented on his face, she realized he probably
talked her into injecting him with a little more than the
recommended dosage. She left him and scurried over to
Jack.

She planned on talking about Tiahuanaco but found
him too in a well-deserved sleep, so she propped her
head against one of the plastic watercoolers in front of
him and watched. He slept with his mouth open—she
always loved that. It made him look like a little boy,
especially when his hair was messy. Her eyes followed
the broad shoulders down to his strong forearms, which
extended from rolled-up sleeves, then at his powerful
hands. She loved Jack's hands. They always made her
feel safe.

His participation in the expedition brought a mix of
emotions for Samantha. She felt uneasy. Still, he brought

back something that had been missing in her life. Jack awakened things in her.

Jack made her feel.

She thought about some of the happy times they had shared, about his eloquent proposal, and the dingy little flat they made warm through life's happenings. She thought about the way Jack gazed at her after they made love. He could make her feel like a queen. She pictured his naked body—rugged, taut, solid. Then her thoughts drifted to the moments of pain he brought when he decided on dragging both their careers through the mud. She always thought he was testing her—seeing how far he could go before her loyalty ended. It wasn't fair, she told herself. She nearly lost everything she'd spent a lifetime building—and Jack didn't seem to care.

The discovery in Mali threatened to undermine all the reasons she had gathered for giving Jack that emotional ultimatum. His theories didn't seem insane now. In fact, they'd been borne out. His rebellion didn't appear as the fabricated defense it once did. *But why did he make it so hard to apologize?* She had been wrong and was woman enough, humbled enough, to admit that she needed Jack. But that didn't seem sufficient. He could still make her furious. She thought a lot about the joy and pain Jack had brought her, and the hidden hurt she had concealed from everyone but God over the last six years, burying it under incessant work.

Then she wondered about Ben Dorn. The triangle she found herself in now didn't help any reconciliation with Jack. Truth was, she couldn't blame Jack for being angry about Dorn's involvement. She'd have felt the same way. But seeing Jack again, even with all the pain that accompanied it, made her relationship with Ben seem even more superficial. She didn't want to think about what the present alliance said about her.

Finally, her thoughts focused on how damn hard the airplane fuselage felt against her backbone before she drifted off to sleep.

\*          \*          \*

"Dammit!"

Dorn slammed down the satellite field phone.

The plane had entered Brazilian airspace over an hour ago, and they would soon be flying over that arbitrary line called an international boundary drawn through the lush mat of endless green foliage. But the only lines that truly broke the dense jungle canopy were the occasional brown rivers that twisted their way to the sea. Still, the plane would soon enter the Bolivian side of this vast wilderness. It meant Dorn was running out of time. Deals still needed to be cut. He had to bribe the necessary custom officials to retroactively process their paperwork, and he'd still failed to procure the necessary equipment for the journey into the Andean highlands. His bargaining power drained like the plane's fuel as they got nearer to the landing strip in Trinidad—the small town where they would begin their trek to the ruins.

"What's up?" Baines asked as he came back from a quick smoke with Anthony and François.

"That call just cost me 96,000 bolivianos."

"Unreal," Baines said.

The portly copilot walked by them from the cockpit and paused. "You might want to switch long-distance carriers," he said in a Jersey accent.

Dorn stared hard at the man as he fumbled for his cigarettes.

"My old lady got this great number from her friends that can really help with the savings. Just dial 32—I think it's 10—32—"

"Thank you," Dorn said. The copilot shrugged and waddled off to the back of the plane. "Where do you get these idiots?" Dorn asked.

Baines chuckled.

"That bastard Checa needs more money," Dorn said.

"I'm not surprised. They'll bleed you dry down here."

Juan-Luis Checa, formerly an attorney, was now the

foreign minister of Bolivia. Before his appointment, he had served as counsel to most of the country's high-ranking politicians. All roads to the dark hearts of most government officials passed through him. The steep payment was for his services. Dorn had met Checa years earlier, when the attorney dabbled in the international arms trade—a profitable side business to his lawyering. He told Dorn not to worry about any permits or visas, and assured him they'd have no problems getting customs papers drawn after their arrival. But he also informed Dorn that he'd need payments for other key players. The ninety-six thousand was his "retainer." That greedy bastard, Dorn thought. This jaunt into the central Andes was getting more expensive by the minute. At the current exchange rate, the payout to Checa alone would be just over forty-two thousand U.S. dollars.

It was no myth corruption ran rampant in Bolivia. Most of the public officials were on at least one drug cartel's dole. Checa himself had deep ties to the Curoz Cartel. And now the expedition had no leverage. Though Dorn possessed a carefully honed skill of imperceptible manipulation, he didn't have time to cut any fair deals. The spring equinox was nearly upon them, and it would take another day through largely inaccessible roads to reach the altiplano highlands, where Dorn hoped to find an even greater treasure than the fossil or artifact. A technology that could be exploited for profit.

"Find out who's in control of Trinidad at the moment," Dorn said.

He needed to know which drug cartel ran traffic out of the small town.

Baines flipped through a faxed list of Bolivian contacts and punched in a number on the SAT phone. "We'll need protection money through the highlands as well," Baines said.

"Don't remind me." Dorn knew they'd probably cross at least two of the cartel's "trafficking zones" on their way to the ruins of Tiahuanaco. They would need to pay

tariffs for "protection money" as they entered each cartel's turf—a medieval practice still flourishing in this
particular region of Latin America. Dorn swung open
the cockpit curtain and looked out the ring of small windows. The ceaseless jungle canopy spread in all directions below them. "You have any idea of our ETA?"

"We should start our descent into Trinidad in little
over an hour," said the pilot.

Dorn looked at the brown dirt rings around the man's
collar and wondered why he ever put his life in the
hands of people like this.

Soon they'd be on the ground. Within the day they'd
be making their ascent to Tiahuanaco. Dorn thought
about the artifact and how they would reveal it to the
world—once he'd studied it in detail in one of his high-
tech engineering plants. There was so much to learn. So
much to capitalize on. The technology he witnessed on
the savanna of Mali had changed things. He now saw
the potential of the device—and whatever it might be
marking.

He saw his future.

Dorn bristled with excitement. If the fabled *Source*
could be found at Tiahuanaco, the technology would be
worth billions. Trillions. Ben Dorn stretched his long
legs and listened to Baines finalize arrangements with
their drug cartel escorts on the phone next to him.

Forty-five minutes later, Baines got news from the pilot
that they were beginning their descent and relayed the
news to Dorn. He walked into the cargo area and found
the entire group of scientists asleep. Samantha had fallen
asleep at the foot of Jack's resting area. A pang of jealousy quickened his pulse. She still looked striking—
even after a day in the dank cargo bay. Within moments,
his jealousy gave way to anger.

He and Samantha had made love once in the last four
months—and then only after some serious wooing. He
knew in his heart their relationship had become one of

convenience. He cursed himself; for some strange reason he still wanted her. Samantha Colby was his most prized possession. An addiction that he couldn't seem to quit. She elicited emotions in him so strong he might call them love—if he believed himself capable of feeling such a thing.

"Samantha." Dorn shook her and she came to groggily.

"Bolivia?"

"We're making our descent now," he said. "I wanted to make sure there was nothing more you needed—other than what's on this list."

She propped herself up and glanced at the paper he carried. "I don't think so."

"Good," he said. "You can't imagine the trouble getting even the basic necessities delivered on time and in one piece down here."

Samantha stared at the list in amazement. She must be impressed, Dorn thought. Even he doubted he could find half the equipment they desired.

"This is fantastic," she said. "I can't believe you actually tracked everything down."

"We're still a little short on the $O_2$." Dorn referred to the portable oxygen units Jack thought the group would need once at Tiahuanaco. The elevation made short work of even the most athletic person. Their progress would be markedly slower without them.

"Thanks, Ben."

Dorn nodded. "We better wake the others. Time to get buckled up."

Samantha looked over at Jack, who still slept soundly. She walked two steps toward him when a loud thump got her attention. It was immediately followed by a few others until the sound of loud banging echoed throughout the plane.

"Rain?" Samantha asked.

Dorn thought it sounded more like hail—big hail. But

before he could answer, the plane banked violently, throwing Dorn off his feet.

Jack imagined hearing the menacing drums of the Dogon beating wildly once more. But then the G forces woke him, and he found the plane in a dive. The engines strained with the added velocity, making it impossible to ask Samantha what the hell was going on. She lay facedown on top of him—having landed on his ribs the instant the plane rolled.

Before either scientist could speak, a screech bellowed from behind them as an engine seized. It quieted, except for the noise of the huge turbine blades, which continued to spin against the wind. The plane changed directions at the whim of the other engines that still powered the aircraft. It took a few more seconds before the pilot could adjust. Finally, Jack heard the remaining engines throttle down and could feel the flaps compensate for the uneven pull. The thumping had stopped.

"What is it?" Samantha screamed.

"I don't know!"

Dorn struggled to push off a toppled canister of propane that had rolled over his legs. "What the hell happened?"

"We must have lost an engine." Jack pulled himself to his feet and ran toward the cockpit. Dorn followed a few steps behind.

On the other side of the cargo bay, François and Anthony stared at something through the far window. Samantha, heading toward them, thought she could make out the tops of trees every now and then. They must be low, she thought. Way too low.

"Holy hell," Anthony said, staring intently at something outside.

"What are you looking at?" she asked.

Neither answered. They simply parted to each side, which allowed Samantha to see rivulets of blood streaming across the small window.

*    *    *

As soon as Jack and Dorn ripped open the curtain to the cockpit, they realized the pilot was effectively flying blind. The wipers worked furiously to clear a solid crimson coating of bloody sludge and feathers.

"Birds!" the pilot screamed. The stick in his hand seemed to manhandle him as he fought for control of the aircraft and its remaining engines. The cockpit window had partially cracked, and wind whistled through a half-inch hole. The pilot stared through a small section of glass that wasn't caked with plasma.

"Came out of a low cloud," the copilot yelled. "Looked like egrets. Thousands of them."

Jack had heard of it happening before. This was a period of mass migrations, and many species of birds flew in dense packs. It was a sight to behold—as long as you weren't flying through it.

Dorn yelled at the pilot over the whine of the engines. "Trinidad shouldn't be more than ten minutes away. Can you land us there?"

"Don't think so!"

They were gliding only five hundred yards or so above the rain forest canopy, Jack saw.

"We lost both left engines," the pilot said. "The right ones must have taken a hit too. They're running at sixty percent. They could seize anytime."

"Are we holding altitude?"

"Not for long . . ."

"Three and four are losing juice," the copilot said. "The intake valves are probably jammed. They're too hot."

He fumbled through charts, looking for alternative landing areas.

Samantha approached from the cargo area and squeezed in next to Jack. "There's blood all over the . . . oh my god."

"We flew through a flock of egrets—the birds fouled the engines," Jack said.

"Could we put down on any roads?" Dorn asked.

"Nothing," shouted the copilot.

"What about rivers?" Jack asked. "If we had to, we might try a water landing."

"Negative," the copilot said. "Nothing big enough anywhere near here." His thick hands shook as he stared at the contour maps. "There's nothing but forest from here to Trinidad!"

"Well, I suggest," Dorn said, "you dig something out of your fat ass. And fast."

Before the man could reply, one of the right engines produced a high-pitch whine and the turbine shut down. No one could muster the courage to speak, aware of the implications.

Panic sped Jack's heart. He thought about losing the extraterrestrial fossil and the artifact. Then he glanced at Samantha and realized he'd lose far more if the plane crashed.

The pilot inched forward in his seat, looking out the clearest part of the glass. Dorn stared hard at the man until he could no longer take it and screamed, "Will you bloody say something?"

The pilot finally whipped around: "Thank god for cocaine."

# DESCENT

"Our pilot's high?" Samantha yelled.

"No," Jack said. "Just damn lucky!" He pointed out what the pilot had already seen—a small clearing cut into the dense forest, an illegal cartel airstrip. There were hundreds of the clandestine landing areas throughout Bolivia. The drug traffickers used them to get processed coca out of the country without having to go through inspections in the larger cities.

"Strap yourself in," the pilot said. "We're going down."

Jack could tell he was having difficulty edging the plane toward the small clearing. They had only seconds to prepare.

Dorn led the others as they sprinted into the cargo bay.

The pilot shouted orders to the copilot: "*Dump fuel— train flaps—landing gear down.*"

"You okay?" Jack asked, helping Samantha with her belt. She only managed a nod. Jack disappeared behind some of the larger crates.

"What are you doing?" she said, panicked.

He appeared seconds later, dragging a limp Ricardo.

"Oh, *shit*. Ricardo . . ." she said.

During the confusion of the last few minutes, Jack had nearly forgotten about him as well. He propped Ricardo next to Samantha, who helped keep his back to the seat while Jack slipped the shoulder harness over him. Ricardo's head bobbed back and forth in half-sleep. He mumbled incoherently to himself. Jack just managed to slide the rusty latch of his own belt into the socket when the plane was jolted with a loud crunch. They must have hit the top of the trees at the beginning of the clearing, he thought.

Seconds later, the huge plane hit the ground. The field hadn't been built for anything like the massive transport they were in; the landing gear plunged into the earth and broke away. The plane slid on its fuselage. With each bump, Jack felt the canvas of the shoulder harness dig painfully across his chest and neck.

From the window facing him, he could make out the blurred jungle. Then the window smashed in, exploding in a shower of wood splinters and leaves. Jack put his head down and prayed for the second time in as many days. There can't be much runway left. We must be out of strip, he thought. He knew that in any instant the plane would reach the end of the clearing and smash into the thick forest.

He didn't have to wait long.

Jack must have blacked out on impact because he couldn't recall how long it took the plane to stop upon hitting the far side of the clearing.

Through the punctured bulkhead, the jungle rang with the shrieks and cries of monkeys and birds disturbed by the sudden violation of their home. Dust hung in the cabin; light filtered in through a huge gash in the side of the fuselage. Coughing and moaning erupted throughout the cargo bay, joining the protests of tapirs and a group of wild pigs from somewhere deeper in the forest. Jack tried to undo his harness, but the rusty latch was completely jammed.

He leaned over and checked on Samantha. "I can't believe this . . ." she muttered.

Ricardo seemed unharmed. He still mumbled to himself, half-conscious.

Through the dust, Jack could make out a body as it wobbled from the cockpit. "This is the pilot," a soft voice muttered. "Is everyone all right?"

Baines and Dorn unbuckled their harnesses first. They soon found everyone largely in one piece—save for a few nonlethal cuts and bruises. François seemed to be worst off. Three of his fingers were broken and bent at grossly obtuse angles. A gash on his forearm leaked blood onto the floor of the plane. The Zulu, Bongane, sat just across from Jack perfectly still, saying nothing. He seemed unfazed.

"Bloody good flying, mate. *Bloody* good flying," Baines told the pilot as they cut through Jack's harness straps. The pilot breathed a sigh of relief. He hadn't lost anyone. He turned to Jack and Samantha, cracking a nervous smile. "Ladies and gentlemen," the pilot said as he passed through the dusty cargo bay, "welcome to Bolivia."

"I'm starting to think something doesn't want us to get to Tiahuanaco," Samantha said.

Ricardo let out a huge sneeze. Jack and Samantha both turned to him, surprised by the outburst. Ricardo's eyes were finally wide open. He looked at Samantha, then Jack, before casually wiping his nose on the sleeve of his shirt.

"Can we get a move on?" Ricardo said. "This Mali dust is killing me."

## RAIN FOREST

The miracle of their survival became more apparent when Jack finally got outside. The pilot had managed to put the huge cargo carrier down on an airfield built to accommodate small planes or maybe an old DC-3—if a trafficker felt lucky. A deep gash traced their landing in the green field for about a hundred yards. The twisted remains of the front landing gear remained half-buried on the farside, an indication of where the plane started to slide on the fuselage.

Jack walked around the sheared-off right wing, which lay apart from the plane's body. He could have hugged the pilot for thinking to empty the fuel tanks. Then he made his way to the nose of the aircraft. It was wedged between two giant teak trees, one of which had dissected the wing, but in so doing, finally stopped them. A few yards either way, and their fate would have been as bad as the birds that were smeared across the cockpit.

Samantha crept up behind Jack and let him know that the fossil and artifact had both come through the landing unscathed. She had argued incessantly for the extra padding before sealing the metal cases. Her paranoia had paid dividends. "The carbon analysis machine wasn't so lucky," she said. "Think we'll be able to get another one down here?"

"I doubt it," Jack said.

He was beginning to doubt if they would even make it to Tiahuanaco before the equinox. They'd already be rushing if all went as planned, but now they were miles from the airfield at Trinidad—their intended point of embarkation. He hadn't the slightest inkling when help would arrive out of the Bolivian forest.

A few minutes after the crash, Dorn and Baines made contact with the reception party at the Trinidad airfield. They gave them an idea of where the plane had gone down but had no clue how long it would take Checa's people to find them and extract the expedition. Dorn said he was loath to associate himself with the likes of Checa and the drug cartels, but they had no choice after entering Bolivia illegally. Jack and Samantha reluctantly agreed.

As the pair carefully supervised the off-loading of the equipment, Jack became keenly aware of each passing minute. It was one less minute they could use to get to the temple, one less ounce of hope. If they had to wait another year, he knew they would never get the unadulterated chance the group had now. The findings from Mali would be impossible to keep secret for that long. He wondered what the US government would do once they learned extraterrestrial technology had been found on Earth. The scenario scared him.

Before the last crates lay on the grass an hour had passed and the jungle had returned to normal. Tree beetles clicked and buzzed and birds called out to one another, as if conspiring against the invaders. Occasionally during the unloading, Jack had gotten the feeling they were being watched. He sporadically scanned the tall trees, whose trunks protested under the choking embrace of thick vines, but he could detect nothing suspicious.

Samantha took a seat against one of the crates. "Look, Jack," she said. "Three quarters up the big tree. Just under all that moss."

High in the upper reaches of foliage, lying motionless, was a dark hairy body. It took Jack's eyes a few moments to draw a clearer distinction between the figure and the shadows, but when he did he realized it was a large monkey. And not just one—a half dozen, all staring at the curious metal bird and the animals who pulled things out of its gut.

"I wonder what they're thinking about all this?" Jack said.

"That their distant cousins are absolutely nuts."

Jack chuckled. When she wasn't making him crazy, Samantha had always made him feel good. He had found in her a communion unlike any other, an intimate, sometimes fiery union, leavened by the reassurance of deep friendship. For a moment he relaxed. Jack wished he still had the bottle of scotch, but Ricardo had commandeered it. The act was an unselfish gesture on his part, for he wouldn't be partaking. Instead, Ricardo revived himself with a few smelling salts before offering the bottle to François. He let the Frenchman take a few swigs to calm his nerves and enhance the local anesthesia Ricardo administered before he went about setting François's badly mangled fingers. The mercenary had been silent as Ricardo stitched together the huge gash in his arm, but once Ricardo began aligning the fractured segments of bone, François's screams disturbed the jungle once more.

By late afternoon the heat of the day had taken its toll on the group. The thick, humid air produced a moist coating over their bodies. Jack had gone through two liters of water already, as he considered possible equations he might use to re-create the position of the temple gateway. Samantha struggled through his crash course in precession and astrology. She understood the Gateway might serve as a shadow marker that could show the group where something might be hidden, but she struggled with the physics behind the solar event. Jack soon realized the task would be his alone. He felt he could wring water straight from the air; his body couldn't evaporate a drop of perspiration, much less the two liters he'd drunk, so he left Samantha to find a suitable place to relieve himself.

The forest intrigued him, and he found himself wandering through it as if it were a botanical exhibit. His eyes followed different sounds from the vast array of living things that called the place home. He saw insects of every kind, mostly big ones, lavishly decorated with splashes of color, not the little pests one found in urban settings. Lush green ferns and bright yellow flowers dotted the jungle floor. He briefly studied an anaconda as it bobbed its head from one of the low-hanging branches of a tree and stared at him with stolid, amber eyes.

Jack had never been this deep inside the *selvas*, as the locals called the rain forest. As he wound by huge rubber trees draped with vines and crossed through shaded areas where the sun was obscured by the high tree covering, Jack couldn't help thinking what variety Bolivia offered in such a small area. Tiahuanaco sat only a few hundred miles away, but in going there, they could be traveling to a different planet. Some 20 percent of Bolivia was arid, over 40 percent was rain forest, while some of it could technically be considered arctic. Bolivia encompassed over a million square kilometers and was split in half by two parallel Andean ranges, or *cordilleras*, which divided the nation into three distinct eco-zones.

The eastern lowlands, the Oriente region, included the tropical rain forests he found himself in now.

The sub-Andean region consisted of the mild to lush intermountain valleys, the *yungas*, where the poppy flowers grown to produce opiates dotted the steep ravines.

Jack had visited the Andean region twice. It included the vast, arid altiplano plateau from the Cordillera Occidental to the eastern range around Lake Titicaca. What lay in store for them at the ruins on that cold plateau sent shivers through him. An extraterrestrial hologram had pointed them toward Tiahuanaco—a place that had first sparked Jack's theories on how ancient humankind might have been helped by visitors from a long-forgotten time or place. Had extraterrestrials given the human inhabitants of the region the technological knowledge necessary to build such structures? Or better yet, what if the entire site was built by extraterrestrials themselves? Jack's spine tingled. His obsession with the enigmatic origins of humankind had only gotten deeper during the last few days.

When the pressure on his abdomen finally reminded him of his purpose, the clearing was well out of sight. He'd probably walked a few hundred yards without even realizing it. Jack stopped in front of a mossy boulder, which seemed as good an object as any to aim for. He undid the zipper on his pants. The wave of relief made him shiver and close his eyes. He kept them shut for the duration. After what felt like an eternity he opened them—only to find himself staring down the barrel of a submachine gun.

Samantha peered into the edge of the trees. Jack had been gone for quite some time. He always had a nasty habit of disappearing, and she both loved him and hated him for it. She found in Jack the fine line between a man who could love a woman—adore her with a totality of soul—without losing his sexy self-reliant spirit. She'd never found the combination before. Or since.

"I know you don't want to hear this, but we're going

to have to leave a good deal of the equipment behind. At least for now," Dorn said. He massaged her slightly burned shoulders, the result of the intense Mali sun. She didn't have the heart to tell him to stop.

She turned around and faced him. "How much will we be able to bring?"

"I'd say about half of it. If we're lucky."

"Damn."

"Once we're at the site, I'll have the rest sent up to us. I've ordered in a proper team. Men I've worked with before. They'll be able to retrieve the rest of the equipment and meet us at the ruins. Right now, it would be wise to bring just the essentials."

"Have you seen Jack?"

"No." The question seemed to annoy him.

"He'll have a better idea of exactly what we'll need." She stood up and brushed the brick-colored soil from her pants. "I'll start separating out the things we don't."

"Do you still have feelings for him?"

Samantha stopped. She looked bothered. "He was my fiancé."

"You care about him."

"Of course. I wouldn't be human if I didn't."

"Not romantically, I'd imagine."

"Romantically?" She chuckled. "You've seen how much he enjoys being around me. I don't think you have to imagine *anything* to figure that one out."

Dorn watched her as she walked toward the supplies.

Samantha worked quickly. She left behind most of the dehydrated food packs they had, figuring they could get food brought up along the way. She brought all the bottled water. Fresh, reliable drinking water would be priceless in Bolivia. She reminded herself that Tiahuanaco was over two miles above sea level and changed her mind about leaving behind some of the expedition's windbreakers and warmer clothing.

She instructed Bongane on how to pack some of the more fragile pieces of scientific machinery inside larger

cases. She used anything she could find, including socks
and dirty T-shirts, to wrap the smaller instruments so
they wouldn't be damaged. Samantha found she had a
knack for remembering what was in what crates and
quickly separated the nonessentials into a growing pile
of wood boxes behind the plane. She blotted the sweat
out of her eyes and stopped to catch her breath.

There was still no sign of Jack.

The barrel was so close Jack could actually smell the
mix of gunpowder, oil, and steel. His eyes pulled back
cautiously to take in more of the scene, briefly glancing
at the figure holding the weapon—a slim, brown-
skinned man whose red bandanna covered most of the
face. The mood was tense. Jack's arms raised in a gesture of compliance.

He kept his hands high in the air.

The figure used the barrel, still trained at his head, to
gesture before asking in a thick accent, *"Dorn?"*

*But it wasn't a man's voice.* Startled, Jack nodded
before saying, *"Sí."*

The figure in front of him pulled off the bandanna.
Jack caught his breath. She was stunning. The woman's
eyes were deep brown, almost black—the perfect color
to match the strands of raven hair that framed her angular face. Her high cheekbones bespoke a European
heritage, probably Spanish. She was slender, small
hipped, but the ammunition clip she wore in a strap
across her chest fell deeply between her breasts, which
were noticeably full, even under her button-down shirt.
Jack tried not to notice.

Dorn leaped to his feet as Jack led a small, armed contingent of a dozen or so to the clearing by the wrecked
plane. Their contacts from Trinidad had arrived.

The woman, who didn't give Jack her name, began
speaking with Dorn in broken English. She told him that
they would have to renegotiate their contract due to this

unexpected turn of events. Dorn cursed heavily before finally agreeing. They had no real options—unless they wanted to take their chances hauling through the jungle to Trinidad on their own.

Jack wasn't surprised that their escorts were so heavily armed. He knew they'd be members of one of the local drug cartels. But given the region, these were probably the safest hands to be in, he mused.

"Thought we lost you," Samantha said nonchalantly.

She looked tired. Obviously, she'd been hard at work separating their supplies into the two piles he saw before him. Jack started to explain, then satisfied himself with a shrug.

Samantha began assigning various crates to various bodies, not wasting any time.

Jack checked the belly of the plane for the rest of his personal gear. Soon he had everything he would need, including his field book. Exiting, he noticed Bongane in a struggle with the large aluminum crate that housed the artifact. The old man glistened with sweat. Jack was surprised the elder African statesman could lift the large case alone. Jack had nearly dropped his half of it in Mali.

He slid his hands under the other end of the case. "Here, I'll give you a hand."

Bongane looked at him with reddish eyes. "Tank you," he said.

They were the first words he'd ever heard the man speak.

Dorn announced the group was ready to start out. Supplies climbed onto backs and shoulders. Their newly hired guides now served double duty as porters. In a few minutes, they would be snaking their way through the forest to Trinidad on foot, where they could get vehicles for the journey into the highlands. Jack's nerves seemed tighter than piano wire. His breathing became fast and shallow. Once there, if his equations held up, he felt sure they would find whatever hidden secret the hologram drew them to. If only they could reach it in time.

Everyone carried equipment, even the skinny pilot and François, who held a large bag under his good arm. All except for the copilot, who rested in the shade of a large palm tree with his eyes closed. The poor whale of a guy must be exhausted, Jack thought.

An angry Baines went to rouse him. Jack came over too. The copilot wasn't moving.

"Does he need Ricardo to look at him?" Jack asked.

"No," said Baines. "He's dead."

# TRINIDAD

"Would you leave *your* friend?" the pilot shouted. "I'm his kid's godparent!"

Dorn had suggested that they leave the body behind. "I see no harm in leaving him here until someone can come back for him."

"He wouldn't last an hour out here before the animals got to him," the pilot said.

"He's right," Jack said. "The man has a family."

"We could bury him," Dorn grunted.

"We don't have time," Jack said.

The flushed pilot looked straight at Dorn. "What if it had been one of you? I hope to God you'd show a little more compassion."

Samantha stepped between them. "We take the body with us."

While the expedition snaked through dense jungle, Jack contemplated the sad twist of fate life had dealt the copilot. The obese man had cheated death in the crash only to go into cardiac arrest a few hours later underneath the large *totaí* palm. Ricardo figured he'd been dead for at least forty minutes, judging by the man's color and body temperature.

Baines had managed to wrap the body in canvas sacks, but it still took two men to carry the corpse. They had to leave extra supplies behind. Dorn looked annoyed. He'd been vetoed, and Jack knew it stung. Dorn was losing control, and Jack could see he hated it.

Brushing by huge palms, they continued deeper into the misty unknown. The *motacú* palm, Jack remembered, was sacred to the local Indians, who used them to thatch the roofs of their *pauhuichi*—distinctive, hand-built mud and wattle houses. Occasionally Jack thought he heard the low growl of a puma, roused from its daytime slumber by the slopping of their boots in the mud. But even among all the natural beauty surrounding them, Jack couldn't help but stare at the slender form of the Latin knockout who walked in front of him. He had discovered her name quite by accident when one of her compatriots called her by name—

*Veronica*.

Jack played with the name in his mind. The woman had a fantastic figure—and an amazing, sensual gait. She appeared to be a mestizo, a mix of mostly Spanish blood, with a touch of local Indian.

Samantha noticed him notice her, as well.

She had caught up to Jack and walked alongside him for most of the last hour. They sporadically entered into conversation on one aspect of the rain forest or another, but Jack seemed to drift away whenever Samantha started talking. She watched as his eyes bounced around in his head, in perfect unison with the butt of the little courtesan in front of them. Jack tripped on a large tree root. He nearly went down under the weight of his immense pack.

"Careful," Samantha said. "Don't want to choke on your tongue."

She sped up and left Jack rubbing his ankle. He chuckled. She had a temper, but he found the idea of her getting in a huff over his appreciation of another woman somehow satisfying. She harbored the same possessive feelings Jack still felt.

Jack eventually caught up to the smallish Bolivians in front of him. Though they looked heavily overloaded with equipment, they offered no complaints. Jack found in Bolivians a gallant heartiness and fortitude. The Bolivian people had endured strife from the very inception of their nation: horrible politicians, bad luck at war, ill-advised land deals. Few Latin American countries were as little known or poorly understood. Sadly, Bolivia's claim to fame lay in the steady stream of narcotics that flowed from its hillsides. No one ever associated the country with its perpetually snowcapped mountain peaks, or its inaccessible Amazonian jungles, or the amazing, enigmatic temples that might be the true birthplace of humanity. No one seemed to be spreading the word either. Tourists were a rarity in this quite inaccessible country, and few Bolivians emigrated to the industrialized nations of the north.

Jack watched a few Bolivians call out excitedly in front of them. Their pace quickened, even they were bent by the weighty crates on their backs and the heavy guns slung over their shoulders. Ahead their escorts found a muddy path cut through the forest—the access road that would lead the expedition into Trinidad. With luck they would soon rendezvous with the waiting vehicles.

The expedition would have to double-time it to Tiahuanaco.

They smelled the town long before they saw it. The humid breeze carried a potpourri of odors: smoke from burning vegetation, gasoline, cooked food, and trash.

Trinidad, like most towns in the lowland section of the El Beni district below Cochabamba, was poor and squalid.

Blisters had swollen, then broken on the heel of Jack's foot. Samantha walked with a noticeable limp. They had been hiking for over three hours.

Veronica told them in Spanish not to walk by the creek.

The small stream ran adjacent to the road, flowing in a hastily dug gully and clogged at various points with debris—little more than an open sewer. It probably drained straight into the Rio Mamore, Bolivia's largest river, which ran adjacent to the town.

"It's putrid," Dorn said, holding a handkerchief to his nose.

The bandannas their guides wore now proved useful in cutting the smell of human waste, which flowed freely in the stream. Jack wished he had one. He explained to Samantha that 65 percent of urban homes in Bolivia lacked potable water.

"It's not human," she said. "It's just not fair . . ."

Ricardo shook his head. "This is worse than I remember."

The group entered the outskirts of the city. A few famished stray dogs came out to greet them after lapping water out of the flowing latrine.

The armed faction led them by a series of shanties where *Kolla*, men who had migrated from even more economically depressed altiplano towns, sat outside smoking and discussing the arrival of the strange caravan.

"They're pretty bold with the artillery," Samantha said, noticing that none of their entourage made attempts at concealing their weapons.

"Certain cartels run certain towns," Jack said. "They're the equivalent of law enforcement here."

Samantha stopped. "Then what do the police do?"

"Most probably take second jobs," Jack said.

He pointed to a man in brown khaki trousers who had helped them out of the jungle. A patch on the man's arm read: POLICíA.

"Great," Samantha said.

Dorn smiled. "At least the police have already been paid off."

Veronica ushered them down muddy side streets between tightly packed tin and thatch shanties. The smell of roasting chicken and *ají*—a hot pepper plant—wafted out of the occasional hut, momentarily replacing the other fetid odors. They found themselves in an industrial district of steel-sided factories and warehouses. A group of skinny children, some lame and deformed, greeted them with smiles.

"The infant mortality rate is the highest in all of Latin America—as many as six hundred fifty per one thousand in some rural areas," Ricardo said after Samantha commented on the sorry state of the children. He went on to explain that most who did survive birth became malnourished. Sixty percent suffered from goiter, nearly half from anemia—a result of iodine and iron deficiencies. "Most don't have parents."

"How do they survive?" Samantha wondered out loud.

"They work," Ricardo said. "Veronica says the average age for working children in Bolivia has dropped. From ten years old to six."

*Six years old*, Jack thought. He listened intently as Veronica explained to them in broken English that most of the homeless waifs survived by either stomping coca, running processed paste, or selling cheap forms of the drug. Nearly all had a habit of using—even those of kindergarten age.

Veronica motioned for them to stop. She approached two well-dressed men in front of one of the larger warehouses.

After a brief dialogue she returned for Dorn. "We talk inside," she said.

Dorn turned to Baines. "Why am I getting the feeling I need my checkbook?"

"Wait here, *por favor*," Veronica told the scientists.

Samantha sat on her backpack. She'd been discussing possible ways in which they could publish the find. Jack leaned his head against one of the expedition crates. He didn't realize she'd finished.

"Jack? Is anybody home?"

"Sorry." Fascinated, Jack stared at two elderly Indian women nearby. Their widely gathered skirts, called polleras, were hiked to their knees, revealing dry calloused legs. The women came from the highlands. They spoke to each other rapidly while stitching a pair of bright red sweaters. The fine wool of the nearly extinct vicuña, a camel of sorts, slipped gracefully through their hands.

"That roving eye of yours knows no bounds."

"They're speaking Aymara." He listened to the linguistic interplay as if it were a symphony.

"Yes. The Aymara Indians speak Aymara," she said. "Why does it enthrall you so?"

"It might be derived from one of the oldest languages in the world."

"I didn't figure you for a linguist."

"I'm not. I read about it. Ivan Guzman de Rojas. Do you remember him?"

The name sounded vaguely familiar to Samantha. "A mathematician, right?"

"A Bolivian computer scientist. He published in the mid-eighties." Jack sat up. "I've always thought traces of the ancient civilization of Tiahuanaco might still be lingering in the language of the local inhabitants. Then I read Rojas's paper. He discovered something more fascinating than the possible age of the dialect. It seems Aymara might be a completely 'made-up' language. One that had been specifically *designed*."

"Humor me here, Jack. I'm outside my field."

Jack paused, slightly frustrated. The fact that most pa-

leoanthropologists did little in the way of linguistic work
was the very thing Jack believed kept the science in the
dark ages. One needed to know linguistics, astronomy,
archaeology, mathematics. Using all these fields to translate riddles from the past was the only method to a com-
prehensive understanding.

"Rojas discovered that the Aymara language possessed an artificial syntax."

"Which means?"

"Basically, the extremely rigid structure is so unam-
biguous it appears to be synthetic. Completely 'made-
up,' Samantha—to an extent that isn't found in normal
'organic' speech," he said, enthused. "Most language
evolves slowly over time. Aymara looks like it was designed from scratch."

"You're saying it was thought up all at once?"

"The language didn't grow from a linguistic childhood. It was 'created.' And its syntax is mathematical."

"Mathematical?"

"Have you heard of the Aymara Algorithm?"

"Ah, that's why Rojas sounded familiar . . ."

"Aymara can easily be transformed into a computer
algorithm—Rojas called it the 'Aymara Algorithm.' "
Jack smiled. "Now what would an ancient people need
a *computer* algorithm for?"

Her knitted brows told Jack she was with him.

"The Algorithm is used as a bridge language. The
language of an original document can be translated into
Aymara and then retranslated into all other languages.
Aymara's like a ready-made translating program. Linguists have found it invaluable."

"An artificial language with computer-friendly syntax—developed in the same place that the hologram has
directed us to . . ." Samantha reflected. "Are you thinking what I'm thinking?"

Jack could see the passion in her eyes. "Yeah," he
answered, barely able to control his own excitement.
"Our extraterrestrial must have left a legacy here too."

A torrent of curses interrupted them. Ricardo was taking another look at François's hand. The man's fingers were swollen and the white gauze around his forearm was tinged with blood. Francois must have ripped his stitches open during the trek out of the *selva*.

Ricardo had resutured the Frenchman's forearm. Disappointed with his sewing skills (he chalked it up to being a bit woozy from his potent travel elixir), he was nonetheless pleased with his orthopedic handiwork. "Come take a look," he told Samantha and Jack proudly. "I couldn't have set the fingers better even if I had X rays." During the whole discussion François smoked a cigarette, incredulous at the doctor's enthusiasm.

The creaking of the sliding doors of the warehouse heralded the return of Dorn and Baines.

"Did you get everything?" Samantha asked. They had been gone twenty minutes.

"And then some."

An engine turned over, followed by the familiar sounds of combustion. Soon, a few other motors echoed from inside the warehouse. An open Jeep pulled out in a flood of smoke, followed shortly by four other vehicles. Two looked like converted troop carriers—trucks large enough to contain all their gear. The other two looked similar to the first Jeep, only larger, perhaps old Toyota Land Cruisers, but Jack couldn't be sure. A tarp covered a large object in the back of one of them—Jack thought the object was shaped like an upside-down *L*.

"They look sturdy enough," Samantha said.

"All four-wheel drive. I don't think we'll have any problems getting up there." Dorn barked instructions to men, who began loading cargo.

Samantha and Jack supervised the placing of their equipment, trying to keep the most fragile devices together in the first truck. Samantha took special care with the two aluminum cases, fastening them down herself.

While Jack threw food packages to one of the Bolivians in the troop carrier, Dorn said, "Only thirty-two hours. Can we make Tiahuanaco before then?"

Jack sensed the nervousness in his voice. Dorn wanted it badly—as badly as he did. "If we're lucky and the roads hold up."

Getting to Tiahuanaco through the muddy roads of the intermountain *yungas* would be difficult enough in thirty-two hours. But Jack knew something the others didn't—he still hadn't settled on his final calculations. If he was wrong about the age of the temple, everything would be futile. Without the exact age, Jack wouldn't be able to place the Gateway properly, and no shadow marker would ever be found. Jack felt the embryonic stages of a headache forming. He had a day and a third to figure out the greatest riddle of his career.

Make that the greatest riddle of his life.

# WATCHERS

The crosshairs of the scope stopped on the tall, silver-haired man. He appeared distinguished, out of place, a rich man in the jungle. Interesting. The two intersecting lines halted momentarily—its center an inch above the eyes, right above the nose.

Click. Whirr. Click.

The field got fuzzy, then refocused on a heavyset Latin man. This one looked disheveled—like he'd just come off a late-night binge. The crosshairs paused briefly—click—whirr—before finding a stunning brunette. The field of focus grew sharper. The woman looked American and had wonderful blue eyes.

"Wow," a voice said. "Now that's a piece of work."

The long lens of the Nikon camera moved gently from one target to the next. Rotating film slipped quickly through the aperture. Click, whir, click, whir.

"Interesting. Who's the girl?"

"I don't know," the voice said.

The man who asked the question had fair skin dotted with light brown freckles. His long nose had turned a deep shade of pink from the sun, as if to match his auburn hair. "You mind if I take a look?"

"Keep your panties on." The burly hands that refocused the lens were smattered with scars. The man behind the camera was slightly larger than his partner and dark-skinned. His brown hair, cropped short, thinned out around his forehead. His name was Pierce. "They're not traffickers," Pierce said.

"No," the fair-skinned one said. "They look more like doctors."

"The fat one looks like he *needs* a doctor." Pierce readjusted the lens. He noticed the dirt and grime that caked their clothes. "Wherever they came from, they had a helluva time getting here. They all look like shit," Pierce said. "Except for the girl, that is."

"I'll have to take your word for it," the younger man replied, unable to conceal his resentment.

"They didn't come with visas. Nothing like their description has come up in the last twelve months. I would have remembered a babe like that."

The fair-skinned man, Miller, pulled out a small cassette recorder and pressed record. "Tuesday, March eighteenth, 1998. Sixteen-forty-two hours."

He propped up the recorder on the vinyl backpack in front of Pierce, who began speaking instinctively without taking his eye from the lens.

"Tall Caucasian, refined-looking, fifties. Obviously the money guy. He deals almost exclusively with Veronica Pena—lucky bastard. Her second, Salcedo, is at her side as usual."

Veronica ranked high in the cartel pecking order. She usually worked the bigger deals, which is why the agents tailed her after the tip from Checa's phone call.

"Mr. Money is followed around by your typical thug-for-hire, fortyish. If I had to bet, the hat is South African. Maybe Australian. Two more younger goons—probably mercs. Taller of the two is injured. Right arm bandaged. We have a skinny little Caucasian. Looks like the pilot. Never seen him down here before. Not one of our trafficking flyboys."

"They could have gone down in the *selvas*," Miller said. "Probably why we didn't pick them up earlier."

"Larger Latin in early forties. Maybe a doctor—looked at the merc's arm. Accompanied by another Caucasian male—could be some damn river guide or something. Then there's a female Caucasian—mid-thirties. Beautiful. Real beautiful." Pierce paused before adding an extra note to the tape, "Boys, I expect you to keep a few of these photos for me, would ya?"

"For shitsakes, Pierce, some of us still care about our jobs."

Pierce chuckled. Young CIA agents were always nervous about losing their jobs—end of the cold war paranoia. Miller was especially fearful. His wife had just had a baby.

"Oh-oh. What's this?" Pierce asked. He adjusted the lens on the Nikon and trained it on the last truck, where it stopped. "Got an older black gent of African citizenship. Wearing distinct African clothing. Large earring. Some kind of a brand on the left shoulder. Could probably trace. Pictures should enhance."

"You think it has anything to do with the Checa call?"

"Probably," Pierce said. "I just don't understand the connection."

The phone taps in Foreign Minister Checa's office had mentioned something about a "present" arriving in Trinidad. Then Checa told the man on the phone that he'd call him back in five minutes from a different line. It was the fourth time this week. Checa knew he was being tapped. *But who tipped him?* Pierce wondered. It was a shame. He had nearly indicted half the country before he got wise that his "safe" line was hot. The CIA had been following his illegal activities in Bolivia for a year and a half, building a case that would help the Bolivian police send him to prison for good. Checa was overtly hostile to US interests—he supplied illegal arms to anti-American guerrillas throughout Central America and played a role in much of the narcotics traffic that ended up in the States. The agency wanted him ousted. Their directive was to use any method they could—short of assassination—to take him out.

Pierce rested the camera on his knee and turned off the recorder, placing the microcassette in his shirt pocket and storing the recorder in his full knapsack. The bag contained satellite communications gear and a few field observation devices.

"What would Checa be doing with some scientists?" Pierce thought out loud.

"Maybe they're here to analyze some paste."

"I doubt it," Pierce said. "They have way too much equipment. I wonder what's in the crates?"

"They've got deep pockets, that's for sure. I see one, two—looks like six trucks all together. Wonder where they're off too?"

"Don't know. Don't care, frankly."

"We're not following them?"

"Not unless they're heading to Sucre," Pierce said, throwing the heavy pack over his shoulder.

"But it might be interesting," Miller protested.

Pierce disassembled the camera tripod. "We don't get paid to follow a bunch of misfit doctors through the countryside. We're here to nail Checa on something serious."

"You're convinced these people have nothing to do with Checa or drugs?"

"Oh, they might have something to do with Checa,"

Pierce said. "But no chance in hell this crew is mixed up in the trade. I'd bet my career on it."

Miller remained silent. The last part of Pierce's sentence obviously carried some weight.

"You know what I think, kid?"

"What?"

"I think this is part of Checa's little zoo operation," Pierce said, referring to the man's illegal exotic animal trade. The minister had shipped thousands of species out of the country over the last eighteen months. But that crime would never stick and certainly wouldn't put him away for life. They needed drugs. Murder.

"You think they're running animals?"

"A bunch of doctors or scientists. Bunch of crates. Trekking through the *selvas*. I'd bet they're out here collecting for a damn zoo."

"You might be right."

"Might be right?" Pierce said. "I'd bet my left testicle on it."

Miller shrugged.

"So. You want to go trekking through the damn jungle to see what little critters they decide to bring back for some five-year-olds to stare at," Pierce said. "Or do you want to get back to Sucre and find the hundred kilos, that you know—as well as I do—will be there."

Miller's blank stare confirmed the young man's agreement.

"Thank you," Pierce said. "You know I've never steered you wrong." He handed the camera to Miller, who, though beaten, decided to take one more look.

Pierce hadn't taken two steps before Miller called out: "Hold on . . . I think you might want to take a look at this."

"What is it now?"

Miller held out the camera and pointed to two men struggling to load a canvas-wrapped burden into the side of a Volkswagen van that had just pulled up. The pilot spoke a few words with the driver.

Pierce put the camera to his eye.

"Sweet Moses," Pierce said. Their surveillance might have paid off. He watched the two men below forcibly bend back the fat, blue arm of a corpse that rigidly extended between the seam of the two sacks.

"I'm glad you have two," Miller said.

Pierce looked confused.

"Testicles, that is."

Pierce's face got red.

"Get out the SAT-link," he said. "We'll transmit from here."

# ALTIPLANO

Within a half hour the convoy of trucks had left Trinidad far behind. The loading of the trucks went smoothly; the twelve escorts worked fast and professionally.

Veronica and another lighter-skinned man seemed to be in charge of the operation. All the same, Jack hadn't argued when Baines suggested he carry a pistol. Most of the Bolivians had probably killed at one point in their lives—he could see it in their hardened, dark eyes. Too, Jack noticed them staring lustily at Samantha, and if they touched her, he'd kill them.

Jack got in the lead truck with Veronica, who had asked him to ride with her. Jack noticed, with some pleasure, that Samantha looked annoyed.

"The woman is your *novia*?" Veronica asked after they rolled out of the village.

"She used to be," he said in Spanish.

She shrugged, her face expressionless.

The caravan would avoid La Paz, the Bolivian capital. Going through it might have made the trip shorter, but their escorts obviously didn't need the attention. Neither did the scientists. Jack reminded himself they were technically fugitives. They carried no visas and had never gone through customs. Besides, he had been in La Paz before; its notorious rush hour lasted most of the day.

For the first half of their ascent into the Andes, Veronica spoke about her family. She disclosed more information than Jack expected. A few times she even caught herself and smiled shyly at him. Jack detected a tenderness behind her hard exterior. He found her quite like Samantha in that respect. She had come up in a man's world, achieved a position of status. Still, the toughness she so carefully projected seemed to mask a vulnerable inner self that had been hurt deeply along the way.

The caravan of trucks crawled up ever steeper hillsides. In the distance, usually hidden between ravines, Jack occasionally made out fields of opium poppies—brilliant patches of red and white tucked among walls of granite.

Imperceptibly at first, then radically, the landscape and fauna changed. After clearing a river that carved the hard rock of the canyon, the road opened to a spectacular vista. Majestic peaks dusted with snow gave way to a savanna of undulating, treeless hills. The place seemed dreamlike—a world hidden by mist and cloud. The road flattened. Jack realized they had reached the highland plains of the altiplano. The winds tore sharply at the trucks now. Veronica slid closer to Jack in order to keep warm. Her shoulder nestled itself behind his back. She looked up to him and smiled comfortably. An electricity pulsed through him. Veronica's breathing got heavier too. He imagined making love to her. Soon, Jack felt her full weight press against his side. Her eyes were closed. Jack knew a night with this woman would be priceless, but he'd also become aware of the superficial nature of his attraction. The magic of her allure remained best untapped. Instead, feeling her warm body against his, he realized how badly he missed Samantha's embrace and the intimacy they once shared.

The trucks soon passed fields of corn and potatoes— Andean staples. Some two hundred varieties could be found here; Jack felt sure he'd tried at least half during his two trips to Bolivia. Though a staple in the Indian diet, along with the high-altitude cereals of *quinoa* and *canahua*, Jack pledged to eat his own hands before sticking another dry spud down his throat. For the last four years, he hadn't even been able to order fries.

The trucks slowed to let a herd of alpacas cross the dirt road along their grazing lane to the high rolling hills. The shepherds wore sweaters and black felt hats. They swung light reed sticks at the animals, which hoofed billows of dust into the air as they crossed. Jack found it amazing the animals could survive grazing on the wild scrub grasses and cacti along the high plateau. As the convoy waited patiently, Jack made brief eye contact with Samantha, who watched him from the truck ahead.

She quickly turned around. Samantha always feigned disinterest whenever she was angry or jealous. Maybe her feelings for him were stronger than he thought.

The gear boxes of the trucks protested loudly and the convoy moved forward once again. Jack pulled out his binoculars from the travel bag at his feet.

*"El lago,"* Jack said. His shifting had awoken Veronica.

In the distance, the blue alpine waters of Lake Titicaca shimmered like a mirage.

# LAST SUPPER

"I didn't know rust could float," Ricardo said.

The convoy stopped in front of a battered ferry. What little paint still remained was peeling off in chunks, regretfully making way for the red iron oxide that coated the craft. The ship floated humbly at a worn wooden dock that extended into the shallow bay. The small fishing town of Tiquine had the only ferry service that would get them and their gear across the lake, although after seeing the floating morgue, Jack knew that if the access road around the icy fingers of Lake Titicaca hadn't been closed, he'd have chosen the longer route.

Samantha climbed down from the first truck and met Jack at the gangplank in front of the small dock. "Enjoy your ride?"

"Yes, I did," Jack said. "Thank you."

Veronica slid out of the truck, wearing Jack's coat. "Let's hurry up and get this stuff on board," Samantha said.

After driving the trucks onto the ferry Dorn was informed by the first mate, an Indian with his upper front teeth missing, that the crew would need to make a few repairs before setting out. "A few repairs?" Dorn looked at Jack, then back at the Indian. "Where the hell is the captain?"

They finally found the captain of the rust bucket hard at work in the engine room. He must have smelled Dorn pissing vinegar because he jumped up and smiled, throwing his arm around Dorn like he was a longtime

friend—before explaining that the few "minor adjust-
ments" he needed to make would take a few hours.

Jack trailed Dorn, who marched angrily up the dirt
road toward the small hamlet.

Discouraged by the delay, Jack nonetheless had trouble concealing a smile as he noticed the perfect black
imprint of the captain's arm across the back of Dorn's
shirt.

The large oxcart provided perfect cover. Bundles of
tightly wrapped *totora* reeds inside the cart concealed
the Jeep, yet left enough spaces to assess the entire area.
Pierce took notes while the trucks rumbled onto the
ferry. Miller needed only two pieces of bubble gum to
enlist a small Indian boy. The newest and youngest op-
erative for the CIA limped back from the ferry and informed Pierce, between bubbles, that the boat had been
chartered for the far side of the lake, the ruins of Tiahuanaco.

"What would the cartel want with abandoned ruins?"
Pierce asked. Miller shook his head, chewing on beef
jerky like a cow on its cud.

Pierce watched the group of doctors and mercenaries
walk up a gently sloping hill toward a cluster of small
buildings. It was getting colder. Pierce buttoned the top
few buttons on his jacket and told himself this was the
strangest narc deal he'd ever witnessed.

"Want some?" Miller held out a stick of beef jerky.

Pierce shook his head. He pulled his coat up around
his ears and slid farther into the seat of the Jeep. Agency
brass in Viriginia had ordered them to trail Veronica
while specialists tried to identify the newcomers. Nothing to do now but wait. The two field agents would
follow their standing directive until further notice: *Remain in visual contact.*

The ferry captain had told the group that the inn just up
the hill served spectacular local seafood. Initially, Jack
was bothered by the thought of wasting time to eat, but

no other options existed—the ferry had a complete mo-
nopoly here. Upon entering the mud and wood structure
Jack smelled the smoking aroma of freshly cooked fish,
and his spirits lifted. A fire raged in a large hearth, casting an orange glow across the room, which served as
both a common area and dining hall. The night chill had
already set in. Samantha warmed herself by the round
stones of the fireplace before joining Dorn, Baines, Ricardo, and Jack at the only available table. A group of
dusty fishermen occupied the other two, seemingly intent
on drinking long into the night.

The proprietors set tables for the rest of the convoy
outside, under a canopy of bright stars. Bongane ate
alone near some of the Bolivian escorts who smoked
*pitillos*, the cocaine-laced cigarettes popular in the Andes, and remained silent during the meal. Jack watched
him, having developed a curious fondness for the old
man, who seemed so out of place and alone. Jack could
empathize with the man's isolation. Within his peer
group, he had been there for years.

The meal itself lasted less than twenty minutes. The
group wolfed down the spicy lake trout without much
talk. Afterward they enjoyed some of the house *cocteles*
and a steamy *pisco* punch. Jack felt a tingling in his
cheeks after only half-draining his cup—the effects enhanced by the altitude. In the distance, music floated to
them from a bar across the dirt road, the sounds be-
speaking eons of South American culture. The melodies
came from the *siku*—the distinctive long wood flutes of
the highland Indians. Rows of these vertical flutes provided a ghostly sound that often, especially on higher
notes, bordered on the macabre. A solo *charango* accompanied the flutes. A cross between a banjo and man-
dolin, it sounded like nothing else on earth.

As the group settled around the fire for warmth, Jack
looked at Samantha, reclining against the finished
stones. Her brown hair was lustrous, teased by the
orange-red demons that flickered about the room; her

sky blue wool sweater was no match for the intensity of her eyes.

He fought the urge to sit next to her, instead finding a dark wood chair nearby. Dorn sat next to him and pressed Jack to elaborate on the Aymara Algorithm. Samantha had filled him in on the way. Spawned by all the necessary ingredients—interesting people, a warm fire, even warmer liquor, and a lack of something to do—a deep conversation commenced. Within minutes it had segued into Jack's notions of a lost civilization— one before recorded history.

"You mean like the long-lost civilization of Atlantis?"

"Yes."

Dorn chuckled. "I can see why some of your thinking got you into hot water. Atlantis is a myth, isn't it? I know it makes for great television, but surely you can't believe it actually existed?"

"I can," Jack said. "But not because I think it's a chic idea. It's just one of the only things that makes sense to me. One of the only things that explains how man suddenly evolved into a great civilization—seemingly overnight—right from the Stone Age."

"Jack doesn't buy into the current notions on the evolution of man," Samantha said.

Dorn said, "I gathered that."

"If you want to put a name on this lost civilization you can. I'm not pretending to know where it is, who it was, or even where it went."

"And you think the extraterrestrials might have had a hand in that civilization's development?" Dorn wondered.

Jack brightened. His bizarre theories now rang with an air of truth, backed by the most wonderful discovery he could have ever imagined. "That's what I would guess. But regardless, common sense assures me this civilization existed. We find clues all over the world. Myths from every part of the globe document it—"

"You can't base science on myths," Dorn said.

"Why not?" Jack stood and walked beside the hearth, which bathed him in soft, warm light. "Myths to me are convenient ways of passing down history—before recorded time. If cultures across the globe speak of the sudden disappearance of a great civilization—cultures that had no contact with one another—I'm inclined to believe them. Just as I'm inclined to believe Alexander the Great conquered Persia or Julius Caesar was assassinated. If you believe those stories, why not the ones from an even older time? Myths *are* history. History before written records."

Dorn chewed on his pipe. "Most anthropologists don't seem to agree."

"There are more and more of us," Jack said. "And not just in anthropology. Astronomers, linguists, historians; researchers like Posnansky, Santillana, Sellers—they're all willing to say something is wrong with our current notions of the past." Jack took a drink of his warm punch. "Graham Hancock says we are 'a species with amnesia.' That's the best I've heard it described. I think the human race has forgotten where it came from. If we'll just listen to our own myths, our prehistory begs to be told. How else can you explain the countless stories of a global disaster that nearly wiped out mankind?"

"You're talking about the flood. From the Bible."

"Yes. A great deluge. A shaking of the earth. An act so horrible, someone tried making sure we wouldn't forget."

"You truly believe it happened?" Dorn asked.

"I know it did." Jack paused. "There are over five hundred deluge legends from around the world. Dr. Richard Andree, who studied eighty-six of them from four continents, concluded that sixty-two were entirely independent of Hebrew and Mesopotamian accounts. All tell of the near destruction of our species—and the few survivors that had to start all over again."

"Like Noah," Samantha said.

"Or like Utnapishtim for the Sumerians; or Tezpi from

Central America; or the Mayan accounts of the Great
Father and Great Mother, who survived the destruction
to repopulate the earth. The Inuit believed the great flood
was accompanied by an earthquake, which occurred so
quickly that only a few managed to survive. The Luiseño
Indians of lower California believed those survivors fled
to the highest peaks until the water receded. The Karens
of Burma tell of two brothers who were saved from the
flood on a raft. In Vietnam, a brother and sister survived
in a wooden chest—along with two of every kind of
animal. In Malaysia, the Chewong people believe that
every now and then their world—Earth Seven, they call
it—turns upside down and everything gets flooded and
destroyed. The Samoans, the Japanese, the Greeks, the
Egyptians—the list goes on and on."

Jack paused, and stared at the flames. "We didn't just
*evolve* from the Stone Age . . . we were blasted *back* into
the Stone Age—by a great catastrophe that nearly wiped
us off the planet."

Wind rattled the shutters outside, and the invisible
Andean chill poured in through the open front door.

"To think we now are the apex of civilization, arrived
at in a completely linear fashion, is not only arrogant
but also sadly contradictory to the facts. Plato insisted
in two of his books that periodic catastrophes ravaged
our planet and left only a few survivors, in his words—
'destitute of letters and education to begin all over again
as children.' "

Samantha gazed at Jack. He had always inspired her.
She followed his every move, aware of why she had
fallen so deeply for him years ago.

"You see, civilization might be circular, not linear.
What if civilization had risen and fallen and risen again?
Plato based his thoughts on the evidence he had about
the great catastrophe that forced survivors to relearn. Re-
civilize. Fact after fact points to a different notion of
prehistory from the one my anthropology professors
shoved down my throat."

"What do you mean?" Dorn asked.

"There are hundreds of anomalies that don't fit into the current notions on our origin as a species—on the history of civilization in general. Take the dating of the Sphinx."

"What about it?" Dorn asked.

Jack began to pace—a habit formed over hundreds of lectures. "The great Sphinx, according to conventional thought, was built around twenty-five hundred years before Christ, by the pharaoh Khafre. That's what's taught in schools. But recently geologists—god bless them—using modern geological dating techniques, discovered that the Sphinx has to be much older. John West and Robert Schoch have bet their reputations that the erosion patterns on the Sphinx could only have been caused by heavy rains over a long period of time."

"But Egypt is dry as a bone," Baines said.

"Exactly." Jack stopped to sip his drink. "Egypt has been dry as a bone for four or five thousand years. But it wasn't always. Ten to fifteen thousand years ago the land that would become Egypt was wet, fertile. It rained a lot. The Sphinx has to have been built *before* then. And not by the Egyptians. The Sphinx was built long before they arrived, and with a technology that rivals ours today."

"Then who built it?" Dorn asked.

"I don't know. A civilization only rumored to exist. Atlantans, if you like. Or a great culture that had been wiped out like so many others. Or maybe . . ."

"You can't think extraterrestrials built the pyramids and the Sphinx?" Dorn said.

"I don't know if they built them. Perhaps they only provided the know-how."

"If you asked me before," Ricardo said, "I'd say you were crazy. But now. After what we've found . . ."

"It seems too damn unbelievable," Dorn muttered.

"So did the existence of extraterrestrials on Earth," Jack said. "Until a few days ago."

"Jack's right," Samantha said. Her eyes were alight with excitement. "We found evidence of probable extra-terrestrial interaction in Mali. And now the hologram is pointing us here—to an important civilization of prehistory."

"Bloody bizarre," Baines said, staring blankly into the fireplace.

"All I'm saying is that sound logic points to some lost connection between ancient humankind and that extra-terrestrial," Jack said. "Think about it—our ancestors' knowledge of astronomy far exceeded ours. They knew the celestial dome is fixed—that the sun, moon, and planets rotate. They knew the exact circumference of the planet—it's incorporated into hundreds of different systems of measure around the globe. Mathematicians and engineers can see the phenomenon in surviving buildings because the ancient people incorporated the figures in their architecture. And these figures were exact," Jack added. "We were only able to obtain exact values like them after Sputnik first circled the globe in 1957."

"Then there's the megalithic structures," Ricardo said.

"The biggest anomalies of all," Jack said. "We're talking about stone blocks, virtually impossible to quarry and move, found throughout the world. They're in the pyramids of Egypt and at Cuzco. The stone slabs of Baalbek, in Lebanon—a temple of totally unknown origin—weigh more than eight hundred tons—each! They're across the lake at Tiahuanaco. We can't move these blocks today. But someone once did."

"How?" Dorn mused.

"I can only speculate. But after seeing that hologram I'd say those crazy scientists who argue that the ancients must have possessed some sort of levitation or antigravity technology might not be too far off."

"Levitation?" Baines asked.

"The Spanish chroniclers who stumbled on Tiahua-naco heard accounts from the local inhabitants about the original builders—long before their time—who miraculously raised huge rocks into the air to the sound of loud noises," Jack said.

*"The Source?"* Dorn said.

"The artifact and hologram are proof such a device could have existed," Samantha said.

"So is the fact that our ancestors used platinum, a metal that melts only at one thousand seven hundred fifty-three degrees, and aluminum, which wasn't thought to be discovered until the nineteenth century. And the existence of advanced alloy staples found in both Egypt and South America that held together stone blocks so large we can't move them," Jack said. "Do you realize what kind of machine it would take to do these things today?"

Ricardo downed his drink, eyes betraying his inebriation. "It would have to be quite remarkable, indeed."

The table of fishermen applauded. The men whistled, blind drunk. Perhaps they had understood a word or two. Or maybe they were just happy he finally shut up, Jack thought. Regardless, the room quieted, leaving just the fire whispering to the warm rocks inside the hearth. Each person seemed to be imagining their own version of such a machine.

"So you think *extraterrestrials* gave us this technology?" Dorn asked point-blank.

Jack was about to answer him—he had a good idea that the ancient accounts of the Shining Ones might shed light on the subject.

But a deep foghorn belched twice in the distance.

It was their signal the ferry had been repaired.

# THE LAKE

The ferry chugged along at top speed—barely faster than a dawdling sea cucumber, Jack thought. The captain of the rusty barge told Jack if he pushed the craft any harder it would quit on them. When Samantha reminded him that another ferry wouldn't come for two days he had stopped hassling the man and instead worked on his calculations for the site. After an hour Jack's brain forced him to take a break.

It had gotten colder.

He pulled on a sweater he had bought from the two Aymara women back in Trinidad. The soft wool cut the chill considerably. Neither the four aspirin nor the coca tea the locals used as an elixir for the extreme altitude of Lake Titicaca seemed to help his aching head. The strong liquor at the inn certainly didn't. Jack left his notes on the weathered table inside the rundown pilot-house, his head hopelessly muddled. The altitude affected him, but he knew had he been at sea level, the calculations wouldn't be any easier.

Jack staggered forward, fighting the rolling of the boat until he reached the bow. Light from a three-quarter moon cascaded across the expanse of water, reflecting on the ripples the brisk wind churned. He fumbled for the Chap Stick that had lodged itself hopelessly into a seam of his pocket and coated his dry lips.

Lake Titicaca rested at an elevation of 12,500 feet, making it the highest navigable lake in the world. It was enormous, covering some 3,200 square miles; to the Aymara, its vastness probably seemed like a sea.

Geologically speaking, the lake was born of a long-lost world. Though more than two miles above sea level, the surrounding land was littered with fossilized seashells, suggesting that at one time the altiplano had been forced upward from a seabed. During this geologic change, great quantities of ocean water could have been suspended throughout the Andean ranges and become landlocked. Though hundreds of miles from the ocean, many of the animals dwelling in the lake were oceanic rather than freshwater types.

Traces of a more recent upheaval could also be seen. Archaeologists had found evidence that at one time Tiahuanaco itself had sat on an island in Lake Titicaca. Now the city's ruins rested twelve miles from the water's edge. Jack had read all of Posnansky's papers on Tiahuanaco. Posnansky was one of the first to claim the city had once been an island port. In his excavations, he uncovered artificially dredged docks that could have berthed hundreds of ships. Some of these huge stone structures weighed over 440 tons. Posnansky believed that a catastrophe occurred at Tiahuanaco. Jack recalled the most chilling of the man's findings:

> Fragments of human and animal skeletons had been found lying in chaotic disorder among the wrought stones, utensils, tools and an endless variety of other things. All of this has been moved, broken and accumulated in a confused heap. Anyone who would dig a trench here two metres deep could not deny that the destructive force of water, in combination with brusque movements of the earth, must have accumulated those different kinds of bones, mixing them with pottery, jewels, tools, and utensils.

Local legend supported the notion that the city fell to a natural catastrophe that separated it from the lake. Jack stared at the black silhouette of the Andes that framed the lake and wondered.

He took a deep breath and reoriented himself. He
needed to have an accurate figure on the age of the temple and the position of the Gateway. There would be no
second chances. He knew no matter what the hologram
revealed, Tiahuanaco would only give up its secret during the morning of the equinox.

Jack sat alone inside the cabin. Two lanterns assisted the
flickering cabin lights, which rose and fell with the throb
of the ferry engine. His eyes imitated the motor's
rhythm, opening and closing in the warm ambiance of
the ship. Most of the group stole naps on the dirty bunks
in the sleeping compartment. Jack would have welcomed
the dingy mattress, but he needed every second before
dawn. On the galley table lay a map of Tiahuanaco. His
field book—opened to the sketches from the Dogon burial ceremony—sat on his lap. He had just settled on his
final calculation—the decision on where to place the
Gateway.

Jack felt two hands on his shoulders.

Warm fingers kneaded the knots in his back, pulling
at the taut muscle between his neck and shoulders. Samantha had awoken. She'd been nesting on the bunk
behind him, having fallen asleep while helping him with
the figures. Jack closed his eyes. For a moment, he was
back at Princeton—getting the same wonderful massage
she would give him during late nights at school. "How's
it coming?" she asked.

"It's coming," Jack said, wearily.

His eyes opened again; they read and reread the dia-
grams on the page before him. He found it hard to con-
centrate. Then, as if Samantha had only just become
fully conscious, she stopped and took the seat opposite
him. She seemed embarrassed. "We've got an hour," she
said.

"I know."

Jack had just spoken to the captain, who promised
they'd dock in forty minutes. That left the scientists

twenty minutes to reach the ruins and another hour to construct the facade of the Gateway before the sun fully cleared the Andes.

An awkward silence followed. Samantha shifted nervously. "So the precession is the key."

"To everything," he said. "The evidence is overwhelming." Jack scratched his scalp with his pen. "The great catastrophe myths are pinned to precessional numbers, as if to give us some cosmic countdown to potential cataclysm. Many speak metaphorically about a mill that keeps turning—perhaps our journey around the sun. A mill that breaks apart every so often . . ."

"And you can find these precessional numbers in myths all over the world?"

Jack nodded. "Sellers studied the Osiris myth of ancient Egypt. She discovered it contained crucial numbers for keeping track of the equinoxes; namely: 360, 12, and 30."

"It's five days off on the days of the year," Samantha said.

Jack smiled. "A phrase in the myth actually says that five extra days were 'won from the moon,' giving us 365 days. But later on the myth gives the most startling figure. The number 72. According to the myth, 'the evil deity known as Set led a group of conspirators in a plot to kill Osiris.' The number of these conspirators was 72."

"Why is that so significant?"

"It's the most preeminent number in precession. Seventy-two years is how long it takes us to shift one degree along the ecliptic. You'll find it over and over again." Jack pushed his field book in front of Samantha. "Sellers proposed that with this last number, we're in a position to 'boot up' and set running an ancient computer program."

Samantha read Jack's scratchy notes beneath a photocopy of Sellers's paper:

12 = the number of constellations in the zodiac

30 = the number of degrees allocated along the ecliptic to each zodiacal constellation

72 = the number of years required for the equinoctial sun to complete a precessional shift of one degree along the ecliptic

360 = the total number of degrees in the ecliptic

72 × 30 = 2160 = the number of years required for the sun to complete a passage of 30 degrees along the ecliptic, i.e., to pass entirely through any one of the 12 zodiacal constellations

2160 × 12 (or 360 × 72) = the number of years in one complete precessional cycle or "Great Year," and thus the total number of years required to bring about the "Great Return"

36 = the number of years required for the equinoctial sun to complete a precessional shift of half a degree along the ecliptic

4320 = the number of years required for the equinoctial sun to complete a precessional shift of 60 degrees (or two zodiacal constellations)

"Amazing," she said.

"You'll see the same numbers elsewhere. A Norse myth tells of '432,000 fighters who sallied forth from Valhalla to do battle with "the Wolf." '" Ancient Chinese traditions referring to a universal cataclysm were said to have been written down in a great text consisting of 4,320 volumes. Thousands of miles away, the Babylonian historian Berossus assigned a total reign of 432,000 years to the mythical kings who ruled the land of Sumer.

"The numbers also appear in architecture. The Cambodian temple of Angkor seems to be built as a giant metaphor for the precession. Five gates are bordered by gigantic stone figures—108 per avenue, 54 on each side—making the total number of statues 540. These are all precessional numbers," Jack said. "There are 72 bell-shaped stupas at the temple of Borobudur in Java; 54

columns surround the temple of Baalbeck in Lebanon. In India, we find 10,800 bricks in the Indian fire altar, *Agnicayana*. In the Rig-Veda—an ancient Indian book of mythology—there are exactly 10,800 stanzas."

"And?" Samantha asked.

"Those 10,800 stanzas are broken down into 40 syllables each. Which means the entire composition is made up of 432,000 syllables—exactly."

Samantha looked stunned.

Jack flipped through more pages of his notes. "Here it is," he said. "In the Hebrew Cabala there are 72 angels who can be invoked if you know their names."

"The repeating numbers in all these myths can't be coincidence," she said.

"No, they can't." Jack looked charged; awake.

"Brilliant," she whispered.

Two dim floodlights snapped on, casting a pale light over the bow of the ferry. Somewhere above them, the captain shouted at crew members. Through the opaque, dew-covered windows Jack could make out a small pier. He stood up.

"We're here," he said.

"Show time." Samantha was on her feet. "You've arrived at an age for the temple, haven't you?"

"Yeah. I just hope it's right."

"What's your number?"

"It sounds absurd."

"So does everything you say," Samantha said, smiling. "But . . . you're usually right."

The words felt like a warm hug. "I think it's at least 32,000 years old."

Samantha's jaw dropped.

"The astrological alignment of the temple corresponds to 23 degrees 8'48". The angle indicates it had to be built during the precessional era that corresponds to 15,000 B.C. That's also what Posnansky concluded, since it aligns perfectly with both solstices and the equinox at that time."

"But your figure's 25,000 years older."

"Actually one year older," Jack said. He seemed invigorated at recalling his newest revelation. "One *Great Year* older. The Dogon obelisk at the burial ceremony was the key. The markings on the stone seemed to calculate Great Years. I counted two Great Years on the obelisk, which meant their artifact came from the 'Wise Ones' *two* Great Years ago."

Jack's breathing had gotten heavier.

Samantha's eyes widened. "That predates the Incas and Mayans by more than 30,000 years. The Sumerians and Egyptians by more than 25,000. Jack, if that's right, it would make Tiahuanaco . . ."

"The cradle of humanity," Jack said.

# TIAHUANACO

The steel gate at the front of the ferry rose, and the convoy of trucks roared onto hard soil. Over the rugged, bleak landscape no roads could be found. From the lead truck, where he sat in front of Ricardo, Dorn, and Samantha, Jack pointed to where two thin lines on the ground disappeared into the darkness.

"We follow those tire tracks," Jack said. "The temple's just east of here."

They'd be racing the sun. Already the soft, blue glow of dawn loomed behind the jagged cutout of the Andes. Slowed by the maze of rocks that peppered the terrain, the trunks bounced and heaved.

Jack explained his calculations to Ricardo, who began

planning the construction of the Gateway's facade. The scientists would use tent poles and canvas to construct a passable mock-up of the Gateway, which could then be moved toward its original and correctly aligned position, but they would have to work fast.

After ten minutes the convoy climbed a gentle slope. In the dim light, Jack pointed to a series of huge furrows in the soil. "We're getting close. Those are Tiahuanaco's ancient agricultural plots."

Scientists had recently discovered the purpose behind the system of trenches that surrounded Tiahuanaco. The series of ditches once held minimoats of water, which kept temperatures constant and protected crops from the killing frosts of the highlands by creating an artificial microclimate. The long-forgotten method had been reintroduced to the local Indians with spectacular results, increasing crop production sixfold.

After another mile, Jack told the driver to stop. In front of them the land rose into a sea of mist. The milky nebula created a dreamscape of pearlescent foam, which hung above lonely gray rock. Moist fingers of fog tickled the terrain, undulating into rifts and gullies. The engines shut off. Silence swallowed them.

A sense of isolation swept through the group. They had climbed into another world. Jack twisted open a steel canister of oxygen and fumbled with the plastic lines that flowed out of it. He placed the plastic cup from the oxygen tank against his mouth and inhaled. The precious gas revitalized him. His thinking became sharp, focused. As if in perfect sync with the clouds clearing from his head, the mist slowly retreated from the hill.

Jack stepped out of the truck. "This is it."

Samantha joined him. "Are you sure?"

As if to answer her a wall of stone showed its smooth face through the fog just fifty yards upslope. The wall trailed away at an angle, the upper portion still concealed in moisture.

"It's the Akapana Pyramid," Jack said. He rifled through his bag, retrieving a flashlight.

Dorn climbed out of the truck. His boots crunched the rocky scree with each step. "It's quiet."

"Sacred," Jack said. "Many Bolivians refuse to come near it."

"Does Tiahuanaco hold religious significance for the Aymara?" Samantha asked.

"In a roundabout way. But their people had nothing to do with its construction. It was here long before them. The first Spaniards asked the local Indians if they had built this place, but the Indians laughed. They said Tiahuanaco wasn't built by the Aymara *or* their forefathers—the Inca . . ."

Jack started up the hill and vanished into the fog.

Samantha, Dorn, and Ricardo followed the sounds of Jack's footsteps and caught him pausing at the crest of the hill on the west side of the pyramid. Below them lay the Temple of *Kalasasaya*, which in Aymara meant literally "The Place of the Upright Standing Stones."

"Is that the temple that measures the equinox?" Dorn asked.

Jack didn't take his eyes off his notes. "Yeah."

The ruins sat on a stone masonry terrace, aligned east to west like most ancient monuments—to be in line with the sun. A long stone wall outlined the enclosure. Spaced perfectly alongside this wall, immense monoliths jutted out of the earth like giant stone fingers. The pillars stood close to twelve feet high. Jack led the three in a jog past the Akapana Pyramid. Its immensity was not lost on Samantha.

"They're huge," she said, touching the megalithic blocks that made up the base.

Out of breath, but refusing to slow, Jack said, "Tiahuanaco seemed to spring up overnight. The locals said these huge stones were magically carried through the air to the sounds of blaring trumpets. Some of the stones weigh over two hundred tons. The Spanish were mystified. No human force could have transported them."

"They're doing a number on me," Ricardo said, wheezing in the thin air.

Their excitement quelled the conversation. They took in the precision of the ancient architecture; the sheer size of the megalithic stones.

The group cleared the side of the pyramid, which ran close to seven hundred feet long and loomed over them with a sinister presence. Then they stumbled down a gentle slope, passing a sunken depression that had been dubbed the Subterranean Temple, though no one understood what purpose the enigmatic structure served.

Just beside this depression lay the infamous *Kalasasaya*. Fifty-four stone sentries surrounded the rectangular enclosure, creating the effect of a huge stockade, but Jack knew the twelve-foot pillars served a benign but no less important purpose. They'd been used to track the earth's position in space. In the center of the enclosure a stone platform looked over the Western Gallery of pillars, which lay directly in line with the main gate. On either side of the Western Gallery the distinct black form of two stone edifices broke up the perfect symmetry.

"That's the Gateway," Jack said. He pointed to the far corner of the temple, where an enormous arch of stone looked out over the tundra. "We don't have much time. I've got to check a few last calculations before you start on the construction of the mock-up. Ricardo, you have to measure the dimensions perfectly—we'll only have one shot." Jack looked at each person in the group. "I guess this is it."

Then he broke in a jog toward the Gateway of the Sun.

Samantha, Ricardo, and Dorn entered the enclosure. The three seemed awed, slowed by the magnificent setting.

"It looks like a fortress," Dorn said.

"That's what archaeologists used to think," Ricardo said. "Until they figured out it was an accurate timepiece. The Swiss watch of ruins, if you will."

Samantha approached a giant stone figurine.

Ricardo whispered, "That monument is nicknamed *El Fraile*—The Friar."

"Why are you whispering?" Samantha asked—in a whisper herself.

He didn't know. "It just felt right."

No one disagreed.

The glow behind the Andes had gotten brighter as the three continued to inspect the statue, as if forbidden to leave by some unseen presence. In the distance, Jack surveyed the other large monument—The Gateway of the Sun—which stood over a hundred yards away. In modern times the edifice had been found lying facedown in a bed of clay and had since been raised up, though no one knew its original position. But Samantha couldn't take her eyes off *El Fraile*. She rubbed the time-worn sandstone. In the predawn, the red hues of the rock stood out against the gray ground. It stood close to seven feet. She studied the face. It was humanoid, androgynous.

"The eyes. They're so big," Ricardo said.

She noticed the huge eyes also; disproportionate to the rest of the facial features, they stared at her as if begging her to answer a riddle. *What was so haunting about them?* On a breeze that rippled her skin with goose bumps came the gentle reminder of her fossil, and its large ocular recessions. Her mind raced. Could this be a representation of the species she found back in that cave? The device *had* led them here.

"What's that he's holding?" Dorn asked, looking at the statue.

The right hand clutched some kind of weapon, maybe a mallet, Samantha thought. "I'm not sure." The other hand wrapped around a large, hinged case. "And how do you know it's a he?"

Samantha studied the rows of scales that adorned the bottom of the figure. Perhaps the shingles embodied the sea, or represented the figure's brilliance or sheen. She couldn't say for certain. Her gaze rose up from the lower portions of the carved stone, then suddenly halted on the hands again.

*The hands . . .*

Her throat dried. She moved nearer, making sure her eyes weren't playing tricks on her. A tempest of thought confused her, excited her. "Do you see what I see?" she said.

Ricardo moved closer. He halted suddenly.

"The hand . . ." Ricardo said after a long silence. "It has only four digits."

Samantha shuddered. *Just like her fossil.*

# VIRGINIA

McFadden was late. He hustled out of his car, finally getting the black plastic box to make the auto chirp twice—the signal his vehicle was locked and the alarm was on. He didn't know whether technology made his life easier or more hectic, he just knew he had to be in the War Room five minutes ago, and he'd be lucky if Director Wright knocked him unconscious before ripping him a new ass. McFadden picked up his briefcase and the pile of manila folders and shoved them under his arm.

He half-jogged through the underground parking structure.

"Good morning, Mr. McFadden."

"Good morning, June."

McFadden didn't stop. He usually chatted up the stun-

ning older woman at the front reception desk. He had a
thing for older women. June, in her fifties and recently
single, became a definite possibility. He couldn't exactly
put his finger on it, but attractive older women had a
certain sexiness that comes only from experience—or
perhaps the accumulated knowledge of having looked
good for a long time. He hoped it wasn't Oedipal.

The first set of guards at the elevator quickly scanned
the laminated card that hung from his neck. The scanners
beeped, signaling acceptance, and the elevator doors
opened.

"Have a good one, Mr. McFadden."

McFadden managed a smile before the thick steel
doors shut out the last traces of the world as most people
knew it.

No matter how many times McFadden rode in the high-
speed elevator he couldn't understand the engineering
behind a machine that could whisk somebody down
thirty-four floors in less than ten seconds with nearly no
sensation at all. Then again, he wasn't an engineer. He
was an analyst. And the pictures he had just received
from the field agents in Bolivia should definitely make
an impression on the director.

The polished steel doors opened, and John McFadden
stepped out, brushing by the state flag of Virginia and
the blue flag of the Central Intelligence Agency, before
causing Old Glory to rustle in turn. He paused to check
himself in the one-way reflective glass he knew housed
the two Special Forces soldiers, who sat bored—no
doubt counting the days before their tour of duty in this
hole was over.

McFadden checked his hair. A-OK. But he reminded
himself to get it cut before his date next Tuesday.

He rifled through the top manila folder, double-
checking everything he would need for the briefing. The
only thing worse than showing up late would be to have
forgotten a vital piece of reconnaissance material. Con-

fident now, McFadden took a deep breath and stepped up to the eye scanner, placing his head in the soft leather receptacle that looked like a pair of night-vision goggles attached to the wall. He waited as the laser scanned his retina.

An awful computer voice said: "McFadden, John. R5622732. Accepted."

McFadden couldn't believe that with all the damn technology down here they couldn't get a sexier voice, something feminine—or at least inviting. The vacuum seal of the large, reinforced door released itself with a whoosh and he stepped into the War Room.

They always kept the dark, underground complex too cold, McFadden thought. Then again he wasn't making any of the decisions that mattered down here. He only influenced them. Still, every trip to the War Room, as members of the agency dubbed the secret command center for the CIA's Directorate of Operations, was accompanied with amazement at what a few billion in taxpayer dollars could buy.

The impetus behind it was initially self-serving—the CIA wanted to be around after a nuclear holocaust just as much as the executive branch did, or the lucky folks at NORAD. Their mission would be even more important after a nuclear conflict, they argued.

The resulting underground building projects that had sprung up across the nation became known as Continuity of Government (or COG), which could house the top layers of government in case of a natural catastrophe, nuclear war, or biochemical attack. The president and his Cabinet, some members of Congress, the Joint Chiefs, CIA, and even a select group of scientists and citizens were "on the list" to be brought into the secret chambers on a moment's notice—the Joint Emergency Evacuation Plan (JEEP). Only an elite few knew who would take part in the JEEP procedure. In fact, the civilians didn't even know they were on the damn list, but McFadden supposed the charges of kidnapping seemed relatively mild within the context of global annihilation. The bases were a Noah's Ark of sorts—except that the people selected to weather out the calamity weren't picked by God. In truth, McFadden didn't know who the hell picked them. If he thought about that fact too long it scared him.

Somewhere behind the concrete walls on either side of him lay water recyclers, food stores, even plants under UV lamps that could keep the lucky inhabitants alive— underground—for more than a decade. McFadden walked by the various workstations and terminals, where agents could instantaneously tap into a vast net of information. The huge overhead displays illuminated a myriad of maps that focused attention on different hot spots across the globe, or different missions the agency was carrying out at the moment. The bunker was a techno-geek's playland.

"How is he?" McFadden asked a black man named Jones.

"Not good," the man answered. "He's flared up something fierce."

"Great."

The director's bouts with "fire-ass," as the man called his incessant battle with hemorrhoids, were legendary. If you caught him during one of these episodes, you just prayed the tongue-lashing was quick. McFadden looked over Jones's shoulder. The director was standing . . .

Not a good sign.

"Did you get all the background info I sent you?" Jones asked.

"Yeah. Thanks," McFadden sighed.

"You ready?"

"Yeah."

"Then let's brief the man."

Retired General Aaron M. Wright still wore the short crew cut of his Special Forces days, though now the sandy blond had been nearly defeated by patches of gray. He had achieved three-star status after his leadership in Vietnam, and had recently overseen the special operations in Desert Storm. Though recently retired from service, he still ran the agency in a military fashion. He was no stranger to conflict and didn't oppose the notion of using necessary force to complete his objectives. Yet he was a fantastic politician—which is why the president appointed him as director of the agency's black-budgeted programs. Billions in taxes went into those clandestine programs each year, the purpose of which no one could guess at—not even Congress. Complete secrecy was maintained, under the notion of national security.

For close to five minutes, McFadden heard more expletives than he knew existed, decorating a speech about the importance of being punctual. McFadden didn't take it personally. All who worked under the director knew this as his style.

Wright smiled when he finished. "Now what do you have for me, John?"

McFadden put the tattered manila folder on the black marble of the long War Room table. The *money* they've got in this place, he thought. He handed a few transparencies to the director's aide, who quickly whisked them off to the AV room. "Our field operatives out of Sucre just sent these." McFadden gave Wright the transcribed reports.

"Which ones?"

"Pierce and Miller."

The director grunted. "Damn good soldier that Pierce."

A voice over the PA system told them the overhead displays were ready.

"Have a seat," the director said as the lights dimmed. "I'll stand if you don't mind."

"Yes, sir."

McFadden rested his report next to a recessed desk lamp that illuminated the paperwork on the table. "Pierce and Miller still think there's a large shipment hightailing it out of Sucre in the next few days. They've turned it over to DEA, who'll assist the Bolivian interdiction forces."

"Great. Is that it?"

"No, sir. Apparently they picked up some interesting information on a phone tap of Foreign Minister Checa's Bolivian office."

"Our old friend, Mr. Checa."

"Yes, sir. Well, while following a lead to Trinidad, Pierce and Miller noticed some members of the Curoz cartel trekking out of the jungle with a few Caucasians we believe to be Americans."

"Interesting. And why should we be concerned with this?" McFadden could tell Wright was getting agitated.

"They entered the country illegally. No visas. No permits. Didn't even come through a sanctioned airfield. They were hauling a ton of supplies," McFadden paused. "And a corpse."

"A corpse?" The director shuffled closer to the table, more interested. "Murdered?"

"We're looking into that now."

"What the hell are they doing there?"

"We're not sure at the moment, sir. Pierce initially thought it had something to do with illegal animal trade."

"Doesn't sound like Pierce to be worried about monkeys or birds."

"No, sir. We think the situation's much bigger." McFadden pressed an intercom button on the desk in front of him. "First photo please."

The overhead suddenly showed a brilliant slide of a small Bolivian town. McFadden described the group of people in the photograph. The woman was Samantha Colby. A paleoanthropologist.

"Cute," the general said.

"We couldn't get a positive ID on the heavy Hispanic guy or the other Anglo. We think he's American. Someone we did ID is this man." McFadden replaced the group picture with a close-up of Dorn.

"Who is he?"

"Benjamin Dorn. Arms trader, businessman."

"Arms? Checa dabbles in the arms trade. Is that the connection?"

"We think so, sir. We traced Dorn to his former arms smuggling operations. But he's smart. Interpol could never nail him on anything. Runs legitimate corporations now. Mining, pharmaceuticals. One of them is Helix Corp. It's a huge bio-technology company. Fortune 500."

Wright nodded. "My wife's got stock."

"From what we can tell, he's legitimate now. Wasn't always. We tracked the girl down from some pictures taken with him. Apparently they've been dating off and on over the last twenty-four months. Here's his file."

McFadden handed it to Wright.

"Somehow they're involved with the Curoz cartel. A dozen men, heavily armed, loaded a bunch of equipment and are en route to the highlands."

"The heroin labs?"

"Possibly."

Wright scanned Dorn's file. "Dorn was involved with the uranium core sales to Iraq?"

McFadden nodded. "Through a tangle of legitimate and illegitimate companies. Most of them foreign. Needless to say, we're concerned about his presence in Bolivia. Especially since he's dealing with Checa."

Another picture flashed on the overhead, this time showing Dorn talking to two men.

"Those two with Dorn are mercenaries. Most recent activity was in the Chechnyan conflict." McFadden paused. "It's reasonable to assume we're looking at some kind of arms deal. Maybe a tactical arms deal."

"But we can't tell for sure?"

"No, sir."

Drops of moisture formed on Wright's brow. He rummaged through his desk. "Where the hell are my silver bullets?" He referred to the silver-packaged steroid suppositories his doctor had prescribed. "John. I want you to divert a KH-14 and two Big Birds. I want constant satellite surveillance. If Dorn takes a shit, I want to know which hand he wipes with. Hell, I wanna know what kind of toilet paper he uses."

"Yes, sir."

McFadden began pulling together his things. He felt a sudden surge of energy. The director had ordered three of their most powerful satellites to monitor the area. With the "eyes in the sky" he would be able to monitor the most exact details from miles away in the stratosphere. He tucked the folders beneath his armpit and made for the door to the rest of the operations center.

"John."

McFadden stopped. The director still rifled through drawers, looking for his suppositories. "If this is an arms deal I want Checa implicated—especially if this has anything to do with uranium or other tactical materials. Have Pierce and Miller continue ground surveillance. And brief Special Ops," he said stoically. "I want them put on standby."

"Yes, sir."

McFadden opened the door to the operations room. He smiled. Wright rarely involved Special Ops if he wasn't significantly alarmed at a developing situation. McFadden had scored.

Good briefing, he thought. Good briefing.

# SUNRISE

Jack glanced back at the crude doorway. "It looks great, Ricardo."

The canvas monstrosity rippled with each gust of the morning wind.

"It looks like shit," Ricardo said. "But the dimensions are perfect—plus or minus a half inch if the wind picks up the canvas."

Supported by a skeleton of aluminum tent poles and wood slats from the side of one of the trucks, the mock-up of the Gateway of the Sun looked like a prehistoric version of the Arc de Triomphe. Ricardo had wrapped nylon tarps and shipping blankets around the crude frame to simulate the solid, stone object. He'd spent the last forty-five minutes creating the mock-up from any supplies he could find.

The actual monolith, standing eighty yards to their west, had been carved from a solid block of gray-green andesite. It was roughly twelve and a half feet wide and ten feet high. The monument resembled a smaller version of the great arch in Paris but formed right angles at the top instead of curves. From a distance the Gateway looked like a giant stone staple nailed partially into the ground. A door, as Hancock had said, "between nowhere and nothing." Experts agreed it was one of the archaeological wonders of South America. But no one had previously guessed its true purpose—or the monument's proper placement. It had been positioned haphazardly in modern times after researchers found the Gateway lying in a bed of clay.

Jack rechecked the long wires pinned beneath stakes that anchored the mock-up to the ground. From the corners of the faux edifice, ropes lay on the dirt at diagonals toward the Western Gallery. These represented the angles Jack calculated for the position of the archway close to forty thousand years ago.

"I've checked my notes," Jack said. "This is where the Gateway was originally placed."

Ricardo looked to his right, where the true monument stood watch over the cold earth in the distance. He wondered what forces could have caused the edifice to tumble so far from its proper position. "It must have been one hell of a catastrophe," Ricardo said.

Along the wall of the Western Gallery, Dorn and Baines carefully stepped over the ropes that formed angles from the center of the makeshift Gateway, to pillars along the side of the enclosure. "Our men will reach the crash site in less than six hours," Baines said, toking hard on a cigarette.

"Good. Have them retrieve as much of the equipment as they can—without sacrificing the firepower I ordered," Dorn said. He looked toward the encampment where the Bolivians still worked pitching tents, before focusing on the rippling canvas mock-up in the center of the enclosure. "If we *do* find something," he said, "we should be prepared to hold on to it at any cost. I don't trust the Bolivians—or Jack, for that matter."

Baines nodded. With a flick, his cigarette butt bounced across the rocky ground, scattering still-glowing embers.

A sliver of a golden disk teetered along the jagged outline of the mountain ridge, preparing to bathe the valley in light. They had less than ten minutes before the sun would directly hit the architecture of Tiahuanaco—testing Jack's assumptions. Anticipation hung in the damp

air. Beside the mock-up, Samantha helped Ricardo re-
wrap a wire around one of the stakes while Jack watched
the pinkish horizon, frantically checking numbers in his
head. She stopped to look at him. She felt anxious—
about the result of their efforts. Anxious that Jack had
staked so much on this one hunch. Her breath couldn't
come fast enough. She prayed he was right, afraid of
what failure might do to him, grateful that the sky was
not overcast. At least the sun was on their side.

"Is there anything else you need?" Samantha asked.
They'd been run ragged in their race against dawn.

"That's it," Jack said. "Now we wait."

The sun rose precisely above the center pillars of the
Western Gallery. The group watched in awe, their eyes
blinking under the intense morning rays, which coated
everything in rose-colored tones. Dorn put on sunglasses. All expected the earth to shake. All expected
the ground to open.

It didn't.

In fact, for almost fifteen minutes they watched the
sphere change colors and rise ever so slowly into the thin
Andean sky, and they could see no shadow markings of
any kind, save for the distorted ripple behind their mock-
up—a shadow even Jack agreed was of no significance.
The exactness with which the two main pillars framed the
sun left no doubt as to the purpose of the temple; the
entire complex had been built to measure the spring
equinox. But it appeared Jack's theory about the Gateway
serving as a shadow marker had been wrong.

Jack started to sweat. *What was missing?* "I'm gonna
check the Gateway of the Sun again," he said. "There
has to be a damn clue."

"We don't have much time," Ricardo said.

"I know."

He jogged off toward the Gateway. He hadn't cleared
forty yards before Ricardo's voice rang over the barren

landscape. Jack turned. Samantha and Ricardo were pointing at something behind them. Something he couldn't see. The ground reflected the sun's light like a mirror. He stumbled back, chasing the four figures, which started running away from the mock-up.

*Why were they leaving?*

Jack's lungs heaved. He broke into a sprint, passing the mock-up. There was no shadow from the facade on the immediate ground around it. When he finally reached the others at the far end of the enclosure, he could barely breathe, much less speak.

It wasn't necessary.

Below them, fifty yards from the *Kalasasaya*, a sharp, distinct shadow grew in the center of the nearby Subterranean Temple, which sat precisely behind the Temple of Upright Standing Stones. Jack looked back at the Gateway. The top of the makeshift arch nearly blocked the entire sun; only minute crescents of the bright circle appeared above and beneath the arch like thin, blinding lemon rinds.

"It's moving so fast!" Samantha yelled.

Jack turned to the shadow again. The dissected sun cast a powerful silhouette of the arch. The shadow ran from them, rippling over the flat surface of the Subterranean Temple. Within fifteen seconds both sides joined in a sharp point over four nondescript stone slabs, choked with weeds. Then, just as quickly as it appeared—the shadow vanished from the floor of the sunken temple.

Jack's chest continued to heave from his run.

"Sweet Mary," Ricardo said. "It's faster than Teotihuacán. . . ."

All Jack's senses came alive. His skin tingled. The Gateway didn't mark anything inside the Temple of *Kalasasaya*. The shadow had fallen in the sunken temple *behind* it. A shadow so distinct, so powerful, so fleeting—that no doubt existed in Jack's mind as to its purpose. The shadow marked the location of something.

Something hidden beneath those four stones.

# PART THREE

# AFTERNOON

The cloudless sky ripened to a rich cobalt blue. The sun—noticeably larger at this high altitude—had made the morning's haze a mere memory. Jack rubbed the back of his neck; it felt raw. The ozone shield in the Andes was practically nonexistent, and the sun had won the battle against Jack's natural melanin defense. He dumped water from his canteen over his head and down the back of his neck; it shot a much-needed jolt of adrenaline through his body. The excitement of groundbreaking had passed long ago, an overwhelming sense of discouragement taking its place. As if carried on the windy gusts, the hours had flown into history, dragging Jack's hope with it. He took off his sunglasses and squinted in the late afternoon light.

The group had dug through ten feet of hard earth and found no trace of anything.

Dorn had grown irritable. He must have asked Jack five times about the fallibility of his calculations. When Jack noticed him approaching the hole again, he decided to avoid what promised to be an ugly confrontation, and instead set off for the Akapana Pyramid to the south of the Subterranean Temple. Jack eased himself onto a large, flat rock and stared at the growing pile of Bolivian dirt.

"Damn . . ." he whispered. His calculations had been off. He had hoped to find whatever the hologram had led them toward. Perhaps the shadow marker was an insignificant anomaly, Jack thought. He massaged the bridge of his nose. His head throbbed from the thin air, from his failure. He allowed the full weight of his head to rest in the palms of his hands.

"Jack?"

He remained motionless.

"Can I talk to you for a second?"

Jack lifted his head wearily. Samantha took a seat next to him. She searched his tired eyes, then looked toward the horizon on which the surface of the lake disappeared. "It looks discouraging," she said.

"It feels worse."

Her eyes, leaving that distant point, found his. "You know, it doesn't matter what we find here," Samantha said. "I mean, we've discovered the existence of extraterrestrial life in Mali. Expecting more would seem . . . I don't know. Ungrateful."

Jack's expression held a hint of gratitude. "You're probably right."

"We've got to keep things in perspective."

"I apologize for dragging you on another one of my wild goose chases." Jack skipped a stone across the pebbled earth. "I promise you before next fall I'll have figured the proper calculations."

"It wasn't a goose chase. No matter what happens here." Samantha watched the rock roll to a stop. "I've been doing a lot of thinking on this trip."

"So have I. Obviously, my numbers aren't adding up."

"No," she said. "I mean about us."

Jack felt his throat dry. "What about us?"

She faced him head-on. "None of my letters ever got answered."

"That's because I never read them."

"Don't do this to me."

"Don't do what to you?"

"Play me. Don't play games."

"I'm not playing games. You can only play a game

when you know the rules—and you've obviously never filled me in."

"How come you never read them?"

"And if I had? What difference would it have made?"

"You would have known how sorry I was. You would have known how much I was hurting too," she said. "I don't know. At least we could have had some closure."

"Closure," Jack repeated. "I thought things were pretty fucking closed when you gave my ring back."

Samantha's breathing got heavy. Jack felt something close to satisfaction. He had gotten her to hurt also; the playing field had evened.

"That's always been your MO," she said. "When the going gets tough you just run away. From everything."

"It beats sticking around answering the phone every five minutes. Explaining our—what did you decide on calling it—'postponement'?"

"You've never given me a chance to explain. I tried. Five times."

"Six," Jack said softly.

"The sixth letter was telling you I couldn't do it anymore. That I had no more energy. No more strength to resolve anything."

Jack shook his head and smiled. "There's nothing *to* resolve, Samantha."

"Really?" Samantha slid closer. "Because when I look at you I feel differently. There's so much . . . stuff. If there was nothing to resolve, then why the hell do I feel—" She cut herself short and stood. A strong breeze ruffled her Gore-Tex jacket. When she spoke again it was soft, barely audible: "Then why do I still care so much?"

Samantha turned and slowly made her way down the hill toward the base camp beside the great pyramid. Jack watched her go. Twice, he choked back the words: *Samantha*. His eyes followed her until she disappeared beyond the knoll. She never looked back.

\* \* \*

Pierce thumbed the electronic zoom of the high-powered binoculars. A stream of red data flashed in the corner of the device, measuring the distance between him and the growing pile of dirt amid the ruins. The group below them had been digging all day. The hole had to be over eight feet deep; once anyone climbed down the rope ladder, they disappeared from view. But what were they looking for?

The two agents had picked a good vantage point. It sat a half mile to the west of the ruins on a small rocky promontory. Their position offered a full view of the encampment, and enough distance to remain visually elusive. But Pierce hadn't counted on the group to start digging. From the agents' position, the deepening pit concealed much of the action around the site.

Pierce found solace in technology. He looked into the crisp blueness above him. Somewhere in that cerulean spacescape the country's costliest spy satellites kept careful watch. One, still just a rumor even within lower levels of the agency, would revolutionize the art of spying. The latest violator of privacy could read a man's watch from miles in the atmosphere, even tell if he had a fever. It could analyze magnetic fields, interpret thermal images. Although Pierce felt confident anything they missed in their surveillance could be picked up back home, the thought of such a device troubled him. He wondered what the world would be like in another twenty years.

"Are they still at it?" Miller climbed up from the crevasse on the back side of the hill, which served as their makeshift outhouse.

"Yeah." Pierce put down the binoculars. "The guys in analysis must be sweating over this one."

"If this is an arms deal, it's the strangest one I've ever seen," Miller said. He lay prone in front of his camera and peered through the thick telephoto lens. "What are they digging for?"

Pierce shook his head. "It just doesn't make any

sense. Why all the ropes? And that twisted mass of canvas?"

There was no transaction. No third party. Nothing. It looked like these people were on a legitimate archaeological dig—except for the fact they had no visas or dig permits and were escorted to the site by heavily armed members of the Curoz cartel.

Over his breakfast of three-day-old tortillas and cold beans, Pierce had paid special attention to the rich guy. The boys in Virginia had processed the film and ID'd him as a former arms smuggler who had dabbled in illegal uranium sales. Benjamin Dorn. From what he could tell, Dorn seemed as interested in the growing hole as the rest of the contingent. Occasionally, he spoke to the South African with the hat, but always alone.

Every three hours Pierce faithfully pulled out the NO-MAD field transmitter and updated Virginia over the Teletype. The last message read simply: STILL DIGGING. If only to satisfy his curiosity, Pierce vowed to get to the bottom of it. He rubbed his tired eyes and yawned. He hadn't slept in twenty hours.

"You mind keeping surveillance?" he said. "I'm gonna steal a little nap." He turned onto his side and pulled the hood of his jacket over his head, shutting out the world. The darkness calmed him, enveloped him like a crib.

Pierce had entered the backwaters of his subconscious only seconds before the sound of Miller's voice dragged him back into foggy reality.

"I wouldn't sleep just yet," Miller said. "I think they've found something."

Ricardo soaked his bare feet in one of the large steel pots used for boiling potatoes, a staple he soon realized—after inspecting the supplies—that would make up a large portion of each meal. His feet had finally adjusted to the hot water. The wisps of steam still warmed and moisturized his dry face when a frantic Bolivian ran down the hill shouting.

Samantha emerged from the field tent.

Jack's stiff, aching limbs cracked as he pulled himself up. He was getting too old for this shit. Judging by the orange hues that painted the rocky terrain, it would be no more than an hour before the velvet mantle of night would fall. The temperature had dropped nearly fifteen degrees. The merciless winds, which always picked up near dusk, bit into the exposed parts of his skin as if a voracious, invisible shark had sniffed out his presence. Jack knew there would be no sense digging through the night. In reality, there was no reason to continue digging at all. If his calculations weren't precise, they could dig to China and still not find anything.

He hadn't walked ten paces before he noticed the commotion at the hole.

A Bolivian at the edge of the pit shouted to someone below, then ran wildly back toward the encampment. Something was happening. Jack quickened his pace. His lungs burned in the thin air. He tasted blood in his throat but didn't slow. Before he could clear the last fifty yards he saw Samantha and Dorn running toward the dig site from camp.

Ricardo hopped painfully across the rocky scree, just behind them. Barefoot.

The sounds from the pit grew more audible. The speech was swift and furious, but through the mumble of voices, Jack heard one word that powered his legs faster. Then he heard it again even more clearly: *"Metálico."*

They had struck metal.

# METÁLICO

Pierce shook the sleep from his head. Miller handed him a pair of light-enhancing binoculars. "At the hole. They've found something!"

Pierce watched one of the Bolivians sprint from the pit toward the cluster of tents beside the pyramid. Seconds later, the Bolivian led Dorn and the girl in a rapid jog back toward the excavation site. The heavy Mexican doctor trailed not far behind.

"Gruff's heading to the hole. He's really moving," Miller said.

The two agents had settled on the nickname for the tall American Virginia hadn't identified yet. Pierce watched Jack sprint toward the excavation from the other direction. He could sense the excitement of the scene playing out beneath them. His heart pounded faster—as if to keep time with Gruff's thumping feet.

"Something's up!" Pierce said. "They've found something in that damn hole."

Jack's boots dug into the loose rock at the edge of the excavation, kicking gravel into the abyss. From the rim of the hole he could make out something oddly reflective from beneath a dusting of red earth. Two Bolivians holding shovels backed off to either side.

Samantha ran up beside him. "What is it, Jack?"

"I don't know," Jack said. "I don't know."

Samantha, on her knees, peered into the hole. "It's definitely metal!"

Dorn shouted for the two Bolivians to climb out of the hole.

As they clambered out, Jack saw a flat metallic slab that extended across the bottom of the pit, vanishing beneath the sides of the excavation. Finger marks arched across the gray surface where the men had cleared the dirt off the object with their hands. Samantha waited for the Bolivians to climb out before hustling down the rope ladder, which hung against the right side of the hole. Jack didn't wait for her to get to the bottom. He sat on his rear and slid down the side.

Ricardo grunted, the sharp stones stabbing his bare feet. "Would someone mind giving me a hand?" The rope ladder swung under his robust frame. Samantha steadied it. Within seconds Ricardo was in the hole with them. Jack overheard Dorn telling the two Bolivians they could take a break, sending them back to the field tents to get Baines. "The fewer eyes that see this the better," he said to the three scientists.

On that point Jack agreed. The thought of cartel members getting mixed up in something of this magnitude was unsettling. He hoped the two Bolivians thought they had uncovered some Inca tomb—and they might have. It suddenly dawned on Jack that he hadn't the slightest inkling about what lay before them. After Mali, it could be damn near anything.

He noticed the layers of different colored soil that ringed the pit. He began estimating how many years' worth of sediment had accumulated over the object.

Samantha's mind worked too. "It's probably been covered for ten to fifteen thousand years," she said.

Jack guessed twenty.

Samantha began clearing more dirt off the metallic slab. Before Jack joined her, he noted the layer of soil at the bottom of the pit—just above the shiny plate. The consistency was granular, less fine than the layers of clay nearer the surface.

"Marine sediments," Jack said. He rubbed the granules between his fingers. Much of the debris in the stratum looked like broken, fossilized shells.

Ricardo said, "It might have been completely submerged at one time."

Dorn asked a stream of questions without answers from the edge of the hole—the pit hadn't room for another person to work comfortably. Meanwhile, on his hands and knees, Jack focused intently on the metallic slab beneath him.

"I can't find any seams," he said. "No holes. No joints. It looks like a solid block."

He hoped to find some edges, some contour that would reveal the exact nature of the object beneath them, but the slab kept extending into the earth.

For the next hour, they handed dirt-filled buckets to Dorn and Baines, who hoisted them out of the hole. It had gotten dark. Two lanterns inside the hole hissed and struggled in the thin air. The tawny light cast ghoulish shadows that rippled along the sides of the pit. Bongane had thoughtfully thrown down to them jackets and gloves, but still the frigid air stiffened Jack's hands and numbed his fingers.

The strange slab twinkled in the glow of the burning propane. "I still can't find any damn seams," Samantha said.

Jack paused and took a hit from the small oxygen tank on the ground beside him. His body ached from the altitude and the cold. They had managed to clear another two feet of dirt from around the sides, but the object's edges were still hidden. He shook his head. For every foot they cleared sideways, they needed to remove the entire ten feet of earth sitting on top of it.

The digging would last well into the night.


"I found it!"

Jack heard the voice through the fuzziness of sleep and awoke with a start.

Dawn washed over the cold ground, twisting sharp black shadows across the rocky earth. The small pup tents the group had set up near the edge of the hole cried small rivulets of dew.

Jack hadn't planned on sleeping. He only wanted to rest his stiff back and hands. His fingers were still caked with dry blood and dirt; tiny granules found painful hospice beneath his nails. The sound of scraping echoed from the excavation.

Jack managed to crawl to the edge of the pit and saw Samantha throw down the shovel and begin digging at something with a small pick. She traced a deep line in the soil—at the edge of the metallic plate.

"I've got one side!"

Other tents rustled nearby as the tired crew revived.

"Hold on." Jack grabbed a small box of digging implements—brushes, picks, scrapers—and scurried down the rope ladder. The hole had nearly doubled in circumference since the Bolivians first struck metal.

"I thought you'd taken a break," he said, hovering over Samantha.

"Hey. The early bird . . ." Samantha traced the edge of the slab with her hand spade; the uncovered surface beneath them was the size of a storm cellar. Jack ran his pick in the other direction. After clearing three more inches on the opposite side Jack yelled: "I've got the other corner!" All pain vanished from his limbs. He shuddered.

"I was beginning to think we might have to call in Caterpillars." Dorn hurried down the ladder and soon was on his knees, helping Samantha clear some of the overhanging dirt.

They continued to trace the edge along the north side of the slab. Outside the hole, Ricardo and Baines handed buckets of dirt to Bongane, who emptied them on the immense pile. Within twenty minutes, all four edges of the rectangular shape were emancipated from the soil's grasp.

"No telling how far down it goes," Samantha said.

"Do you think it's a container?" Ricardo asked.

Jack ran his fingers along the edges of the cold metal. They had cleared two inches of earth from around the sides, but the object continued on into the ground. "It could be. The dimensions seem familiar though. It's the same size as an Egyptian door."

"A door?" Dorn said. "But it's seamless. There are no holes. No indentations."

Jack looked up. "Ricardo. Is my tape measure up there?"

Ricardo rifled through Jack's backpack alongside the edge of the hole and tossed him the tape. "Tuck this at the corner, Samantha," Jack said. She held it down as he backed up, pulling the tape taut until he found the other edge. "Hundred and fifty inches."

Dorn put his foot on the end of the tape measure while Jack extended it sideways across the smaller edge of the rectangle. "Seventy-five inches—exactly." Jack smiled.

"You and these damn numbers," Dorn growled. "What the hell does it mean?"

"It means that whoever set out these dimensions knew the existence of the golden section—a mathematical principle ancient humans weren't supposed to have known."

"It's the same ratio as the king's chamber," Ricardo said, peering into the hole.

"Inside the pyramid at Giza?" Samantha asked.

Jack nodded.

"You think the pyramids and whatever we've found here are related?" Dorn asked.

"They have to stem from the same body of knowledge. The dimensions of doorways and rooms in the great pyramids follow the same mathematical model that this slab seems to follow—phi."

"Phi?" Dorn said. "I thought the Greeks discovered that thousands of years later."

"Obviously not," Jack said. He joined Samantha, who dug at the sides of the slab.

At the edge of the hole, Ricardo attempted to explain·

the notion of phi to Baines. "It's an irrational number," Ricardo said. "Like pi. It can't be worked out arithmetically. Basically phi is the value of the square root of five, plus one, divided by two. Which is roughly"—he punched in numbers on his watch, which doubled as a calculator—"1.61803. Outside of mathematics the numbers seem unimportant. But phi ends up being a very integral part of the Fibonacci series—a series of numbers where each integer is the sum of the previous two. Like 0,1,1,2,3,5,8,13—and so forth. A principle that ancient man shouldn't have known—but obviously did."

"And you're sure this is a door to something?" Dorn said.

"I said it follows the same formula by which doors were built in Egypt," Jack said.

"But there's no possible way in," Dorn said. "No seams. No holes for any keys."

"And if it's a container, and it's built to phi, we'd have to dig down at least twelve feet," Ricardo noted. "That's tractor time, my friends."

Samantha ran her hand along the cold, seamless surface. "It looks like it's made from the same alloy as the Mali artifact. If it is, we're not going to be able to cut our way in. The alloy's impenetrable."

Jack's spine chilled with a sudden realization. "That's it." He stood abruptly and brushed by Dorn, climbing the rope ladder.

"That's what?" she said.

"Our key," Jack answered.

Then he vanished over the rim.

Jack and Bongane deftly avoided large stones as they carried the aluminum case that held the artifact. At the dig, they found Samantha pacing nervously inside the pit.

As they set down the aluminum case, she covered her eyes from the glare of the sun. "What are you thinking, Jack?"

"Oxygen first," Jack said, breathing heavily. He turned the dial on the small tank next to one of the tents. Frustrated, Samantha crawled out of the hole, followed by Dorn.

"I don't know if this will work. But it's worth a shot." Jack sucked deep drafts through the mouthpiece. "I want to activate the hologram once inside the hole."

Samantha's eyes widened. "It *could* trigger something."

Jack got more animated. "The hologram itself had different virtual panels, remember? One shut the device off. I think another might serve as a key. An electronic one."

"It's a fantastic idea," she said, excitedly.

Jack turned to Ricardo.

Ricardo was suddenly alarmed. "Don't look at me. I'm not going down there playing Russian roulette."

"Relax. I just wanted to get your opinion."

"My opinion? My opinion is that we're trying to accomplish entirely too much on our own. We need to get back to the States, file our papers, and come back with the right equipment—with the whole scientific community at our si—"

"Ricardo."

Ricardo shook his head. "Yes. If you're asking if I think it could serve as an electronic key. Yes, it could. It might also do a hundred other things."

Samantha stepped up and flicked open the latches. "As Thomas Fuller said, 'He that won't sail until all dangers are over must never put to sea.' " She lifted the lid. At once the sun caught the artifact, bouncing light into their eyes like a slashing scimitar. Jack helped her lift the object from the case. Both pieces of the kite-shaped device were still connected, forming that ominous eye that stared at the group with its pitch-black pupil.

"Slowly," Dorn said from the rim.

Jack steadied the artifact in his left arm. A rope had

been tied around the device to help steady it as Jack climbed down the ladder. Baines and Bongane fed the line to Jack, whose right boot poked about for the bottom.

"A little more," he called up.

At last Jack swung his other leg off the ladder and knelt down in the cleared earth to the side of the metallic slab. He threw off the rope around the homing device. Anticipation filtered among the group. It had grown quiet, as if they'd been forbidden to speak.

Samantha peered over the edge. Worry had begun to replace her excitement. Enthralled by the possibilities, she now wanted to tell Jack it was too risky.

He looked up at her.

With a trembling hand she signed: *Be careful.*

Jack nodded. His pulse quickened and he wiped the sweat of his palms on his pants. He managed a good grip on the device and stood up fully, turning to face the metallic slab. It lay two feet in front of him. Jack took a step toward the metal sheet below him. Almost instantaneously, he felt a sudden surge rifle up his back.

"It's creating some kind of electric charge!" he yelled.

Just as the device broke the plane above the slab, Jack felt numbing energy pulse through his hands, then up his arms.

Before he could explain the sensation, Samantha screamed.

Inside the Bolivian sleeping tent, Veronica had just started a fifth game of solitaire when her cellular phone squawked loudly. She grabbed it from the leather pouch on her waist and turned down the volume. "*Veronica.*"

The voice on the other line was desiccated by static. She said in Spanish, "I can't hear you." She stood up from the table in one of the tents and brushed by the thin mosquito netting that floated across the entrance. Once outside she realized the reception wouldn't be made any better.

Something was disturbing the connection—though she could have sworn she charged the phone before leaving Trinidad.

She finally recognized Gustavo's voice—Checa's point man—and her uncle by marriage, a man who filled her with anxiety. The voice sounded different, high-strung. She explained that Dorn had asked for a large cargo chopper.

"A large cargo helicopter?" her uncle said.

"*Sí.*"

Her uncle relayed the news to Checa, who'd become especially interested in what was happening at the site.

Veronica described the excavation. She explained that two of her men had found something metal—in the ground.

"Do you know what it is, angel?"

"No." She told him that Dorn had forbidden any of her men to get near the dig site.

"Interesting . . ." the voice said. "Senor Checa will want you to find out exactly what it is they have dug up."

"I understand," she said. Veronica read deeper into the comment. She understood that if anything valuable was brought out of the earth, Checa would want it confiscated. She knew the two men would be formulating a plan. It would mean bloodshed. Killing.

"Keep us informed, angel," her aunt's husband said, and broke the transmission.

Veronica walked back into the tent and sat down in one of the plastic fold-out chairs. She felt dizzy—a melancholy tinged with anger. She pulled her satin hair back, wrapping it in a makeshift knot around itself. She was tired. Tired of the killing, of the constant deception. She felt nothing but disdain for her country. She despised the world of drugs and violence, which had initially rescued her, given her an outlet for her hate. Since childhood she despised most things, especially men. The majority were vile, unprincipled creatures, like her uncle.

Veronica shuddered. It had been a while since she consciously revisited the painful memories. She could see her room in Sucre—the lace pillows, the flowered wallpaper, the wooden ceiling fan that worked only on its lowest setting. The same fan that cut the thick air in slow circles and provided the throbbing background of her nightmares.

Veronica's heart began to beat harder—just as it did then.

She remembered his ominous silhouette, backlit by the faint glow from the hallway. Then the noise—that horrific squeak—as her uncle carefully closed the door.

It took him six steps to reach the edge of her bed.

She always counted them. They fell slowly, each one cracking the floorboards, all the while getting nearer and nearer. By the sixth step her nightgown stuck to her body with sweat. Then that voice—that malevolent half-whisper followed by the wafting odors of alcohol: *"Hola, Ángel."*

Then her uncle smiled, as he always did, before lifting the sheets and crawling into bed.

She was nine years old.

Energy pulsed through Jack's body, firing nerves in a blitzkrieg of motion. The artifact dropped from his hands and landed in the soft earth.

"Jack!" Samantha pointed to the slab.

He couldn't be seeing what he was seeing. A deep seam manifested itself from nowhere—crawling from the center of the slab in a straight line, dividing it in half. The atoms had to be rearranging themselves. The solid alloy morphed into two distinct sections with fluid ease—like the parting of the Red Sea. The energy field vanished—as quickly as it came—replaced by a whoosh as a vacuum of air escaped from beneath the two sections, now divided. The air vaporized in the colder temperatures, creating wisps of steam that curled toward the sky before dissipating in the atmosphere. Jack wiped the condensed vapor from his face and watched speechlessly as the two doors receded effortlessly to the sides of the pit, triggering diminutive earthslides.

The scientists looked on in shock. Inside the dark cavity between the doors Jack began to make out some forms through the vapor.

"Stairs?" Samantha called out, trembling.

Through the last whisps of steam that floated through the newly created opening, Jack could see stone steps disappearing into the darkness below.

Dorn stood reverently at the edge, his eyes wide with wonder. "It *was* a door."

"But for what," Jack mumbled.

Samantha and Ricardo hurried down the ladder. Jack left the artifact where it lay on the earthen border.

From the rim of the hole, Dorn told Baines, "Keep everyone else away. Set up a perimeter. No one's allowed in without my permission." He began climbing down the ladder.

Inside the pit Ricardo breathed heavily. "The device must have triggered some sort of hermetically sealed doors."

"But why hermetically sealed?" Samantha wondered.

"I don't know," Jack said.

"The technology," Dorn said. "It's unbelievable . . . Think of the applications."

"The metal actually morphed." Ricardo traced the opening with his hands. "Metals *are* slow-moving liquids, but you have to heat them thousands of degrees before they change states. These atoms changed and re-changed on demand. They liquefied into seams and returned to a solid state. . . ."

Dorn shook his head, awestruck. "My God. Who built this?"

Jack looked down the stone stairs, which led to darkness below him. "There's only one way to find out," he said. Jack took a step toward the subterranean entrance.

Samantha grabbed him.

"The hell you are." She smiled, then moved in front of him. "I'm going first."

# ENTRADA

Samantha stepped cautiously into the shadows. Jack followed her down the long stone steps, which ran the entire width of the opening, approximately six feet wide. Her boots left perfect imprints in the millimeter-thin layer of dust which coated the stone. Jack inhaled. The thick, dank air reminded him that the environment inside the tunnel had remained unstirred for thousands of years. The stairs dropped into a stone corridor that smelled musty, fungal.

"Do you feel the wet?" Jack asked.

Samantha rubbed her forearm. "Yeah. The air. It's . . . humid."

"Like it was bottled in another era," Jack said. "The climate was much wetter when this place was built." Just the thought of breathing air that had remained sealed for thousands of years intoxicated him. It was like drinking a fine, aged wine. He breathed deeply, despite the pungent, damp taste it left in his throat. *Whoever built this place breathed the same air.*

"Incredible," Ricardo said. "The stairs are cut like the blocks outside. But still, they look like any other ancient site. Which doesn't make sense, because the covering—"

"Is the same material as the artifact," Jack finished. "Whoever built this place, quarried huge stones like at other ruins, but used a piece of extraterrestrial metal to seal off the opening."

Jack could have spent hours studying the craftsmanship of the stairs, yet the unknown at the end of the tunnel kept pulling him forward. He nearly bumped into Samantha, who paused after reaching a landing. "Thirty stairs," she counted.

"The number of degrees allocated to each zodiacal constellation," Jack said. He touched the joints at the walls, which were perfect right angles, and smiled. "Could be just a coincidence though."

"There's no sign of weathering at all," Ricardo said.

Except for the fine layer of dust and a few small cracks that splayed the solid stones, the stairs remained as pristine as the day they were cut. "If this place was hermetically sealed, it would be preserved—forever," Ricardo said.

Dorn scanned the walls in awe. "Amazing."

"The hallway's abnormally large," Samantha said.

Jack noted it as well. He wondered what that could have meant for the people who built it. *Were they large themselves? Or was this a sacred hallway, built spaciously for effect?*

Sunbeams from the top of the long flight of stairs pierced the thin veil of dust their boots kicked up. The molecules sharpened and defined each ray of light. Jack's finger traced the joints between two immense blocks of stone that sat one atop the other, and made up the entire ten-foot wall of the corridor.

"These blocks probably weigh two hundred tons each," Jack said. "They're cut from solid andesite."

Dorn flicked open his pocketknife. The wafer-thin edge of his blade wouldn't fit anywhere along the seam between the blocks. "Astonishing," Dorn said. "And all done without grout. How in bloody hell do you cut something so big—so perfectly? If any of my companies were to build to these specs we'd need diamond-tipped quarry saws, laser guided. It would be a nightmare."

"The tricky part would be moving these monsters in the first place," Jack said.

The corridor extended for another thirty yards. The back wall was barely visible in the darker reaches. "Could be a dead end," Samantha said. "Maybe it branches off."

Jack followed closely as she continued down the corridor. The cocoonlike confines of the tunnel muffled the shuffling of their boots. Halfway down the underground passage, the stone walls changed color—deepening from the light gray of the andesite blocks. He bumped into Samantha.

"What is it?" Jack demanded, his chin over her shoulder.

"Hieroglyphs. Look." She pointed to the far wall. "Thousands of them."

Across from him, the whole wall of the tunnel was adorned with laser-precise glyphs—cut right into the stone. They scrolled from left to right in perfect rows, covering floor to ceiling. Although the light from the stairs had begun to fade, Jack could make them out with no trouble. "They're the same as the glyphs from the Gateway of the Sun," he said. "And it's a complete rendering! It's all here—the equations are finished."

Ricardo peered at the glyphs from behind. "They look like some kind of formula."

"This alone will make my career," Samantha said. "Finding the rest of these glyphs."

Jack grinned. "Just a drop in the bucket now."

The thrill of the new discoveries felt palpable to all.

Dorn traced one of the icons with his finger. "Will we be able to translate these symbols?"

"Maybe," Jack said. "We have the complete glyphs now. We can run it through some code-breaking programs and hope for the best."

Samantha had slipped away to the end of the tunnel.

"It's not a dead end!" She stood, staring down another corridor, which branched off to the right. "Look here."

That woman always has to be first, Jack thought. He jogged over to her.

"L-corners," she said. "Same as in Egypt."

"Societies in the Middle East *had* to have sprung from the same source as here," Jack said, enthused. "On either side of the Atlantic, cultures share more than just architecture—the civilizations both practiced the art of mummification to preserve their dead. Believing either in life after death—or some notion of reincarnation."

"And both built pyramids," Ricardo added. "Pyramids that may have helped preserve and sterilize organic matter such as human remains."

"What do you mean?" Dorn asked.

Ricardo explained. "Biologists have discovered that somehow the shape of the pyramid preserves or sterilizes organic matter. Even small pyramids made from cardboard or plastic."

Samantha was staring at the walls of the connecting corridor. The colossal gray stones disappeared under a glaze of yellowish lathing.

"It looks like plaster," she said.

Jack ran his hand across the wall; it felt smooth, microtextured. "I've never seen plasterwork this fine before."

"Not at a site this old," Samantha added. "We'll have to sample this later."

Samantha led the group down the passage. "The hallway's rising again," she said.

Jack agreed, but with each step a sense of wrongness welled in his gut. Something about the corridor troubled him. He felt dizzy, almost drunk.

"Something doesn't feel right," Samantha said.

She noticed too, Jack thought. He knelt down, cocked his head. "My equilibrium's whacked. But why?"

He looked up the long passageway, which inclined at an eight-or nine-degree angle, Jack guessed. *Or did it?*

He reached in his pocket for a pencil, which Jack laid on the floor.

"What are you doing?" Samantha asked.

The pencil began rolling—uphill. The others watched in astonishment.

"Impossible," Dorn said. "It's defying gravity!"

Jack watched the pencil pick up some speed before stopping it with his foot. "No. Just an optical illusion," he said. "The corridor's not rising. It's still descending."

"Descending?"

"It's an illusion. You've probably seen it on television a thousand times—a mysterious roadway where people can shut off their engines and roll uphill."

Samantha walked forward again. "But why was it designed like this?"

"I haven't a clue."

The knowledge that the hallway actually descended helped Jack's equilibrium, as long as he didn't look too far down—*or up*—the corridor. But after another twenty yards the same nagging anxiety came back. This time, stronger.

Samantha said, "There's no sign of any more hieroglyphs."

This new tunnel felt sterile in almost every way, out of place. Maybe because it lacked any engravings. The pace slowed.

Ricardo looked around. "Something's bugging me about this whole corridor. . . ."

"Maybe it's the air," Dorn offered.

Jack took a breath. The air seemed less stale, but already a cold, fresh current began to filter in from outside.

"It's not the air," Samantha said slowly. "It's the walls."

*The walls.*

"They're luminescent," she said. "They glow."

Dorn examined the walls closely. "I'll be damned."

Samantha said, "We can see perfectly. With no flashlights."

Jack put his cheek to the wall. It cast an ethereal luminescence upon the side of his face. "You're right. After that ninety-degree angle we shouldn't be able to see a darn thing."

"And there's no sign of indentations for torches," Samantha said. "Have you seen any traces of oil or smoke residue from lamps?"

"Nothing," Jack said.

The hallway grew narrower; the group formed a single file. Samantha led less brazenly than before, her gait cautious, even tentative. Everything about this new tunnel seemed different, Jack thought. The feel of antiquity at the entrance had vanished.

Ricardo's voice cracked. "This isn't like any site I've ever seen."

"I know," Jack said. "It looks—modern."

Samantha walked on, blocking Jack's view of the rest of the underground passage. He was about to ask Samantha if the corridor opened to an anteroom, but just then she disappeared in a blast of mist so loud it overpowered her scream.

# MIST

Vapor exploded from the sides of the small tunnel. Samantha disappeared in a fraction of a second. Jack fell backward, shocked by the blast. The eruption continued for a short moment, clouds of spray cutting off his vision.

Then the hissing stopped.

Jack, Ricardo, and Dorn slowly picked themselves off the floor; looking ahead in stunned silence. Jack thought he heard Samantha crying somewhere beyond the wall of mist that still floated eerily throughout the stone enclosure. "Sam! Are you okay?"

The sound of coughing, then sobbing, grew louder as Jack's ears adjusted from the loud blast. "Can you hear me?"

"Yeah." Her voice trembled. "I can hear you. I'm okay."

"What the hell just happened?" Dorn yelled.

"I don't know. I'm still in one piece," she said. "Just scared."

Jack made out Samantha's crumpled form on the stone floor a few yards ahead of them. She rested on one arm, her clothes soaked.

"Are you guys . . . all right?" Samantha managed.

"We're fine," Jack said. "Whatever happened was contained to a few feet."

"The vapor smells sweet," Ricardo said.

Jack licked his lips. "But tastes alkaline." The thought crossed Jack's mind: *Maybe we shouldn't be tasting anything*. He crawled toward Samantha. She still didn't get up. He scanned the sides of the tunnel and noticed a small series of recessed holes.

"The holes are on the ceiling, too," Dorn said from behind him.

Jack's hand broke the pockmarked plane on the wall. Nothing happened.

"I thought it might work on some scanning principle," he said.

"Like department store doors?"

"Yeah. Maybe it's pressure sensitive," Jack said. He stood.

Ricardo looked at him fearfully. "All this stuff—it's *mierda*."

"But *amazing* bullshit," Jack said. He put a reassuring hand on Ricardo's shoulder then turned toward the holes. Closing his eyes, he stepped forward, transferring his weight onto the lead foot.

At once, the mist again erupted in a blinding fulmination.

Samantha screamed at the noise, amplifying the panic Jack felt. He stumbled through to the other side—feeling like he had just traveled through a cold sauna.

"Don't do that!" Samantha yelled.

Jack gasped. He wiped a few strands of wet hair from his face. "That gets the ole adrenaline going, huh?"

"At least *you* knew it was coming."

Jack sniffed his clothes; they smelled like a disinfectant. He looked back down the hallway. Ricardo and Dorn peered through the last of the mist. The ringing in Jack's ears lessened.

"It operates like a pressure pad," Jack called out.

"Is it safe?" Ricardo asked.

"We're still here."

A discussion ensued between Dorn and Ricardo about the relative aegis of the unknown device before Dorn decided he would go through. With each misting, Jack noticed the sound of the spray machine grew softer—as though the years of inactivity had to work their way out. The group waited for Ricardo, who comforted himself in Spanish before yielding to the mist.

He appeared, eyes closed, wet, and obviously unhappy.

"What is this thing?" Dorn asked, looking back at the multitude of holes.

"The mist smells like disinfectant," Samantha said.

"I was thinking the same thing," Jack replied. "Which would make this some sort of decontamination device."

"Like the spray room at the Centers for Disease Control," Ricardo said.

Samantha looked puzzled. "But a decontamination device for who?"

"Or what," Dorn said, after a silence.

Jack shook himself off. "And was it supposed to keep infectious agents out . . . or *in*?"

The question hung in the air like a hangman's noose.

Samantha peered down the corridor and fidgeted. The hallway appeared to branch off just ahead of them, but Jack couldn't see past her.

"Well?" he asked, urging her forward.

"Why don't you lead?" she finally said.

The glow from the walls provided ample light, as if thousands of invisible candles were still shining. Jack took soft, deliberate steps. Choking down a sliver of spit, his throat as dry as chalk, he felt like a child in some house of horrors—not wanting to see whatever was around the next corner but inextricably pulled toward it anyway.

They branched into a smaller passageway. "Damn," Jack sighed.

Two immense granite stones had fallen from the wall into the tight tunnel. One had broken in half, sealing the right portion of the corridor. The other had fallen toward the middle of the passage but remained intact, resting against the wall like a lean-to. Head-size chunks of rock filled the gap, cemented by a snarl of ancient tree roots and dirt.

"Roots?" Ricardo tugged, and the brittle wood snapped in his hand.

Samantha began pulling out some of the debris. "We just might be able to get through," she said. Soon the others joined her.

"I've only seen a few trees on the whole altiplano," Dorn said.

"Another indication of the age of the site," Jack said. "There are only a few trees now, but judging by the thickness of this root system and the humidity we felt once we entered, the climate was totally different here fifteen thousand years ago."

"Could that be due to a subsequent ice age?" Samantha asked.

"No. I think the climate change was triggered suddenly. By the same thing that caused the global catastrophe spoken of in so many flood myths."

"The climate changed because of a flood?" Dorn asked.

"Flooding was involved. But the underlying mechanism is known as earth crustal displacement. It probably caused all the damage around here."

"Earth crustal displacement?"

Jack tossed back more debris. "Charles Hapgood first formulated the theory, which was later endorsed by Einstein. He believed that every forty thousand years or so, a massive shifting of the earth's outer crust occurs, distinct from the slow process of plate tectonics, where pieces of the earth's crust move separately rather than in unison. Hapgood said the entire outer crust—which sits like a thin orange peel on a molten core—could move rapidly and in one piece."

"Be a hell of a disaster," Dorn muttered.

"The shift might put Antarctica on the equator and the United States near the pole. Einstein and Hapgood weren't positive about what triggered the event—probably the gradual accumulation of billions of tons of ice at the poles. But the theory explains the historical accounts of massive human extinction, and the strange fossil finds of the last century."

"What finds?" Dorn asked.

"Paleontologists on the northern tip of Vancouver Island found fossils of hundred-foot palm trees, fauna that can't grow in that climate. In the Arctic Circle, only a few hundred miles from the North Pole, explorers discovered gigantic fruit trees frozen in the ice with fruit and green leaves still on branches. The only way a warm weather tree freezes with its fruit is if the event happens all at once. Those trees were thrown from a temperate climate into a frozen one overnight. We've also found the preserved remains of mammoths in Siberia that had been frozen solid with warm weather flowers still undigested in their stomachs."

"Good god!" Dorn said.

"Each year new findings support the theory," Jack added. "Just recently I heard that oil exploration crews working the polar regions uncovered frozen coral."

"Coral exists only in extremely temperate waters," Samantha said.

"Exactly."

They continued to clear debris in silence, each left to ponder his own thoughts on such a cataclysm until Samantha eventually managed to crawl beneath the slab. After some poking, she backed out of the tight space. "I think we can squeeze through soon."

"Fantastic," Dorn said.

The man's demeanor had changed, Jack thought. Ever since the spectacular scene on the Mali savanna, Dorn had become more focused, more calculating. He cooperated with Jack; deferred to him. But Jack sensed the compliance masked something deeper—something akin to lust.

Within minutes the four formed an impromptu passing line, handing back chunks of debris. A mound grew by the side of the cave-in. Samantha scurried past the slab; her small frame navigated easily through the remaining debris.

"I can see the other side!" she said.

She broke through a mesh of brittle tree roots that hung from the stone ceiling. They snapped away at her touch, allowing a faint glow to filter in to the others. Samantha snaked through the breach. Jack waited. He could just make out her movement as she stood up on the other side.

"What is it?" Jack's heart hammered in his chest. "Does the hallway continue?"

She didn't answer.

Jack could see her head turn. He thought about grabbing her legs and pulling her back. "What is it? What do you see?"

"Jack," she said, "it's incredible."

# THE ROOM

The enormity of the space shocked them.

Ricardo labored to pull himself off the floor, slapping at a ring of dust that clung to his midsection just above the belt. He looked past the other three. "Oh my god."

Jack stood under a portico of giant stones that opened into a massive room. The light seemed more diffuse, perhaps because of the distance between the walls. The walls did, however, cast enough glow to give them an idea of the dimensions of the complex. Towering stone walls rose to majestic ceilings nearly twice the height of the previous corridors. Sixteen columns, spread in four lines through the great hall, supported the weight of the stone-lined ceiling.

"I think we've found the living room," Samantha finally said.

Jack followed her as she entered the banquet-size room. Ricardo pulled out a flashlight.

Jack looked surprised. "You've had that the whole time?"

Ricardo shrugged. "Didn't feel it until it nearly poked a hole in my chest just then."

"Looks like the same architecture as the Mortuary

Temples at Giza," Samantha said. She ran her hand up one of the gigantic columns.

"Or the Osireion," Jack said, referring to the subterranean complex he had visited in Egypt five years ago. He walked toward some stone chairs and tables. "Definitely looks like living quarters."

"But there's nothing ornate," Samantha said. "The whole thing looks like it was built for sheer practicality. There's no gold inlay, no elaborate patina work. Nothing to suggest this room was used by high officials or priests or royalty."

Dorn nodded. "It's quite bland."

The blandness, Jack knew, was an important clue to whoever built the structure. Jack agreed with Samantha's conclusion that the room served no religious purpose. In fact, he couldn't discern anything elaborate at all. The complex seemed to follow a simple maxim: function over form.

The scientists fanned out, pulled in different directions.

The faint sound of Jack's footsteps echoed as he passed uninterpretable sculptures carved from a melange of quarried stone. Jack couldn't decide what the forms represented. *At least art hasn't changed*, he concluded.

Jack paused at a long stone table. Scattered in disarray lay six stone chairs. A few had been broken. Nearby another stone edifice looked intact. Carved from granite, the container seemed built for holding foodstuffs. Jack's mind spun. What had taken place here? What purpose did some of these objects serve?

Samantha noticed a few piles of debris scattered about the room. The mounds looked like bizarre heaps of whipped malt. A few metallic threads plaited the pasty matrix.

"What do you think this was?" she wondered.

The dry, cakey substance crumbled between Ricardo's fingers. "Wooden furniture once upon a time," he said. "Digested by termites."

"Don't tell me you have a degree in entomology too," Dorn said.

Ricardo shrugged. "Just a nasty problem with my porch."

Like hypoglycemics in a candy store, the four explorers examined the great room. Occasionally one of them would call out, noticing an interesting artifact. The others would then focus on the sublime implement and guess what some of the uses for it were. The scene felt like that stupid game show, Samantha said—the one in the late seventies where celebrities made up stories about an old tool and contestants had to guess which person was telling the truth.

"But why underground?" Samantha asked. "It looks like this was purposely constructed as a subterranean complex."

Jack thought. "It might have something to do with the misting device."

"Or maybe . . . they wanted to keep this place secret," Samantha said.

Jack walked to a metallic chair behind one of the support columns.

"What is it?" Dorn said.

"A chair."

"I can see that."

Ricardo crouched down and buffed the coat of dust off one of the legs. "It looks like aluminum."

Jack held it up with one hand. "I can't believe it! But it has to be."

"What's so important about a bloody aluminum chair?" Dorn asked.

"To extract aluminum from bauxite ore requires electrolysis. You also need to heat it to over a thousand degrees," Jack said. "Ancient man wasn't supposed to possess technology capable of accomplishing that! Advanced metallurgy requires sophisticated methods and a powerful energy source. Some kind of extraterrestrial technology must have been used."

After a brief discussion, the four agreed to split up. They would inspect the adjoining rooms that branched off the main hall. No one was to enter any room beyond that. "It could be a bloody maze down here," Dorn reminded them. All agreed.

The room behind the alcove lay barren, but it led to another passageway on the far side. Just ten yards in Jack stopped in dismay. Three huge ceiling stones had caved in, sealing the adjoining corridor. The toppled megaliths must weigh sixty tons apiece, Jack guessed, and unlike the rubble they had circumvented before, here there was no way around. He began looking for a possible breach when he heard Samantha yell his name.

Rushing back into the great hall, he heard Samantha's voice again: "Jack!"

He nearly ran by an archway that connected another smaller chamber to the great hall. Samantha knelt in the dimness, in front of a few rectangular stone blocks that sat on raised platforms of andesite.

Jack stopped.

Samantha had pulled off a dust-coated metal covering from one of the blocks. The tegument must have been made from aluminum for she propped it on end beside the edifice with ease. The curved surface—larger than a full-length mirror—distorted Jack's reflection as he approached. Behind him, an out-of-breath Ricardo followed Dorn into the room. Jack counted four of the massive raised blocks. Samantha stood on the extended base of the center block.

*What was she staring at?*

Jack closed the distance. The stone block now looked more like a container that had been laid upon the raised foundation like an Egyptian sarcophagus—only larger. His heart pumped blood like a bellows. The hair rose on his neck. Jack blinked.

Something was inside.

Jack stepped onto the dais where the massive sarcophagus rested. He focused on the form resting within, forcing his eyes past the intricate engravings that adorned the sides of the repository.

*It couldn't be . . .*

Jack grabbed the edge of the coffin; suddenly he felt as if he might faint.

In the container, a gray face stared back at him through hollow, sunken eyes.

# SARCOPHAGUS

Jack felt weak. For a moment, the blood escaped from his brain—or rushed into it—he couldn't be sure. The effect made him feel as if his head had become disconnected from his body and was in danger of floating away.

"It's . . . it's the same species as our fossil," Samantha uttered.

"But . . . mummified," Jack managed.

The figure in front of them—the angelic eyes that had long since closed; the four-fingered hands, the gray skin that sagged wrinkled and tight against an intact skeletal frame—was a corpse, an actual body. The idea washed through Jack in chilling waves. The fossil had been an incredible sight. But this made everything real. The figure before them wasn't a pile of fossilized bones—ones that led to wild conjectures on the part of anthropologists and artists as to what the species looked like. This corpse, which lay with its arms crossed over its thick chest, left no room for errors. No hypotheticals on skin texture, or hair, or build. The long, blanched robe covered most of the body, the edges delicately embroidered with gold fabric.

No mummy wraps had been used. No saturated solutions. Yet something had preserved the resplendent body with near perfection. Jack's trembling hands traced the large face. Even though the skin had dehydrated and stuck tight to the facial bones underneath, the mummification was a far cry above even Egyptian standards. The face didn't look grisly. It looked peaceful. Jack dared himself to touch the long, silver-white hair that still clung to the large head.

Samantha's glittering eyes met Jack's.

"They had hair," he said. A small tear tracked down Jack's cheek. It wrapped around his strong jaw and hung on his chin for a few deep breaths. Then it fell, landing on the long four-fingered hand. The images of the bald extraterrestrial vanished from Jack's mind. This wasn't a hairless creature closer to an insect than a man. This was something quite human. Something with a beard. Something that needed haircuts; that had to groom itself. Something more human than the ancient Neanderthals. This figure in front of them seemed inexplicably like family. The four fingers, large eyes, and the slightly larger head seemed extraordinary, but if one looked past that and the corpse's height—which must have been close to six four or five—many could mistake the form for a tall man.

Like a viewing casket at a funeral, the opened sarcophagus allowed him to connect with the form. The sight created in Jack an inexplicable empathy, a visceral, shocking sense that he was paying respects to a distant relative. He *felt* for this figure. A feeling quite different from observing a chimpanzee and noticing it had hands, feet, ears, breasts, and acted at times like a human. An altogether different experience from seeing an artist's rendering of a Neanderthal man, shaved and showered in a three-piece suit—the one that anthropologists made famous for so long as they theorized on how closely related the two species were. That is, until the recent genetic studies completely destroyed the familial connection.

The sight of the whole body, with a complement of facial hair and long, flowing locks that fell from the head so delicately made the existence of extraterrestrial life personal; much more personal than the evidence they found in Mali.

"Could these be your Shining Ones?" Samantha finally said.

Jack tried to answer, but his larynx had balled into a tight, dry knot.

Dorn looked confused. "The same people the Dogons spoke of?"

"Not just the Dogons." Jack's voice caught and wavered. Years of struggle and pain seemed to find their way out from some dark, heavy place in his spirit.

Ricardo put his hand on Jack's back. "This is your proof, my friend. Enjoy it," he said.

A reverent silence fell.

"I can see why they were called the Shining Ones," Samantha said at last. "The historical descriptions are nearly perfect." She shook her head. "Your lost people are lost no more."

"Yes," Dorn thought aloud. "Your paper—on mankind's forgotten benefactors . . ."

Jack touched the broad arm of the corpse. "I almost can't believe it. But they're here. Staring at me."

"And others knew of these Shining Ones?" Dorn asked.

"They're accounted for in the histories of dozens of cultures," Jack said. "Countless oral and written traditions document the arrival of a small band of mysteriously embodied beings. These strangers apparently possessed great wisdom. They were physically unlike the local inhabitants. Considerably taller. They had shining faces with large and brilliant eyes." Jack paused, looking down at the strong, hair-covered face. "And beards . . ."

Samantha's eyes met his.

Jack noticed the flush her face radiated. "They were spoken about in Hebrew texts, like the book of Enoch. There it is written that: 'Their faces shone like the sun, and their eyes burned like lamps.' Even Daniel and a few other Old Testament prophets refer to the same beings.

"But their appearance wasn't restricted to the Middle East—or to Africa. The Tibetan Book of Dyzan speaks of 'luminous sons' who are the 'producers of the form from no-form.' Thousands of miles away, the same luminous beings were mentioned in various Sumerian texts like the Kharsag Epic."

Dorn remembered the epic from Jack's paper. "The eleven clay tablets?"

"Exactly. The Kharsag Epic speaks of a group of wise sages, luminous beings 'who set about teaching the inhabitants the cornerstones of civilization.' Writing, metalworking, planting, building. It goes on to say that before the coming of these Shining Ones, 'Man had not learned how to make clothes, or permanent dwellings. People crawled into their habitations on all fours; they ate grass with their mouths like sheep; they drank stormwater from the streams.' There are even accounts of them coming out of the sky in a 'ship of fire.' "

Samantha stared at the corpse. "You were right. All these years . . ." she whispered.

Jack heard it but looked at Dorn, who asked, "Did these extraterrestrials actually interact with early man?"

"Yes," Jack said. "In almost every account, whether the Mayans or the Sumerians or the Egyptians spoke about these people, the Shining Ones taught the locals. Protected them. They brought law and order to a race that hadn't known any. Just think of it. It all makes sense. These bearded ones—whether they were known as Viracocha here, or Quetzalcoatl in Mexico, or Kukulcan or Elohim, in other parts of the world—they were always described as tall, pale-skinned men with beards. The natives claimed they possessed magical powers. Power to levitate rocks. Power to create magic. Power to heal."

Jack's breathing quickened. "Power that can all be explained by the remarkable technology we've witnessed. Think about that hologram. You saw how we reacted—how the Zulu reacted. We're products of the twentieth century. Just imagine what this technology must have seemed like to the peoples of prehistory."

"Arthur C. Clarke's Third Law," Ricardo said. " 'Any sufficiently advanced technology is indistinguishable from magic.' "

"They must have been like gods," Samantha said.

"The Shining Ones *were* revered," Jack said. "Many saw them as omnipotent beings in a time long before Judeo-Christianity. Some scholars believe many of our angel legends could have begun with them."

"Why didn't they take over the whole earth?" Dorn asked. "Their technology would have allowed even the smallest group to dominate the entire planet—wipe out the primitive people."

"It wasn't their nature," Jack said. "They were healers who preached against violence and war. When the word *war* was mentioned, the natives of Mexico said these Shining Ones would plug their ears—refusing to listen. They even preached against human sacrifice."

"But how did they die? Where did they go?" Samantha asked.

Jack began taking off the other three lids. Each one held the same noble form, in the same position, though the last body was smaller than the others. "Most legends have them disappearing over the seas. Some have them simply vanishing. A few have them fading into the heavens again," Jack said. He touched the smooth, gray skin of the last mummy. "Maybe with some tests we'll be able to figure out exactly what happened to them."

"Did the legends speak about the number of Shining Ones?" Dorn asked.

"Accounts vary, but most speak of an extremely small group of three or four. But no matter how many appeared, all the legends have them vanishing just as fast—after ushering in all manner of great things."

Dorn stood speechless.

"Finding out how they died shouldn't be all that difficult," Ricardo said. "By the looks of it, this process is much perfected from even pristine Egyptian samples. I should be able to extract as much information as we want, given the proper machines and time. It's one of the benefits of mummification," he said. "We can retrieve perfect DNA—even after thousands of years."

"Mummification's another area that ties the ancient cultures together," Jack said. "On both sides of the Atlantic, civilizations habitually used the custom. To most of them, preserving the physical remains of the dead was the only way one could have an afterlife."

"Maybe they weren't so far off," Samantha said.

"What do you mean?" Dorn asked.

"Well. If we can get perfect DNA from a mummy, we'd have the complete building block of that person genetically. What if these visitors knew that. And what if they possessed the technology to reanimate life? Or knew that it was possible?" She paused. "I can't help but think this custom had its roots in something scientific, rather than religious. Like the fact that they knew it would preserve DNA."

Jack realized she might be right.

Dorn said, "C'mon, Samantha, you can't think they mummified their dead in the hopes that they could be brought back to life?"

"Did you read *Jurassic Park*?"

"Saw the movie."

"Well, they did it with dinosaurs."

"That's a bloody movie," Dorn said.

"Samantha has a point though," Jack said. "Look at

all the recent work in cloning. We're nearly done mapping the whole genome, and we've even transplanted an actual human gene into other living animals. The writing's on the wall. DNA is the building block of life. Why not the rebuilding block of life?"

"Which brings up another point," Samantha said. "It takes a living being to mummify the dead. There's no trace of any skeletons . . ."

"You can't think one of these creatures is still alive?" Dorn said.

Silence again filled the room.

"All it says is that someone was alive at the time these four were mummified," Jack said.

Ricardo wiped his brow. "After the last few days, I'm not sure I'd rule anything out, my friends."

Jack walked between the four coffins, wondering what lay behind the blocked passageway he'd stumbled upon. The group decided that they should draw a detailed plan for the careful analysis of the entire site. Samantha helped Ricardo put the aluminum coverings back over each stone sarcophagus while Jack and Dorn made notes.

"The notion of bringing back the dead . . ." Dorn shook his head. "You really think it's possible?"

"Let's put it this way. After everything I've seen happen in the world of genetics lately, I'm thinking about rewriting my will," Jack said.

"What. Now you're going to mummify yourself?"

"I'm sure as hell not opting for cremation."

# SURFACE

Jack made sure Ricardo took a few carefully selected samples of tissue from the last of the embalmed bodies before they left the complex. He hoped that when the rest of their analysis equipment arrived with Dorn's men, he would be able to answer one mystery: how the creatures had died. Coming back through the misting device had been easier than going in, largely because they knew it was coming. The jets sprayed them once again, but the mist seemed stickier, as if it were a different substance. Ricardo thought it was. The device, Jack told Samantha, must be able to sense direction.

"If the device performs some sort of decontamination process on entering, and a similar process with a different substance on the way out, then the extraterrestrials were concerned not only about bringing contaminants back in with them," Jack said. "They were also desperately worried about going outside."

Near the entrance to the complex, a whitish glow illuminated the hieroglyphs at the entrance corridor. The group paused to take notes while Jack filled Samantha and the others in on the blocked passageway he noticed off the great hall. Dorn suggested they wait till his men arrived with more equipment before trying to breach the obstruction.

After seeing the immense blocks, Jack knew they didn't have a choice.

\*　　\*　　\*

The harsh Andean light hurt Jack's eyes. The glow of the underground chambers seemed so peaceful in comparison. The sun had passed noon a few hours ago, and already the highlands had begun to succumb to the inevitable nocturnal chill. Bongane sat at the edge of the excavation with Baines, who had already donned his jacket.

They had been underground for six hours. It seemed like six minutes.

"I hope it was worth it," Baines said, helping Dorn out of the pit. "The whole friggin' camp is curious. I couldn't even take a bloody leak."

Dorn pulled him aside immediately and explained what the group had found. Jack could imagine the dialogue. Baines's eyes grew larger—confirming Jack's suspicions.

Bongane helped Jack place the artifact back in its case. Baines told the scientists and Dorn that the expedition had navigated most necessary channels—if not entirely legal ones—which granted them permission for their field work.

"Things are shaping up," Dorn said. "I think I'll finally be able to relax."

"Speaking of which—we haven't eaten anything since last night," Samantha said.

Only then did the grumbling in Jack's stomach get his attention. After finding the entrance in the morning, they hadn't paused once, not even for lunch.

Bongane smiled. "You hungry?"

"I'd eat anything right now."

"Good. I cook all day."

"What are we having?"

"Soup."

Jack's stomach demanded more. "Is that all?"

Bongane picked up his end of the case. "And potatoes."

Jack picked at the boiled spud in front of him with his fork. You could mash it, bake it, boil it, fry it; but still, Jack thought, the bland root remained tasteless. Why did people insist on eating the damn things? The only flavor came from the mountains of merciful toppings you smothered it with—and out here on the altiplano none could be found.

A discussion began on the obstruction Jack found in the anteroom.

"Do you think it leads to another series of chambers?" Samantha asked.

"I don't know. It was sealed tight. I don't know if we'll even be able to clear it."

"What about explosives?" Dorn asked.

Jack put down his fork. "I wouldn't suggest blasting down there. And I don't think standard blasting powder will do the job anyway."

"My men are bringing C-4," Dorn said.

"Plastique?" Ricardo's eyebrows raised. "Nothin' like toting a cannon to a knife fight."

"We've used it in my mining operations," Dorn said. "A little goes a long way."

Reluctantly, Jack agreed to check the feasibility of the process in the morning. In less than twenty minutes the meal had been devoured. The next hour passed sipping warm Andean tea. Still, the elixir wouldn't overcome the urgent call of sleep. Half-opened eyes belied their fatigue and the contentment their stomachs now relished.

Before the group went to bed, Dorn received a radio transmission from his men en route to the ruins that all the expedition equipment from the crash site had been retrieved.

Samantha warmed both hands around her coffee mug, cradling it like a porcelain child. "When will your men get here?"

"Sometime late tonight. They've informed me all the necessary paperwork has been filed. We're completely legitimate now."

"That's good to know."

"The analysis machines will be up and running in no time," Dorn said.

For Jack, no time wasn't soon enough. There was so much data to process, so much information to record and sift through. The scientists decided that the group would set up a work camp inside the subterranean complex at daybreak.

"It would save a lot of transport time," Jack said.

"And keep us from passing through that torturous machine every two seconds," Ricardo added.

The group discussed the possibilities of contaminating the facility, but reasoned there was no way around it, and that the misting machine—if indeed it served as a decontamination device—should help.

Besides, Dorn pointed out, there's nothing alive down there to contaminate. "Is there?"

No one could answer him.

# VIRACOCHA

Four soft-white skeletons crawled across the rocky terrain, glowing in the thin night air. Pierce's night-vision goggles clearly defined the long axle of the lead truck as it spun; pushing the protesting back wheels over the landscape. The warm engine blocks of the four vehicles shone clearly beneath their metal hoods. The steel exoskeletons glowed bright against the green-gray background of rock. Pierce counted five bodies. One in each cab, and another form asleep in the back of the last truck. He shook Miller, who had fallen asleep sitting upright. Pierce handed him another pair of night-vision goggles.

"Keep an eye out. I'll transmit."

"More trucks?" Miller asked after a moment.

He monitored the phosphorescent convoy, which snaked to the ruins, while Pierce followed the small trail to the covered Jeep. Feasting on electric current from a car battery, the satellite communicator roared to life with beeps and clacks. Pierce attacked the keyboard in a two-finger assault. He could anticipate the orders—and felt the deep pang of adrenaline.

At 06:21 local time, the KH-14 noticed a brief, powerful electromagnetic disturbance at the dig site. The lean-to the scientists had constructed to shield themselves from the sun had blocked both the photo view of the satellite and Pierce's and Miller's. The disturbance had gotten someone's panties in a twist—from Virginia came orders to update on the hour. Pierce felt one step closer to intervention, though he couldn't understand what the scientists had been doing in that hole for over six hours. Maybe some subterranean weapons test? Pierce finished his message about the incoming convoys and pressed send. The transmitter scrambled his message and sent it bouncing off two satellites thousands of feet in space.

Whatever was going on, Pierce thought, it was getting weirder by the second.

Wind whipped the tents.

The convoy of Dorn's men had arrived just before the weather picked up. Samantha could still hear Baines and Dorn coordinating the off-loading of the last equipment. She warmed her hands inside her down-filled Gore-Tex jacket, then decided to refill her mug with spicy Andean tea. As the steam rose from the kettle, she noticed that her watch had misted over—probably from passing through the decontamination device. Through the condensation she saw it was past two in the morning. She was exhausted, too tired to sleep. Everyone had worked into early morning, unpacking materials. They'd already connected the two large generators. The machines would be up and running for tomorrow's tests. The convoy brought all the equipment from the crash site, and then some. Ben had spared no expense in Mali, even before they discovered the fossil, but now he'd ratcheted up the resources. It scared her. Ben seemed more invested—too invested for her liking. The expedition now felt conquistadorial—like some massive treasure hunt.

Jack had thrown down a cot inside the big lab tent. The gentle hissing of the swaying lanterns put him to sleep soon after. Samantha never thought about waking him. Instead she pulled his notes gently from underneath his arm and sat down to decipher them for herself. She felt the hot tea warm her stomach. The bottoms of the tent flapped in the winds as if the entire structure could take flight at any moment. Jack slept through it all. Samantha's eyes felt heavy, but she couldn't stop perusing Jack's research.

Viracocha.

The name emblazoned the top of his worn, yellowed papers. It stood out in bold, as if he'd traced the letters a countless number of times. Beside it in smaller script was a string of other names: Kukulcan, Votan, Orejona, Ta'aroa, Maoui, Elohim. He had written the words "Shining Ones" over and over again. A few rested beside question marks—as though his doubts had doodled their way onto the page.

Samantha found more information on Jack's laptop.

His file under Shining Ones listed fact after fact. Her hand tapped the touch pad, scrolling the screen upward. With each page her conviction grew: the veracity of Jack's theories was sound. These mysterious Shining Ones apparently performed great acts of power and taught the inhabitants the cornerstones of civilization before they mysteriously vanished. Samantha was familiar enough with the myths of the South American peoples—she knew about the legendary Viracocha—but until yesterday, Jack's interpretations of them felt too bizarre.

Now they read with the sweet ring of truth.

The myths dared people to believe. Most of the texts were only as far away as the local library. No matter what name ancient peoples gave these figures, the descriptions were similar: a small group of civilizers. Wise sages. Great men of science and magic who helped heal the world, yet who also possessed terrible weapons of fire. Samantha pushed words onto the gray screen as fast as she could read them. Under each name the same story appeared. The universal accounts shocked her. Whether they had been sourced from oral or written records, from Middle Eastern scribes or Spanish chroniclers recording the oral beliefs of the native inhabitants, the accounts all spoke of the arrival of these beings before the Great Flood. Bearded pale men of large stature. Men whose big eyes and faces shone with power like the sun. They couldn't have been native Indian—Indians possessed little facial hair and most didn't break five and a half feet. The fossil and bodies stood close to six feet five.

Samantha's heart raced. Facts reemerged from her own experience. She recalled reading something about the Time of Giants in the Bible. *This was all related.* Her hands shook on the touch pad. The facts had rested in front of humanity for all recorded history. Most of us have just chosen to overlook them, she thought. Every story—every description—of Viracocha, Kon Tiki, Thunupa, Tupaca—they all read the same.

The evidence didn't just exist, it existed beyond a reasonable doubt. Samantha thought about the fossil in the steel case. She thought about the four mummified giants resting peacefully in their stone coffins. The skeptics— like herself—couldn't deny the physical proof the expedition had uncovered. What would it mean for the world? What would it mean for Samantha Colby?

She wondered—hoped—it would mean something to her father.

Samantha took deep controlled breaths; she ought to calm herself. A scientist doesn't act like a giddy schoolgirl. She could handle this. But how does one handle the fact that Earth had been blessed with visitors from another world; visitors who taught civilization to humanity and who possessed great powers, but acted kindly. Visitors who didn't come to conquer but healed the sick, who taught medicine and mathematics.

Samantha read a quote Jack had copied from one Spanish chronicler who told how the great Viracocha instructed men in the ways of peace: "They say in many places he gave men instructions how they should live, speaking to them with great love and kindness and admonishing them to be good and to do no damage or injury one to another, but to love one another and show charity to all."

Samantha set her mug down. These extraterrestrials weren't evil space voyagers hell-bent on destroying earth. They were guardian angels.

No matter what source or people the legend stemmed from, Viracochas, the Shining Ones, were remembered as those who brought order and taught the cornerstones of civilization. In Peru, they were credited with teaching medicine, metallurgy, writing, farming. In Bolivia they were credited with building great temples with huge stones, and teaching the inhabitants about engineering, architecture, and the stars.

No wonder Jack felt so adamant. For a moment, Samantha's mind drifted back to Princeton. She had felt so sure that he was simply acting out. An extraterrestrial presence on earth? It seemed like good television, not good science. Her eyes found Jack again, asleep on his cot, his arm draped off the edge. While she couldn't attribute all their problems to a simple theoretical disagreement, she took Jack's insistence on fighting the establishment personally.

But he was right.

All his obstinacy—the years of rebellion—felt different to her now.

She had been too afraid to make waves. Too afraid to

raise issues that might slow or even devastate her career. A thought floated through her mind—maybe it's why she learned to hate Jack. She could see in him the courage she couldn't find in herself. Maybe it wasn't his stubbornness she hated—maybe it was his courage. If she looked deeply enough into her soul now, the truth could be found. Her insecurity might have ruined their relationship. Sure, Jack's pride played a role, but she had forsaken someone she loved deeply. All because she was afraid. Jack had stood up to a scientific system hell-bent on the status quo. An establishment that had everything figured out and didn't want anyone or anything to muck it up. Jack paid the price—banished by his colleagues and abandoned by someone who should have been there for him all along.

Samantha dared not make a noise. Instead she wiped her tears on the arm of her parka. She had been reminded of a long-forgotten Bible story she had learned in Episcopalian grade school. The story about Peter's denial of Jesus in the face of adversity. As a child she always told herself she'd never do that to someone she loved.

She shut off the laptop, then turned down the lanterns. In the near darkness she found her cot and collapsed. She needed to talk to Jack. No, do more than talk. She needed to humble herself and apologize, not because she'd been wrong in doubting Jack's theories, but because she'd been wrong in doubting the man behind those theories. A man—she now realized—she still loved, always loved.

Samantha covered herself with the wool blanket. Her head gradually found the perfect indentation in the small travel pillow. Outside, the cold winds howled at the moon like a pack of wolves. She pulled the wool just under her chin. Her lids closed. As her body warmed, she recalled another cold night she spent with Jack. A quiet Christmas Eve eight years ago. She savored the memory of the colorful tree, the scattered clothes on the floor, the crackling fire, the feel of his body . . .

Then Samantha fell asleep, dragged into unconsciousness by images of tall bearded men who performed great acts of magic.

# OBSTRUCTION

Fog shrouded the encampment. Pierce awoke groggily at half past six in the morning and climbed out of his sleeping bag, rubbing the swollen crescents under his eyes. He took up position on the rocky outcropping next to Miller.

"They're bringing a lot of their equipment underground," Miller said. He snacked on a dry cereal bar, washing it down with water. Below them, the camp already bustled with activity. "I would have woken you earlier but I figured you needed the beauty sleep."

"You look like shit, too," Pierce grunted and ripped open a cereal bar himself.

A sputter from the truck got his attention before he took a bite. "I got it," he said, walking to the satellite communicator that descrambled the code before splaying the text onto a small screen:

Sept. 12. STOP. 0800 STOP.
DO: #3566577 DOCUMENT TRANSMISSION
ANALYSTS WANT MORE GROUND DATA ABOUT
ELECTROMAGNETIC DISTURBANCE AT SITE. 06211.
SEPT 11. WHICH LASTED SIX SECONDS.

FURTHER SATELLITE OBSERVATION YIELDS NOTH-
ING.
NEED ON-SITE VISUALS. POSSIBLE?
PLEASE ADVISE.
#3566577. STOP.

Pierce shook his head.
"What is it?" Miller asked.
"Too damn early for this."
Pierce pecked back the response on the keyboard. The
agency wanted them to go in; get more information.
Though he could hardly believe what he typed, Pierce
sent the return message:

SEPT. 12. STOP. 0801. STOP
FLD. FO. #27AV43 DOCUMENT TRANSMISSION
MESSAGE ACKNOWLEDGED. STOP.
NEED 24 HOURS TO RECONNOITER POSSIBLE AP-
PROACHES TO SITE. STOP
IF MISSION FEASIBLE: WILL ATTEMPT CLOSE-IN VI-
SUAL IDENTIFICATION.
WILL NOTIFY WITH FINDINGS. STOP.

Since dawn, supplies had filtered into the subterranean
complex in a procession of wood crates. The group had
transferred half of their equipment from the encampment
near the pyramid to the great hall and its expansive
chambers. The line of bodies carrying gear into the hole
reminded Jack of an ant colony. The generator that
would supply their energy needs droned loudly in a
chamber just off the great hall.
"Any ideas on the cause of death?" Jack asked Ricardo.
"I'm just not sure." Ricardo probed the flesh of the
mummified extraterrestrial. The skin felt like cured
leather. Ricardo's scalpel made a small incision. Then
he made three more, tracing a half-inch square on the
first mummy. Using the edge of the blade like a ladle,

he freed the section of skin from the corpse's thigh. Ricardo carefully dropped the patch of skin into a test tube and sealed it with a rubber plunger. "The hair I took earlier this morning is dissolving in solution right now. It should give us a better idea of its genetic makeup. I've also run diagnostics for trace toxins."

Biogenetics was the next frontier. A simple strand of hair could yield a plethora of clues. Dissolved in solution, molecules were freed, allowing scientists to retrieve information about the past life of the deceased. Recently, using the same procedure, scientists had found strong traces of cocaine in the hair follicles of Egyptian mummies. It proved that the ancient Egyptians used cocaine— just like the Mayans. The cocaine mummies, as they were later called, bolstered the argument that Jack and others had been putting forth for years: The South American cultures and Egyptian cultures were not only related, but had sprung from the same source of civilization. It certainly raised questions on how Egyptians came to possess coca—a crop grown exclusively thousands of miles away in South America.

"They look fairly healthy," Jack said, "for being thousands of years old."

"This is the second time I've looked at them," Ricardo said. "And I still don't see any signs of trauma. No broken bones. No skin lacerations of any kind. Whatever killed them probably did so at a microlevel. Viral. Maybe bacterial. They might have been poisoned. I'm just guessing without performing a complete autopsy. For that I'd have to rip one of these guys apart, look for signs of internal hemorrhaging. Although I'm not ruling out the most logical explanation."

"Which is?"

"That they simply died of old age." Ricardo put the lid back on the sarcophagus. "But I have no way of knowing that. They aren't an earth-born species. I don't have a clue as to what their normal life span was."

"I'd guess it was long," Jack said. "Biblically speaking, even humans seemed to live longer in ancient times. Abraham lived for a hundred and seventy-five years."

"I'll have a better hypothesis once I get the results from my first tests back," Ricardo said.

He and Jack stepped over the cable that ran toward the generator. The power source sputtered loudly from down the corridor.

Samantha met them in front of the small chamber the scientists had already dubbed "Ricardo's study." The room brimmed with medical equipment and analysis instruments. "I think we'll have to blast through the obstruction," she said, out of breath. "The drills aren't even making a dent."

"And disturb all this quiet?" Ricardo shouted.

"I'll ask Bongane to move the generator," she said.

"I will be forever in your debt," Ricardo said and vanished back into his makeshift laboratory.

A pneumatic drill banged the rock with a noise that overpowered the rumble of the generator. The huge andesite block fought valiantly against the diamond-tipped metal tongue that hammered incessantly at a small crack. It took Baines and Bongane thirty-five minutes to widen the fissure by half an inch.

"This will take us all month," Baines said, exhausted.

Bongane laid down the drill so Jack could assess their progress. It didn't look good. The block wasn't weathered at all and the drills had trouble finding cracks big enough to exploit.

"Blasting's the only real option," Dorn said.

Baines agreed. "These blocks didn't serve as a true hanging wall. They're not part of the structural integrity of the tunnel."

Jack peered at the crack. "I don't know. We have no idea what's behind this. Blasting might get us in—but it might also blow whatever's behind here to smithereens."

"I don't think we have a choice," Samantha said.

Jack thought for a moment. He told himself it wasn't just a matter of instant gratification—he'd used explosives on a few digs, but only in extremely controlled settings and when no other options existed. "Can you control the blast?"

"I've been mining for twenty-three years," Dorn said. "We know what we're doing."

Feeling a few pangs of guilt, Ricardo set the samples in the specimen rack beside the fold-out table, which held a battalion of machines. He doubted if any of the Bolivian hospitals had half the equipment. Sighing, he pulled out a plastic chair near the powerful microscope. The chair bent in protest under his cumbrous frame.

Ricardo rubbed his eyes. The cell structure of the extraterrestrials was remarkably similar to our own. But he still hadn't come up with a probable cause of death. He got up and shook his legs before perusing the sixteen sheets of results from his battery of tests. He flipped through them, looking for everything and nothing. The findings over the last few days had overwhelmed him. So had seeing Jack and Samantha together again after six years.

Ricardo had always found himself caught in the middle. He had met Samantha first. She was warm and brilliant and beautiful. Ricardo met Jack a few months later—introduced by Samantha as "The One." She'd fallen head over heels. In a way, Ricardo did too. He and Jack hit it off right away. They shared the same spirit of mischievousness. The two men loved knowledge but also had no qualms letting loose in a pub or two or three. Jack, never at a loss for women, would always provide Ricardo with "assists"—usually women who'd given up trying to court Jack. But it seemed to Ricardo that most of those relationships invariably became strong, platonic friendships. Jack always teased him about how he could have so many "girlfriends"— that is, girls who were just friends.

Ricardo explained that some guys were like that.

He could spend weeks analyzing the data in front of him. Ricardo decided long ago that his great love would be books—knowledge. It was enough for him, he thought. *Almost* enough. He paused halfway through the stack of cell counts, toxic analysis, and antibody tests. Signs of a very peculiar virus showed up—without any antibodies. He looked again. His heart began to drum. The answer to what had killed the extraterrestrials might have just reared its ugly head.

Ricardo read and reread the initial viral analysis as he awaited confirmation of his findings. He felt short of breath—on the brink of an important revelation. *Surely this couldn't be*. Finally he heard the laser printer spit out the data sheets. He ran past the centrifuge, collecting the stream of pages straight into his hand.

Page nine.

His findings were confirmed. He yanked the top sheet from the stack. The rest of the papers dropped onto the floor. Ricardo knocked over the chair and ran out of the room.

Thin red wires trailed down the face of the rock, snaking their way onto the stone floor where they reunited in a taped bundle. Explosive charges sat carefully packed into seams on the immense stones. The six squares of plastique looked like they had given birth to the laminated serpents. Baines's fingerprints pockmarked the pliable substance in the center of the packs where the red fuse wire had been burrowed into the C-4. He rolled two wooden spools of fuse down the hallway, and paused next to Jack. "The charges should be just enough to get us through. They'll break this bloody mammoth with no problem."

"Let's hope they don't break anything else," Jack said.

"We'll be fine. We used just enough C-4 to cut those blocks into small pieces." Baines handed Jack the other spool. "If we detonate from beyond the anteroom, I reckon it'll give us enough of a safety cushion."

The two men rolled the wooden spools past Dorn and Samantha, who helped Anthony with the tenuous but critical task of getting the crates of unused C-4 as far away as possible.

"I'd be mighty careful, miss," Anthony said.

The fuse extended all the way past the anteroom and into the great hall. Baines directed Jack to roll the last coils around the corner while he retrieved the wood crate that held the battery terminal.

Jack had just finished laying out the blasting cords when Ricardo ran down the corridor toward him, shouting: "I found it!" His cry echoed throughout the entire space. Samantha, Dorn, and Anthony rushed into the anteroom. Baines jogged in, carrying the crate with the battery terminal.

"What's going on? Are you okay?" Samantha asked.

Ricardo slowed. "A virus!" He put his hands on his knees, trying to get his breath. Ricardo held up a paper in his hand. "The extraterrestrials . . . they died of a virus . . ."

Panic began to fill the void. "Are you sure?" Dorn asked.

Jack wasn't surprised. The decontamination device was a dead giveaway. Fear and anxiety clutched his chest. He grabbed Ricardo's shoulders. "What virus?" Ricardo sucked in more air. Jack repeated the question: "What virus, Ricardo?"

"Coryza."

Baines dropped the wood crate. "Oh shit."

Jack exhaled sharply. "Shit is right." He threw a relieved glance at Samantha before pointing to Ricardo. "Don't ever do that again. You scared the hell out of me."

"Do what again?" Dorn said, dismayed. "How can you be so smug? We're talking about a virus that might be infectious!"

"It's very infectious," Samantha said.

"But at least it's earthborn," Jack added. "And relatively mild."

Baines squirmed. "It sounds bloody horrible. What is it?"

"The common cold."

It took a few moments before Dorn regained his composure. He seemed slightly embarrassed.

"I agree," he finally said to Ricardo. "Don't *ever* do that again."

While Baines wired the fuses to a copper screw on the battery terminal, which would serve as the detonator, Ricardo elaborated on his findings.

"From what I could tell they had weak immune systems," Ricardo said. "At least weak for the microbes on this planet. I found a high concentration of virus in all four samples, but I found no antibodies for it. No traces of anything that would suggest the beings were able to fight off the infection."

"It would explain why they took so many precautions about decontamination," Jack said.

"And why they probably built this whole structure underground," Samantha added. "They feared the microbes on the surface. Thus the hermetically sealable entrance corridor."

"It's ironic," Dorn said. "A race so advanced—taken down by a little virus that's been around for millions of years."

"A little virus we still have no cure for," Jack said.

"From what I can tell, they must have had trouble adapting to life on Earth. I'm curious to know how long they lasted before succumbing," Ricardo said.

Jack stared introspectively at the long fuses which ran toward the obstruction. "The scenario fits with the historical records. Almost every account has the Shining Ones vanishing quickly. There are also stories of temples that man was forbidden to enter."

Jack retrieved his field book from the top of one of the crates.

"The legend says only a select few humans ever entered. Enoch said he had been allowed to visit one of these temples."

"Who's Enoch?" Baines asked, still fiddling with the terminal.

"The three great chronicles of Enoch were compiled many years before Christ—from sources even earlier—thousands of years earlier. Enoch was Noah's grandfather, literally known as 'the man who spoke the truth.' His writings always seemed pragmatic, historical—the man always wrote without religious or supernatural trappings." Jack's finger scanned the page. "He tells of a House of Joy and Life, the bright dwelling, Where the Destiny of Man was established; the splendid place of Flaming Brightness," Jack read. "This 'Brilliant, Glowing House' stood out from all the other mud dwellings in the surrounding areas, which were lit by torches. He says: 'In every respect, the inside was so magnificent, and spacious, that I cannot describe it to you. Its floor was brilliantly lit, and above that were bright lights like planets, and its ceiling, too, was brilliant.' "

"Sure sounds like a description of this place," Ricardo said. "For someone who lived in prehistory the technology must have seemed mystical. It seems mystical enough to us."

Baines interrupted. "The detonator's ready." He waved everyone away from the terminal. "Careful now," he said. "This is live."

Dorn turned to Jack. "Ready?"

"Yes," he said, less sure than he sounded. "I suppose I am."

Samantha said, "We're only seventy yards away. Is this safe?"

The short distance they stood from the charges surprised Jack also.

"In a diamond or platinum mine we'd be behind a reinforced wall," Dorn explained. He patted the immense cornerstones of the anteroom. "But these huge blocks are sturdier than anything we use in Johannesburg, believe me."

Baines's leather boot rested on the "hot wire" destined for the other end of the terminal. "Here we go, then."

The group crouched next to the comforting forty-ton block of solid stone that served as their shield. Dorn plugged his ears. The rest shielded their eardrums with the palms of their hands. Dorn nodded.

Baines yelled, "Fire in the hole!"

Samantha closed her eyes. Jack sensed everything as if it were happening in slow motion. He noticed the pea-size arc of electricity jolt the wire even before Baines tapped it onto the steel screw.

The explosion came in at hyperspeed.

Jack felt as if his eardrums might rupture as the shock waves from the blast carried by them on a quick rush of wind. A deafening roar followed, as if a pride of crazed lions had been unleashed. A few moments later, thumping echoes replaced the tumultuous growl as loose rocks bounced down the hallway. A cloud of dust carrying the strong odor of spent explosive followed. Heavy particles of smoke and dust blinded them momentarily. An occasional cough broke the settling silence as the group held a hand over their mouths and noses. They spoke through the muffle of fingers.

Samantha's eyes teared. "Do you think it worked?"

"Doesn't sound like there's any more settling," Dorn said.

Jack stood, dusted himself off. "Let's take a look."

"By god, we've done it," Dorn said—as if doubting they would.

The stone obstruction had disintegrated into a mass of small boulders that spread out across the length of the tunnel. The pungent smell of spent C-4 burned their nostrils. Heavy smoke from the plastique still curled around their ankles as they sifted through the tons of rubble. Jack climbed the heap of crumbled rock. Near the top he noticed a small crawlspace between the pile of shattered stone and the ceiling. Excitement coaxed him on. "It's clear to the other side," he yelled.

Jack crawled along the apex of the debris. After a yard, the slope descended again to the far side. He slid down the mound of split rock, his boots pressing onto wet stone at the bottom. Jack found himself staring down a long corridor. A series of rooms opened on both sides. The solitary stone cubicles stood guard over the hallway with spartan indifference. To his immediate left, before the first of the rooms, Jack noticed a large square hole cut into the side of the passageway, about waist high.

It looked like a shaft.

His heart sped. Explorers had found the same peculiar ducts in the Acapana Pyramid at the surface. As yet, no one had been able to figure out their exact purpose. Some scientists thought the stone channels served as ventilation shafts. Others believed the Tiahuanacans had been involved in a water cult, and that these sluices funneled water through the structures. The shaft measured almost three feet diagonally, just wide enough to fit a man—with the possible exception of Ricardo. Jack took a few steps toward the hole, sloshing through the thin layer of water that glazed the stone floor.

Samantha watched from atop the mound of rubble. "What is it?" she called out.

"It's some kind of stone duct," Jack said. "Just like the ones in the Acapana Pyramid. Only larger." Jack's head disappeared into the shaft. The stone channel cut into the darkness at a sharp decline. Jack felt a lightness in his stomach. He knew what the decline meant. "This channel descends at a thirty-degree angle!"

Samantha's voice wavered. "There might be a second level to the complex?"

"Maybe a whole series of levels."

Samantha relayed the findings to Dorn, who had joined her on the stones.

A slight breeze cooled perspiration on the side of Jack's face. *A slight breeze?* Maybe these *were* ventilation shafts. Jack watched some of the smaller rocks on the pile begin to vibrate. He thought Samantha might be coming down the slope, but she hadn't moved from the top of the mound.

"Do you feel that?" he asked.

The vibrations caused ripples in the water at Jack's feet. The thought of water made him queasy—it had crept above his shoe soles.

"What is it?" Samantha sounded alarmed. "An earthquake?"

A growl bellowed from the dimness down the hallway. The breeze became a gust.

Jack's gaze found Samantha's, her eyes were wide with fright. Then he felt a massive liquid wall slam into him from behind. He floated toward the pile of crumbled rock in front of him, but time seemed to coagulate. Images passed before him like a series of still photos. Foam. Brown. Rocks.

His body must have been thrown into a state of shock. Jack's face smacked the hard stone at the base of the pile, but he felt no pain. For a fraction of a second his universe consisted of his mouth. He felt two of his bottom teeth rip free from his jaw. Even amid the turbulence, Jack clearly experienced the strange sensation of swallowing those teeth.

Then he slipped from consciousness.

# MUD RUSH

The wall of brown water consumed Jack in an instant. Samantha watched in horror as he slammed into the bottom of the rock pile, then disappeared. The force of the onrushing wind knocked her over the apex of the mound and down the side she had climbed. Rough stone peeled layers of skin from her flesh. She tumbled to the bottom. A torrent of mud followed, sweeping her, Dorn, and the rest of the group out of the anteroom in a stampede of boulders. Samantha felt caught in a powerful wave. Tumbling. Hitting rocks. Walls. She knocked into bodies. Felt an arm. A leg. She careened for thirty yards before the force of the flow dissipated. Five mud-covered figures appeared from the muck. Moist coughs echoed in the chamber. The dirty water drained away. One set of eyes appeared, then another, as Ricardo, Dorn, Baines, and Bongane wiped away their silty bath.

Samantha tried standing, but stumbled.

Ricardo held her. "Hold on. Are you okay, Sam?"

Samantha managed a nod and looked at the floor, trying to get her legs back.

"Mud rush," Dorn said between coughs. "It must have been caused by the blast."

Samantha looked around, the image of the wall of mud coming back to her. "Oh my god. Jack!" She squirmed out of Ricardo's grasp.

The rock pile had been decimated. The wall of water succeeded in sweeping half the obstruction away. Samantha scrambled over the flattened pile without heeding Ricardo's calls for caution. She reached the far side of the mound and watched in horror as the water backed up against the rocks.

The water level was already dropping.

The foamy reservoir gushed through the hole in the side wall—the shaft that Jack had been inspecting. Behind her Dorn's and Ricardo's shouts bounced off the stone ceiling as they climbed the slope. The knot on the side of her skull ached, but she ignored it, forcing her eyes to focus into the draining corridor.

"I can't see him, Ricardo! I can't see him."

Ricardo slid beside her. "Where was he when it hit?"

"Near the base of the pile." She pointed to the remnants of the brown pool rushing down the shaft. "He was looking at that opening. He said it might be some kind of ventilation shaft to another level."

Dorn put his arms around Samantha. His touch made her feel worse; she backed away.

"Do you see him?" she said, panicking.

"We'll find him." Dorn pulled muddy strands of hair off her face. "We'll find him."

Samantha continued to watch the water, which was quite shallow now. "He could have survived," she mumbled. "He's a swimmer. He could make it."

The surface foam dissolved as the muddy tide found new ways of responding to gravity's perpetual call—but still no sign of Jack.

Samantha didn't notice the motion behind her. Dorn turned to Baines. He answered the man's nonverbal question—with the trace of a smile—as if Jack's disappearance came as a blessing.

Dorn shook his head: *No way.*

Samantha sloshed through a foot of mud at the base of the pile. She felt something against her leg and pulled up a large tree root. The swollen red knot at her hairline throbbed painfully. Still, her limbs probed through the muck. She called Jack's name, but only her echo answered from the hallway.

He was gone.

"He must have been swept down the duct," Ricardo said.

Looking down the mud-coated chute, Samantha called his name over and over.

No one answered.

The group searched the ankle-high mud for twenty more minutes until even Samantha acknowledged his body wasn't anywhere in the newly opened section. Half of her felt sick. The other half clung to hope. At least they hadn't found his corpse. Jack could still be alive. Somewhere.

While Baines and Bongane went to retrieve any rope they could find on the surface, Dorn began explaining the physics behind a mud rush, evidently a common threat to miners. Samantha caught only small snippets of the discussion as she rocked back and forth, biting her nails. Dorn explained that blasting often liquefied portions of a subterrane—ripping open underground reservoirs of water, or rupturing natural barricades that kept back the water table. The result was a deluge of mud that could fill a tunnel instantly.

"I'd say we were lucky it was only a small liquefaction," Dorn finished.

"Lucky?" Samantha stopped rocking. "We might have lost Jack, dammit!"

Her outburst startled Dorn.

Samantha didn't care about the physics. She just felt a sick sense of helplessness. Jack was gone. Fifty minutes had passed since the mud rush, and Baines and Bongane still hadn't returned. Samantha knew each passing minute decreased the odds of Jack's survival. Her anxiety shook her body.

When she finally saw Bongane and Baines climbing over the rubble shouldering coils of vinyl cord, she leaped to her feet.

*       *       *

She hadn't imagined anyone else going down the shaft after Jack. She was the smallest and lightest, and her skill at rock climbing made her perfectly suited for the job. Ricardo handed her his flashlight. Bongane checked and double-checked the knots around Samantha's waist, then tightened the coils between the six rope sections. She could be lowered to a depth of 180 feet.

"What if we need more rope?" she asked.

"That's all we have," Baines answered. "We had to scour the entire camp for this."

"If we need more rope," Dorn said, "this whole exercise will be useless anyway."

Samantha peered down the shaft. The stone tunnel disappeared into an inky void. She flicked on the flashlight. The beam parted the blackness with a sharp four-inch beam. She twisted the top and the torch's beam widened, illuminating more of the shaft.

"If you need to be pulled out give us a signal," Dorn said, "try two tugs."

"How 'bout if I scream: 'Get me the hell up'?"

"That would work too."

Bongane hoisted Samantha into the small chamber, where she paused to take a few deep breaths. Her feet dangled beneath her, her buttocks on the ledge. "You checked all the knots?" she asked. If one of them unraveled, there would be no way back up.

Bongane nodded.

Baines said, "Try to keep the rope from fraying against any edges."

Samantha started down, on her back. Her shorts slid easily over the mud-coated stone. They fed the rope down to her at a steady pace. Samantha prayed for strength in those knots. Her terror had no outlet. The tight confines that boxed her in like a stone coffin seemed resolutely indifferent to the whole affair.

"You've got forty more feet," Ricardo called out.

Every now and again she shouted Jack's name. It wasn't long before the rope stopped feeding down to her.

"What's the problem?" she shouted.

Ricardo's voice boomed: "That's it. A hundred and eighty feet."

Samantha stared down the rest of the shaft, then flicked on the flashlight. She couldn't tell how much farther the duct continued. "Jaaackk!" She waited as her voice echoed back at her. *Why couldn't they have brought more rope?* She called again and again.

Still no answer.

She felt a hormonal panic roll through her lower abdomen and into her chest. Jack was dead and there was nothing she could do about it. She rested her head on the cold surface of the incline. A tear streaked through the dirt on her cheek. She should have opened up to Jack last night. Now she'd never have the chance. She thought about losing Jack twice in a lifetime—this time forever.

She didn't answer the calls from above asking her if she could see the bottom. Instead, she put the flashlight in her pocket and wept.

# SHAFT

The men continued to shout, but Samantha couldn't answer. After a few minutes she felt the rope tighten around her waist; the men had begun hauling her back up. An emptiness consumed her. The despair of a few moments ago evolved into something closer to despondency—a whole body numbness. She ignored their calls. Her chin rested on her chest; her eyes stared off into the dark. She got closer to the concerned shouts from above. About halfway into the return trip, her belt snagged on a seam between two stones. She could feel the men tug in vain and finally realized she'd have to help them.

"Samantha," Dorn yelled. "Can you hear me?"

Samantha didn't move for a few moments. "Yes," she called out weakly.

"Thank god!" he shouted back. "We thought you might be dead."

"Did you see anything?" Ricardo called.

"No." The answer drifted from her lips in a whisper.

"You seem to be stuck. Can you move?" she heard Ricardo say. His tone was gentle. Reassuring. "We need to get you out of there. We can try to look again when we get more rope."

*They could try again.* The thought encouraged her numb limbs. "Lower me a few inches," she managed. "My belt is snagged."

As the rope lowered her, Samantha managed to twirl herself onto her side, freeing her belt. As she flipped onto her back again, she felt the flashlight scrape against stone. It came out of her pant pocket and bounced down the shaft.

She never heard it land.

She paused. Above her, two backlit heads stared down from the shaft opening. She wondered whether there were enough reasons to go back. The rope tightened again around her waist, constricting her already shallow breathing. Samantha prepared herself for the final ascent. As she was hoisted, she peered one last time into the confines of the abyss. Then her mind began playing tricks on her. From below, she thought the walls of the shaft glowed for an instant.

She shook her head.

"Wait!" she yelled.

Samantha saw it again. This time twice—in rapid succession. A light blinked off and on. Off and on.

*A flashlight.*

"It's Jack!" she screamed.

# ELOHIM

Jack's stomach expelled muddy water in an agonizing contraction. Pain overwhelmed him. His lungs seared with each short breath, as if a hundred daggers lined his rib cage, waiting to pierce him if he inhaled too deeply. Jack willed his fingers to work, forcing them to click on the flashlight that had nearly fallen on him. He heard a jumble of shouts but his brain refused to process any peripheral information and instead issued orders only his hands understood. His thumb pressed the button: off and on. Off and on. His hands would have to cry out because his mouth couldn't.

*The mud . . .*

The memories came back to him—the onrushing mountain of water—the rubble pile. But where was he now? His bleary eyes looked for signs of the obstruction. *Maybe it had been washed away.* His tongue noticed a small gap between his bottom teeth. Jack tasted the coppery edge of blood mixed with gritty soil.

His energy was fading.

Jack's fingers couldn't hold the flashlight any longer—it slipped from his grasp. Soon the darkness would overtake him, Jack thought. Through silt-clogged ears, Jack made out voices again. Shouts seemed to echo off the ground to him—from which direction he couldn't tell. Jack tried to respond again but couldn't. Exhaustion overtook him. His mind wanted sleep. He needed rest. More rest.

Just for a minute.

Jack's face slopped into the mud. Instinctively, his survival instincts jolted his body into action. His head jerked up. Out of his nostrils foamed muddy bubbles. *Think!* Jack demanded of himself. Semiconscious, he propped himself up against a wall. His chest again seared with pain. But the pain kept him thinking, kept him awake. His eyes blinked, tearing mud. He was confident he wouldn't drown in the pool of mud, but the haze again threatened to overtake him.

He must have been passing out. For an instant Jack imagined he wasn't alone.

Across the room, against the wall, a tall figure watched him.

Jack hadn't the strength to clear his eyes. His head bobbed from shoulder to shoulder—his neck straining to keep still. He was dreaming.

Or dying.

That was it, Jack thought. *He was dying.* For the glowing figure in front of him didn't go away. Through the whirlwind of his mind, Jack made out the long face, the thick beard, the flowing gown, and the big eyes.

Large, luminous eyes.

They seemed to beckon him, but Jack couldn't move. He felt peaceful. More peaceful than he had in all his life. Through growing obscurity Jack could still make out the wondrous glow of the figure. It *must* be an angel. The angel opened its arms. The apparition got closer. It came to him.

He *had* died, Jack thought.

# SLEEP

Jack awoke suddenly. His brain craved stimuli—and soon it came. Light streamed into his eyes, searing his cortex with pain. He squinted. A warm wetness dragged across his forehead. He heard a soft voice. Jack tried to get up but felt a sharp ache on the side of his chest, which he soon noticed was wrapped tight with a flexible bandage. He felt the delicate touch of a woman holding his shoulder down.

"Stay still. Everything's okay," he heard the voice say.

Jack stared up at a ceiling of canvas, trying to get his bearings. Then the figure next to him got closer, blocking out the light, which allowed him to see the long black hair and sharp angled features of Veronica.

"What's going on?"

"You had a serious fall," he heard her say. Her delicate hands wiped a few strands of hair from his face. Slowly, his mind began processing things. The wall of mud. The shaft. His eyes followed the seam of the canvas tent. *The field tent at the surface.*

He had survived. But who'd gotten him out?

Veronica dabbed his forehead with a warm sponge. Jack felt the wool blanket at his waist and pulled it higher.

"You sleep for long time," Veronica said.

Jack managed to sit up. "How long?"

"Since morning."

Jack heard the hiss of lanterns. Outside the night

winds moaned over barren ground. He'd been unconscious for at least twelve hours. "Where is everyone?"

"Your friend will be back soon."

"Samantha?"

"*Sí.*"

Jack breathed deeply. Samantha was okay.

"She get more hot water and medicine," Veronica
said. Then she mumbled something softly in Spanish.
Jack thought he heard: "*Esa mujer te quiere . . .*"

Jack closed his eyes. *That woman loves you . . .* Is that
what he heard?

"Jack?"

The voice startled him; there was no accent. His eyes
opened.

Samantha stood at the entrance to the tent. "You've
been out for quite some time." She approached the cot.
Veronica got up and quietly slipped out.

Samantha sat beside him. "How are you feeling?"

"Worse than I look." Jack struggled, propping himself
straighter.

"Careful. You probably fractured two ribs. At least
dinged them pretty badly."

"You haven't seen any spare teeth?" Jack said, feeling
his lower bridge.

"Things could have been much worse."

"What happened? I remember . . . mud. Tons of it."

Samantha touched Jack's arm. "I know. You were
covered in it. It took me an hour just to clean you."

Her touch felt gentle. "Thanks."

"The blast liquefied a portion of the complex. Water
flooded the corridor. You disappeared right in front of
me. I thought I . . ." She paused. "We thought we'd lost
you. The water carried you down the duct."

"I just remember that stinking pool of mud."

"That mud saved your life. You must have landed in
three feet of the stuff when you hit bottom."

"Bottom?"

Samantha nodded.

Memories came back. "There's a second level, Samantha."

"I know."

"How did you—"

"We only had a hundred and eighty feet of rope. Not enough to get down to you. After you signaled with the flashlight we ended up looping extension cords together before I could finally reach you."

"*You* went through that duct?"

"I've got the cherries on my *derrière* to prove it."

"How did we get back up?"

"That was the easy part. We took the stairs."

"The stairs?" Jack tried to get up.

"Try to rest." She handed him two tablets of Vicodin. "Take these."

Jack reluctantly acquiesced. "What stairs?"

Samantha paused. "In the morning." She bent over and kissed him lightly on the forehead. "In the morning." She started out of the tent.

"Wait! Samantha!" Jack tried to get out of bed. He wanted to know more. He wanted to explain the miraculous thing he had seen down in that mud-filled chamber, but the pain in his side doubled him over. "I'm okay!" he said—but only to himself.

Samantha had already pushed through the tent flaps.


Pierce didn't breathe.

He had made out the vapor of a man's cigarette seconds before the infrared signature of a body came into view from behind the pyramid. A pat on his back signaled that Miller—who watched their flank—had also noticed the sentry.

Pierce had only managed a few series of very low light photos from the fourth step of the pyramid, which afforded a good view into the pit. The specialized camera with the enormous lens trembled in his palm. He could see the figure clearly—and the man, who carried an Uzi draped over his right shoulder, was coming straight toward them. *Should they move?* The nearly full moon would reveal their presence if he got too close. They either needed to make a break for it now or stay completely still, but he had no way of communicating with his partner. As the sentry neared, instinct held Pierce motionless. He prayed Miller would stay put.

Miller did.

The guard circled the far side of the excavation pit— just twenty yards away. Pierce couldn't get to his weapon without betraying their supine presence on the ledge. He took the shallowest, slowest of breaths. The man stopped. After one last drag the sentry flicked the glowing cigarette butt against the mound of dirt beside the hole. *The guard was staring right at them.* No movement, Pierce thought, while his mind—as if possessing telepathic powers—urged the armed watch, one of the Caucasian mercenaries, to head back.

Perhaps the human brain could perform such feats under tense circumstances, Pierce thought. Because a few seconds later the guard retraced his steps around the crater and headed back around the pyramid.

With only a hand motion, Pierce signaled to Miller to retreat. The first series of pictures would have to suffice—their brazen mission seemed far too risky now. Once behind the heap of earth Miller broke into a jog toward the gully they had used for cover while traversing to the site. Pierce followed, his lungs burning in the thin air, the night-vision goggles jostling painfully against his forehead. The two men continued away from the campfires near the tents before disappearing into the shallow arroyo just west of the encampment. The painful adrenaline of a few seconds ago had been transformed to pure exhilaration, the rush Pierce craved as a spy. The venerable agent had just seconds to enjoy it. As he neared the apex of the gulley and slid down, Pierce noticed *two* glowing figures—in a heated struggle beneath him.

*       *       *

Veronica paused under the brilliant, porous umbrella of space. She stared at the platinum moon and wondered just where in that pockmarked surface lay the Sea of Tranquillity. As a girl she dreamed often of that special place the astronauts landed. She imagined it was the most peaceful place in the universe. If only she could go there, to a place of tranquillity. The moon had become a talisman of hope—its presence somehow comforting, even if she knew nothing so serene would ever save her from her brutal existence. Nothing maybe, except a kind man like Jack. For a special twenty-four hours she had believed there would be a future for her—with him. That he would be the one to lead her to that placid existence. But the handsome stranger held the special honor for another woman. At least, Veronica thought, she'd been blessed to witness the prospect of one relationship unmarred by violence or incest or apathy. This gave her hope—however fleeting—that one day she would find the same. Veronica took out a cigarette and cupped her palms together to shield her lighter from the winds. Her thumb worked the dial until a flame danced between her palms.

Then she heard a cry—from the gully to her right.

The man shouted a millisecond before Pierce's serrated blade passed cleanly through the Bolivian's trachea, just below the brainstem. The body fell in front of Pierce, still writhing but muted—save for the gurgle of breath from the wet gash in the man's throat.

Miller scrambled to his feet, holding his shoulder, tinged with blood. "I didn't even see him till it was too late," he whispered.

"Are you okay?"

"He stuck me good with a ring knife, but it's not deep." Miller eyed the corpse. "Shit. I blew our cover—it's a cartel member."

"Nothing you could do."

"We could bury him. It might buy us a little more time."

"Leave him. If we're lucky the Bolivians will think it was a fight among themselves," Pierce said. "Let's get."

"He ripped off my goggles," Miller said, probing the ground with his foot. "I can't see a thing."

"To your right," Pierce said.

He located them with his own scope, then heard the sound of footsteps above them. Scrambling toward Miller, Pierce scooped up the goggles and grabbed the agent's arm. Without looking back, the two men ran through the rocks and shrubs and vanished into the darkness just as the footsteps reached the ridge.

"I can tell you none of my men did this," Dorn said with a scowl. The lantern illuminated the bloody soil surrounding the Bolivian corpse.

"Then who did? We?" Veronica asked. Her black eyes shone with anger.

"That would be my guess," Dorn said as matter-of-factly as if he'd been commenting on the weather.

Veronica continued to stare at Dorn and Baines, while two of her men lifted the limp form of their fallen comrade. "This no part of the deal," she said.

"You can feel secure that I will reimburse you for the trouble," Dorn said. "I'll have Baines write up a check tonight."

"You give me check for body?" Veronica seemed to take the comment like a sword thrust. "If I discover you do this . . ." Then she cut herself off.

Dorn remained silent.

Veronica grabbed the lantern. Without another word, she joined her men as they transported the corpse up the ridge. Illuminated by Baines's heavy flashlight, the blood on the ground between the two men appeared oddly reflective, like a surreal crimson Rorschach.

Dorn waited until the three Bolivians disappeared over the ridge before speaking. "What do you think?"

"I don't know," Baines muttered. "I don't like it though."

"You think one of the Bolivians murdered him?"

"She seems to be telling the truth, but it wasn't one of my blokes."

"Who then? Another cartel? A guerrilla group?"

Dorn's question remained unanswered. Baines bent to one knee, his flashlight trained before him. He picked up a detachable lens from a pair of goggles. Baines turned to Dorn.

"Someone," he said, "with night vision."

On the way back to the encampment, Dorn walked in thought. A wild card had entered the equation, and he didn't like it. On the outskirts of the camp he stopped Baines. "Pay off the Bolivians. I want them gone from here in the morning. They've become more risk than protection."

"I'll take care of it tonight," he said.

"I want it done quietly. Not a word about this event to Samantha or the scientists."

"I'll make sure there's no contact."

"Good. Extend the security perimeter and beef up the armament. Your men should be ready to move on a moment's notice," Dorn said. "Whether it was the Bolivians or bloody leftists—someone is taking peeks at our site."

"Which means what, I wonder?"

The South African fumbled inside his pocket for his pipe. "That we'll be leaving sooner than planned."

# MORNING

McFadden rubbed the corner of his eyes with his thumb and forefinger. He found the term "sleep"—for the dried secretions in the corner of his eyes—ironic. He hadn't gotten much last night. He'd spent most of the evening at the agency's photo enhancement facility, examining the night photos Pierce and Miller got of the excavation site. The two agents reported a termination of one of the Bolivian escorts. It made the analysis of the photos that much more crucial. McFadden didn't think the agency had much time before the field agents' cover was blown.

"And the analysts think the structure is man-made?" Wright, the agency director, asked.

"Yes, sir." McFadden handed him some more photos. "These were taken just forty yards from the excavation. You'll notice the distinct square edges toward the bottom of the pit. We enhanced them. The sides were definitely engineered."

Director Wright stared at the opaque photos. The image resembled an open storm cellar, with four clearly distinct sides surrounding blurred darkness.

"We think those ridges inside are stairs," McFadden added. "But we can't be sure."

"Get sure," Wright said.

McFadden nodded. Exhausted, he found the intensity of the most recent developments were keeping him tightly wound and sadly awake.

"And the electromagnetic readings?" Wright asked.

"The satellites haven't picked up anything like the energy spike at 0621 yesterday. But they do confirm a metallic presence inside the pit—along each side."

"I'm running this through channels. This doesn't sit right with me. . . ."

McFadden knew the channels Wright spoke about would lead straight to the president himself.

"Have the field agents continue surveillance," Wright said. "If it looks like they're going to be made I want them out of the area at once."

"I'll do that." McFadden stood up to leave.

"And John?"

"Yes, sir?"

"Get some rest," the director said. "You look horrible."

Veronica and her men had left Tiahuanaco before dawn. She wasn't even able to say good-bye to Jack. As the trucks wound their way down from the highlands, she explained the latest happenings to her uncle on her cell phone. The man seemed far too intrigued with what the scientists might have found and far too nonchalant about the death of one of her comrades. She stared behind her at the covered corpse and wondered how much more she could take.

"Señor Checa and I want you to stay in the area," her uncle said. "Out of sight, of course. We'll be sending reinforcements to meet you."

Veronica's breathing quickened.

"Do you understand, angel?"

"Yes," she finally said. "I understand."

Vicodin ES is a fantastic drug, 750 milligrams of pure pleasure.

The analgesic guile of the sedative still fogged Jack's mind when Samantha brought him breakfast. He didn't bother adding water to the instant oatmeal. Instead he choked down the mixture dry, straight from the bag, as he made his way to the excavation pit.

She had to help him out of bed, but once outside, the crispness of the morning air invigorated him. His sore limbs seemed to loosen with every step, and the pain from his ribs had nearly vanished. They passed through the security perimeter. François, keeping watch, nodded to them from the cab of one of the trucks. The Bolivians had departed before dawn, Samantha told him. Jack couldn't say he was sorry to see them go—except for Veronica.

"Now about this second level," Jack asked.

"The whole level was concealed," Samantha said. "After I was sure you were going to be okay I did a little exploring and found a flight of stairs that had been sealed off."

"Sealed?"

"From the outside. Someone had purposely disguised the plaster patchwork. The wall crumbled beneath the butt of the flashlight. It only took me twenty minutes to poke my way through to the other side. That's when I realized the stairs opened into the far cubicle near the cave-in."

Jack breathed hard in the thin air.

"Need to rest?" she asked.

Jack shook his head. "I'm fine." The memories of his ordeal seemed so real. But they couldn't be. He must have been dreaming. "I don't want you to think I'm crazy . . ."

"About what?"

"I remember seeing something, Samantha. In that room." Jack stopped. He gathered every ounce of courage he could muster. "I saw a Shining One."

Samantha stopped and looked at Jack with serious eyes. "I know."

The bones in Jack's legs became rubber. *She knew?*

# PART FOUR

# SHINING ONE

"You know?" Jack swallowed hard. He felt faint.

"You weren't hallucinating." Samantha took his hand in hers. "C'mon. I'll show you."

She helped Jack down the stairs of the entrance corridor. Barely conscious of the glyphs on the east wall, momentarily forgetting the luminescent plaster, hardly noticing that no one else was around, Jack followed Samantha without speaking. She stopped in front of the decontamination device.

"Are you ready?" Samantha asked.

Jack nodded, speechless.

The spectral image danced in the dust-filled stillness of the great hall. The long, delicate beard hung beneath spectacularly piercing eyes. The graceful luminescent robe rippled in breezes spawned long ago. Jack's heart hammered beneath his rib cage, as if demanding freedom.

"The images were activated when I found you," Samantha said. "Scared me to death."

When they entered the great hall, Samantha had asked Jack to sit down beside a fold-out table. From an expedition case she pulled a small metallic cube, slightly smaller than the fuzzy dice classy people hang from rearview mirrors. Jack noticed small, circular depressions on each side, save for one. Samantha walked a few feet in front of Jack and put the cube down on the stone floor, activating it by turning it on its side—the one without a concavity.

"Welcome to the future of home movies," she said.

Light issued from the depression on each side. The beams spread outward and upward, creating a twenty-foot square field. As Jack's eyes adjusted, he made out a three-dimensional, statuesque extraterrestrial who walked in front of him as if he'd actually been in the room.

"This is unreal," Jack said.

Finding the fossil in Mali was unforgettable. Seeing the preserved remains of an extraterrestrial had outdone it. But now, the strange sensation of watching one of these creatures move in three dimensions felt entirely surreal.

The holographic scene playing out before them took place on the surface at Tiahuanaco, except the stone structures looked new and marvelous and the surrounding land was lush. Groves of green trees swayed in the breeze.

"You were right about the climate change," Samantha said.

Loaded with gear, as if planning to travel, the figure walked away from the camera—actually toward the other side of the three-dimensional stage—making his way toward a shimmering lake in the background. On either side of the "stage," two larger extraterrestrials watched him go. Jack got up from the table.

"Go ahead," he heard Samantha say. "You can actually walk through it."

Jack glanced at her before stepping into the grid.

He felt as if he'd stepped in front of a movie projector. The images from the side of the cube played over the back of his legs. Though he knew the images were translucent, the fleshed-out form of the extraterrestrial seemed close enough and real enough to touch. Jack reached out. His hand disappeared into the shape. Excitement played along his spine.

*This was too much.*

Jack caught the reflective properties of something on the figure's back.

"I think he has the artifact," Jack said. "He's wearing it . . ."

"That's what we think too," Samantha said. "He must have been the one to reach Mali—the fossil we found."

The images vanished for a millisecond.

"Don't worry. It's another scene," Samantha said as a new set of images reappeared.

Jack walked out of the grid. "How many times have you seen this?"

She smiled. "This will be thirty."

"Thanks for starting without me."

She pointed. "You'll want to see this."

Within the matrix a different extraterrestrial—Jack could tell because of the different fabric that lined his robe—walked toward a semicircle of smaller figures with their backs to the viewer. Jack moved forward. The smaller figures approached the larger one with no fear. The smaller shapes had black hair and olive skin, and wore furs and rough fabrics.

Jack circled the grid to get a frontal view of the smallish forms, their faces. "Samantha . . . those . . . those are . . ."

"Human beings," she said. "Probably a late strain of *Homo erectus,* or early *sapiens.*"

"They're interacting," Jack said. "We're watching interaction with an extraterrestrial . . ."

Samantha grinned. "I thought you'd enjoy it. We've counted five different extraterrestrials in the various scenes."

"The others are definitely human," Jack said. He noted their five digits, then examined the skulls beneath the black hair and weathered skin. Humans—every one of them. The smaller shapes greeted the extraterrestrial with kindness. They showed the Shining One woven baskets filled with some sort of grain. The form took the basket and began dropping seeds into a long furrow. He then bent over and covered the seeds with soil, like he was demonstrating the procedure to the onlookers.

"The extraterrestrial's teaching them agriculture," Jack said, awash with excitement.

The holographic image bounced, then grew dark.

"We don't know why the scenes don't finish," Samantha said. "The device must have been damaged."

A new, darker scene coalesced.

"We think this is somewhere inside the temple," she said.

Against a backdrop of gray stones, a smaller extraterrestrial worked beside a table. Jack noticed that this Shining One's tunic fit tighter, like a doctor's smock. Using his four-fingered hands, the Shining One moved a form beneath an opaque sheet. Jack walked around the scene and was able to tell that the shape beneath the sheet was a body, though he couldn't tell if it was male or female. But he had no doubt as to its genus—*Homo*.

"It looks like he's performing some kind of surgery," Jack said.

The image froze. Ripples flittered around the cube like high-tech static.

"That's it," Samantha said. "It jams in that same spot every time."

Jack picked up the cube. The scene vanished instantly. Jack blinked, holding the cube in his outstretched palm. "Incredible," he said.

He walked the cube over to Samantha and held it in front of him. She took it with both hands but didn't pull it away. The sides of her hands rested in his palms.

"What else did you find on the second level?" Jack asked.

"Just you."

Their lips remained still, but their eyes spoke. Hers revealed a willingness. Jack fought the urge to bring her closer.

His voice came in a whisper. "Nothing else?"

The moment ended. Samantha shook her head, her voice holding a trace of disappointment. "Just a catacomb of empty rooms and dead ends. Except for the stairway I discovered."

"The one you carried me out through?"

"Yeah."

"Where is it?" Jack asked.

Samantha placed the cube back in its packing crate. "The entrance was hidden. Plastered over in the last of those empty chambers. I'll show you."

# LEVEL THREE

They entered the corridor where the mud rush had nearly killed him. The once-impassable pile of rubble was now a maze of boulders. A thin layer of mud covered the walls and floor, the majority of it having been shoveled into piles along the sides of the corridor.

"We discovered another shaft," Samantha said, "just like the one you fell through. The others are seeing if it opens to a third level right now."

Jack paused in front of the shaft. "I'm surprised you're not with them."

Samantha led him past each of the empty rooms on either side of the corridor. Jack glanced into each. They had been painted at one time; he could make out faded designs beneath a coat of dust. Samantha turned left into the last of the cubicles. In the center of the back wall a large hole had been punched through. A mound of plaster covered the stone floor just beneath it.

"A secret entrance," she said.

Jack inspected the hole, ran his hand along the wall.

"We would have never found the entrance from this side unless we used sonar," she said. "The patching's perfect."

Jack agreed. The concealment of the archway was expertly done.

"Why would they want to seal a whole level from the outside?" Samantha asked.

"The extraterrestrials must have known they were dying," Jack said. "They might have sealed the lower levels to keep out grave robbers—or future explorers. Maybe they hid something important."

He knew that many cultures, particularly the Egyptians, sealed important rooms behind similar plaster facades.

Samantha squeezed through the tire-size opening, Jack following close behind, his sore ribs objecting.

"It gets a little darker down here," Samantha said.

A saber of light sprung from her flashlight. She widened the beam, casting large circles on the plaster walls. Jack noticed something lustrous on her shirtsleeve. He pulled at it; glowing dust rubbed off on his fingers.

"Your shirt."

Samantha looked down. "The glow from the walls comes off here. We don't know why." She moved forward. "Ricardo discovered the paint is actually a biological agent. A 'glow in the dark mold' he says."

"Amazing," Jack said. "I should have realized it earlier." He knew of hundreds of species of plant and animal that possessed phosphorescent qualities.

"Ricardo thinks the mold was specially developed for this subterranean habitat."

Jack touched the wall. His fingertips glowed. "Organic paint," he said. "Organic *luminescent* paint."

They continued down the long, straight stairway. Voices echoed up to them before they reached the landing. At the bottom, Samantha pointed to a mud-filled antechamber on the left. "That's where you landed," she said. "Be careful. The mud's still slippery."

"Is that where I saw the Shining One?"

"You and me both," Samantha said. "Scared the hell out of me until I figured out it was just a holographic image."

Jack peered into the mud-filled room, the vision of that angel still imprinted on his mind. Samantha led him farther down the corridor, which branched at a hard right after twenty yards. Their boots squeezed tiny treadmarks out of the dark goo that coated the floor, a slight sucking sound accompanying each footstep.

As they completed the turn, Jack saw a pile of boxes and coiled ropes that partially concealed three figures. Backlit by two hissing lanterns, Dorn approached them. "Good to see you up and around," he said. "Sorry we couldn't wait. How are the ribs?"

"What?"

"Your chest. How does it feel?"

"Oh. Much better." Jack had nearly forgotten about his wraps.

"Good. Because we lowered Baines down the ventilation shaft to the next floor," Dorn said, smiling. "And apparently he's reached the bottom."

Jack, Samantha, Ricardo, Bongane, and Dorn listened for Baines's signal, each in their own empty chamber off the corridor. The series of empty cubicles mimicked the floor plan above them. Baines was to scout the lower level and see if he could find another concealed entrance like the one they discovered above. He'd been gone forty minutes when his first thuds echoed not from a room but from the corridor itself. Jack pinpointed the area halfway down the corridor wall, just ten yards from the previous flight of stairs. The group rushed to the muffled noise.

The expedition picks made short work of the crumbling yellow plaster, which dropped in large chunks into the thin bed of mud. Ten minutes after the first taps, their digging had produced a hole in the wall wide enough for Baines's head. The man looked like a child playing with his mom's flour-dusted cookie sheet—his crew cut was powdered white from the digging. The veins in his neck bulged, pumping blood into his face. For a second, he looked like a human wall mount, Jack thought. A taxidermied *Homo sapiens*.

"Well?" Dorn asked. "What took so damn long?"

Baines wiped sweat from his eyes. "I think we hit bloody pay dirt."

Stairs disappeared into a pool of black water that had flooded a whole catacomb of corridors. The flooded passageways reminded Jack of the canals in Venice—except this water didn't stink.

Baines was wet from the chest down; thick muscles shook over the entire length of his body. "Like I said—there's been some flooding."

"The water's not stagnant," Jack said. "It must be getting fed from somewhere."

Ricardo looked at the ceiling. "Which means we're into the water table." A *kerplunk* answered him as a droplet hit the pool. "And this place is leaking. . . ."

"It's draining from the lake," Jack said.

Dorn looked puzzled. "But we're a few miles away."

"Tiahuanaco used to be a port at one time," Jack explained. "This whole hill was an island within the confines of the lake. Posnansky discovered those huge stone docks just a few hundred yards from here. Whatever catastrophe caused the uprising of land, didn't lower the water table. Remember, we began digging only a hundred and twenty feet above lake level."

"And we're a lot farther underground than a hundred feet," Samantha said.

"At least three times that. We were under the water table the second we came down the entrance stairs." Jack bent over and scraped a line in the wall with his pocketknife, just above the pool. "The water might be rising."

"Damn." Dorn looked into the flooded corridor with concern. "Let's hope not."

Other drips struck discordant notes throughout the chamber.

The mood sobered as the group considered the possible implications. Jack took the flashlight and aimed the beam about twenty yards to the right, where he could make out more stairs on the opposite side of the flooded passage.

"There they are," Baines said, still shivering. "The room's right up those stairs."

"How deep's the water?" Ricardo asked.

"Just be prepared to get wet," Baines said. "And bloody cold."

Jack turned to Samantha. "You feel up to it?"

She was already taking off her boots.

The dark pool felt like a charged chemical vat.

Jack's body shuddered. Frigid water streamed into his boots and numbed his shins. His bum knee ached as the cold attacked the joint, before crawling up his thigh. Jack let out a muffled groan as the icy bath proceeded to attack even more sensitive regions of his body.

Bongane remained on the stairs with the flashlight, helping to illuminate their path across the inky lagoon. If the water rose by any significant amount, he was to alert the expedition at once.

When the men hit the floor of the corridor, the water reached a good six inches above their belt lines. It rose high enough on Samantha's smaller body to produce a high-pitched squeal.

Jack's toe touched a stone ledge. "I think I've got the first stair."

He pulled himself onto the stairs, which offered only small respite from the bone-chilling bath. Ricardo sprung onto the stairs as if he'd been shot from a cannon. Jack didn't think he could move that fast. Baines and Dorn followed, dragging more water with them onto the already slippery rock. Then Jack helped Samantha from the icy pool.

The five wrung the water from their clothes and rubbed their limbs back to life. Though eager to see what Baines had found, no one questioned the time spent trying to regain the slightest sense of feeling. Anywhere. Jack could make out Bongane's thin form crouched on the steps at the far side of the underground lagoon.

"Just up the flight of stairs," Baines said.

"Everyone ready?" Jack asked. Teeth chattering, only Samantha nodded. "If anyone starts feeling faint say something," he said. "Hypothermia's a real possibility down here."

He looked at Samantha, who lacked the bulk that most of the men carried. "You understand?"

"Yeah," she said.

His boots squeaking, Jack started up the stairs. Samantha followed, deftly avoiding his wet footprints, which made the stone treacherous. Ricardo softly cursed each step as he lumbered close behind.

Hesitating at the edge of the pool, Dorn pulled Baines aside and whispered in his ear, "If this is what you say it is, we'll have to be even more careful with security."

"I know," Baines said, softly. "I know."

The two men looked up the stairs at the three scientists before beginning their ascent.

Jack stared at the long room in awe, not sure if the cold bath or the scene in front of him kept his hands trembling.

"Jackpot . . ." Samantha said.

The importance of the hangarlike chamber became clear as soon as Jack passed beneath the archway at the top of the stairs. Though they were not fully discernible in the gloom, Jack saw piles of stacked objects.

"What is this place?" Samantha asked.

Jack squinted in the dim light, thankful when Ricardo handed him his flashlight. He pointed the beam into the room and could now make out the forms clearly. Organized piles of metal sheets, coils of wire, and pieces from a steel exoskeleton lay along the walls. Makeshift cubicles holding finely machined parts and computer panels formed aisles between larger pieces.

A layer of dust coated everything.

"This is as far as I got," Baines said, leading an amazed Dorn between rows of metal fixtures. The group spread down different aisles. The excitement in the air felt flammable, capable of igniting at any moment. Light from the walls allowed them to navigate, but Jack had to move close to each pile to distinguish the finer details. A theory began forming in his mind.

Samantha picked up a small section of luminescent cable and turned to Jack and Ricardo, who had paused next to a pile of twisted, scorched steel. Her soft voice trembled in the dim light.

"Do you know what I think this is?" she said.

Jack picked up a tarnished scrap. "Wreckage . . ."

# WRECKAGE

"You think these are the remnants of a ship?" Dorn asked.

"It has to be," Jack said. The whole scene—the neatly ordered piles of debris and parts—reminded Jack of the aftermath of the 747 crash off Long Island. The remains of that aircraft had been pieced together in a large warehouse by the FBI and FAA agents.

"Sumerian tablets spoke of luminous beings who

drove through the sky in a ship of fire. The Akkadians, Babylonians, Persians, Mayans, all describe a bizarre machine that could fly. An Indian seer described one in exact detail in a Sanskrit text. That account, in the *Mahabharata*, dates back to at least 7016 B.C." He picked up a sheet of metal. It gleamed with a brilliant sheen—reflecting even the trace amber rays from Jack's flashlight. "If this is a wreck, then I think we have our answer."

"To what?" Dorn asked.

"To whether or not the extraterrestrials ever left."

"So they were stranded here?" Samantha said. "They didn't have a choice."

"The parts *do* look salvaged," Ricardo said. "They're all grouped into related elements."

"Like a used parts store," Samantha added.

"An *extraterrestrial* used parts store," Dorn whispered.

Steam rose from the five wet bodies in the room, as if each person were percolating.

"Can you imagine what all the technology in this room is worth?" Ricardo asked.

No one answered.

The question seemed rhetorical—at least to any scientist or engineer. The technology that lay scattered around them would be worth trillions—the equivalent of patenting every new technology for the next thousand years. One spare computer chip, a small piece of revolutionary optic cable, a new metallic compound, could yield a blueprint for a science centuries ahead of anything on earth.

Samantha turned to Jack. "You think they crash-landed?"

"It looks like it," Jack said. "These pieces of metal—the ripped parts—all look like they're damaged. If they could have managed interstellar space travel after putting down, they probably would have eventually left."

"That would explain why the crew stayed and built

this complex," Samantha noted. "Especially if the atmosphere or biological conditions weren't conducive for them."

Jack looked around the room. "And it explains the Piri Reis map—and how the ancients knew the circumference of the planet."

"You think the extraterrestrials analyzed the earth from space?" Ricardo asked.

"It's the only logical conclusion."

"Piri Reis?" Dorn asked. "Is that the map of Antarctica?"

"Made by a Turkish admiral in Constantinople in 1513," Jack said. "But the admiral couldn't have gotten the necessary information from the explorers of the day. Antarctica wasn't even discovered until 1818—more than three hundred years after he made the map."

"Then how did he know Antarctica was even there?" Dorn said.

"Piri Reis said he got the information from earlier sources—some old maps made thousands of years prior. The cartography's more remarkable, though, because the coast of Queen Maud Land is shown in perfect detail."

"And it shouldn't have been?"

"Damn right it shouldn't have been. The coast sits under miles of ice."

Dorn nodded. "So it would have been impossible to know what the coast looked like unless one had been around before ice covered the continent."

"Right," Jack said. "We only discovered the hidden coast in 1949, after a seismic survey. Then there's Philippe Buache's map in 1737—also based on earlier sources—that showed a seaway dividing Antarctica. Geologists recently confirmed that was what the continent would have looked like before the last ice age."

"I guess it's obvious where the information originally came from," Samantha said. She gestured at the room. "From our friends."

Jack moved toward an archway that looked like it

might lead to another chamber or corridor. He crossed a line of floorstones that had buckled, dividing the room.

"More signs of geologic disturbance," he said. He bent to one knee, shining his flashlight down the length of the cracked surface. "Fantastic . . ."

"What is it?" Samantha asked.

"Mica."

"Mica?"

"A two-inch sheet of it. Beneath the floor stones. See the black material beneath the crack? It probably lines the whole area."

"The whole room? That would cost a fortune," Baines said.

"In solid sheets like this it would," Jack said. "I've only seen this done in one other place. Teotihuacán."

"At the Pyramid of the Sun and the Mica Temple," Ricardo recalled. "Except most of the mica has already disappeared."

"Why?" Dorn asked.

"Stolen," Ricardo said. "By the man the Mexican government hired to restore the pyramid in 1906. The mica had considerable commercial value, so it was removed and sold during the excavation."

"Why go through all the trouble?" Samantha wondered. "I mean the original builders. Did mica have some kind of religious significance?"

"I've asked myself that too." Jack stood up. "The locals went to great lengths to obtain those sheets. Mica contains traces of metals like aluminum or lithium—depending on the rock stratum in which it was quarried." He paused. "The particular form of mica in the Mexican temple is found in only one place in the world. Brazil. That's two thousand miles away."

"Then it *had* to be religiously significant," Samantha said.

"Not necessarily. I know it's hard—but forget you're an anthropologist. Just use common sense. Drop the old notions about ancient man as primitive, extraordinarily superstitious people. After everything you've seen down here, you have to. Those people didn't travel two thousand miles to get a certain type of mica for religious or cultural reasons. They did it—"

"For technological reasons," she said.

Dorn asked, "What do you mean? The mica serves a scientific function?"

"Mica has properties that make it suitable for a variety of applications," Ricardo broke in. "It's used as an electric and thermal insulator. It's used in capacitors. And mica's been found to be especially opaque to fast neutrons."

"What the hell does that mean?" Dorn asked.

"It can act as a moderator in nuclear reactions," Ricardo answered.

The silence that followed was palpable.

Samantha moved to the archway, reminding Jack about the next room. As the group shuffled behind her, Jack broke off a small chip of mica, rubbing the surface between his fingers before standing again. *Why did the Shining Ones shield the floors of the third level?*

An emotion welled within him, the expectant feeling he got when the cards began lining up in computer solitaire—when he knew all of them would fit.

He took a deep breath.

The technological accomplishments, precession, the Aymara Algorithm, the Dogons' knowledge of astronomy—all began to fall into place. The bearded tall men, the time of giants from the Bible, the traditions of the Eye Goddess, the ancient maps—everything made perfect sense. The mysteries of the past—which had begun to align long ago for Jack—seemed destined to finally make sense to the world.

Jack shivered at the thought. The puzzle that had tormented him could now be solved, thanks to findings both too simple and too extraordinary to believe.

"Jack," Ricardo said. "Are you okay?"

"Yeah. Just thinking. Why?"

"Because you're really gonna want to see this."

# LABORATORY

The starkness reminded Jack of a morgue. Immaculate white walls glowed throughout the chamber. All the stones in this room had been plastered over; the bio-luminescent technology was more alive, the light much brighter than in the salvage hall. The ceiling glowed too, providing more than ample illumination. Jack no longer needed the flashlight. Long metal shelves lined one section, upon which sat various tools.

The back wall was plated with a solid metal sheet.

In the center of the large room, three rectangular tables made of aluminum sat precisely equidistant from one another. Metallic arms with multiple hinges were attached to the long sides of each table. Samantha lifted one up. It straightened automatically, sticking out from the table like a stirrup. Samantha shuddered. "Reminds me of my OB-GYN."

"Or a laboratory," Dorn said. He inspected two huge curved chairs that sat next to a finely cut worktable by the long shelves. "Look at the size of these."

"Would fit a tall extraterrestrial nicely," Jack said.

"It's definitely a lab," Ricardo said. He held up a cylinder that resembled a futuristic ice-cream maker. "This looks like some kind of centrifuge."

Jack agreed. The room looked like a chemical or biological facility. The sterile floors and walls, the metal tables and shelves, the eclectic mix of modern implements and bare, functional furniture gave it a high-tech air.

"The scene from the viewing cube," Samantha said.

"I think these are the same tables the smaller extrater-restrial worked at."

"You're right," Dorn said. "In the last scene before it jammed."

"If this was a hospital it would explain these X rays." Baines said, waving sheets of flexible opaque material.

*X rays?*

Jack took them from the man. "They're not X rays," he breathed. "They're gene charts . . ."

Jack grabbed another sheet off the nearby table. The flexible material had a reflective backing, which allowed dark patches of intricate bands of DNA to stand out without the use of any backlighting.

Dorn took the sheets from Jack and flipped through them with Ricardo.

"These had to be laser-generated somehow," Ricardo said.

"Can you make any sense of them?" Jack asked.

Ricardo held up a sheet. "This one looks like a human gene pool." He pointed out the distinct number of forty-six chromosomes arranged in twenty-three pairs.

"A woman," Dorn said. "You see, both chromosomes in the pair are X-shaped. Males have one X, one Y."

Dorn was an expert in genetics, Jack recalled. His firm, Helix Corp., had helped revolutionize the field.

"But these . . ." Ricardo turned a few more sheets over and over, as if they were confusing road maps. "I can't be certain, but they might show early hominid DNA. The structure looks similar to the human charts but with a few noticeable exceptions."

Jack handed another gene chart to Ricardo. "What about this one?"

Ricardo inspected it. "There are a few common se-quences to humans . . . but there are *way* too many chro-mosomes."

"Could the genes be extraterrestrial?" Samantha asked.

Ricardo shrugged. "I would think they have to be. I'll

compare a sample from the DNA I took from the sarcophagus. We'll have an answer in a day or so."

"Assuming we're looking at extraterrestrial DNA—
the next question is why?" Samantha wondered. "Why
would they've charted their own genes?"

"They were probably looking for ways to combat the
virus," Ricardo said.

Dorn shook his head. "There'd be more effective
means for that than gene manipulation. Besides, the benefits of gene manipulation are long-term. They couldn't
have made themselves any less susceptible to the virus
in a single life span. One sees the effects after repairing
or adding genes in offspring."

"That's a technocentric view," Ricardo said, "true of
genetic research now. But we're only in the embryonic
stages of gene work."

"Are you implying the extraterrestrials could have
changed DNA inside their own bodies?"

"No," Ricardo said. "That's improbable. I'm just saying we shouldn't put constraints on their technology simply because we can't see past our own. I mean, look at
this." He held up the laser-imprinted gene chart. "What
created this little beauty?"

"Maybe this," Jack said.

He had wandered behind a partition wall at the back of
the room. The others joined Jack behind the wall, where
he motioned to a metallic object that sat on a raised platform of stone, cocooned between three tight slabs of rock
that resembled a doorless shower stall. Engraved icons
and hieroglyphs covered the entire enclosure.

"What is it?" Samantha asked.

"I don't know," Jack said.

From a distance, the object looked like a cylindrical
water heater. But on closer inspection, the intricate panels that overlaid its exterior silently told of a much more
elaborate function. The object stood approximately five
feet tall and tapered to a cone on top. Its diameter was
perhaps two and a half feet—just narrower than a large

outdoor trash can. A series of multicolored panels collared the "neck" of the instrument, just below the cone. Jack couldn't help but think it looked like a taller cousin of the *Star Wars* droid Artoo-Deetoo—though he hoped this one wouldn't walk or talk.

More unlit panels peppered the front like an advanced audio system. Between these panels, starting just below the collar, four equidistant modular sections ran one below the other, down to the base. Each section measured four inches from top to bottom and spanned the entire two-and-a-half-foot width of the device. Thin seams gave the appearance that the modules could open and close, though whether like drawers or on hinges was unclear.

"Look," Jack said. "More glyphs. They look like they were lasered onto the machine." He pointed at some icons that had been cut directly onto the alloy above each of the four modules. "These look like labels. Or operating instructions."

Ricardo said, "The device probably performs a variety of functions using the same power source."

"I bet you're right," Samantha said.

"Can you make anything of those symbols?" Dorn asked.

Above the top module two wavy perpendicular lines extended top to bottom like a crude symbol for a river.

Above the next receptacle the lines wound around each other horizontally like two intercoiled snakes.

The lower, middle section had an icon that looked like a flat line, above which three squares of different size hovered at different distances.

The last icon, lasered just above the fourth door, was the largest and most interesting. Above engravings that resembled Morse code—a dot on either side of a straight line—Jack noticed three thin, twisted triangles that were set around a small circle. The triangles looked almost like the slashes one would find in Chinese writing, and the way they wrapped around the circle made Jack think of a present-day hazard symbol, only more crude.

"The icon on the lowest section looks familiar," Jack finally said. "But whatever they represent, the engravings look like an afterthought. Like they were lasered in long after the machine was built. See the newness of the grooves compared to the rest of the alloy."

Samantha stood directly behind him. "And the same symbols and equations are repeated on the back wall."

"They repeated everything in here," Baines said. "Why?"

"The equations are obviously meant for someone who might discover the device. Not the original makers," Jack said. "I suppose it was very important to convey the proper use."

Ricardo's voice was emotion charged. "Like they were prepared by the extraterrestrials for someone who might not understand their science."

"Similar to the hieroglyphs we sent out with Voyager," Jack said. Earth scientists launched the deep space probe in 1977, intending to communicate the story of our world to extraterrestrials.

"You reckon each chamber has a different use?" Dorn asked.

Ricardo inspected each of the four doors, then the rounded cone above them. "That's what it looks like," he said. "The idea is probably to incorporate multiple functions in a device that runs from the same power source. Like a fax machine that serves as a copier, answering machine, and phone. NASA's been keen on developing equipment like that to reduce payload and increase efficiency."

Dorn nodded. "Why bring four different machines into space if you could run different applications from the same power source?"

"But what does each one do?" Jack wondered, gently tracing the outline of the lowest module with his finger.

With a whisper, the panel opened, disappearing to the left.

Jack flinched.

Before he could catch his breath the entire bottom section extended itself out of the machine like a CD tray, eliciting shouts from the four. Samantha looked at Jack, who had backed away. "Have to be careful what you touch in here," she said.

Inside the tray lay an object that reflected light brilliantly, like an oversize, diamond-shaped compact disc.

"There's something inside," Samantha said.

"Don't take it out," Ricardo said. "We have no idea what might happen."

"Whatever's in that tray looks like it might act as a power pack—a function card," Jack noted. "What do you think, Ricardo?"

"Probably. Judging by the design it sure looks like it."

Jack's hand moved to the door above the tray. As his fingers passed by its top right corner, the door slid open and another tray extended outward. The entire machine resembled a common audio system—a giant four-disc CD changer, Jack thought. Except that this jukebox would have played angular, almost tire-size CDs.

"It must work by invisible sensor," Ricardo said. "Maybe infrared."

Jack opened the next two doors, but the top one looked different.

His eyes grew. "It's empty!"

The others crowded in. "You're right," Ricardo said. "The disk's missing."

"Missing?" Dorn said.

Jack's breathing got faster. He had just realized why the disks in the other three chambers looked so familiar.

Samantha peered over Jack's shoulder. "Are you thinking what I'm thinking?"

Jack thought so. "Our artifact from Mali is the missing disk. . . ."

It took forty minutes to bring the piece from Mali down from the great hall. Ricardo and Bongane rigged two expedition air mattresses together, and the inflatable beds became a raft to transport the case across the flooded corridor with minimal effort. It was followed by a crate with Ricardo's engineering equipment. Soaked again, Jack undid the latches on the case. Inside, the artifact shone as brightly as a diamond. "Gimme a hand," he told Ricardo.

The two men lifted the artifact out of the case.

"It looks like it'll fit," Samantha said.

Dorn and Baines watched Ricardo and Jack raise the homing device to the proper level. The artifact's weight strained Jack's shoulders, but as he and Ricardo slid the kite-shaped disk over the tray, Jack felt the weight in his hands vanish. Ricardo took a step backward. The homing device sat cantilevered in midair.

"Electromagnetics," Ricardo said. "The same technology we noticed when the two pieces joined together."

Samantha asked Jack if they should slip the entire artifact into the tray. Before he could answer, it dropped of its own accord. The whoosh of a vacuum seal sounded. Then, as if responding to preprogrammed instructions, the top tray disappeared into the larger device and the door slid shut. The three other trays followed, whisking inward with blinding speed. With barely a whisper, long rows of lights activated across the machine, settling into a steady, pulsing pattern. Then panels along the collar of the device burst into color. A vibration filled the room, raising a thin layer of dust from the laboratory floor stones. Armies of hair follicles came to attention across the whole of Jack's body as the unseen force surged about like a karmic whirlpool.

"Do you feel the energy field?" Ricardo yelled, holding out his arm. A compass—built into his tacky watch—spun wildly.

"Feels like static electricity," Samantha said.

Tiny pins of light reflected off Dorn's eyes. "It's incredible!"

Jack heard another sound to his left. He turned just in time to see wisps of vapor curl toward the ceiling in front of the metal wall—which had begun to slide open.

Jack looked at Samantha. Something from the device had triggered the wall to open.

"Should we check it out?" Samantha said.

"Let's make sure the device is stable," Jack said. "I'm hoping we just booted it up."

"What do you think it does?" Dorn asked, motioning Baines into the new room while the scientists examined the machine.

"I'm not sure," Jack said. "But I don't think we should press our luck any further."

"He's right," Samantha said. "We don't have any idea what each of those modules could do. For all we know this could be a weapon. Or a potentially dangerous power plant."

"It would take years to safely de-engineer," Ricardo said.

"At least the light panels look constant now," Dorn said.

The device seemed to have completely stabilized.

"Ricardo?" Jack asked.

The scientist had already opened the crate that held his diagnostic equipment and retrieved a black case the size of a shoe box. He inserted one end of a small, steel wand into a socket on its side. When Ricardo turned the box over, Jack saw a glass panel covering a series of needles and a gray computer screen. Ricardo tapped the box twice against his knee and toyed with two small dials before needles within the device began bobbing back and forth.

"What is that?" Dorn asked. "A Geiger counter?"

"No. A Geiger counter measures levels of radioactivity exclusively," Ricardo said. "It's a little late to be worrying about that."

Sensors cried out sharply.

Ricardo turned down the gain before proceeding with more readings.

"This is an electromagnetic remote sensor. It reads and analyzes a variety of electromagnetic fields," he said. "Electromagnetic radiation is a form of energy characterized by its wavelength or frequency. Radio waves—visible light—generate some sort of field. Even our bodies do."

Jack watched waves of energy register on the small, blue screen that Ricardo stared at, now obviously concerned.

"I've gotta get a printout of this," Ricardo said.

He entered commands on a small field of touch pads. In seconds a feed of thermal paper snaked out. As if reading a ticker tape on Black Monday, Ricardo gravely analyzed the series of lines. "You're not going to believe this. But it's producing the magnetic signature of a fusion device."

Jack leaned closer. "A fusion device?"

"No doubt about it," Ricardo said.

Jack's excitement widened his eyes. "Then this has to be *The Source*!"

Dorn turned to him. "You think *this* is the lost source of power?"

"It must be," Jack said. "It would explain the myths . . . the sketches of strange devices in old tombs that seem to have electromagnetic coils and filaments. A technology the ancients said harnessed the power of the sun!"

"The sun *is* a giant fusion reactor," Samantha said, gazing at Jack. "This has to be it."

Dorn approached the device. "This little thing is a bloody nuclear reactor?"

"Nuclear, yes. But much different from today's fission reactors," Ricardo said. "Fusion is fission's reverse process. Two nuclei come together and fuse, forming a new nucleus with a greater weight than either of the previous two. The small portion of mass that is lost is converted into energy. Powerful energy," he said. "The key ingredients in the reaction are hydrogen and helium. They fuel the reactions inside the sun."

"And these reactions can occur forever, right?" Dorn asked.

"Almost. The sun is so massive, those reactions can take place for billions of years before it burns itself out, even though in just one second the energy it releases could keep our entire civilization running at present rates for over a million years. As far as fusion reactions here on Earth—there's enough hydrogen fuel so that the energy could be practically limitless—in terms of human consumption." Ricardo paused and looked back down at the remote sensor. "But I'll tell you—this device could be even more remarkable."

"What do you mean?" Jack asked.

"Because we're not completely fried, I'm guessing the power being generated is not hot fusion—but *cold* fusion."

Jack repeated the words in his mind: *cold fusion*. A process that could generate the same reactions without the intense temperatures of the sun or a standard nuclear plant. Cold fusion promised clean power that produced no greenhouse gases or world-threatening by-products.

"Then, we've just found the key to mankind's future," Dorn said excitedly. "Centuries ahead of its time."

Jack shuddered at the thought. He knew fusion would shape technology in the coming millennium—already scientists exploring with hot fusion in giant magnetic reactors called Tokamaks were making significant advances. The race had already begun—fossil fuels would soon be depleted, and the toxic gases from combustion still threatened humankind with extinction. "If we're really looking at a fusion generator, it explains how these temples were built," Jack said, thrilled. "And the countless records of how the Shining Ones levitated giant stones to the sounds of trumpets. And maybe why the locals attributed the legend of *xiuhcoatl* to the Shining

Ones. The extraterrestrials were said to have a 'fire ser-pent' that could pierce and dismember human bodies. Other stories mentioned they possessed a power that could destroy the world."

"Which is another reason not to mess with this thing anymore until we know precisely what we're dealing with," Ricardo added.

"I agree," Samantha said. "We'll have to leave that to the world's top physicists. They should be able to de-engineer the technology safely."

"Let's not be too hasty to call in outsiders," Dorn offered. "Do you have any idea what this device—what all the technology down here could be worth to us?"

"Us?" Jack asked. "I hope you're referring to the en-tire human race."

Dorn paused. "The world would eventually see the technology, but after we patent the advances—through private corporations. This machine is priceless, as long as we keep its existence between ourselves."

"This isn't a case of shipwreck salvage," Jack said. "The extraterrestrial technology belongs to science—to everyone in the world."

"He's right," Samantha added. "We're not dealing with gold bars and silver coins."

Dorn looked pensive. "Maybe. But how and when we make the findings known will have serious repercussions for us. That's all I'm saying. We should talk about this in depth."

Baines appeared through the adjoining chamber.

"Anything of interest?" Dorn asked.

"Just some more observation tables," the man said. "And a few skeletons."

# THE GRAIL

The room was smaller than the last. Jack paused to examine the metal partition that had slid back into the wall between two rubbery seams that extended from the floor to the ceiling. He guessed that the room had been the last defense against airborne microbes.

Inside, a series of raised stone slabs were covered with blue mats. The pads, though deteriorated, had the sheen and pliability of rubber or soft plastic. Beds, Jack thought, not observation tables. He counted ten, though all but two beds were empty. He stopped by the first, where he saw a long, distinctive skeleton resting on a decomposed pad consisting of a woven matrix of blue threads over a honeycomb interior. The sheer size of the skeletal frame left no doubt in Jack's mind about what he was observing—the big skull, the hollow sockets, the four digit bones of the hand.

"Our fifth extraterrestrial," he said.

"It's another male. Look at the pelvic structure," Samantha said. "I wonder why we haven't found any females."

"The legends speak only of a band of men. I'm guessing the crew had been all-male, just like our space crews were until a few years ago." Jack gently brushed dust from the large skull. "This one hasn't been mummified."

"Is that significant?" Dorn asked.

"Very. I'd say he'd been the sole survivor for a time—the last to die of the virus. The care with which

the extraterrestrials mummified their dead leaves no
doubt about that. Had any others survived him, they'd
have seen to it that the same mummification process was
performed. There was obviously no one left after him."

Ricardo sighed. "The last of the Mohicans . . ."

Across the room, Samantha examined the other skeleton resting on a similar raised bed. "Oh my god . . ."
she said. "You have to see this."

As Jack joined her, his eyes took in the new set of
bones. They were noticeably smaller. The head appeared
human-size. The rib cage was much shorter. His gaze
followed the arms to the hands . . .

"Five digits," Samantha said.

Jack felt the cranium. His fingers tingled as he traced
the pronounced brow ridges above the eyes. "This is
*Homo erectus!*"

"I know." Samantha's voice cracked. "And look at the
pelvis. It's a female."

Jack nodded. He didn't need to analyze the pelvis
structure of the creature to determine its gender. Beneath
the lower ribs a tiny skeleton lay cradled inside the hip-
bones. Jack felt flush, red splotches blossomed along his
neck. He moved to the side of the table. Though his
throat felt dry as sand, he managed, "And she was preg-
nant."

Jack's trembling hands carefully maneuvered between
the larger bones until he reached the tiny, flawless skull
and, with the tenderness reserved for a living child, carefully removed it. He studied the skull without saying a
word. It had a small hook in the back; the brow ridges
were less defined than its mother's. Jack fit the lower
jaw against the diminutive, thin skull. The joints made
a perfect seam. "Samantha . . ."

Jack turned. He noticed tears in Samantha's eyes.

"It's *Homo sapiens*," she said.

The gene charts, still in Ricardo's grasp, began to
shake. Ricardo shuffled through them. "One gene map
is from *Homo sapiens*," he said. "The others aren't—

though each shares similarities. One might be *Homo erectus*. The other . . . extraterrestrial."

Jack cupped the skull like the Holy Grail.

For him. For Samantha. It was . . .

"What does this mean?" Dorn asked. He stepped closer.

"It means we've found the missing link," Jack said.

"And it's"—Samantha could barely speak—"an extraterrestrial."

Jack set down the small skull as gently as if it had been made of papier-mâché. Ricardo hugged Samantha, pausing only to wipe away tears of his own. The scene took on the feel of a wake. Dorn stood still, trying to piece things together in his mind. Baines stared in wonderment at the three stunned scientists but kept his distance. All the moisture from Jack's mouth seemed to collect under his lids. Raw emotion manifested itself in the tiny skeleton that lay before him; a tempestuous surge of pathos, delivered in the form of a small skull.

He couldn't speak. It didn't appear anyone could. In front of them lay the answer sought by all those who studied humankind's past—the very embodiment of a lifelong quest.

*The* answer.

The riddle that haunted so many had finally been solved. The origin of our species—that elusive link to the past, the bridge between *Homo sapiens* and our nearest relatives, *Homo erectus*, the wanderers—had been found.

"This . . . ahhh," Jack tried. "I can't believe this. *Not even after everything we've learned.*"

"We found it," Ricardo said. "We finally found it."

Baines pointed at the tiny bones. "The skull's human?"

"As human as you or me," Jack said.

Samantha sat on the stone floor. "This is too much."

After a few more moments Dorn asked, "This baby is the actual missing link?"

"No," Jack said. "Not the baby." He walked over to

the large skeleton on the other side of the room and pointed: "*He's* the missing link."

"The extraterrestrial?"

Jack began to gather himself. "The clues were right in front of our noses the whole time. But even I couldn't fathom it."

Dorn's complexion got ruddy. "There are historical records of extraterrestrials fathering the human race?"

Jack's gaze remained fixed on the long, graceful skeleton. "They weren't known as extraterrestrials. They were known by different names in different cultures, but the descriptions are always the same," he said, fighting for the cool reserve of a person of science. "Whether the ancients called them Shining Ones, or Elohim, or Viracocha—the cultures explain how these beings actually had children with the daughters of man. It isn't just one obscure account buried on a stone tablet somewhere. Cultures on both sides of the Atlantic share the same myths."

"I'll be damned."

"Tibetan, Hebrew, Egyptian, Sumerian texts, all tell the same story. An Akkadian text, the *Atra-Hasis*, speaks of an actual genetic experiment conducted with the local tribes. In that account, seven females were supposedly impregnated with male cultures. Two of their offspring had been given the names Adam and Chawwah—which translates . . . Eve. According to the epic, the entire ordeal had been a controlled experiment designed to combine some of the qualities of the 'Lords' with those of the native inhabitants."

"The device. The gene maps," Samantha mumbled from the floor. "It all makes sense."

"A completely different story found on a Sumerian tablet tells how luminous beings 'impregnated the daughters of Man in order to create a new kind of conscious being.' A different story in the *Atra-Hasis* claims that man was created from the 'blood' of a 'Lord' mixed with a mysterious clay."

"Sounds like the story from Genesis," Samantha said. "God created Adam by mixing spittle and clay."

"Imagine it," Dorn said. "Shining Ones or extraterrestrials—or whoever, performing genetic experiments."

"Another ancient Hebrew text describes an offspring born as a mixture of these peoples and the local inhabitants. The story is told by Lamech, the supposed father of the biblical Noah. The man was said to be terrified 'of his weird baby who filled a darkened room with light.' Records from the book of Enoch say Lamech realized the child was more likely to have come from the loins of—as he puts it—the 'Sons of the Lord in Eden' than his own. He even tells his wife that Noah 'is not like you and me—his eyes are like the rays of the sun and his face shines. It seems to me that he is not born of my stock, but that of the Angels.' "

Jack began pacing next to the raised slab. "I know it sounds crazy but everything we found seems to fit the paradigm. Suppose a crew of astronauts—like the men we sent to the moon—had somehow put down or crashed on this planet. They had problems adjusting to the conditions. The Shining Ones were obviously extremely susceptible to the earthborn microbes. Why else would they have needed the decontamination device?"

"Or built this underground complex," Ricardo said.

"And we've already seen that the beings had the technology to manipulate genes."

"So to try and adapt," Dorn said, "they decided to breed with the local people."

"To share genes," Jack said. "The extraterrestrials sought the ruggedness and immune system of *Homo erectus*. They chose the best, most apt, human types they found here—those with the highest potential—and combined the two species. The historical accounts say the Shining Ones 'took only the best of the daughters of man.' "

"But it still wouldn't have helped their own survival chances," Dorn said.

"You're right," Jack said. "It could have been an altruistic act on their part; to leave a legacy. But that fits with the portrayals of them as gracious and merciful."

Ricardo knelt beside the extraterrestrial skeleton. "I'll take it one step further," he said. "What if the Shining Ones knew they were dying. Knew they were hopelessly stranded. But what if they were also aware that if they saved their DNA in the form of mummification—perhaps one day, when their own children became advanced enough . . ."

"Humans could bring them back," Jack said softly.

The group pondered the implications. Each hypothesis, which would have sounded incredibly insane a few days ago, built upon another. "Remember the icons on the device?" Jack asked. "Those two intertwined lines on the second module. Maybe they weren't snakes. Maybe they represented—"

"A double helix," Ricardo said. "They must!"

"That module was probably used in their gene-splicing procedures. I assume it's what they used to successfully breed with the native inhabitants," Jack said. "Though I'm not saying these men never got horny. The historical evidence suggests the Shining Ones took many wives. And the descendants of these beings—known in some records as the Watchers—in Hebrew the *Eyrim*—later developed a healthy lust for the daughters of man and begat many children by them."

"Which would explain the lab room with the gynecological instruments next door," Samantha said.

"I'm guessing that in subsequent generations, artificial insemination was done away with completely. Initially though, to successfully create a hybrid race from both species, more intense gene manipulation would have been needed; a better than random process whereby the strengths of both species could be properly combined," Jack said.

"You'd see the changes immediately," Ricardo agreed. "In the first generation."

"And if the extraterrestrials were around long enough before they all died of the virus—say covering even one or two generations of early humans—only about thirty years reproductively speaking—they could have easily imparted not only their superior intellect in the form of genes, but also their wisdom and teachings, which spawned civilization as we know it."

"And they couldn't have died out too soon," Samantha said. "It must have taken years to build this whole complex."

Ricardo said, "It explains the sudden emergence of *Homo sapiens*—seemingly overnight—without any traces of nearby evolutionary links, from primitive *sapiens* or *erectus* populations that used crude stone tools."

"*Homo sapiens* never evolved," Jack said. "We burst onto the scene and dominated straightaway—in thirty thousand years or so—a mere fraction of a millionth of a second in terms of the life of our planet. We've excelled beyond all expectations. We've driven thousands of species into extinction, including our hominid forebears. We fly. We've harnessed the power of the atom. We've put our kind on the moon. We've mapped our own genetic structure; effectively found ways to fight disease. No other creature on Earth has been able to accomplish these things. Why all the advances? Why so fast—if we weren't suddenly given the innate intelligence?"

"And then been taught to use it," Samantha added.

"Then we've also proved that a biblical God doesn't exist," Dorn said smugly.

"Not true," Jack said. "If anything we've *proven* the existence of God. We've proven the existence of a creator. Evolution has long asked us to believe that we evolved by random acts of chance over time. These bones prove we weren't the by-products of random mutation. We were *designed.*"

"You're going to tell the world that God's an extraterrestrial?" Dorn asked.

"Biblically speaking, God *isn't* of this earth," Jack said. "No one would argue that. God's an *extra*terrestrial any way one looks at it."

No one spoke.

Each person struggled with his or her own thoughts. Jack finally said, "Look, I'm humble enough to know that I don't understand all the answers. I believe in God. I always have. And I believe that same God created everything in the universe—including those extraterrestrials. If that omniscient presence decided to create mankind here on Earth, who am I to question the method?"

Samantha looked on pensively.

"I'm not pretending to know how and why God decided to bless this world with our species," Jack continued. "Whether it was space voyagers—or spit and dirt—the only thing I do know is that we were *created*. Created by a God—by a presence greater, more mysterious, than simple random mutation."

The five humans stood in silence, reordering their preconceptions of the history of the world and humankind's place in it. The long silence broke to sounds that came from the laboratory room: The slapping of bare feet on stone.

A few seconds later Bongane ran into the room, soaking wet.

"The water," he said. "It rises!"

# EXHUMATION

The black pool had risen half a stair above the high-water mark Jack had scraped into the wall. Bongane told them that the corridor had begun filling more quickly after a loud rumbling noise. *The activation of the fusion device*, Jack thought.

"At this rate, the whole level will be under water within two days," Ricardo said.

Currents within the black mass now rippled the once-still surface. The thought of losing everything panicked Jack. They would have to move fast.

Ten minutes of furious discussion erupted. Reaching a consensus was less difficult than Jack would've imagined. Conflicting personalities shared a singular purpose now: They would exhume as much of the contents on the lower level as possible. Best case scenario, the expedition had forty-eight hours to clear the level—that is, if the water continued to rise at the same pace. Their problems were compounded by the fact that the Bolivians were gone—though Jack wasn't sure he would've resorted to using them anyway.

It was decided that the artifacts on the lower level would be exhumed in order of importance. On this fact, however, disagreement emerged. Samantha, Jack, and Ricardo stood firm in their decision to retrieve the skeletons and gene maps at the same time as the fusion generator. Dorn reluctantly agreed, leaving the contents of the salvage hall for last.

\*   \*   \*

Ricardo's system of rafts and pulleys had taken over three hours to set up but would save them valuable time in the race to retrieve as much gear as possible. "Besides," he argued, "the system should keep things safe and dry. I don't want to risk wetting the fusion generator."

Samantha and Jack waited patiently as Baines, Bongane, Anthony, and François brought down the cases in which the scientists would carefully pack their prize.

"I still can't believe this," Samantha said while photographing the position of the fetus skeleton within the *erectus* womb. Jack and Samantha carefully photodocumented the room, as the position of the skeletons could prove important in further analysis. Jack gingerly packed the small skull into its padded aluminum case.

Through the entire procedure Jack acted like an automaton, his mind in a haze. He felt that his life had stopped five days ago, that the whole expedition really wasn't happening. It *couldn't* be happening to him; it all felt too benevolent. *But oh, what sweet justice.* The prospect of losing everything they'd found had given him a singular inspiration. He felt like an ant, obsessed only with protecting its colony—a colony that would be destroyed by floodwaters if the contents weren't moved to higher ground.

Back and forth. Back and forth.

For twelve straight hours Jack labored with packing. His lower jaw ached and his ribs felt worse; his medication had worn thin. He arranged and rearranged the order in which equipment would make the difficult water crossing—only to be challenged by the endless, worn stairs. The group had set up a series of oxygen canisters at regular intervals between the levels. Transporting equipment up the stairs felt murderous in the high altitude.

Crating the fusion generator and moving it to the flooded corridor had taken more time than expected but went reasonably well. The device and the wood crate that they built around it must have weighed over six hundred pounds combined. Baines and François had fashioned a makeshift dolly from a few scraps of wood and the rubber wheels from one of the expedition's gas generators.

But transporting the fusion device across the water was another matter entirely. The raft had to be improved to carry the heavy object. It had taken nearly two hours to build outriggers that would help stabilize the system and support the added weight. Each person took turns wading into the frigid water to help build the add-ons. Five minutes was the longest anyone could tolerate the water's icy grasp. The blankets and heat lamps at the top of the stairs provided little respite—they only reminded one of the excruciating pain that waited for them upon their next trip into the murk.

When they finally got the crate to the other side safely, more than one scientist thought they might never thaw out.

The water level had risen more or less at a constant rate.

Jack took notes on how long it took each stair to become submerged. It seemed Ricardo's forty-eight-hour figure would hold, though Jack did notice that the water had been flooding at slightly different rates occasionally.

The fusion generator had already been hoisted up a flight of stairs. Now the machine rested in the corridor on the second level. No one had the strength to move it to the first level at the moment. Samantha and Jack did manage to bring the case that contained the gene maps and the three skeletons to the surface. If they left with anything, Samantha said, it would be with those bones.

After fourteen hours, the group decided that catnaps were essential. Fatigue had already caused too many mishaps. Each person would get an hour and a half of sleep before resuming the frantic scramble for higher ground.

Jack found Samantha soundly asleep on the cot in the field tent—right beside her precious aluminum case.

Jack watched her for a few moments before waking her. Her face was smeared with dirt and her wet clothes hung beside a portable gas heater. Her hardness, the austerity, all seemed to fade away in sleep. Jack no longer saw the intimidating terror of the Princeton academic establishment—the fiercely independent woman hell-bent on standing against the male-dominated winds of the world.

He noticed the gentle curls of her brown hair, her small nose. "Samantha." He woke her with a gentle touch.

She sprang up in the cot, startled. It took only seconds before the determined glare returned to her eyes. "Thanks," she said. "How's it coming?"

"Good," Jack said. "Ricardo's been sifting through the wreckage, pulling out what he thinks are the most important pieces—technologically speaking. With any luck we might be able to save ten percent of the salvage hall by morning."

"What time is it?"

"Five-fifteen," Jack said.

Samantha swung her slender legs off the cot and pulled on her dirty, damp trousers. "At least we have the fusion generator. And this." She patted the aluminum case. "We can always retrieve the rest with divers."

Jack nodded, his lids heavy.

"Here. It's still warm." She ushered him into the cot. The warmth from her body radiated through him like angelic coals; the temperature change made him shudder. He could still smell traces of her body lotion and shampoo on the pillow.

She tucked him in. "Snug as a bug in a rug."

"Thanks."

"Get some sleep. Someone will get you up at dawn."

Samantha bent over and kissed him on the forehead.

Jack could still feel the imprint of her lips when Samantha closed the tent flaps behind her. He concentrated on the sensation.

Moon-rays illuminated the tent through the large vent

opening. Jack slid to the side of the cot and stared through the hole at the brilliant moon, just a sliver from full. The dimpled surface seemed close enough to touch. Jack's species had been there. Members of his genus had traveled through that dark void and walked on its surface. Pride welled within him. Why did mankind yearn to reach out into space? Why the insatiable desire to explore the universe? Why had his species—*Homo sapiens*—been so fascinated by the stars throughout history?

Perhaps we've unconsciously yearned for home, he thought—wherever that might be.

His body settled into the small cot. The platinum sphere left an incandescent imprint on Jack's lids as they closed. Just moments from sleep, Jack thought more about the moon. Something about it troubled him. You're just being paranoid, he told himself, before dozing off.

# MOON

Jack awoke to find Bongane holding a cup of hot coffee.

"Your turn?" Jack said, indicating the cot.

"No. I'm okay." Bongane would continue working.

Bundled against the dewy dawn, the two men walked to the excavation pit under a pale morning sky that hung the full moon as clearly as it had during the night. The pile of aluminum cases and wooden crates had grown during Jack's nap at the excavation site. Dorn's men bustled about the small stack.

The decontamination device sufficed as a shower. Jack wiped the vapor from his face and continued into the great hall. Bongane said he'd go farther down to help Samantha. Jack found Ricardo instructing Anthony on keeping a particular crate upright.

"You look exhausted," Jack said.

Puffy mounds framed Ricardo's droopy eyes. "You missed all the fun," he said. "We pulled that damn fusion generator onto this level." He pointed to a large crate that sat just outside the anteroom. "We're bringing it to the surface in a few minutes."

Ricardo grabbed both sides of his waistband and pulled his pants up his hips.

Jack watched with a smile.

"I know," Ricardo said, tightening his belt. "But let me assure you, this forced diet ends as soon as we're out of here."

"Dinner's on me," Jack said. He put his empty cup on the long stone table. "Where's the water level now?"

"Still under the lab. But rising much faster. We've only retrieved two crates of equipment from the salvage hall." His head bobbed forward with exhaustion. "I don't think we have more than four hours before the level's submerged."

"Damn," Jack said, searching through a corral of boxes. He found his camera and a few rolls of film. "We better finish photo-documenting as much as we can."

Loading film as they went, Jack told Ricardo they should start by photographing the hieroglyphic stone wall that had surrounded the fusion generator on three sides. "I'm sure those inscriptions are instructions. They might be the most important thing we can salvage."

Ricardo agreed.

They passed Samantha and Bongane pulling a crate up the stairs. Samantha's concern showed through damp exhaustion. "We don't have much time," she said.

"I know."

Jack asked the whereabouts of the other members of the crew.

Dorn was at the surface, she told Jack. She hadn't seen Baines or François in hours.

Jack and Ricardo pulled themselves across the submerged corridor on the raft. The water had risen dramatically. Jack managed to disembark safely, keeping the merciless pool at bay. In the lab room, he took a quick light reading and set his camera. He shot a few wide series before resetting his lens for a series of tight shots. He hoped the entire mural might be translated with the aid of computers.

"At least the generator came with instructions," Ricardo said. "We've been way too brazen with some of this technology already. We're not dealing with holograms anymore. We're dealing with fusion reactions."

"I hear you," Jack said. "Which is why we make the generator public knowledge the first chance we get. I don't give a damn what Dorn says."

"I agree, *amigo*. It's a Pandora's box—especially in the wrong hands."

Jack found an angle where the flash wouldn't obliterate the delicate engravings. For backup, he fired off another roll using the light from the chamber's walls after changing the shutter speed. Jack placed another plastic container of film in his shirt pocket and took a last look at the four engraved icons—the large symbols that had been repeated on the systems module.

"What's wrong?" Ricardo asked.

"This last icon," Jack pointed. "Does it remind you of anything?"

Ricardo stooped over to take a look. After a few seconds he shook his head. "The two spheres separated by a line could signify the fusion process."

"Probably," Jack said. "But what do you make of the triangles around the circle above it? Does it look like a hazard symbol to you?"

"Could be."

Why did it look so familiar?

"Is my field book still down here?"

"I didn't move it."

Jack had left the leather notebook in the hermetically sealed chamber after noting the position of the skeletons. Ricardo peered nervously over his shoulder. Finally, Jack found a worn photocopy with some Tibetan script on it. His finger scanned by drawings of different idols. "I knew it."

"The same symbol?"

"No. But darn close." Jack started into the other room. "C'mon."

The similarity shocked both of them.

Jack held the photocopy against the wall, just below the fourth icon.

"Chinese?" Ricardo asked.

"Tibetan." The scripted word looked like an elaborate version of the hieroglyph on the wall. "It seemed curious to me because I've seen the same symbol on some Aymaran tablets."

"What is it?"

"The Tibetan word," Jack said, "for Armageddon."

He pointed to the icon on the wall. The same icon had been engraved on the fourth chamber, the one nearest the base of the device. "That resembles both the Tibetan and Aymaran symbols for the end of the last age—the end of the world. It also looks like it denotes the fusion process."

Ricardo shifted nervously. "What exactly are you saying?"

"That one of these modules might be something we don't want to activate . . ." Jack stood up slowly and folded the paper. "Ever."

Jack took a last few pictures of the fourth icon. "I've got enough," he said.

Ricardo stood up. "Good. Let's get out of here. All this stuff is disturbing enough without talking about the end of the world. Besides," he said. "Tonight there's a full moon—and I haven't been feeling lucky."

Jack adjusted the camera strap around his shoulder. He couldn't shake the image of the moon, which had defied the morning sun. *Why did it trouble him so?*

He walked by the three tables in the front of the lab, then suddenly stopped. "That's it!"

"That's what?"

"That's why the damn water's rising so much faster."

Jack finally understood the increased rate of flooding. Twice every season the tidal pull of the moon joins the constant gravitational pull of the sun, resulting in an especially high tide. That tide was now attempting to bury them in a liquid grave. The effects of a strong spring tide would raise the level of the water table. The sun and moon would together work to weaken seams and increase pressure on the already strained retaining walls.

As the two men picked up the pace, weaving through stranded piles of equipment in the salvage hall, Ricardo cursed himself for overlooking such a simple phenomenon. Already a thin layer of water glazed the floor.

"The stairs have breached," Jack said.

The sound of their sloshing footsteps echoed off the walls, overpowering the incessant dripping from the seams of the massive stone wall on the south side. Tiny ripples vibrated over the sheet of water. Winded, Jack refused to slow. The scientists had nearly cleared the last of the wreckage when both heard a crash.

"What's that?" Ricardo yelled.

A roar carried through the hall on a strong breeze. The sound sent jolts of adrenaline through Jack's body. He turned but didn't have time to answer. A wall of water barreled toward them, lifting metal sheets in its wake before knocking Jack's legs out from under him.

# BREACH

The last of the four aluminum cases slid into the truck. Samantha urged Dorn's men to be careful. Completely unaware of the precious cargo inside, the reinforcements who'd brought up the rest of the supplies worked with careless indifference. Each aluminum case housed the body of an extraterrestrial. Samantha read the huge block letters that were plastered on the side of the cases: PROPERTY OF HELIX CORP.

The implied ownership didn't sit well with her.

At least the worn case into which she packed the skeletons of the *Homo erectus* female and her precious hybrid baby was hers from the expedition in Mali. Already loaded on another truck, they sat next to the case that held her extraterrestrial fossil.

She approached the excavation pit. The wooden crate that housed the fusion generator was being hoisted out of the pit by one of the trucks. Attached to a steel winch, two half-inch ropes trailed down to a cargo net that cradled the case like an Italian prosciutto.

"Careful with that!" Samantha called out.

The crate dragged against the sides of the pit. Samantha would never have agreed to move it so hastily, but Dorn had been adamant about securing the generator in the truck—even though the device seemed out of imminent danger. He shouted commands from inside the excavation like a film director. On the surface, his men secured the crate and backed one of the trucks toward it.

"Safe and sound," Dorn said.

"Has the water taken the third level?" Samantha asked.

"I haven't been down there. I don't think so."

"Good," she said. "I'm going for another load."

She started down the stairs.

"Wait. I'll go with you," Dorn said.

The decontamination device went off when Samantha and Dorn were still twenty yards away. Baines ran through, nearly slamming into them. He looked wetter than the misting device would have warranted.

"The east wall . . . has breached," he said, out of breath.

"Breached?" Samantha's stomach tightened.

"The whole third level is gone! The second will be under in minutes."

"Good god!" Dorn said. "Where's everyone else?"

"François is dead," Baines said. "I don't know about the rest."

Samantha felt as if a python had wrapped itself around her chest. "Jack and Ricardo?"

Baines's chest heaved. "They were down in the lab taking pictures."

"That's on the third level." Samantha looked at the two men, then forced her way past them.

Dorn held her wrist. "You can't do anything—except get yourself killed."

"They could be trapped down there."

"It's too dangerous," Dorn said. "We can only hope they made it to higher ground."

"Hoping's not good enough," she said. "I'm going after them."

She struggled in Dorn's grasp, freed herself, and ran down the hallway.

"Samantha!"

She stopped and turned. Dorn looked at her with pleading eyes. "Please! Don't do this. I'll send someone else down!"

She stared down the tunnel toward the great hall, then back at Dorn.

Then she sprinted through the decontamination device.

Jack's lungs felt like bursting. Pain tore through his sinuses. His throat burned. His ears were muffled by underwater chaos, his body shocked by the icy onslaught that roiled around him. The waters tossed him like driftwood in heavy surf.

*I have to breathe!*

Jack's hands speared through the water. *Where was the surface?* The urge to inhale would soon overcome him.

*I have to breathe!*

He slammed into something hard. *The far wall?*

Jack felt himself rise. An instant later the muffled noise became a roar as his ears cleared the water. The surface! His lungs screamed and he sucked in oxygen a millisecond before the cold world recaptured him.

But he could think now. Two kicks from his strong legs and his head cleared the surface again. Piles of debris floated in a swirling mass. Off to his right, Jack made out the back of a head as it bobbed in the backwash of current. "Ricardo!"

Jack coughed, his lungs clearing water. The head turned. Ricardo's face was matted beneath coils of hair. "Here . . ." he said, weakly raising an arm.

Jack swam to him as the water leveled in the immense salvage hall. Pushing by islands of steel and floating cables Jack managed to grab hold of Ricardo's collar.

"You okay?" he shouted.

Ricardo nodded just above the swirling blackness. Jack probed the depths with his feet and found bottom. Ricardo also righted himself. The water was rising fast.

Ricardo pointed to the submerging archway that led to the stairs. "That's the way out!"

\*          \*          \*

Samantha slipped down four stairs, her back scraping
against the stone. Her head slammed into the ledges
twice before she picked herself up and took the remaining stairs to the lower levels two at a time. Beneath her
she heard a muffled clamor. At the bottom of the first
flight, Samantha ran by the room where she had discovered Jack and the hologram. She stopped by the jagged
hole punched out in the hallway. Once inside the hole,
the sound of rushing water became a roar, amplifying
off the walls. She continued down the next flight of slippery stairs.

She prayed and ran. Prayed and ran. *Oh, God.
Please . . .*

She repeated the three words over and over, never
getting past the *please.*

Surely God knew what she meant.


Just ahead of Ricardo, Jack swam beneath the archway.
A strong current whisked him into the corridor where
the raft had been. The once placid pool had become a
swift underground river. The water must be filling areas
west of them, Jack thought. He swam hard. Over the
roar and crash of metal objects slamming against stone,
he heard Ricardo call out behind him, "The stairs!"

The two men were drifting toward the stairway to the
second level, the current carrying them faster than Jack
had expected. His arms dug into the water in heavy
strokes. He kept his head above water, searching through
the chaos for the steps. He couldn't let himself miss
them. There was no way to fight the current for a pro-
longed period of time.

Jack's legs burned. His clothes felt like hundred-
pound manacles. The current swept him even with the
opening of the stairway but he was still two yards away.
*Kick!*

Jack buried his head in the water and reached for the
stairs. His fingernails scraped against stone. He opened
his eyes but could see nothing. One hand slapped onto

a dry stair. He looked out of the water just in time to grab the far wall. His fingers held firm, pulling his body out of the swirling current.

Behind him, upstream, Ricardo stroked madly in the water, coming toward him fast. "Kick!" Jack shouted. "Kick!"

Leaning his back against the wall for leverage, Jack reached his arm into the current. His hand coiled around Ricardo's forearm just as he passed. The force nearly yanked Jack back into the water. He dug the fingers of his free hand into a seam between two stones.

"Swim, Ricardo . . . I can't . . . hold you."

Ricardo had drifted against the wall past Jack, past the stairway. The man buried his head against the current and tried groping his way back with his free arm. Jack was being pulled down the stairs. He gritted his teeth and tried desperately to pull Ricardo in. His biceps shuddered.

He couldn't hold Ricardo anymore.

In a millisecond Jack's mind processed a sickening fact. He had to decide if he would let go of the wall or let go of his friend. Something inside him made a plea for survival—but conceded to a more powerful force: loyalty. He wouldn't let go of Ricardo. His body slid down another stair, his fingers dragging across the wall. Maybe they could swim back when the level filled— when the current slowed, Jack thought.

Then he felt two hands grab the collar of his shirt.

Samantha leaned all her weight against the stairs, dragging Jack back to safety. Her boots slipped on the smooth steps, but Jack managed a foothold and backed up. Ricardo hooked an arm around Jack's knee and fell onto the stairs.

"What happened?" Samantha yelled.

"A strong spring tide coupled with the blasting, maybe." Jack massaged feeling back into his arm. "A retaining wall must have ruptured. This whole complex will be underwater in a matter of minutes."

"Then let's get the hell out of here," she said.


The three scientists passed halfway through the great hall when Jack heard a muffled voice in the distance. He stopped. "Did you hear that?"

"Sounded like a groan," Samantha said.

"It's coming from over there." Ricardo pointed to a small alcove behind a series of immense support pillars.

Behind a pile of unpacked crates and debris they found Bongane.

His hair was matted with blood that had coagulated on his scalp and neck like purple syrup. He tried to get up. Jack held him down.

"Don't move, Bongane. You've been injured."

"We must get out," Bongane said.

Samantha inspected the man's head. She found a three-inch gash just behind his left ear. The skin had separated, forming two swollen ridges between a valley floor of blood and skull. "It looks pretty deep," she said, applying pressure to the wound. "Don't worry. We're gonna get you out of here as soon as we stop this bleeding."

"No"—Bongane turned himself on his side, trying to get up—"time."

"There's time," Jack said, supporting Bongane's head.

Ricardo saw the Zulu's shirt above the abdomen—the white cotton soaked in blood. He gently pulled it toward his chest and cleansed the source of the bleeding with his sleeve.

"It's an exit wound," Ricardo said. "Bongane's been shot."

"Shot?"

Jack felt a queasiness overtaking him. Bongane still struggled. His fingers probed for something between two large crates.

"What is it?" Jack said.

Ricardo pushed away the boxes and lifted a long wire. "Blasting cord," he said.

"Blasting cord?" Jack stayed with Bongane, whose head rested in his lap. "What happened?"

Samantha and Ricardo began pulling up blasting wire, which wound through the network of rubble.

"Holy shit," Ricardo said.

The cord terminated in small packs on three support pillars. Just below the pillar, François lay dead in a pool of his own blood.

Ricardo examined the satchels that were hidden behind expedition equipment. Bricks of gray putty were packed against the base of the columns. A small plastic box with an LED display was wrapped onto each satchel with black tape. The display read: 000:00.

The devices looked like detonators.

"C-4," Ricardo said. "Attached to the support columns."

"C-4?"

"There's enough of it here to take down the entire hall."

As Jack rounded the corner—Bongane's long arms draped around his and Ricardo's necks—a desperate eruption of panic stole the wind from his lungs as if he'd been whacked in the gut with a lead pipe. No light came from anywhere down the entrance corridor. In front of them, Samantha ran past the hieroglyphs that heralded the entrance, stopping at a mound of rubble sloping into the corridor.

Jack climbed the slope with Samantha, leaving the dazed Zulu in Ricardo's care. The entrance had been completely sealed. Resting against the high mound, Jack looked through the dust that now danced in the beam of the flashlight. Samantha remained silent. In the pale glow Jack saw her face flush, bright splotches trailing down her neck like crimson ivy. Her breathing had grown heavy.

"I think we've just been fucked," Jack said.

# ENTRANCE

Dorn watched as a truck, using the steel sled attached to the bumper, pushed the last few heaps of red earth into the excavation pit.

He mumbled quietly to himself, "I'm sorry, Samantha."

There was nothing else he could do. She would die underground with Jack. With the man she had made painfully clear, of late, she still loved.

Baines said, "It was inevitable."

Dorn turned to him.

"She would have been a bloody pain in the ass, that one," Baines said, in a coarse attempt at consolation. "And dealing with Jack now instead of later is Christmas come early far as I'm concerned."

Dorn felt deep satisfaction at the mere notion of Jack's passing. His spirits lifted. "We leave as soon as possible," he said. "Activate the detonators."

Baines turned toward the truck.

Dorn watched the last of the red earth grow level with the surrounding terrain. For a brief moment, when Baines said the third level had breached, Dorn felt everything might actually work out. Jack and Ricardo would have been killed—quite innocuously—by a benevolent force of nature, saving Dorn the trouble. He knew Jack would never agree to use the extraterrestrial advances for profit. He would merely have had to persuade Samantha of the inordinate value of keeping the technology secret.

But she went back for him.

Perhaps it *was* better this way, Dorn thought. Though losing her hurt him more than he ever imagined it would.

He cleared his head with a breath of crisp air.

At least his destiny was secure. Tied down in the wood crate of a heavily armed truck sat *The Source,* a device that would make him the most powerful man in the world. In a few weeks only traces of the dig would exist. By that time he would have left Tiahuanaco far behind.

Samantha looked blankly at the corruption of rock and soil. "But why?" she finally said. "What the hell is he doing?"

"Dorn knew we'd never agree to keep the technology secret. Any one of his high-tech corporations has the resources to de-engineer the technology and make trillions."

"We've been sold out, my friends," Ricardo said, still tending to Bongane.

Samantha began to shake.

Jack had seen the look before—the one fueled by rage.

"They were probably planning to blow the whole complex once we got out with all the equipment," Jack said. "Which tells me there wasn't a chance in hell Dorn planned on sharing the technology—no matter what we decided."

Samantha bit her lower lip. Her blue eyes glared straight in front of her—as if the sapphire lasers might soon disintegrate the pile before her. "That bastard. What do we do now?"

Jack scraped at the stones. "We're not getting out through here."

"But this is the only exit," Samantha said.

"No. It's an entrance. And the Egyptians and Mayans built concealed exits in precise stellar alignment with an entrance. We've seen the same architecture—the same techniques demonstrated here." He turned around and looked down the corridor. "There has to be another way out."

"Where would it be?" Ricardo asked. "None of us noticed one."

"Like I said, it might be concealed. But everything in here should be built precisely and mathematically according to the same notion of the precession."

"We don't have much time," Samantha said. "Maybe an hour—no more—before all three levels are submerged."

Jack's mind rushed through calculations. He thought aloud: "The exits were calibrated with the entrances according to the four cardinal positions," he said. "If the spring equinox revealed the entrance corridor, I'm hoping the autumnal equinox reveals the exit corridor."

He climbed back down the crumbled hillock.

*"Hoping?"* Samantha asked. "Don't sound so sure of yourself."

"Hope," Jack said, "is all we got right now."

# PART FIVE

# ANALYSIS

McFadden nervously flipped through the *Cosmopolitan* magazine he had lifted off the reception desk above the Directorate of Operations. In the dim light of the War Room he had problems finding the article that had hooked his interest—the one about the new technique that would deliver the most intense orgasm of a woman's life. He slipped it back in his briefcase. He'd take it home—though he suspected there'd be another mind-shattering "O" piece next month.

Reading women's magazines had been a gold mine for him—a bible of sorts. McFadden always said it was like having the battle plans of the opposite sex. A successful romancer needed to have a finger on a modern woman's pulse. He had developed the habit after agent training, where he and his classmates were taught that placing one's self in the mind-set of an adversary was the only way to anticipate their actions.

He sipped the cold water he'd gotten from General Wright's aide from a paper cup the size of a thimble. McFadden looked down and noticed that in his hurry to brief the director on the latest satellite findings, he'd developed two crescent watermarks on the armpits of his light-blue dress shirt. He started to put his blazer back on when Wright appeared from his office.

Two overhead displays flashed various images taken by the eyes in the sky during the last hour. A stream of data

had been fed into the Cray supercomputers, which delegated tasks to smaller processors that analyzed specific
characteristics of every byte of information that came
into the agency. Fingerprints; spy reports; satellite feeds;
computer records: all got delegated to an array of processors that interpreted data with the proper software.

"Enhance that," Wright said.

The black-and-white photographs were digitally clar-
ified. An audiovisual officer magnified the area around
the large wooden object tied down in the back of one
of the trucks at Tiahuanaco. McFadden pointed to the
enlarged image of the crate.

"That's what our analysts say is generating the magnetic signature," McFadden said.

Two fusion specialists briefed the director on the
physics behind fusion and the magnetic fields that today's experiments with controlled fusion exhibit—the
same magnetic field they began picking up when the
wooden crate was brought out of the hole.

"And you're saying that this device is armed," Wright
asked. "Or at least operating now?"

"It seems that way, sir." McFadden slid two transparencies to the director's aide, who handed them to the
AV officer.

Within seconds, one of the monitors showed the results of the electromagnetic analysis.

"Normally you wouldn't pick up any abnormal magnetic disturbances other than the slight field that all objects generate. In this case," McFadden said, "you can
see a severe magnetic field around the wooden box. A
controlled magnetic field."

"Is that important for fusion?" Wright asked.

"Yes, sir. It creates a contained environment, a sort
of 'magnetic bottle' in which fusion reactions can occur
without melting the device around them." McFadden explained that experiments with fusion today used enormous magnets the size of trucks to create such fields.
"Which makes whatever's inside that crate even more

suspicious. Our fusion experiments and the Russian Tokamaks are housed in immense structures. The object
inside that crate can't be larger than a standard warhead.
That's why the analysts believe it might be a new form
of tactical weapon."

Wright looked grave. "A tactical nuke?"

"Yes, sir. But unlike anything we've ever seen."
McFadden thumbed through a few more papers before
finding the temperature data from the latest satellite pass.
"Sir, we're not reading any kind of temperature change
that would suggest hot fusion reactions. We think we're
dealing with something completely new—perhaps cold
fusion."

"Cold fusion?"

"Either that or the device is somehow shielded from
generating a heat signature."

Wright stopped pacing and ran his hand across the
marble surface of the table. "Get a contingency plan on
my desk ASAP. I want this thing confiscated."

# DEPARTURE

The camp bustled, and tents collapsed like earthbound
parachutes. For the last hour Pierce had watched Dorn's
contingent, which now consisted of seven men, refill the
excavation pit and pack supplies. Neither Pierce nor Miller had seen the three scientists reappear. Dorn had obviously added them to the growing list of corpses. The
South African had been agitated ever since the termi-

nation of the Bolivian, widening the perimeter and arming his men more heavily.

Dorn and the analysis team back in Virginia were both
interested in something in the large wooden crate in the
back of the lead truck. Pierce increased the magnification
but could only make out a nondescript shipping label
burned into the wood slats of the crate: DGS. A global
shipping company Pierce assumed Dorn owned.

Miller, who had been monitoring their satellite scrambler in the Jeep, walked over holding a thermal paper
printout. "Just like you thought," Miller said. "It looks
like we're moving in. McFadden wants us to coordinate
with the DEA."

Pierce set down the binoculars. "The DEA? Who is
he kidding?"

"Virginia's scrambled Special Forces but they won't
be in the area for another twenty-two hours. They say
the DEA's our only capable reinforcements."

"Capable . . ." Pierce chuckled. He would rather be
backed up by one extra agency man than a hundred DEA
agents—Rambo types who carried out missions with all
the subtlety of a Viking berserker on crank.

"I'm supposed to contact the DEA field commander
right away," Miller said.

Pierce shrugged. "At least we won't be sitting up here
on our asses."

The large wooden crate rested securely in the bed of the
first truck. A faint blue glow escaped from the spaces
between the wood slats and reflected off Dorn's eyes.
Inside the crate, the fusion generator and its four modules awaited instructions from the team of researchers
that Dorn had already assembled back at his private engineering complex in Cape Town. He ran his hand along
the ropes for the third time, tugged at the knots. The
device inside the crate was the greatest treasure ever
found by mankind—the most priceless machine in the
world. One that would send his corporations light-years

ahead of all others in gene therapy, fusion generation, engineering. His company would patent the world's first fusion reactor. One that performed a variety of functions. The possibilities coerced a smile.

Baines appeared from out of the long shadows of the Acapana Pyramid. "The charges are set." He looked at his watch. "Twenty-five minutes now. They'll detonate, underwater or not."

"Each device responded?" Dorn had faith in the quality of the remote arming system, which he had sold quite profitably in the Middle East.

"All six," Baines said. "Trust me. When those charges go they'll pancake all three levels. No one will be excavating anything unusual anytime soon."

"What about the chopper?"

"It's still down," Baines said. "Our men in Brazil say the repairs will take at least a day."

"You tell them that's not fast enough—I want to be in Pôrto Alegre by nightfall."

"Right," Baines answered.

"Ride up here with Anthony. I don't want anyone else near the device. Understand?"

Baines slung his M-5 automatic into the cab of the truck. "Safer than the crown jewels of England."

"Good. Because that bloody machine is more valuable," Dorn said. "A lot more valuable."

# DETONATION

Water cascaded across the floor of the great hall. The first level had started to fill.

"We don't have an hour," Samantha said. Long tendrils of water had already entered the great hall from the anteroom.

"Not even half an hour," Ricardo said. "The devices are armed."

"What?" Jack left Bongane propped against a wooden crate and joined Ricardo next to a satchel of explosives wrapped around a column. The LED display, which once read 000:00, now ticked down from 024:52.

"Can we disarm it?" Jack asked.

A groan rasped from Bongane's throat. He managed to shake his head. "You touch . . . goes off. . . ."

"Could be," Ricardo said. "And I'm no demolitions expert."

Samantha splashed over to the three men. Already a half inch of water covered the floor. "I hope you're right about this exit."

"C'mon," Jack said, struggling to hoist Bongane to his feet.

The Zulu shook his head. "I slow . . ."

"You're coming. We're getting out of here."

Bongane sat motionless. His head bobbed forward.

The thin man weighed much more than Jack expected, but he managed to shuffle down the corridor with Bongane slung across his back. A viscous liquid crawled

down Jack's shoulder. Bongane was bleeding badly from
his stomach. Jack was about to admit he didn't know
how much longer he could carry the man when Ricardo
shouted that he had come to the end of the passage.

Ricardo's watch had been a godsend. Not only had
Jack used its calculator to correct for the effects of precession—its compass had provided accurate headings for a
passage aligned to 22.1 degrees WNW. At the end of the
corridor, Ricardo helped Jack rest Bongane against the
wall. The Zulu had lapsed into unconsciousness.

"He needs help soon," Ricardo said.

Jack picked up the crowbar they had lifted from the
scattered supplies in the great hall and slammed it into
the wall. Vibrations jolted his hands, numbing his cold,
wet body.

"It's stone!" Jack said.

According to his calculations, the dead end was in
precise astrological alignment with the autumnal equinox. Jack felt convinced the wall would give—just as
the walls to the other secret passages had. The exit *had*
to be here, he thought.

"Try again," Samantha said.

The crowbar's two steel teeth tore through the thin
layer of plaster and ricocheted off the stone beneath.

"It looks solid," Jack said, dismayed, as water began
backing up against the dead end where they stood.

"Again!" Samantha yelled.

Jack swung the crowbar in desperation, this time high
above his head. The teeth sunk deep into plaster almost
three feet above Jack's shoulders. Jack wiggled the
crowbar free. Plaster cascaded onto the floor.

"That's it!" Samantha yelled.

Jack swung again, this time punching a fist-size hole
through the wall.

Ricardo helped Jack jiggle the crowbar loose. More
plaster fell into the three inches of water that now
flooded the chamber. Jack reached for the hollow. He
felt a slight breeze through the opening.

The concealed passageway started some eight feet off the ground, as if the exit had been purposely built for emergencies only. Jack tore at the plaster, finding the opening was more like a window than a door.

"Okay, let's go," he finally said.

Ricardo and Jack formed a makeshift stepladder by interlocking their hands and hoisted Samantha through the opening. Using her flashlight, Samantha saw that flat floor stones made up another cramped chamber. At the back wall, a narrow opening housed a tight, stone staircase that trailed away into the black.

"Stairs!" she yelled.

"C'mon, Bongane! You gotta help me!"

Ricardo got on the other side and reached beneath Bongane's armpits. They lifted him toward the opening, but his arms hung limply at his side. Samantha reached down and tried to hook the man's collar. Bongane felt too heavy; Jack was losing his grasp.

"Let's try from farther underneath," he cried. The water had reached Jack's shin.

Near complete exhaustion, Jack began to raise the man again, this time from Bongane's belt, when Ricardo said, "He's gone, Jack."

Jack propped Bongane against the stone wall. He took the Zulu's hands out of the pooling water and placed them across the man's lap. Then he undid the leather necklace from around Bongane's neck and slipped it in his pocket. He would try to notify his family. He ran his fingers over Bongane's lids, pulling them down over expressionless eyes.

Jack took the stairs two at a time, but still the ascent up the stepped passageway seemed endless. They'd been climbing for six minutes. Near exhaustion, Jack had to believe they'd be near the surface by now.

Samantha called out, "I see something up ahead."

Jack raised his flashlight beam from the stairs immediately in front of him and trained it into the blackness.

The glow illuminated a buckled wall above. He took a few more stairs. The object in front of them wasn't a wall.

Jack's flashlight revealed the roots of a huge tree gripping the corridor. The thick runners blocked the entire passage like a complex net. The ceiling of the corridor had been broken into fist-size mounds of rubble by the roots. Red dirt covered the stairway.

"It's jammed solid," Samantha yelled.

"We have to be close to the surface," Jack said. "We're seeing root systems."

"And the red soil," Ricardo said. "Clay. Just like the first couple of strata."

Jack clawed at the obstruction with the crowbar. Dirt rained down on him, covering his head and shoulders. He stopped, out of breath. A slight draft caressed his face.

"Do you feel a breeze?"

"It's coming from above us," Ricardo said.

"We'll never be able to hack through that tree in time," Samantha said.

Jack sifted through the clumps of soil he'd dislodged. It was moist and peppered with fungus. Mixed throughout the viscous mess he made out small white shapes. He picked up a translucent form between his thumb and forefinger.

"What's that?" Samantha asked.

Jack turned, holding a transparent insect nearly an inch in length. "Termites."

Samantha recoiled. "Why are we playing with bugs?" she yelled. She looked at her watch. "We've got less than five minutes before the charges detonate."

Jack inspected the insect. It was of a large South American variety. He scanned the soil again. This time, he retrieved a living pupae that squirmed in his palm like an oversize maggot.

"The tree's hollow," Jack said.

Samantha's eyes remained locked on the repulsive

worm. Jack saw the blood drain from her face. "Wait a second," she said. "What exactly are you thinking?"

Completely underwater, the protected case of the LED display reached 00:001 before the circuit that ran the timer tripped another circuit, which allowed the electric charge to travel to the blasting caps. The current pulsed into the charges—igniting 250 pounds of plastique explosive on the third level. Molecules of plastique set off larger groups of molecules, which set off even larger groups with the force of ten thousand sticks of TNT. The blast sheared the support columns in two and took down the back wall. Because the level had flooded, the intensity of the shock waves carried much farther and with better results. The salvage hall, the laboratory, the sealed rooms, all underwater, fell like stone dominoes.

Had anyone been standing on the second level, the stone floor beneath their feet would have launched them into the ceiling ten feet above. Consciousness would have ended there—in a potpourri of cartilage and hemoglobin. But had one's spirit remained in the physical realm just a fraction of a second longer, that same essence might have perceived the plastique in the back corner explode, twisting the entire frenzied mess. The confused anima would have witnessed such chaos and fury in the collapsing walls, the roiling water, the invisible demons called shock waves, that hell might have seemed an appealing destination.

In the great hall, two-hundred more pounds of C-4 rested snugly around crucial stone supports. The jumpy molecules of explosive felt the shock waves hit the large room. Barely able to contain themselves, they waited two hundredths of a second longer before they too saw God.

Samantha fought the overwhelming urge to scream.

Though something primal begged her to open her mouth and shriek, she couldn't, else the mass of insects covering her face would find their way down her throat. Her right hand pinched her nostrils shut. Her left pulled herself through the hollowed trunk of the dead tree. She navigated by touch, keeping Jack's boots within an arm's length in front of her. Termites crawled across her closed eyelids. The sharp feet of thousands of insects pricked at her skin on their journey down her shirt. The army collected in the valley between her breasts.

She was going to die.

They were crawling inside her ears. *Oh, God. Oh, God.*

Samantha's body ached for the comfort of unconsciousness. But the intermittent burns from soldier termites kept her from slipping into that tranquil netherworld. Using mandibles as big as their bodies the soldiers clamped into her skin. Samantha literally floated—in a biomass of termites so heavy it felt like thick clam chowder. She felt a tingling along her calves, and realized the swarm had found its way beneath her pants. A few insects crawled up her thighs.

She had to scream.

*No! Keep moving. Don't give up. Stay in control.*

Her hand poked blindly for Jack's leg but couldn't find it. He'd moved too far ahead. Panic swelled inside her. She'd have to open her eyes. She couldn't make it. This had to end. *Please God make it end.*

Paralyzed, Samantha stopped, then sensed a palm on her buttocks—Ricardo, pushing his way up behind her. A chill struck her, and she realized the source of the sensation had been cool, dry air—not fright.

A strong hand grasped her arm, whisking away her equilibrium. In the next instant she was on level ground.

Her hands clawed at her face, brushing at anything that moved. Samantha blinked in the sun; she could just make out Jack's blurred form. Then she looked down and saw a skirt of living termites still squirming across her legs. She screamed and rolled over the ground. The cracking of their juicy bodies rang for her like Christmas bells. Her body shuddered in waves of fear and nausea and relief.

A few seconds later Ricardo fell onto the earth behind her, spitting pale bugs from his mouth. She noticed Jack crawling to her when her body jerked and her ears popped from a painful explosion.

Jack fell to the ground. Behind him a howl of wind blew a wave of insects and soil out of the hollowed tree. The earth trembled. She watched small rings of dust ripple over the ground in expanding circles heading off toward the looming Andes.

Large cracks formed in a hundred-yard circle behind them as the terrain settled in on itself. As termites and soil rained on the three, Samantha inhaled deep breaths of air.

Just beyond lay the desolate remains of the camp. Dorn had disappeared.

# WAR ROOM

Nerves inside the agency were wound tighter than strung piano wire. The tenseness brought on by war or crisis permeated every conference room, computer cubicle, even the granite-walled bathrooms. Resources and manpower at the DO's disposal had been siphoned from assignments with lower priority. The War Room buzzed with activity.

Wright pulled up a leather chair beneath the overhead displays. Using his arms for support he slowly lowered

himself into the soft, full seat. McFadden could see the
director's frustration manifested in small creases along
his forehead. "John," Wright finally said. "This is a
doozy."

"Our agents are still following Dorn," McFadden said.
"They have the convoy in visual contact."

"But no sign of the scientists?" Wright asked.

"No, sir. The field agents are confident he killed all
three."

McFadden was ready to suggest the few intervention
options devised to secure the mysterious device when a
bespectacled agent ran into the room. McFadden recognized him as Kirby, one of the satellite analysts.

"New readings from the site just came in, sir," Kirby
said.

Wright's voice was hoarse. "Go ahead, son."

"Eight minutes ago, our sensors aboard the KH-14
picked up vibrations from a subterranean explosion."

Wright winced and pushed himself out of his chair.
"An explosion?"

"Yes, sir." Kirby leafed through a manila file. "We've
got corroborating evidence from seismic ground sensors
in the region."

"It couldn't have been an earthquake?"

Kirby shook his head. "Too brief for a natural seismic
event. No aftershocks."

Beads of sweat formed on the director's upper lip.
"But nothing on the magnitude of a tactical weapons
test?"

"No, sir. Nothing that strong. Maybe conventional explosives. We may see something when the newest satellite photos are downloaded and processed."

"I want those pictures while they're still wet," Wright
commanded.

Kirby pushed his glasses up his thin nose and scurried
out of the room.

"Shit." Wright placed both hands on the table, letting
his weight fall on his locked arms. "Don't go anywhere,

John," he sighed. "I have to make a phone call."

The director walked to a back office and closed the door behind him.

McFadden's pulse quickened. The phone call Wright made would be to the president himself. McFadden imagined the conversation—one that technically would never have occurred. The CIA and its DO were the president's secret warriors—the loyal branch that would serve as a clandestine and potent force if need be. The shield of plausible denial would be maintained, but McFadden knew the president himself would now be giving the orders. There'd be no paperwork—no way to prove the orders.

After several minutes, Wright emerged with a grave expression on his face. McFadden knew instantly that surveillance time was over.

"John, we've got some work to do," Wright said. "It's a go."

The president had spoken. McFadden shuddered. This was about to get personal.

# AFTERMATH

Samantha trembled beside Jack. She had stripped to rid herself of the insects before putting her khakis back on, but Jack knew the chill she felt resulted from more than revulsion.

"The symbol for Armageddon?" Samantha said. Jack had just told her about the message on the stone wall behind the fusion generator.

"The glyph looks like a fusion reaction," Ricardo said.

"You think that fourth module's some kind of a weapon?"

"Though they were peace loving, history said the Shining Ones possessed a deadly device that could destroy the world as we know it," Jack said. "We already possess simple fusion devices, which could do a tidy job."

"The hydrogen bomb," Samantha agreed.

Ricardo said, "Truth is we aren't sure what the fourth module's function is. We only know what it *could* do."

"But something that could cause a *global* catastrophe?" Samantha asked.

"Maybe the device triggered the catastrophe—maybe it was earth crustal displacement—that wiped out Tiahuanaco and other ancient civilizations," Jack said. "In some ancient texts, the emphasis was that the Shining Ones had been associated with a terrible catastrophe that overwhelmed the earth and destroyed the greater part of humanity." Samantha's expression was distant, always a sign of concern, Jack remembered. He continued. "All the information points to something—a weapon—a physical phenomenon—that the extraterrestrials possessed that could wipe out the world."

"The technology of the device is thousands of years more advanced than ours," Ricardo said. "And we already possess weapons of mass destruction. In the sixties—before the ban on atmospheric explosions—the Soviet Union tested a hydrogen weapon the equivalent of a hundred million tons of TNT."

"We know what the equivalent of twenty thousand tons will do to a city," Jack said, referring to the crude fission bombs dropped on Hiroshima and Nagasaki. "What about a hundred *million* tons?"

"That was a hydrogen weapon of the sixties," Ricardo said. "Trust me. We've devised even more effective ways of killing people with a single device over the last thirty years."

Jack stared out toward the horizon. "I'd hate to think what the extraterrestrial technology is capable of."

"Do you remember your Bible?" Ricardo asked.

Jack motioned for him to go on.

"You told me that the Kharsag Epic and other ancient references call the land where these Shining Ones settled Eden, right?"

"Yes."

"Well, in Genesis, the Tree of Knowledge existed deep inside Eden. The tree of the knowledge of both good and evil," Ricardo said. "God instructs that the world he created be open to man's will. But he said, 'You must not eat from the tree of the knowledge of good and evil, for when you eat of it you will surely die.' "

"Genesis two," Samantha recollected.

Ricardo paused. "I think the Tree of Knowledge was analogous to the technology of the fusion device. Maybe it was a metaphor about the power to use that knowledge—technology—for both good or evil."

A gust of wind blew dust across the altiplano.

"Someone might have been trying to protect us," Jack said. "From ourselves."

Samantha paced among the charred campfire circles. "Dorn will never give up the device. He'll try to de-engineer it himself. We have to stop him now—before he gets out of Bolivia."

"Where would he would be heading?" Ricardo asked.

"He has a high-tech lab outside Cape Town. He wouldn't dare bring it to the States." Hate beamed from Samantha's eyes. "I really don't know what the creep will do."

"Could we contact the Bolivian government or the American Embassy?" Ricardo asked.

"Not enough time," Jack said. "Besides the Bolivians are already taking bribes from Dorn. And even if the U.S. government believed us, the second they realized

what they had, the device would get buried in some secret federal lab."

"We could track him down in South Africa," Ricardo
offered.

Samantha shook her head. "He'd have already hidden
the device, the fossil, everything. Besides, if he found
out we were still alive . . ."

"If he leaves Bolivia, everything's lost." Jack began
to follow the tire tracks in the ground. Samantha and
Ricardo joined him on the downslope.

"How will we catch him?" Samantha asked. "And
what could we do if we did? He's got armed mercenaries."

"And almost an hour on us," Ricardo said. "Besides.
We've got no transportation."

"We still have four things going for us," Jack said,
picking up the pace. "Three strong minds," he said, then
gestured toward the faint outline of Lake Titicaca. "And
the fact that he still has to get across that."

# LAKE

Veronica's men waited patiently. Their numbers had
doubled with the arrival of Checa's reinforcements. Her
pulse quickened as she listened to her uncle. A DEA
agent on Checa's payroll had informed him that a joint
CIA/DEA operation was mobilizing to apprehend a
group of Americans.

"Are you sure it's the scientists?"

"Our informant at the DEA mentioned the name Benjamin Dorn. Whatever they found at Tiahuanaco is invaluable," he said. "We can wait no longer."

Veronica felt sick at the thought of more violence. She couldn't respond.

"How far are you from Tiquine?"

"Where is it?" Miller asked.

"It's on the other side of the lake—where the ferry lands. Population forty-five. Mostly Indian fishermen. The DEA guys want to hit 'em there," Pierce said, scanning the waters of Lake Titicaca.

"Where's the boat?"

"ETA in five minutes," Pierce said.

Miller began off-loading equipment from the Jeep.

A high-speed boat was on its way to ferry them across the lake. The craft, confiscated from the drug cartels, had once been used to out-pace local police. The floating bullet would get them to Tiquine with time to spare. The agent bringing the speedboat would be left behind to monitor Dorn's activity until the trucks boarded the ferry. Both agencies had confirmed that Dorn had booked the ship for the crossing.

Pierce and Lieutenant Drew of the DEA agreed to take the convoy into custody at the dock in Tiquine—the only logical place that the drug enforcement agents could get to in time. It made sense as a site for an ambush. The officers could use the cover of the local buildings to go unnoticed until interdiction. When Dorn's men finally arrived in Tiquine, all of their trucks would be bottled up on the ship with no place to go. Pierce had warned Drew to be prepared for a fight. Dorn's men were heavily armed with automatic weapons.

"You ready for this?" Miller asked.

"Better believe it." Pierce sensed the adrenaline rise in his body. He felt much younger than his fifty-two years. He was about to lead a multiagency operation that would seize a nuclear weapon before it got sold on the black market. If word of his actions ever reached the

States, he would be an instant hero. But word wouldn't. The Bolivian government and press would be told of the successful DEA raid that confiscated hundreds of pounds of cocaine—god knows the DEA had enough of the shit lying around in evidence warehouses. The price of failure could mean death. The possible rewards of success? The quiet, unheralded confidence of a job well done.

Suddenly, it didn't sound like a great deal.

He pulled his Kevlar vest from off the floor mat of the truck and fastened the straps over his shoulder. As he put his windbreaker over the armored suit, he recalled the sentiments of the DO: *Get the crate into custody at all costs. Don't worry if things get messy.*

If Pierce's prior experience with the DEA was any indicator, he knew things would.

The three scientists walked three miles from Tiahuanaco before hitching a ride with a local Indian harvesting potatoes on the ancient agricultural plots. His Chevy pickup was shared by eight families—the inhabitants of an entire hamlet by the shore of the lake. Ricardo had persuaded the old man to accept the wet bills he pulled out of his jacket—enough pocket change to feed his family for a week. The old man pointed the scientists to the approximate location of the ferry dock, which lay a mile down the steep hills to the north, before driving away.

They proceeded slowly. The slope was wet, the foliage thicker than that of the mostly barren highlands. Though lower in altitude the air was still thin, and the group lacked any oxygen. After three quarters of an hour of fighting underbrush, Jack finally spotted the dock just a quarter mile to their left, some two hundred yards of elevation below them.

Now the same rust bucket Jack had cursed three days ago became their ally. The dilapidated ferry had apparently held up Dorn's transit from the highlands. From

their ridge the scientists could make out the four trucks
waiting on the lakeshore.

The ferry chugged toward the small dock, spitting
black smoke from two pipes above the pilothouse. Its
bow parted the water into an angry foam.

One by one below them, the trucks rumbled to life.

"We have to get the device now," Jack said.

"There are seven men with Dorn. Most of them are
armed," Samantha said.

Jack knew what they lacked in firepower would have
to be made up with brainpower. "The device is in the
lead truck," he said. "Looks like there are two men in
the cab. None in the bed with the crate." A tarpaulin
covered something large in the truck bed behind the
crate, but Jack could see no other mercenaries. "If we
managed to take out the drivers and commandeer the
truck, we'd have a fighting chance of getting away."

Jack looked down the hill they would have to descend
to reach the dock. A few shrubs and trees would help
conceal them on the way down, but they would have to
traverse twenty yards of open road at the bottom. Jack
looked back to the lakeshore. Dorn spoke with two of
his men at the end of the dock, far from the trucks.

"What we need is a diversion," Jack said.

"Or an act of God," Ricardo added.

Samantha knelt between the two men. "I wouldn't
mind both."

"Well, we better think of something," Jack said.

The ferry was just a hundred yards from the dock.

Jack swung over the ridge and began to half-walk,
half-slide his way down the hillside. Ricardo made the
sign of the cross, then followed Samantha down the
same path.

About a hundred feet above the trucks, Jack paused
behind a clump of bushes. A few yards to his left, a
long-fallen tree trunk rested against a rocky outcropping.

A drone came from nearby. It seemed to emanate, in
fact, from inside the rotten log.

Jack whispered that he had a plan that just might work.

"I can't wait to hear this," Samantha said softly. "How are you proposing to take out a highly trained, heavily armed group of mercenaries?"

Jack smiled. "By enlisting some of our own."

Samantha followed Jack toward the tree trunk, where industrious bees congregated on a large knothole that opened to the hollow interior. The hum grew louder as they neared the hive. Samantha swatted at a few inquisitive bees that darted in the air around her.

"Don't do that," Jack whispered. "If just one stings it will alert the entire hive."

"What the hell are you thinking?" She grabbed Jack's arm. "Your love affair with insects has gone too far. These are bees. And bees sting."

"These aren't just any bees," Jack said. "They're Africanized." Samantha slid back away from him as he gestured toward the flying sentries. "Which is why we have to stay calm."

Samantha froze. She had heard the stories of hostile hives that had killed hundreds of people across Latin America. The insects had spread over the entire Latin continent after 1956, when an experimental breed escaped into the wild. In recent years, swarms had entered the southwestern United States.

"You see how hostile they are. Normal bees wouldn't even pay attention to you. Africanized bees can apparently smell fear and react to it by attacking."

"Your friend has lost his mind," Samantha told Ricardo, who stopped beside her.

"He's a genius," Ricardo said. He crouched next to Jack. "It just might work. The lead truck is right beneath us."

"If we can free this thing," Jack said. He eyed the raised ledge that held the log in place. "How are those old legs of yours?"

Ricardo grabbed his thighs. "These soccer legends? Stronger than steel. Leading under-sixteen scorer in Chihuahua state history. They'll hold up."

"Good," Jack said. " 'Cause if we don't manage to get the log over this ledge in the first few seconds thousands of angry tenants will be calling on us."

The ferry had nearly reached the dock.

Blood raced through Jack's body. "It's now or never."

Ricardo nodded. "I'm ready."

"Samantha?" Jack asked.

She shook her head. "There's no way . . ."

There was no time to argue. Jack sat down slowly, careful not to make any quick movements. He slid himself toward the log, lying on his back, until his boots rested on it, knees bent to his chest. Ricardo assumed the same position next to him, muttering something that sounded like "*loco gringo*."

"On three," Jack said. Ricardo braced his palms on his knees. Behind them, shielded by brush, Samantha looked on.

"One . . . two . . . three—"

Jack kicked. At first the log felt cemented to the hill, but just as bees began to filter out, it began to move. Jack and Ricardo battled gravity, edging the log up the outcropping. Clouds of bees emerged from the trunk. Jack's legs shook. Pain burned through his thighs.

Then the log stopped.

"Oh . . . shit—" Ricardo managed.

A venomous sentry found the side of Jack's neck and stabbed a stinger into the soft flesh. In the next instant Jack's neck was stung again. Then once on his forearm. The assault pheromone had been released. The hive started to attack. Jack's vision blurred. He was lightheaded from the oxygen deficit. His legs threatened to give out and drop the log back onto Ricardo and him.

Then, in the haze of his peripheral vision, he saw Samantha next to him. She threw her shoulder at the bottom of the log—and it began to move again. With a last heave, they wrenched the log free and watched it disappear over the precipice.

# REUNION

The log bounced down the hill, scattering the few birds that had nested in the thick bushes below the escarpment. The men by the vehicles noticed the commotion too late, turning just as the dead tree jumped another embankment, bounced twice on the dirt road, and slammed into the side of the lead truck. In an explosion of wood chips, the tree snapped in half. Inside the cab, Baines and Anthony leaned toward the driver-side window, startled by the impact. In the milliseconds following, Baines tried to process what had happened. The spilled coffee in his lap; the dust; no gunfire; it must have been a landslide, he told himself. Baines asked a startled Anthony if he was all right before noticing the black cloud around the truck.

The collision must have ignited the fuel tanks, he thought. He kicked open his door.

Dorn felt something was wrong a few seconds before Baines yelled, "Landslide!" That sixth sense of his. Dorn walked toward the truck, then began to run as a black cloud enveloped the lead vehicle.

His fusion generator couldn't be allowed to burn.

Dorn saw Baines tumble out of the passenger door and realized the black cloud wasn't smoke. The billows were a moving mass. He heard droning as a finger from the cloud shot toward him.

Jack and Ricardo stumbled down the steep embankment to a natural gully by the side of the road. Jack thought he could make out the flailing arms of the driver in the cab of the first truck.

The truck jolted into gear.

Jack jumped onto the muddy road just before it passed. Hidden by the thousands of bees covering most of his face and shoulders, Anthony could only be identified by his reddish hair. The truck rumbled on. The Englishman's screams made Jack's blood curdle. Ten yards down the road, Anthony lost control of the truck, which veered to the left and plowed into the steep hill.

Jack ran to the truck.

As he neared the vehicle, the passenger side door flung open. A moment later Anthony fell out of the cab amid a living haze. His wail pierced the late afternoon sky. The Englishman struggled to his feet, pursued by a swarm of Africanized drones. He wobbled, stumbled down the road, his body a pulp of blood and stingers. Jack got one last glance at the deformed, swollen face before the man fell headfirst into the mud.

Jack pulled his jacket over his head.

The bees had begun another attack, this time their aggression directed at the two scientists. The burn of venom ignited the uncovered portions of Jack's body. He reached the open truck door and clawed at the glove box, pulling out a bundle of maps that he quickly lit with his lighter. As Ricardo neared the truck, the papers caught fire. Jack waved the torch rapidly, getting the blaze under control. The maps began smoldering. He spread the smoke through the cab.

"Hurry!" Jack said through his jacket. "Get in!"

Coughing in the thick smoke, but thankful most of the

stragglers had evacuated, the two men shut the doors.
Even Africanized bees hated smoke. Jack threw the engine in reverse. The wheels spun wildly, clawing
through the mud that coated the ditch. The tires caught,
pulling the truck back onto the road. In the rearview
mirror, Jack saw that Dorn and most of the men had
taken refuge in the lake. One man remained cocooned
in a truck cab. Jack watched as it swerved out of the
parked column, picked up an agitated Baines, and
headed toward them.

Samantha staggered through the thick undergrowth at
the bottom of the hill.

The lead truck sped toward her, smoke coming from
both windows. Already stung, she dodged more attacks
as Jack slowed the vehicle. Samantha leaped for the side
rail and pulled herself into the bed of the truck without
its stopping. She felt the engine accelerate. Then she
noticed a Jeep, which quickly closed on them.

A flash erupted an instant before Jack heard the impact
on the steel of their rear bumper.

He heard Samantha yell, "They've opened fire!"

Jack depressed the accelerator. The engine screamed.

"They've got automatic weapons," Ricardo said, looking in the right-hand mirror. The mirror exploded, showering him with glass. *"Mierda!"* Ricardo yelled. "I sure
hope we have a plan B!"

"I can't lose them in this truck," Jack said. "It's not
fast enough."

The truck swerved dangerously around a curve in the
road. The muddy causeway led through a thicket of
trees. They would be entering the intermountain *yungas*
soon, which would make the roads even more treacherous.

The Jeep got closer.

                    *        *        *

Samantha bounced around the bed of the truck. Bursts of 9mm tracers blew wood chips off the side rails. Some of them ricocheted off the steel doors. Baines fired whenever he got a clear shot, Samantha seeking refuge behind the large, tarp-covered object. She noticed the ammo box shortly thereafter.

*Ammo box?*

Samantha found the tarp tie downs and loosened them. Wind caught the tarp, which blew off the back of the truck and revealed an imposing black shape that made her shudder.

Jack turned around in the cab. "Look! There it is."

"There what is?" Ricardo had dropped to all fours on the floorboards.

"Our plan B."

The long black barrel of the mounted machine gun hovered at eye level before Samantha.

The weapon could mean their salvation—if Samantha could: (1) quickly get over her fear of firearms, and (2) figure out how to work the damned thing. The ammunition belt flowing from the mechanized beast held cartridges longer than her fingers. It had to be a fifty-caliber.

She heard Jack call her into action. He yelled something about the gun being self-feeding. *Self-feeding?* She didn't want to be around any weapon that fed itself. Behind them, Baines unleashed another fusillade.

Rounds bounced off the steel around Samantha, the pings of impact ringing in her ears.

She knew Baines was trying to take *her* out now. This encouraged her to find the firing pin safety, which she disengaged.

For a person afraid of guns, this was something akin to flood therapy.

Afterward, Samantha retained only fragmented images: the shaking of the gun as it spit heavy shells; the vibrations that jolted through her body as if she were holding an electric wire; the cries of birds and monkeys as the gun rained lead on the wooded thicket—just after Samantha fell on her ass.

Jack tried avoiding the deep ruts, but a recent rain gave the obstacle course an unfair advantage. Crossing a small bridge that spanned a ravine, Jack hit a buckle in the road that nearly tossed Ricardo through the passenger-side window. The impact toppled Samantha in the back of the truck.

But she didn't let go of the trigger.

Jack watched in amazement as the gun cut trees in half. Sitting, Samantha continued to hold the trigger, and the thicket exploded behind them. Branches tumbled. Birds that survived the assault fled into the sky.

Jack slowed the truck as they approached the other end of the bridge.

Samantha got to her feet and steadied herself. Heat poured off the gun. The smell of cordite hung in the slipstream of the truck bed. She lowered the barrel of the weapon once more. Behind the truck, the Jeep slid to a halt. Though squinting in fright, she saw Baines and the other man leap off the bridge—just as she squeezed the trigger again.

Round after round slammed into the Jeep. Its fuel tanks erupted. Samantha released the gun only after a fireball rose in a black-bordered cloud and dissipated up the canyon.

Jack stopped the truck and Samantha straggled out of the back. She opened the passenger door and slid in beside a bewildered Ricardo.

The only noise was the crackling of flames as the Jeep continued to burn atop the wooden bridge, that was now twisted, its shorings having been damaged in the blast.

"Unreal . . ." Jack mumbled.

He put the truck back in gear and resumed their descent on the winding road.

Samantha could only stare blankly out the window.

# DEA

Pierce, Miller, and Lieutenant Drew, their counterpart from the DEA, had finished picking sites for the two Drug Enforcement Agency snipers atop a small mud building that directly faced the ferry dock. Pierce was in the midst of placing the other dozen DEA agents at key areas along the road that ran out of town from the dock when his field phone squawked. He answered it.

"What?" Pierce shouted.

His tone caused Lieutenant Drew to stop talking to one of his men and try to pick up on the conversation. Pierce shook his head in disbelief. Barely audible from the handset of the field scrambler, the agent who'd brought them the speedboat and monitored Dorn's convoy, inflected wildly. Pierce's face became a shade darker than the near-crimson sky that hung above the lake.

"What happened?" Miller asked impatiently.

Pierce waved him off. "Maintain surveillance on the main body," Pierce said into the handset. "Don't let Dorn out of your sight. We'll be there as soon as possible."

Pierce hung up the scrambler. "We have problems," he said.

From an earthen home just off the main road, Veronica watched the confusion outside through a dusty window. The DEA agents became agitated, but there was still no sign of Dorn. The Americans abandoned their positions. She pushed the cloth curtain to the side. The two snipers stationed on the roof of the next building began breaking down their scopes. The agents were preparing to leave. Stupid *gringos*. Veronica turned and lifted the door to the cellar. A dozen of her heavily armed men peered up at her. They would do whatever she said. She had that power.

"It's off."

Her men shifted nervously. She heard one sigh. Checa and her sick uncle had been willing to waste all their lives—pulling strings from the safety of their powerful positions. She was ordered to ambush the DEA during the confusion of the arrest and take possession of the expedition's find. Veronica would've made sure Dorn died in the process—a *proper* payment for her murdered conscript and friend. But she feared for the safety of her men. And Jack.

Veronica grabbed a walkie-talkie from her waist. "The ambush is off," she told the other group of men at the inn. "Keep hidden."

She knew the bloodshed had only been postponed. Checa would be notified of the DEA's new destination and plan. For now, though, the scientists had avoided this trap. Veronica closed her eyes and thanked God—who had finally listened.

# BREAKDOWN

Ricardo's boots protruded from beneath the front of the truck. Under the engine block, his flashlight cast a warm glow that the truck's grille dissected into scores of thin beams. He'd been hard at work for the last forty minutes, cursing. Mechanics and doctors—nothing frustrated them more than a lack of proper tools.

Jack had managed to pull into the small clearing just off the main road seconds before the truck died. Ricardo said they'd been lucky—two rounds had pierced the fuel filter and an injector. A half-inch either way would have ignited both gas tanks. Ricardo hoped to bypass the filter and repair the clogged fuel system, which was now littered with shell fragments and debris from their hourlong escape from the ferry site. A five-gallon container of reserve fuel would be all the gas they had when—and if—Ricardo could get the truck started again.

No doubt hindered by the damage done to the bridge in the wake of the Jeep's explosion, Dorn's men showed no signs of pursuit. Jack felt confident that an effective search couldn't be mounted for at least another hour or two—and in the cover of the forested regions, the South African might never find the small side road they'd taken. Dorn had packed the expedition laptops in the lead truck—obviously hoping to contain (and possibly use) all of Jack's data. Jack's plan now was to get to the nearest phone line. The scientists would contact Samantha's department chairman at Princeton. They would send all the research data to him. While they were at it, Jack thought they would copy the data to every research university on the Web. The more public we make this, Jack had said, the less chance of a cover-up. "And the greatest chance we'll all remain alive," Ricardo added. Everyone agreed. But until Ricardo got the truck fixed there was nothing to do but wait.

From a nearby ridge, howler monkeys cried at the night. In the still, humid darkness the primates sounded as if they were undergoing some bizarre jungle torture. Jack felt thankful for the cover. They'd only just entered the intermountain forested region before the truck died. Jack lay next to Samantha on a mat of large ferns, breathing the oxygen-rich air his body craved. A small stream meandered nearby. In the more temperate climate of the *yungas*, there was no need for their jackets, which now served as pillows tucked behind their necks. The stars punched holes in the black canvas of Bolivian night. In the absence of pollution or lights, they looked close enough to touch.

"It frightens me," Samantha said, staring into space.

"What does?"

"All of this."

The flickering glow from the nearby lantern painted a kaleidoscope of shadow and color on her face. In the distance, just down the hill, Ricardo's curses echoed up to them.

"All of this. The fossil . . . the wreckage . . . the fusion device."

"The link?"

Samantha sighed. "The missing link." Her words came slowly, deliberately. "Knowing the answers is worse than the ignorance." She turned to him. "Do you know what I mean? I felt more at ease when I *didn't* have all the answers."

"Truth can be terrifying."

"It's worse than that. It's like everything you've grown up believing was a lie. Everything you've come to know as fact turns out to be wild conjecture. Conjecture that made so much sense before. I feel so stupid. So wrong."

Jack said nothing.

She bit her bottom lip. "What is this going to do to the world of science? Religion? Most scientists are die-hard evolutionists."

"Darwin proposed a theory," Jack said, "parts of which may still be valid. I think we've just proven that there's more to it. Much more. The establishment's accepted Darwinism as fact—not theory. But then, that's always been the problem with science. Once a view becomes entrenched, people stop questioning it. They start to see things with certitude. That's when real science dies—when people become confident enough, maybe lazy enough, to stop asking whether there's another way to see the universe."

"But evolution makes perfect sense."

"Because we've convinced ourselves to stop looking for other explanations. Evolution is a fantastic idea. But it's not *the* answer. What we found down there didn't refute every Darwinian principle—just most of them."

She sighed. "That's comforting."

"The world relies on people like us to muck up the waters," Jack said. "To create the ripples that will eventually spawn new ideas—maybe lead us closer to truth. But we've lost a valuable tool."

"What's that?"

"Common sense."

Samantha played with a lock of her hair. "I just can't help thinking what this will do to the world. I mean what am I supposed to tell my family when I get home? What will I tell my dad—my children someday?"

They had talked about children before. *Their* children.

"You tell them everything," he said. "Which won't be too far from what the Bible has been telling us all along—that the universe was created by a great omniscient presence—one who obviously cared enough to create and nurture us."

"And what do we tell the Darwinists?"

Jack paused. "*That* could be a little stickier."

"Evolution is wonderful in its simplicity. I can see it at work," Samantha said. "The way families of animals seem to share some of the same characteristics. The one family tree that branched into so many different forms of life."

"The links that connect all the species you mean."

"Yeah."

"The links that Darwinists have relied on to explain how evolution works but still can't produce. Do you recall their infamous link between fish and amphibians?"

"Coelacanth?"

"Coelacanth," Jack said. "The fish had a long, flat body, and thick fins that protruded from its underbelly—they looked like the precursors to actual limbs. Scientists said the coelacanth became extinct seventy million years ago and put it in the neat evolutionary chart as a link between fish and amphibians. Geologists even used the fish as an index fossil—dating whole strata of earth where they found a coelacanth fossil as being at least seventy million years old.

"Now if that fish doesn't say something about the fallibility of Darwinism . . ."

Samantha remained silent because she knew, as well as Jack did, that coelacanth should never have been used to date strata at seventy million years or older. The extinct species should never have been used as a link between fish and amphibians. Because in 1938, off the coast of Madagascar, a group of fishermen caught a *living*, seventy-million-year-old index fossil.

"That's what's wrong with evolution. It's a failed attempt to organize everything in neat little charts. Life is not neat." Jack propped his head up on his palm. "Darwinists keep insisting the links will be found, that the fossil record isn't complete enough yet. But no one is producing any of these transitional species. And unless we can get samples of DNA there will be no way to prove them."

"Then why is the theory so widely accepted?"

Jack collected himself. "Remember when Thomas Kuhn proposed that scientific theories shouldn't be seen as dealing solely with pure objective facts?"

"Yeah—we need to interpret a theory within a wider context of scientific, social, and even political beliefs."

"Exactly. He called the larger ideological context a paradigm. The power of such a paradigm is so strong that some scientists will continue to believe in it even in the face of powerful contradictory evidence," Jack said.

Samantha agreed. "Leon Festinger called it cognitive

dissonance. But do you think the theory of evolution is still accepted because we just can't break free from the current paradigm?"

"I do. Evolutionistic thought permeates business—the survival of the fittest being at the heart of free market capitalism, politics, almost everything. When theories become entrenched and so interlocked with a broad worldview, it becomes hard to distinguish valid research from invalid research. Consequently it takes mountains of overwhelming new evidence before a new theory can take the place of the old one—"

"Kuhn's 'global paradigm shift,' " Samantha said.

"The same thing happened when Darwinism initially burst on the scene," Jack said. "When his theory was first introduced, most scientists shared an implicit belief that the colored races were genetically inferior to white European races. 'Evidence' supporting this view was generally quickly accepted because of the social climate of the time. Hell, most of Darwin's biggest supporters thought no rational person could believe that the Negro is the equal of the white man."

"I see what you're saying." Samantha looked enthralled. "Even Darwin himself based much of his evolutionary thought on the same racist, generally accepted beliefs of that era."

"Remember in his book, *The Descent of Man*? He wrote that the Negro races were more closely related to the apes than white people. He also thought that because of this the civilized races would soon exterminate and replace the Negro savages—by natural selection, I imagine," Jack said smiling. "Thankfully, cultural influences like the civil rights movement have helped chip away at that notion—but I can't help but think that on a subconscious level, Darwinism continues to subtly propagate racism."

"I hope our find will usher in a new paradigm."

"It will," Jack said. "But I think the shift would have happened eventually, even without the find, because the very foundations of evolution are absurd when you examine it rationally."

"How do you figure?"

"Look, we're told that sometime after the great explosion that formed the sun and the planets in our solar system, an incredible chance accident created the first living cell, even though statisticians estimate that the odds of that happening spontaneously are virtually impossible—even if the earth *is* billions of years old," Jack said. "But even so, explosions don't create order. They create disorder. Evolution asks us to believe that this great cosmic explosion not only formed the universe but also started making life from inorganic material, which then proceeded to get more complex. Remember the Second Law of Thermodynamics?"

"Over time, things always proceed from order to disorder," she said.

"Right." Jack grew excited. "It's an observable law of the universe. Evolution asks us to throw out that observable law and believe that over time things grow *more* ordered and complex."

Samantha watched Jack's eyes in silence.

"That's like believing that if the earth possessed every component part for an automobile—even laid out in the same field—those parts would begin to assemble themselves, and a few million years later we'd have a working Hyundai."

"A working Hyundai? That's an oxymoron."

Jack smiled. "Okay," he said. "But even if a finished—and working—Hyundai was left to its own devices, it wouldn't *evolve* into a Mercedes-Benz. If you let the law of thermodynamics work, that same car would become a heap of rust and completely degenerate over time."

"But a car's not a living thing that reproduces."

"And neither was the molecular soup in which life supposedly spontaneously combusted."

Jack rolled on his side, closer to Samantha, whose

eyes told him she agreed. "You can see the Second Law of Thermodynamics at work in every aspect of life. Our bodies degenerate over time. Our sun is slowly degenerating—burning itself out. Systems left on their own will *all* degenerate. It doesn't work the other way around. *Something* has to be behind evolutionary progress. It can't just be blind and random, as Darwinists say it is."

Samantha and Jack talked about life and the earth and they hypothesized and debated, just as they had when they were a couple. For a moment, next to the tepid stream that whispered over smooth rocks, Jack felt as if things had never gone sour between them. The intellectualizing had become beautiful, intimate. The discussion had blossomed into one of those fantastic conversations college kids claimed to have only on drugs.

"What about natural selection?" Samantha asked.

"That part of Darwin's theory I'll subscribe to—in part—even though it's misunderstood as a mechanism in evolution. Natural selection helps to sustain a species by assuring that its strongest members survive to breed again. But natural selection doesn't change one life form into another, it just preserves the best of one species."

Samantha's initial reluctance had turned into a curiosity to match Jack's. "What about random mutation as a contributing factor in evolution? Over thousands of generations, mutation could eventually cause a species to evolve, right?"

"It might," Jack said. "But don't you think there has to be more involved there too? Mutations are ninety-nine point nine percent harmful. Most are degenerative."

"But over time, millions of those little changes might build on one another until an animal becomes a new species."

"Ernst Mayr attempted to find that out at Harvard, remember? But what they discovered—which is nothing new to horticulturists or stock breeders—is that selecting traits and then attempting to breed changes in an organism over successive generations inevitably leads to something he called 'genetic homeostasis'—a natural barrier that inhibits further genetic change. In fact, subsequent generations often revert back to the original makeup of a species, sometimes after horrific results."

Samantha traced circles in the soil by the side of the great ferns.

"And why should time be a factor?" Jack asked. "Time is the savior that evolution's hung its hat on. Without millions and billions of years of time the theory wouldn't make any sense at all. And if time is the only explanation of how mutation works, how is it that some species haven't changed at all?" Jack pulled a leaf off a fern. "Ferns of 250 million years ago are the same as today. Mosquitoes are the same. Sharks are the same. Crocodiles haven't evolved. There are hundreds of species, including simple bacteria, that haven't changed at all."

"And I guess we can't be sure if we're even measuring these time periods accurately," Samantha said. "Truth is we're about as capable of realistically dating the age of the earth as a child building the Sears tower with an Erector set."

Jack agreed. No one would bet their life on any means of dating. He stared at the stars. "What we found is going to change everything."

Samantha looked into the sky. "Yeah. It will."

"Exactly what we'll learn I'm not sure," Jack said. "But I *do* think our universe was designed. The proof that these extraterrestrials aided in the emergence of our species suggests a design. A building is designed by an architect. Books require authors. Paintings have painters. Complex things demand a designer. None of us would ever expect the molecules that form computers to have been randomly assembled by chance into a PC. So why is it any easier to accept that the human brain—the most complex computer the world has ever known—is the result of chance. How can we possibly think this majestic organic processor came about randomly?"

"I don't know," Samantha said softly. "But I do love yours."

"What?"

"Your brain."

Jack hoped Samantha couldn't see him blush in the dim light. He caressed her arm, feeling a few bumps. He'd forgotten about the welts. Her arms had taken the brunt of the attack.

"They hurt like hell," she said.

Jack checked her scalp, pulling a few remaining stingers from above her hairline. "You know," he said gently, "some people swear by bee venom. MS patients, arthritics—some sting themselves on purpose hundreds of times a day."

"Yeah, well, I'm not a masochist."

"I think I know just the trick." He walked to the edge of the stream, collected some moist clay, and kneaded the mixture in his hands, softening it further. He motioned Samantha over and spread the reddish clay onto her arms, then he started on the back of her neck.

"It feels good," she said. "That's supposed to take care of the stings?"

Jack covered the few welts on her face. "I don't think so . . ."

Samantha pulled away, confused.

Jack smiled. "I've just been wanting to do that to you for six years."

It took Samantha a few seconds to realize Jack was kidding. She managed a chuckle—only after Jack promised the mud really *was* good for the stings. He'd learned of its medicinal applications from a lowland Indian tribe. Still suspicious ten minutes later, Samantha finally conceded that the mineral-rich soil had dissipated much of the burning.

"I guess I've been wanting to say something to you for a few years," she said.

"You don't need to."

"I do." Samantha took a deep breath. "I was afraid."

"I know. You worked hard for your career."

She shook her head. "No. It's more than that. You scared me because you could hurt me," she said. "Somewhere along the line I gave you that power." Even in the moonlight Jack could see tears build in the corners of her eyes. "I had never let that happen, before or since. Do you understand?"

"I've got an idea—" Jack bit his tongue, quelled the familiar anger that in the short silence that followed became pain. He went with it. For the first time the pain felt free of rage. The hurt brought moisture to his own eyes. As he submitted to the feelings for the first time, Jack shuddered—as if his body had untied a last knot of hate.

Samantha stared into his eyes without speaking.

Jack finally said, "Let's get you washed off."

Samantha's boots sat on a rock beside the slow stream. Jack watched her slip out of her pants and lay them folded atop her shoes. The flaps of her shirt covered her long legs at the thigh. She felt the water with her foot, then again caught Jack's gaze. She took off her blouse. Jack felt anxious, almost scared, but he never took his eyes off her. With one hand she undid the clasp on her bra and let the lace straps fall from her shoulders. She breathed heavily. Deliberately. Jack stared into her blue eyes as she bent over and pulled off her panties. Then she stepped into the water.

The mud on her body washed away in the gentle current. She smoothed water over her shoulders, then the back of her neck. Jack found himself near the side of the stream. Samantha turned to him and stood up in the pool, the water just covering her navel. Then, as if reading some unsaid signal, Jack found himself taking off his shirt.

*       *       *

Her body lay cold and wet beneath him on a bed of moss at the side of the pool. Jack pulled back a strand of wet hair and held her face. He kissed her. First gently, on the lips. Then deeply. His mouth traced down her neck. Samantha's eyes closed and her stomach got light. When his mouth found her breasts, she uttered a soft sigh. Her breath came in short gasps of anticipation.

Samantha opened her eyes and held his unmoving gaze.

Then her head fell back against the thick moss and they were one.

# TRAIL

Jack gently shook Samantha awake.

The night seemed darker than before. Her body more relaxed than it had ever been. This one night had made up for six years of pain, she thought to herself. She loved him. Now more than ever.

"Ricardo rigged something he thinks will get us out of here," Jack said, already dressed.

"Did you sleep?" she asked.

"Do I ever?"

Samantha found her clothes. For a moment she had forgotten about the fossil and about the incredible happenings of the last few days. She'd been lost to a contentment she had nearly forgotten. But now, while she slipped her clothes over a few painful welts, the urgency of their situation became clear again. She remembered the betrayal by a man who now seemed as distant and foreign to her as the fusion device and its potentially dangerous applications.

"Have I been out long?"

"Half hour since I left to help Ricardo," Jack said. He didn't mention the twenty minutes he let her sleep in his arms—or the solace he found breathing the sweet smell of her.

The remote sensor sat silent on the dashboard as the trucks slogged through the muddy causeway. Covered with welts alleviated only with cortisone, Baines's strong hands strangled the steering wheel as if it were animate. The headlamps of the trucks illuminated nothing but forest and mud. "This thing isn't doing us a damn bit of good," Baines said vehemently. The black box continued to monitor the surroundings, creating fluctuating waves on its light blue display.

Dorn twisted his pipe angrily between his fingers. "We don't have many other bloody options, do we?"

Dorn had entrusted that most precious piece of technology—*The Source*—in which sat all four modules—to Baines, who had let it slip away. Just hours ago Dorn'd been imagining the bright future that lay ahead for him once his own researchers discovered the function of each of the four modules. Now he contemplated Baines's future if they didn't recover the device—one that looked bleak for the man. Worse than bleak—one that didn't exist.

Fixing the bridge had taken far too long. Now the scientists had a huge jump on them. The instrument on the dash was their only hope, but it would only detect electromagnetic disturbances within a half mile or so. They would have to practically stumble onto the fusion device if they had any chance of finding the scientists at all. Dorn had already been led down one false trail—when the instrument detected an electromagnetic disturbance that ended up originating from a small gas generator, used to power lamps and a TV in a squatter's shack.

Rage filled him. As he looked through the hopelessly thick forest on either side of them he slammed his fist against the dashboard. "How the hell did they get out of the temple?"

"You've got me," Baines answered. "It wasn't through the entrance. I'm sure of that."

"If we don't find them soon," Dorn said, "that bastard will spread news of the fusion device all over the world. He said he wanted to make the expedition's findings public." Dorn couldn't fathom how the man could piss away trillions of dollars. "We have to stop him before he reaches a phone line."

As if Baines sensed what would happen to him if they didn't find the scientists he gunned the engine faster.

Dorn retreated to his own thoughts about Samantha. Initially relieved at her survival, that relief had been replaced with anger. He would never let Jack win. Things had been so clean before he arrived—and they would be again after he was gone.

After a mile more of jolting over the primitive dirt road, words began to spatter out of the truck radio. Words that fell like a warm blanket across Dorn's lap.

"The Sikorsky's up and running," the voice said.

Dorn sat up in his seat. He looked at his watch: half past two in the morning. Then he grabbed the handset. "What is your ETA?"

"From the coordinates you gave, we should be over you in forty minutes."

Dorn breathed a sigh of relief. The men at his shipping operations in Brazil hadn't thought the cargo chopper could be made operational for another twenty-four hours. Obviously, Dorn's powers of persuasion had sped the repair process. Though far too late to extract them from Tiahuanaco, the Sikorsky would at least be able to aid in the search now. Dorn knew he would need all the help he could get. He had just started to reflect on what could happen if the scientists managed to stay alive long enough to report him to the authorities.

Then, as if the gods of fate had somehow heard Baines's silent pleas, the man stopped the truck in the middle of the road and pointed to the remote sensor. "It's picking something up," Baines said. The instrument began clicking. A strong signal registered on the machine; the fluctuating waves spasmed.

The signal came from somewhere off the south side of the road.

"Could be another damn generator," Baines said.

Dorn needed to make a decision. He needed to be right.

"Check it out," he finally said.

# PLANTATION

The three scientists stayed off the main road.

Instead, guided by a luminescent moon, the truck continued slowly down the access path, in hopes of finding a small village. Jack followed the compass readings on Ricardo's watch. He knew a grouping of tiny hamlets lay somewhere west of their location; he just hoped the last five gallons of fuel they added would get them there. Ricardo winced at every jolt, lest his handiwork come unraveled. After twenty minutes, Samantha told Jack to stop. She pointed to a thicket of trees, just past a clearing in the forest. Beneath the trees, speckled by paisley patterns of dark shadow and silver moonlight, Jack saw a few wood buildings.

"Maybe there's a phone," Samantha said.

"What's that smell?" Ricardo said. An acrid odor hung heavily on the damp morning air. Jack let the engine idle. He sniffed the same scent: a chemical.

"Like gasoline," Samantha said.

They decided to investigate.

Leaving the truck on the access road, the three scientists pushed through the calf-high grasses in the clearing. Still fifty feet away from the thicket, but more aware of the smell, Jack knew exactly what they had stumbled on.

After five minutes of surveillance, Jack felt confident the series of huts that made up an old coca plantation were indeed deserted. He led Ricardo and Samantha through a maze of hastily erected buildings. Electrical wires hung bare, connecting the various huts from rooftop to rooftop in a dangerous web. Decaying coca leaves carpeted the ground.

Jack headed for the largest structure, a long, barracks-size building with plywood walls.

Heavy forty-gallon steel barrels sat in rows against its outside wall. A plastic tarp covered some of them. Jack pushed the edge back and sniffed.

"Kerosene," Jack said. "It's used to process cocaine." He lifted the lid on another barrel. "And alcohol."

Ricardo's eyebrows raised.

"Chemists in the cartels have recently discovered that substituting pure alcohol for kerosene increases extraction rates from the coca base by another fifteen percent," Jack said.

"Then why was it abandoned?" Samantha asked.

"The plantation's dormant," Jack said. "They'll use it again. Every six months or so a processing plantation like this shuts to 'cool' down before local police or American drug enforcement tracks it." Jack knew how advanced the trade had become. The rotating processing plants were capable of harvesting $14 billion in cocaine each year—a big part of the $74 billion global retail market. "And if they're advanced enough to use alcohol they're probably patched into phone service."

Jack started for a small shed that had been padlocked shut.

The padlock snapped easily under the leverage of a lug wrench from the truck. With dawn still an hour away, Jack hoped to find the generator that would give them added light in the search for phone lines.

"Bingo," Jack said, peering inside.

The generator gurgled outside, still working out the kinks after Jack started it. He and Ricardo made another forced entry into a long building at the center of the complex. A pungent chemical musk filled the room. Jack felt his way past a row of steel barrels before a group of fluorescent lights fluttered on.

"The wiring's still good," Ricardo said, his hand on a light switch.

The strobing of the few neglected bulbs dimly illuminated the abandoned room. Exposed wires hung from the plywood ceiling, feeding bare sockets.

Jack's eyes adjusted. "Do you see any phone lines?"

"Not over here," Ricardo said, peering for signs of a jack. Ricardo and Samantha inspected the far side of the room while Jack weaved through a collection of dusty desks and plastic chairs, cobwebs joining them in an elastic bio-matrix. Jack tore at the webs, which stuck to his arm like cotton candy. He scraped most of the sticky mess off on one of the chairs before noticing a drilled hole in the rotted floor.

"I think I found it."

Jack knew that processing labs often ran their cable and phone lines underground through plastic pipes for up to a half mile before the lines surfaced and ran exposed to the nearest phone line. Though many cartels used cellular communication, those signals could be picked up by the DEA, which scanned for them. The old system of pirating unauthorized lines straight into the phone system suited them better.

Jack wrestled the end of the lug wrench into the hole; the brittle floor gave way. Within minutes, the three had opened the entire corner section. Jack used his flashlight to supplement the flickering room bulbs. In the two feet of space between the floor and the foundation Jack saw plastic conduits that led out of the side of the building. Just below them, drilled into the sideboard, were two empty phone jacks.

Ricardo peered past Jack. "Will they work?"

"Let's hope so," he said.

Samantha stood up. "I'll get the laptops."

"I'm into the University at La Paz," Ricardo said. He tapped on the keyboard. The first line had been dead, the second still had tone. The fax modem squeaked like a pained bird as it connected with the university's system. Outside, on the horizon, a tinge of blue fought its way out of the blackness. The laptop beeped and a barrage of Spanish prompts floated by. Ricardo typed like he had twenty fingers. "I think I've got it!"

Jack read the familiar University Research Lab connection to the World Wide Web.

"Export all the files. Everything," Jack said.

Samantha typed furiously on her own laptop. "I'll E-mail the anthropology chair at Princeton, telling him where we are and what the hell happened. I'll have him contact the embassy here if he can," she said.

"This is gonna take a while," Ricardo said. "The bandwidth on this line won't let us transmit data as fast as we're used to."

Jack couldn't imagine the Internet being any slower than he'd experienced at home. The computer sat for long pauses as it communicated with the Web site.

"Okay, we're sending the first files," Ricardo announced. "I've used the University Forum system. I've copied every research institute on the Web. We'll hit hundreds."

"Good," Jack said. "Think of it as our insurance policy. Once we've disseminated the data there's no way *anyone* will be able to cover this up. Not Dorn. Not the Bolivians. Not even our *own* government." He put his hand on Ricardo's shoulder. For the first time in the last twenty-four hours Jack felt something close to relief.

Then the lights cut out.

# GENERATOR

Outside, the generator coughed twice, then grumbled to a stop. An eerie silence occupied the early morning, peppered only by a few crickets singing their last ballads before dawn.

"What happened?" Samantha asked.

"Maybe the generator's out of gas," Jack said. "Maybe."

"I'm running on batteries now," Ricardo said. The gray glow of the screen illuminated his face. "But I'm already low. I don't know if I'll be able to transmit if we don't get some juice back in here."

"Shit," Jack mumbled.

Power outages in Bolivia were almost a daily occurrence, which is why most people who could afford them kept gas-powered generators on hand. But the generator failing—that troubled Jack. "I'll check the genny," Jack said.

He picked up the flashlight.

\*    \*    \*

Jack waited until he was within the generator shed, then turned on the torch. He hadn't seen or heard anyone outside. He got onto his knees, darting the flashlight beam across the machine, looking for the gas cap. He found it on the left side of the generator and unscrewed the rusted top. Jack trained the light and shook the heavy engine. A blue opaque film sloshed inside. The generator had gas. He began a search for other possible problems. He could see no oil leaks on the two-by-fours beneath the machine. He poked about for the spark plugs when a distributor cap fell onto the ground in front of him. Jack froze.

"Need that?" a voice asked. Then all went black.

Jack felt himself being pulled up. He couldn't see. Everything was dark, everything fuzzy. He heard more voices, felt himself leave his feet. Jack crashed into a desk and toppled onto the floor. Heavy beams of light cut the space of the long building like sabers. Jack blinked the wet from his eyes. He couldn't get his mind to focus. The room shook back and forth. He saw shapes. Just figures. Movement. A struggle. Grunts. Jack shook his head out. Something was ripped from the wall. A laptop.

A heavy thumping began to echo in his ears. He needed his mind to work. Pressure around his triceps—a hand. Jack was yanked to his feet. He fought for balance and recognized the man holding him—Baines. Another man grabbed his other arm. Jack winced. A painful blast of light shone directly into his eyes. Jack could feel the heat from a halogen bulb on his face. "You white knights are so bloody predictable."

Dorn's voice. An angry voice. Jack couldn't open his eyes. A hand held his face and squeezed. "You've made a mistake. A huge mistake, you son of a bitch."

The light moved from Jack's face. In front of him, Dorn's blurry image slowly came into focus. Jack

looked around the room. He saw no one else. "Where's
. . . Sam?" Jack managed.

"That's none of your business anymore," Dorn said.
"In fact, nothing is."

Adrenaline pulsed through Jack's veins, dissipating
the fog in his mind, but still, the incessant thumping
noise would not stop. Dorn's voice held a certain final-
ity. "Listen," Jack kept his eyes trained on the fuzzy
image of Dorn. "Don't touch the fusion generator—"

"Jack," Dorn said, "I'm quite tired of taking orders
from you."

"You can't activate the device," Jack said. "Kill me.
But don't activate the . . . fusion—"

Dorn let Jack go.

"I'm not going to kill you." The South African's voice
struggled for composure. "But I can't say I don't envy
Baines."

"Wait—" Jack struggled against the two men. "You
don't know—"

Jack's feet came loose from the floor. He hit the plywood wall hard enough to loosen the nails, then crumpled to the floor. Dorn paused at the doorway. "I know
*exactly* what I'm doing."

On his left, behind a desk, Jack saw Ricardo. Conscious and aware, his friend bled from a cut above his
eye.

Jack looked back into the room. Dorn had disappeared.

Jack felt beneath him for anything on the floor he
could use as a weapon. Baines was to his right. Another
man walked by Baines and flanked him. Jack focused
on Baines's hand. The man pulled a 9mm Ruger and
slapped in the clip.

"Jack . . ." Ricardo said, propping his back against the
wall.

Jack didn't answer. His eyes followed each wave of
the black pistol as Baines strode toward them. Jack ex-

pected some parting speech from Baines, who obviously disliked the scientists from the start.

There was none given.

The man pointed the gun at Ricardo and fired.

# HELICOPTER

The wash of the double-rotor Sikorsky CH-53 Super Stallion parted the thick grass of the clearing in two huge circles. The cargo helicopter had lowered its rear ramp in the moist soil of the clearing. The large wood crate housing the fusion device had already been loaded. Dorn bent over and held his glasses as he ran through the rotor wash to the ramp.

"Up front with me," he told one of his men who had accompanied the helicopter crew. The man pulled a semi-conscious Samantha into the Sikorsky. The five aluminum expedition cases followed, then a few wooden boxes slid into the stomach of the machine.

A moment later three more of Dorn's men ran from the truck.

"That's everything, Mr. Dorn."

"See what's keeping Baines," Dorn said. He climbed into the chopper.

Jack shuddered. Blood misted his leg with each beat of Ricardo's heart.

Ricardo screamed in agony, clutching his boot, which had been nearly blown from his leg. The leather toe hung loosely by only the thick sole.

Jack caught eyes with Baines—the man looked expressionless. *This man enjoys killing. Enjoys torture.* Strangely, Jack's fear disappeared, replaced with venom spawned by the writhing of his friend next to him.

Jack started to get up. He'd kill Baines. Or be killed in the attempt.

The man pointed the gun at Jack.

The blast seemed louder than before. Everything went white in Jack's mind. His head rang. *I've been shot in the skull.* Jack felt no sensation whatsoever. No pain. Only whiteness. Everywhere. A loud ringing in his ears. For a few more moments, Jack waited—he saw no bright tunnel. No relatives. He was still alive.

His vision came back.

Intense gunfire had erupted inside the large room.

The man standing next to Baines was now on the floor, rolling toward the cover of some steel barrels. Jack couldn't find Baines through the smoke; he must have escaped in the confusion. Automatic weapons fired from every direction. Jack reached for Ricardo, instinctively pulled him toward the safety of the overturned desk.

His senses cleared.

The white flash must have come from a stun grenade, he thought. He could still smell the cordite from the blast. Dorn's man next to the barrels was engaged in a gun battle with someone who had charged in the door. Jack watched the man near the barrels empty his clip through the rising smoke before a round exploded in the side of his neck. The man stood, clutching his pierced carotid, then took another slug in his chest, which knocked him to the ground.

Jack waited, not moving. As the smoke filtered out of the room, he saw another body lying by the entrance. He could see a vest and helmet on the body. The steel shell lay askew to the man's head, showing tufts of sandy blond hair. A thick puddle of dark blood had already begun to congeal beneath the man's face.

Outside, automatic weapons continued to crackle from all directions.

"You hanging in there?" he asked Ricardo.

"*Sí.*" Ricardo had already stuffed his handkerchief into the wound in his foot, to stem the blood loss. The rag was soaked. Jack ripped off the bottom of his shirt and tied it around Ricardo's calf.

Ricardo winced. "What the hell happened?"

"Maybe it's the cartel," Jack said.

He couldn't say for sure. He just knew that whoever lay dead before them at the entrance had just saved their lives.

# PIERCE

Pierce discharged his clip. The barrel of the Sig P226 was hot. He slammed another fifteen-round magazine into the handgun—his last before he'd have to load manually. Still no word from his partner inside. *Dammit!* The mission had gotten out of control. The DEA agents had taken up position behind the wrong shed—leaving Pierce, Miller, and Boyett, their surveillance man from the lake, ass-out with no cover. Pierce's team covered the back of the long wood structure. The DEA boys were to loop in front and cut off any escape. In the sixty seconds it took the DEA agents to realize their mistake, Boyett had taken a round above his collarbone and Miller hadn't reappeared from the warehouse. *Interdepartmental missions never worked.* Pierce felt helpless, pinned down by a rain of automatic weapons fire from at least three more of Dorn's men who'd joined the fray from the clearing.

They must have come from the chopper, Pierce thought. The agencies hadn't been expecting any kind of aerial intervention. Dorn had unwittingly led them all the way to the plantation, but had the agents known reinforcements would be arriving via chopper, Pierce would have never tried to take them now. To his left Lieutenant Drew crawled toward him in the shallow depression behind the building. The man wore a helmet and vest over his green DEA jacket.

"Have you located the target?" Drew asked.

A round exploded through the plywood just above their heads.

"No!" Pierce shouted, keeping low.

"I've got my men doubling back along the road," Drew said. "A helicopter put down somewhere near here. I'm going to check it out."

"I know that, asshole." Pierce grabbed the man's vest. "But you're staying right here to cover me—one of my men is stuck in that warehouse!"

Jack knelt by the body of the man who worked for Baines. He grabbed the dead mercenary's pistol and found two extra clips in his blood-soaked jacket pocket.

Baines had escaped.

Performing CPR, Ricardo hunched over the other body by the entrance.

"What are you doing?" Jack asked. He got closer to the crimson pool before realizing the man looked American. Not a cartel member.

"DEA," Ricardo said. He bent over again and exhaled into the man's mouth.

*DEA?* Jack felt for a pulse. The slightest hint of life flowed through the man. Ricardo compressed the chest again. The man's face tilted toward Jack. The sandy hair was caked in black slime that oozed from a hole on the side of his head. The freckled face looked pale, the eyes glazed, distant. The face looked so young. The agent couldn't have been a day over thirty.

Ricardo stopped. "He's not gonna make it."

An explosion rocked through the side of the plywood wall, showering Jack and Ricardo with splinters. Jack picked himself off the floor. One of the kerosene barrels had ignited. The plywood building was now kindling.

"Where's Samantha?" Jack asked, panicked.

"Dorn . . ." Ricardo answered.

Jack pulled Ricardo through the flaming opening. "He can't get away."

Jack knew his friend was in pain, but Ricardo too realized the gravity of the situation. They *had* to find Dorn now.

Jack stopped at the edge of the clearing. A double-rotor cargo helicopter blew dust and debris into his eyes as it rose above the grassy field. The red rays of dawn gleamed from the top of the empty truck by the side of the path. The gray chopper rotated ninety degrees. He could just make out its black nose cone. Then the machine banked east and disappeared behind the trees, taking the last of his hope with it.

Before Jack had time to contemplate their options— or lack thereof—the earth exploded at his feet.

"The thicket," Ricardo shouted.

With Ricardo's arm draped over his neck, Jack struggled toward the cover of the trees. He couldn't see who was firing at them.

He guessed it really didn't matter.

The searing heat of the flames had no effect on Pierce.

He held his partner's head in his lap and felt for a pulse. There was none. While the warehouse ceiling burst into flames above him, Pierce closed Miller's eyes, which stared at him, as if asking for something. The kid just *had* a kid, Pierce thought. He pulled his dead partner from the flaming structure.

\*   \*   \*

Branches tore at Jack's face. Vines reached for his ankles and tripped him. The jungle seemed relentless in its
obstacles. Jack's legs burned, and he tasted a hint of
copper in his throat—ruptured blood vessels from his
wheezing. Jack imagined Ricardo's pain—the man bit
tightly on his bottom lip with each step. They plunged
deeper into the thick trees behind the plantation. The
sporadic firing got thinner. The roar of the flames became the main noise around the plantation. Jack had no
clue where he was going. Just get away, he told himself.
Survive. Regroup. The two men reached a berm. Jack
didn't slow. Halfway down its backslope, they stumbled
and slipped into a muddy ravine below. Ricardo muffled
his pain by screaming into his arm.

Jack listened for footsteps but heard nothing. Only the
crackling of the fire behind them. It washed the trees
above the ravine in shades of orange.

"Where are we running?" Ricardo gasped.

Jack didn't have an answer. He didn't know. He
wasn't thinking—only feeling. Samantha! He had to find
her. Noises on his right, down another long slope, got
his attention. He thought he heard an engine. He blocked
everything else out of his mind—the roaring fire, the
shouts of men back at the plantation, Ricardo's heavy
breathing. Yes! A vehicle.

"Do you hear it?" Jack said.

Ricardo nodded.

Below them, they could see a wide river. They slid down
the second slope, dodging thick *totaí* palms. Jack stumbled, lost his grasp on Ricardo, and fell five feet onto
the lush bank of the river, landing on the hard steel of
the 9mm Glock, which had dropped from his hand. He
heard someone shout in Spanish—only thirty yards
downstream. Then he noticed the revving of the gasoline
engine again. The sound echoed off the river, but it
didn't sound as if it came from a boat.

*A plane.*

"Hurry," Jack whispered and helped Ricardo onto his feet. Together, they hobbled along the water's edge, navigating a maze of bushes. Jack didn't have time for stealth. The engine noise seemed farther away now. He smelled the aviation fuel and heard the plane but still couldn't see it.

The engines throttled down. Finally, Jack could see the pontooned seaplane emerging from behind a large palm, thirty yards downriver. The prop blew water between its two floats as it headed away from them.

Ricardo stumbled. Each breath was strained. "I don't know if I can keep going."

"You have to," Jack said. "The plane's right there."

"That's what I mean." Ricardo managed a smile.

"Stay put." Jack left Ricardo on the riverbank and waded into the water. The plane would be their only means of escape, and their only realistic chance at pursuing Dorn.

The pilot revved the engine. River water misted from the surface, caught the glow of dawn, and left a small, glimmering rainbow in the prop wash. Jack checked the breeze. It blew strong from behind him—in the same direction the plane was heading. Thank God, he thought. The plane would be turning around and heading upstream—into the wind—for takeoff.

The engine throttled back and the seacraft pivoted in the brown water. Morning light bounced off the cockpit glass. Then Jack made out the Bolivian pilot and one passenger through the windshield. Drug runners checking on the disturbance at their plantation, Jack thought. They'd probably seen more than enough to conclude it was a DEA raid.

The plane crept slowly in his direction. Jack would have only one chance. He pushed himself out into the river from the tangle of roots on the bank. The plane came closer—only twenty yards away. The pilot's arms flicked switches above him. The copilot scanned the commotion on the hillside. Jack would have to move— before the plane picked up speed. He dove.

The right pontoon grazed Jack's head as he surfaced. He grabbed the steel brace on the vinyl float. The plane picked up speed. Tendons in Jack's wrist stretched under the strain. Pain shot through his shoulder socket. Jack's grasp on the brace loosened. There'd be no second chances. He couldn't let go. He managed to swing his other hand onto the pontoon support, and his body began to hydroplane across the water as the pilot throttled the engines further. Spray from the props blinded him. The plane hit the small wake it made turning. Jack used the momentum to throw his body onto the pontoon. He pulled himself even with the copilot's door panel. His hand found the aluminum latch.

The startled Bolivian found himself kissing the barrel of Jack's Glock.

Jack watched the copilot swim to shore on the far side of the river. Keeping his gun trained at the pilot's head, he gave directions calmly in Spanish and reached for the AK-47 lying in the backseat. Jack tucked it next to his right leg and patted the pilot down. Confident the man was unarmed, he ordered the drug runner to swing the plane toward the small sandbar near the edge of the river and stop it there.

Jack spotted Ricardo's white shirt on the bank. He wanted to go to his friend but knew he couldn't leave the pilot alone. He waved his arm above the fuselage. *C'mon, Ricardo.*

The scientist hopped off the riverbank and stroked against the current. A thin slick of blood floated away behind him. Shouts of another cartel member barked from the plane radio. The voice asked the status of the plantation, repeatedly asking the pilot to respond. The

Bolivian looked at the radio. Jack shook his head and turned it off.

"Let's go! Let's go!"

Ricardo breaststroked, keeping his head above water until Jack saw him feel for the edge of the sandbar with his feet. Soon he was aboard.

Pierce watched the plane turn downriver. His partner was dead. The truck was empty. There were only three dead suspects—none of them major players in the surveillance. The device that Virginia thought was a tactical nuke had been whisked away by helicopter to God knows where. He had failed his country. His partner. The shitty morning would only get worse when everything set in. Pierce grasped the handle of his SIG. He would stop this plane and take a few heads.

The morning mist crept through the forest, galvanized by the twinkling of dawn through the trees. It all seemed like a dream—or a nightmare.

He heard the DEA agents behind him. They had seen the plane too. Pierce pushed his way through bushes, tripped on a root. He got up and stumbled down an escarpment, landing on the riverbank. The plane's engine throttled up, the craft turned into the wind and gained speed.

Ignoring the pain in his ankle, Pierce steadied his handgun with both hands.

Shouts filtered down to them from the hill. Jack made out a half dozen green-vested forms who appeared sporadically from the trees some forty yards upriver.

The men along the bluff shouted in English before opening fire.

Rounds tore into the water. The pilot swore. Bullets pierced the left pontoon. Another round ripped through the Plexiglas windshield and tore a hole in the vinyl backseat next to Ricardo.

Ricardo, curled on the floor, prepared for the inevitable crash. The engines whined. The pilot held the throttle forward. The prop-swept water exploded under a new barrage as they got closer to the agents. *We'll never make it*, Jack thought. The gunfire grew more intense with each yard they closed. Rounds slammed into the cabin, showering the interior with fiberglass debris. Then, as if he'd been dreaming, the chaos in the cockpit—the hail of bullets—abruptly halted.

Through a shattered window Jack watched the soil of the riverbank fracture in a fusillade of gunfire. The confused agents dove for cover, returning salvos toward a position upstream. The plane had neared lift-off speed when Jack saw the cause of the distraction. Above the DEA agents, behind an outcropping of worn rock, a group of Bolivians had opened fire. The smallest of the attackers had long jet-black hair.

For the briefest moment, the slight figure stopped and faced the plane. Jack could feel the plane rise but didn't take his eyes off the woman. Veronica! Her intense black eyes followed the rising cockpit. The pilot groaned, pulling the stick back as hard as he could. The plane banked to avoid a bend in the river. A last image froze in Jack's mind as the G forces pressed him into his seat: Veronica, automatic rifle raised above her head, pumping the weapon up and down in salute.

A wall of trees rushed them in a blur. The plane banked sharply as the right pontoon grazed the treetops. Then, as the wings leveled, Jack looked below him out the shattered window. The river had vanished. All was unbroken, green forest.

Pierce watched the plane take flight above the tree line, its wings catching the sun. He squeezed off one more round, then slowly lowered the pistol. Oblivious to the new commotion on the ridge, he wiped the sweat from his face. He fell to his knees in the moist sand and wondered what he would say to Miller's wife. His hand smelled of powder.

# EAST

Wright paced back and forth in the War Room. Just inside his office, the small cot he had brought down to catch some sleep went unused. The director still looked impeccably groomed, but the oily sheen of his face and his tired, bloodshot eyes bespoke the long night.

The director was enraged—and as one of Wright's top roosters, McFadden didn't have to hear axes grind to tell him to keep his mouth shut. Wright spewed rarefied and obscene curses spawned from three prior wars. Then he pulled out a leather chair and sat down, exhausted.

"Can we track the weapon by satellite?" Wright asked Kirby, the skinny analyst.

"No, sir," Kirby said. "Our satellites would have to make almost a direct pass to pick up the device's electromagnetic signature at its current charge." The man pulled off his glasses, revealing two red indents on either side of his nose. "The KH-14 and Big Bird satellites were trained in geosynchronous orbit above the site, sir. Even if we located the target again on one of the other passes, it would take us at least twenty-four hours to position a satellite in the area."

"Shit." Wright leaned back in his chair, which needed some oil. "Do the field agents have any idea where the helicopter might be heading?"

"No," McFadden said. "It was flying east, toward Brazil, when they lost it."

"East?"

"Yes, sir."

"Well, there's a whole lot of fucking east out there!" The director's hands balled a crumpled tissue that had nearly disintegrated. Wright calmed himself. "Any ideas?"

McFadden stood up. "Most of Dorn's industrial base is in South Africa. He wouldn't dream of trying to slip a tactical weapon into the States. I'd bet my money he's heading home. By water, sir. They wouldn't risk customs at the airports. And there's a million places to disembark."

Wright grunted. "Alert the agent-in-charge in Cape Town. I want him briefed immediately. Do we have the make of the chopper?"

"It's a cargo transport—double prop," McFadden said. "That's all we know."

"Check out the vehicle registry. How many double props work out of that part of the world."

"Hopefully not many," McFadden said. "I'll start with the ports, sir." He collected his papers, then added, "Assuming they were heading for Brazil."

It took twenty minutes to enter Brazilian airspace and another two and a half hours before the Atlantic became visible on the horizon. During the time, Jack cleaned Ricardo's wound. Using an old first-aid kit he managed to butterfly-tape it closed, sterilizing it first with alcohol and peroxide. Jack didn't think humans could scream that loud.

The port Samantha mentioned Dorn's shipping line was based out of also had a small airstrip.

"They have to be putting down there," Jack said, as if trying to convince himself.

Ricardo agreed. "*If* Dorn was going to transport the device by ship. And *if* he was heading for South Africa."

The nervous pilot had calmed down during the flight. Jack discovered the man was only hired occasionally by the cartel. He knew who he was working for—and probably what he was transporting—but he had a family to feed. Augustine showed Jack the faded picture of his family in front of a small Catholic church. Jack assured the man that they weren't going to harm him. Without going into details, he also explained how important it was that they find the large cargo helicopter—important for Jack's family—for Augustine's family.

Important, Jack thought, for the world.

# PORT

The airfield at Pôrto Alegre consisted of two short runways capable of landing the more adventurous 737, but usually catered to smaller planes. The Cessna had no problems. In fact, the rubber wheels beneath the pontoons seemed glad to feel concrete again. The plane taxied briskly toward a row of aluminum hangars. The pilot had only been at the airport once before but had no problem guessing where the helipad would be.

They passed a few small helicopters in various states of disassembly, but Jack couldn't see the Sikorsky anywhere. The Cessna passed row after row of small planes on their right, anchored to cement blocks in what sufficed for parking berths. Then, behind a large domed hangar, Jack caught a glimpse of the gray paint of the cargo chopper. "There!"

He waited a few more seconds—until the entire helicopter was in view—before he let his heart succumb to the emotion. Jack slipped the AK-47 into a long, nylon sports bag Ricardo had found in the backseat. Then he adjusted the 9mm Glock in his waistband. He had a few

words with their pilot, begging the man not to get involved or drag the cartel into this.

"Don't worry," Augustine said. "It is better if I disappear for a while."

Jack believed him.

Jack and a limping Ricardo approached the cargo chopper from the side.

It stood on a large concrete pad branded by a yellow
X surrounded by a circle. Its back loading gate was still
down. Jack heard whistling from inside. He scanned the
area but could see nothing but hangars and an occasional
fuel truck. Jack glanced at Ricardo and quietly unzipped
the sports bag. Ricardo took the weapon, keeping it in
the bag, and took up position in the blind spot of the
helicopter, just to the side of the loading ramp. He would
make sure no one surprised Jack, who pulled out his
pistol before tiptoeing up the ramp.

The pilot lay beneath a circuit panel in the front cabin
of the helicopter. He wore a green flight suit and black
cap, but two worn vinyl flight seats concealed most of
his body. He whistled a familiar Brazilian tune, sadly
off-key: "The Girl from Ipanema." Jack didn't think the
man was Brazilian though—he caught glimpses of red
hair beneath the baseball cap. Jack's eyes scanned the
belly of the chopper. A few stray boxes. A large steel
case sat open to one side, but it was empty save for a
few candy wrappers and empty Coke bottles.

Jack passed a pile of cargo nets. The shell of the helicopter lay mostly barren. Dorn had long since unloaded
the device.

Jack's pulse pounded. He wasn't even sure the pistol
he held would fire. He checked the safety—which was
on. A silent sigh pursed his lips as he considered the
implications. Then he unlocked the safety and continued
forward.

Jack got to within three feet of the man before the

pilot noticed him—probably from the floor vibrations. The man sat up from beneath the portable mechanic's light that hung from the seat. "Who the hell are you?" he said in a thick South African accent.

Jack pointed the pistol at the pilot's head. "Not the girl from Ipanema."

Steaming 038 degrees ESE, the cargo trawler *Cape Indigo* would head straight into the swell for the next thirteen hours. A tropical depression born a thousand miles away off the coast of West Africa had rumpled the satin ocean with high winds before dissipating over the mid-Atlantic. Defiant of the cloudless sky, ten-foot waves tore at the bow of the trawler, raising the ship on fists of foam before slamming it down again.

Dorn stood at the bow of the ship, holding on to a steel rail that led below decks. He cursed the lines of undulating waves that jolted the ship with each pass. The crate holding the fusion generator sat on the flat steel surface of the bow beneath a tarp secured on both sides of the ship. Dorn wanted the device below decks in the cargo hold, but would have to wait until the captain off-loaded a hundred tons of raw sugar. Had it not been for Dorn's haste to reach international waters, he would have had them begin the procedure back at the port.

"I don't care what you do with it," Dorn yelled. "Get the sugar out of that hull. All of it."

The captain nodded. "We'll use the crane as soon as the swell subsides."

"No," Dorn said. "You'll do it now. I want this box secured below deck!"

Reluctantly, the captain called for two members of the crew.

Inside the galley, Samantha awoke groggily. She felt sick, medicated.

One of her hands had been manacled to the bottom of a long, built-in bench, but she could move her body freely. Her eyes searched the surroundings. Laminated Formica floor. A wood table. Two small round windows against a bulwark of steel and rivets. She knew instantly from the rolling motion that she was in a ship. Dorn's ship. The health inspection permit, which hung above the stove, bore the name of Dorn's shipping company. She stood up, extending her shackled arm so she could see out one of the forward portholes. The window looked directly over the length of the ship. She watched Dorn and another man inspect something—the fusion device maybe—underneath a large vinyl cover, tightened securely to cleats on either side of the deck. She truly hated him now.

What had happened to Jack? He had gone to check the generator just a minute before Dorn's men entered the warehouse. Where was he? Was he alive? The thought intensified the queasiness brought on by the swell and whatever drug pulsed through her system. She desperately struggled against her restraint. If she lost Jack she wouldn't be able to bear it.

For the first time in her life, Samantha felt totally helpless.

# PENDULUM

At gunpoint the pilot swore he was nearly out of fuel.

Jack made him prime the rotors and checked the gauge himself before agreeing to let him call for fuel service. It put them another twenty minutes behind Dorn's ship. Once airborne they'd make up the distance quickly, but finding the ship on the endless expanse of Atlantic would be difficult. During the wait, Jack checked the cargo area again and devised a plan. By the time the helicopter's thick blades lifted them off the airfield, the first steps of that plan had already been put into motion.

Ricardo sat in the copilot chair with a headset on, monitoring air traffic and making sure the pilot didn't decide to radio the ship. The AK-47 Ricardo kept nearby would ensure compliance. The spare flight suit Ricardo slipped on fit much too snugly.

The pilot assured Jack no contact would be made. Dorn had ordered strict radio silence. "I don't even know if he'll let me land," the pilot grumbled.

"How is he going to stop you?" Jack asked.

Jack sat directly behind the pilot on a fold-down bench that faced the interior of the craft. He glanced at Ricardo, who looked peaked. Though he'd lost a lot of blood, he refused to be left behind at the airstrip. Jack felt anxious. Ricardo had only agreed to go back for help once Jack got on board the ship, acknowledging he'd only be a hindrance when they landed.

A few minutes after takeoff, Ricardo noticed a black box inside a navigation pouch by the copilot's chair. The box turned out to be the expedition's remote sensor. The same one he'd used to monitor the fusion generator.

"That's how Dorn must have found us, even though we'd bypassed the main road," Ricardo said, examining the instrument on his lap.

"Could it help us track them, now?" Jack said into the headset.

Ricardo shook his head. "We'd have to be within a mile or so before we got any readings. And there's bound to be a million different things that will interfere with the signal."

"Like what?"

"The rotors of the helicopter are complicating things

now. We'll probably see the ship long before we detect the fusion generator—but it can't hurt to try."

The bow of the *Cape Indigo* fell into another ocean furrow.

"Watch that line!" the captain yelled.

Half of his eight-man crew struggled with the large wood crate as they attempted to move it below decks. The captain silently cursed Mr. Dorn. Moving the crate in this swell endangered not only his men—but also the damn equipment Dorn so wanted to protect. The lost tonnage in sugar would cost Dorn a small fortune—but worse, the captain already visualized the future jobs he'd lose with the distributors in Cape Town.

"Slowly," the captain cried while the crane lowered a hook above the cargo net. Getting the hook to thread the support straps of the net took much longer than usual since the swells swung it dangerously back and forth. Eventually a crew member climbed atop the crate and fitted the hook to the cargo loops by hand. Before raising the crate even a foot off the deck, the captain knew they had problems. It swung wildly beneath the fulcrum of the crane. Eased into a rhythm by the swell, the pendulum effect grew more pronounced. Before the captain could shout to the winch man, the crate slammed twice into the crane's base.

"Put it down. Down!" the captain ordered.

Inside the crate, the straps that held the device upright in its container continued to strangle it. The lowest belt, however, was losing its grip on the base of the machine. The strap began to creep upward.

The cargo crashed onto the deck just a few feet from where it sat before.

While his men once again secured the crate to the deck of the ship and covered the wooden box with a heavy tarp, the captain turned to Dorn. His hands still shook in anger. Why did wealthy people find it so impossible to trust someone else's judgment?

"It's too difficult now," the captain said. "Just like I said."

"When can you get it below?" Dorn asked.

"A few hours. We're passing through the tail end of this."

"Fine," Dorn said, irritated. "But I want it doubly secured to the deck. This is an unbelievably important piece of machinery. You understand?"

"Yes," the captain said. "I understand."

Beneath the black tarp, cradled in the confines of the wooden crate, the fusion generator seemed suddenly aware of its own importance. The panels on its front twinkled to life, teasing the dark with colorful thrusts of illumination. Small beacons came on-line, beacons that remained undetected by anyone outside.


The ocean spread to infinity. The midmorning haze kept visibility to under ten miles. For forty minutes Jack scanned the blue mat beneath the chopper but found absolutely nothing. He had just decided on plan B when Ricardo bolted upright in the copilot chair. His eyes were glued to the remote sensor in front of him. "Jack!"

Jack unbuckled his shoulder harness and slid behind the throttle controls next to Ricardo. A lump formed in his throat. "Is something happening?"

"More than something," Ricardo said. He held up the remote sensor. Light blue waves undulated wildly. The signal got stronger when Ricardo pointed the device south. "We've got them!"

"Where?" Jack demanded.

"Just southeast of our present position," Ricardo said. "That's the good news."

"What's the bad news?"

Ricardo's hands shook. The sensor squealed. "The readings are stronger than anything I've seen so far. A hundred times stronger than the readings I took when the device booted up."

Jack paused. "What exactly does that mean?"

"I think it's charging," Ricardo said.

"Charging?"

The two men held each other's gaze.

Jack pointed his pistol at the pilot. "Follow that signal. Now!"

Kirby ran into the War Room. "We've found it, sir!"

McFadden, half asleep in a chair in front of the monitoring station, jerked forward. He rubbed his eyes.

"Where is it?" Wright demanded, putting on his spectacles.

"Forty-two miles off the coast of Brazil," Kirby said, still shaking from his run.

"Don't lose that signal," Wright said. "Plane? Ship?"

"Ship, sir."

"Do we have visuals?"

"In just a few minutes, a KH-12 will make a pass a few miles away," Kirby said. "We're prepping for pictures now."

Wright stood up. "I want a rundown on our tactical capabilities within a thousand miles of the ship's position. Put all forces in the region on alert."

Kirby nodded and left the room.

The director turned. "You were right, John."

McFadden grinned. This mission would make him, he thought. "I think we have a carrier group near Argentina, sir. I'll notify Admiral Lilly."

"Good," Wright said. "Take them to battle ready."

The helicopter had gotten within two hundred yards of the ship before the radio crackled in Ricardo's headset.

"They want to know what the hell the chopper's doing out here," Ricardo said.

Jack motioned to the pilot. "Tell them in their rush they left a steel case and you're here to return it. You didn't want to break radio silence. Make it convincing," Jack said. "If you don't we're putting down anyway."

The pilot hesitated, gathering his thoughts.

Finally he repeated the message into his headphones. After an unbearable wait Ricardo finally caught Jack's gaze.

"We've got the go-ahead to put down," Ricardo said.

"This is it." Jack patted Ricardo's shoulder. His friend's robust tan had been drained to a jaundiced saffron. "Promise me something."

"Anything."

"Get yourself help first," Jack said. "Then worry about us."

Ricardo shifted his foot painfully. "Nothing a fiery Latin blood transfusion won't cure."

Jack looked at Ricardo. "I mean it."

"I know."

Jack walked back into the cargo area to prepare the empty case.

He could see nothing in the blackness.

His damp palm made the stock of the pistol slippery. He dried his hand on his shirt then tightened his grasp around the 9mm. Hidden inside the steel case, Jack could only imagine the sensation of the chopper descending onto the helipad of the trawler. In reality, he felt nothing until the helicopter jolted on the listing deck of the ship. Jack's heart hammered, on pace with the thumping rotors that cracked the air above like giant eggbeaters.

His left shoulder was jammed into the side of the case. Someone was sliding it across the cargo bay. Like a rock climber wedged into a crevasse, Jack pressed his arms and legs against the sides of the container to prevent his body from moving. He prayed that Dorn's men wouldn't dally too long with the pilot, wouldn't recognize Ricardo beneath his aviator glasses, flight helmet, and green jumper. He prayed that somehow he would manage to find Samantha still alive, that together they could find the fusion generator before it headed for God knows what.

The case was lifted, then banged down.

The impact jarred the wind from his diaphragm. They dropped the chest, Jack thought. He struggled against panic—his inability to breathe was compounded by the dark, tight space. *Calm. Calm. Just wait. You'll breathe.* But Jack's lungs refused to take air. His mind became muddled just when it had to be razor sharp.

"It's bloody heavy," he thought he heard a voice say. *Breathe, dammit, breathe.*

Jack heard one latch on the case open. Not now, he thought. Not when he had no breath. The sound of the helicopter faded away. Jack forced a quick gasp just before he heard the snap of the second latch. His stomach knotted tightly.

The lid was raised.

# PICASSO

Wright stared at the overhead display in silence.

The War Room held twice the number of agents it normally did, but an uneasy quiet filled the space. On the overhead display system a colored photo-image beamed down to them like a futuristic Picasso. Taken by a nearby satellite, the remote sensing image showed the position of the ship at sea within the surrounding electromagnetic spectrum. The ocean appeared dark blue—almost black. The coast of Brazil appeared yellow, rivers light blue. What bothered the director was the fuzzy mass of green that surrounded a small area in the ocean.

"What you're seeing is the entire electromagnetic spectrum in the area," Kirby said and wiped his forehead with a tissue. "The green-shaded portion indicates an electromagnetic disturbance. It occupies a fairly large area around the ship."

"And do we have pictures of the vessel?" Wright asked.

McFadden held open a file with the latest satellite photos. "Our KH-12 came closest on a pass twenty minutes ago."

Wright picked up the black-and-white, digitally enhanced image of an ocean trawler. A few workers appeared as pinkie-size people. A tarp covered something on the bow.

"We picked up the heaviest electromagnetic readings from the bow of the ship," Kirby said, looking over McFadden's shoulder.

"It's still charging?" Wright asked.

"Yes, sir." McFadden paused. "Exponentially. Sir."

Kirby motioned to a team of analysts in white lab coats who huddled behind a small alcove of telecommunications equipment. They seemed nervous. The dark, foreboding world of the War Room could do that to the uninitiated, McFadden thought. They briefed the director on the latest electromagnetic readings.

"According to our experts, it seems to be approaching critical mass," Kirby said.

Wright put down the photos. "Critical mass?"

"The point where intense fusion chain reactions become possible," McFadden said.

"I know that," Wright said, annoyed. "Our hydrogen bombs use a detonator—a fission explosion—to generate enough heat and temperature to induce the fusion reaction." He took a few paces across the floor.

"If it's a tactical weapon—an H-bomb—something we haven't seen before," Wright said, "what would happen if it reached this critical mass?"

"We've already run a few programs," Kirby answered. "Some postulations. If what we're detecting is a fusion weapon, it would have the force of a 2,200 kiloton hydrogen bomb when it reached critical mass."

The overhead displays dimmed. A new global map outlining the Atlantic Ocean and the South American coast appeared on the screens. A green triangle with coordinates marked the ship's position. Faint ghosts of that same triangle traced the ship's route from the coast.

Wright took off his glasses and wiped his forehead on his sleeve. He remembered what the 20,000-ton fission bombs had done to Japan. He knew what a 100-kiloton weapon like the one the Russians atmospherically tested could do to the entire District of Columbia and its three surrounding states.

"Sir, we can give you an idea of the affected area."

Wright nodded.

Kirby spoke to one of the analysts, who punched in commands on the central computer monitor. The room dimmed again. The red glow from the overhead image drenched the entire room in crimson, as if the underground bunker had become a photography darkroom.

The entire space hushed.

All thirty-two people stopped their business and stared at the overhead display. Red concentric circles radiated from the light green marker, which represented the ship. The widest circle covered most of Brazil.

Wright cleared his throat. "My God . . ."

"Those rings are the shock zone, sir. Obviously the force at the epicenter will be greatest with the energy dissipating through each successive zone. Those are the figures if the device detonates from a position forty-two nautical miles off the coast of Brazil. The initial shock wave will make landfall. We figure sixty percent of the rain forest. Potential casualties . . ." Kirby's voice cracked. "Excuse me. Well, the two major coastal cities—São Paulo and Rio. And then the capital, Brasília."

"Those cities probably have a population over eighteen million," Wright said. "What the hell are you saying?"

"Because we aren't familiar with the actual device generating the signature we've played things a bit conservative—assumed there would be survivors in those cities."

"Assumed?"

"In the short run, four to six million casualties. Medium term—probably double that."

For the first time in his two years as the director of operations, Wright noticed the blowing of the air-conditioning unit. A paper fluttered on a desk. The only other sound came from the cooling fans behind the overhead units.

"Of course the long-term effects would be global, sir."

The director wobbled, almost imperceptibly, McFadden saw. In the office behind them, an aide held a red phone linked by its cord to the center console of the desk.

"The president's holding, sir," the man said.

Wright cleared his throat and walked toward the office.

# DECISION

Daylight blinded Jack.

He couldn't breathe—he couldn't see, but he had to make his move. Before the trunk lid opened fully, Jack fired six rounds from the Glock. Two shapes fell.

In another second Jack was out of the case and on his

knees on the deck of the ship. He blinked, waving the gun to both sides, checking for anything that moved. His breath came in painful contractions. On the ground next to him, Baines stared at him with lifeless eyes. A quarter-size hole in the man's upper chest fed a growing pool of blood. Jack kicked away the automatic weapon next to him.

He found the other man by following a trail of blood. Bleeding from his abdomen, the man was alive but unconscious, lying behind the aluminum cases that held the extraterrestrials and the precious fossil from Mali. Jack recognized him as one of Dorn's reinforcements in Bolivia. He grabbed the man's M-5 automatic weapon and ran across the pitching deck toward the superstructure near the stern.

He had to find Samantha!

Wright came out of the back office with an expressionless face. He had been on the phone with the president for the last ten minutes.

McFadden knew he wanted to appropriate the mysterious device and find out exactly what weapon Dorn had gotten his hands on, but that had been before the device began charging; before the words "critical mass" came into play. McFadden could tell by the director's eyes that something had changed. The agent knew, even before Wright spoke, that the director wouldn't be retrieving anything.

The director looked back at the overhead displays before turning to McFadden. "We're go," he said. "Take the device out. Now."

McFadden hesitated. Then, with the room once again abuzz with activity, he picked up a blue phone and asked to be patched through to Admiral Lilly.

# ATLANTIC

Aboard the carrier USS *Carl Vinson*, fresh from two days of shore leave in Buenos Aires, a half squadron of F-14 Tomcat pilots and their navigators listened to the mission commander in the briefing room. Four GE-powered nuclear turbines hummed through the steel walls of the dark chamber. The mobile reactors pushed the aircraft carrier at a healthy twenty-four knots—six slower than its top speed. CVN 70 had left the muddy, polluted waters surrounding Mar Del Plata behind and now cruised on the open Atlantic.

Over five thousand men and women called the *Carl Vinson* home for months at a time—which is why shore leave kept the sanity of both seaman and pilot alike. But now those two reckless days in BA seemed comatose compared to the exhilaration Lieutenant Dekansky felt. Part of the contingent that flew the complement of over eighty aircraft, Dekansky choked down lukewarm coffee and took notes. The carrier's present location, the commander said, was 342 nautical miles northwest of the target—a civilian cargo vessel smuggling a tactical weapon.

Dekansky's heart raced as he learned the heavier than usual ordnance they'd be carrying—MARK 83 laser-guided bombs. Men below decks were already arming the planes. The mission would be black—national security issues were involved—and the target had to be completely neutralized. He wouldn't be able to tell his wife what he had done, wouldn't even get to brag to his buddies back on the ship. The mission commander gave five pilots their launch order. Lieutenant Dekansky and Lieutenant Hinkel would launch first. Two other F-14s would launch next in a backup wave. A fifth would stand by on the thousand-foot deck.

Nerves dried Dekansky's throat. Briefly he contemplated the scenario if he didn't return. His family would be told that his plane went down on a routine training mission, and Dekansky suddenly grew afraid his unborn son might grow up thinking his father a failure.

The commander finished by wishing the pilots good luck.

The briefing had taken three minutes. There were no questions.

"Let's get it done, gentlemen."

Assisting the carrier group in the Latin American tour of duty, the USS *Vicksburg*, a Ticonderoga-class guided missile cruiser, cut easily through the heavy swell. The ship's four turbines created eighty-six thousand horsepower, pushing the sleek vessel through the rough Atlantic like a knife through Jell-O. The cruiser prepared for launch. The coordinates of the target had been fixed. The captain ordered the stabilizers into position, which would keep the floating missile silo steady. Missile compartment doors pulled back on the bow of the ship. One of the launch tubes had been armed with a TASM nonnuclear missile. The 454-kilogram warhead had a range of over 1,000 nautical miles. The officers and men of the *Vicksburg* began for real the drills they had repeated hundreds of times.

"Twenty-four Romeo one. All systems clear."

"Ordnance armed."

"Inertial guidance functioning."

"Stand by."

Klaxons blared over the ship.

The captain gave the order to fire.

A missile appeared from a billow of smoke in the square firing canister. It paused a split second, guidance fins extended from four sides of the missile, and the weapon traveled at an angle—nose skyward until it reached its cruising altitude of thirty meters. When the nose fell, the vapor trail leveled, and the missile hurtled low across the sea at Mach .07.

The brilliant white plume the Tomahawk left looked glorious in the afternoon sky. The launch went without a hitch. The 358 men on board cheered and hugged one another.

No one knew exactly why they had fired.

# GALLEY

Unaware of the disturbance at the helipad, Dorn talked urgently to Samantha inside the trawler's galley, but nothing he said softened the fury in her eyes. He tried to explain that his destruction of the underground complex was for the benefit of everyone. He hadn't planned for any of the scientists to get hurt, things had just gotten out of control.

"So you leave me to die with the others! You've lost your mind," Samantha said. "You care about nothing! Except that device. It's consumed you."

"I do care for you," Dorn said.

Dorn watched her pull against the plastic riot cuffs that kept her restrained at the galley bench. Red lines from her struggle crisscrossed her wrist. He would try to reason with her once more when she'd had time to rest.

"I'm going to send up the medical assistant to give

you some more Thorazine," Dorn said. "You're going to hurt yourself."

He opened the door to the galley and stepped onto the side deck. A brackish mist from the pitching waves dappled his face. Samantha had made it quite clear that persuading her of the merits of keeping the technology secret was useless.

It upset him just to think it: Samantha wouldn't finish the trip.

Dorn knew that the same stubborn qualities that he once found so attractive in her would be the catalyst for something he dared not think about. If it became necessary he would have it done painlessly—somewhere mid-Atlantic—where the sea and its creatures could claim her corpse. Dorn walked toward his cabin. He was in need of a scotch—self-doubt was not a feeling he was familiar with. It left a horrible taste in his mouth.

Halfway toward the entrance to the officers' quarters Dorn heard a commotion on the deck below. Leaning over the rail, he watched two men fighting. His eyes widened. Anger and panic made his hands tremble as they gripped the siding. One of the men looked like Jack Austin.

# JACK

The sailor's hands felt like a vise. Jack couldn't free himself from the hulking figure that rammed him again into the rails of the ship. Pain spread through his ribs. On the third lunge, Jack's handgun disappeared over the causeway and into the ocean. The whiskers of a four-day beard rubbed against the side of Jack's face as the sailor tried to throw Jack onto the deck. The stock of the automatic weapon, still draped over Jack's back, dug into his spine. He couldn't get to the weapon.

Jack kicked the man off and managed to scramble a few yards down the deck, which pitched to the side, further disorienting him. The sailor chased him, bent at the hip like a linebacker. Jack prepared for a collision. The deck sloped toward him. Again he felt the metal rails on his back and almost without thinking remembered a basic physics principle from high school. *Bodies in motion tend to stay in motion.* With the grace of a matador, Jack grabbed the sailor's shirt and guided him toward the rail. The man's chest only skimmed the top. His howl followed him off the deck and into the wake of the ship.

Samantha's fingers gouged at the restraining bracelet, which peeled the skin off her arm in response. She couldn't allow herself to get sedated. She had to make a move. Beside the galley sink she noticed a carver. It glistened each time the ship rolled. Perhaps she could knock it off the ledge and onto the ground where it would slide to her. Extending her manacled arm, she dropped onto the teak floor. Her shoulder nearly ripped out of its socket, and she stopped, still three feet from the sink. The pain in her wrist was excruciating. Then she noticed a latch to the panel beneath the wooden galley seat—a supply drawer that ran the length of the bench.

Samantha looked around the room. Dorn hadn't returned and the medical assistant was nowhere in sight. With her free hand she opened the latch. Two dirty life vests fell out. With one arm she rifled through the locker. More life vests. But maybe she'd find a first-aid kit with a scalpel or scissors. Her pulse began to race. She didn't have much time. Probing toward the back of the locker,

Samantha's fingers felt plastic, and she made out a red case with a handle.

Momentarily, she forgot about the pain in her wrist. Her fingers groped for the handle. The tips touched. She clawed at the case, trying to knock it down from its perch on the back of the locker. With a lunge, Samantha's nails caught the back edge of the handle and lifted it off the pegs. The box almost fell into her lap. She opened it.

Flares.

She cursed. Nothing inside would cut through her painful bonds. But she might be able to use it. Samantha freed a stubby gun with one hand, then grabbed two flares. She dropped one into the gun and closed the barrel, placing the other flare inside her shirt pocket. She pivoted, hearing a disturbance outside. A scream? *Someone was coming back*. She stuffed the life vests in with her foot, slamming the locker shut just as someone's head passed one of the portholes. She kept the metal flare gun hidden beneath her thigh and held the locker door closed with the back of her heel.

She didn't have time to latch shut the locker because the door to the galley opened.

# LANGUAGE

Jack pushed open the door with the barrel of the M-5 automatic. His eyes scanned the galley. Empty, save for a few tables. He was about to shut the door, when he heard someone call his name.

It sounded like Samantha!

He entered the room and saw her huddled in the far corner. He ran to her.

"Jack?" Tears streamed down Samantha's cheeks. She couldn't speak for a few seconds, as if her breath had left her. "I thought I lost you. . . ."

Jack held her tightly. "Not twice in a lifetime."

He looked around the room. "We have to cut you loose," he said.

"The knife—by the sink."

Jack grabbed the blade. He set the compact submachine gun on the table and knelt over Samantha to cut through the riot cuff.

"Don't move!"

Jack froze at the sound of Dorn's voice behind him.

"Stand up slowly, Jack," Dorn said. "And drop the knife."

Jack did, straightening up with his hands out at his sides. The knife rattled onto the wood floor. Dorn stood in the doorway. He held a pistol—trained at Jack's skull.

"Now back away from the gun, slowly."

Samantha's eyes were wide with fear. She glanced at the automatic weapon—just out of reach on the table— then behind Jack at Dorn.

Jack stepped back slowly. His mind raced to formulate a plan. He knew Dorn would shoot him in the back if he went for the gun, and that he wouldn't have time to rush Dorn before he fired. Dorn had tried to kill him once and would no doubt do it again. The next few seconds would determine whether he lived or died. Maybe Dorn wanted to clear Samantha from the line of fire before pulling the trigger.

"Don't do anything stupid, Ben," Samantha said. "Please."

Dorn didn't answer. He told Jack to step to the left.

Dorn was going to shoot him. Jack could feel it in the pit of his abdomen. In his terror, he barely noticed Samantha's right hand—which was moving almost imperceptibly. His eyes focused.

*She was signing!*

Jack read the ASL letters Samantha signed with her free hand: *U———C———K.*

In the millisecond it took Jack to wonder why she signed "uck" he saw Samantha's other hand pull something from beneath her thigh. He'd missed the first letter . . .

Jack dropped to the floor. Duck!

A flash exploded from the barrel of the flare gun, the missile grazing the top of Jack's head as he fell. He felt its heat and smelled the fumes. Jack heard a gun burst from behind him. The wood next to Samantha splintered. Jack rolled to his right and looked up. The flare had struck Dorn in the chest, knocking him back through the doorway.

The heated projectile bounced off the wall inside the galley, then exploded in a starburst of light. The flash blinded Jack. Thick smoke filled the room. He crawled toward Samantha and found her. The knife lay next to her. Jack cut off her cuff and grabbed the submachine gun from the table. Samantha followed him, coughing. Shielded by the wall, they walked toward the doorway.

Dorn lay on his back, still stunned by the impact of the flare. Particles of sulfur burned holes in his shirt. Jack picked up Dorn's pistol. Before he could stick it in his belt Dorn's leg swiped across the deck, knocking Jack's already unbalanced feet out from under him. Dorn charged. His speed shocked Jack, who couldn't get his arms in front of him in time. The collision sent Jack flying into the galley's outer bulkhead.

The pistol dropped. Daggers of pain tore through the cartilage around Jack's chest. Dorn ripped the M-5 from Jack's left hand. He fell to both knees. The pain in his chest was paralyzing. Dorn aimed the muzzle of the submachine gun.

Jack raised an arm—but there was no gunshot. Instead, Dorn's head rocked forward, and the South African crumpled in front of him, his chin splitting open on the steel deck. Through the smoke, Jack saw Samantha standing over the fallen man, holding her flare pistol by the barrel.

Jack held out a hand to Samantha, who hoisted him to his feet. Dorn lay unconscious, blood pouring from his chin, a knot rising at the base of his skull.

"The other sailors will be here any second," Samantha said in a panic. Heavy red smoke filtered out from the galley toward the pilot-house one deck above.

Jack scanned the gangway. "Where did he put the fusion generator?"

"I'm not sure," Samantha said anxiously.

Jack took her hand. "We have to find it now," he said. "It's charging."

# CHARGE

Wright waited for the news.

An aide at the communications alcove turned to him and said, "The F-14s from the carrier are supersonic." The man paused, listening to the small plastic headphone that led from one side of his face to a boom microphone. "The *Vicksburg* reports no problem with the Tomahawk launch. . . . Bird should reach target in six and a half minutes."

Wright looked at the updated remote sensing image. The green field around the ship had grown dramatically. "Will the missile get there in time?"

"We don't know," Kirby said. The group of analysts hovered over two computer terminals like agitated birds. Sweat beaded down Kirby's neck—a sure sign of a man with no answers. "I don't know what we're dealing with here, sir. A typical hydrogen weapon would have already reached critical mass. This . . . this is like nothing I've ever seen."

McFadden said, "Are you saying if this thing detonates it could be worse than the projections you gave us?"

"That's exactly what I'm saying, sir."

"Are you updating the damage postulations?" Wright asked.

Kirby peered over the other thin analyst at the computer terminal. "We can't update things fast enough."

"What do you mean?"

"The device is still charging exponentially. We can't keep up."

"Sweet Jesus . . ." Wright fell back into his chair. The director looked back at the screen, in the seconds his glance had been averted, the green electrical field had grown.

Sitting behind the director, McFadden felt the urge to vomit. This project was supposed to have made him in the agency. Now it had gotten entirely out of control. His excitement had been replaced with the unfortunate precognition that things were about to go horribly wrong. All he had done was become part of something so terrible that generations would speak about the event only in hushed tones. For the first time since he could remember, McFadden didn't worry about tomorrow.

He didn't know if there'd be one.

Jack thought it might take hours to search the trawler for the device.

It didn't. As soon as he and Samantha reached the bottom deck they felt the intense energy field emanating from the bow. They made their way forward.

The air tasted strange to Jack. It pricked at his pores like an astringent. "The atmosphere's ionizing!" he shouted to Samantha over the sound of the wind and waves. He approached the rippling tarpaulin. Jack had no doubts what sat underneath.

"Something terrible's happening," Samantha said.

"We've got to move fast!" Jack yelled.

Vibrations pulsed from beneath the tarp.

A yellow glow shone on the steel deck of the ship through gaps at the base of the tarpaulin. Jack's fingers tore at the rough cord that held the tarp down. "I can't get it off!" The rope cut his hands as he pulled against the tight knots. He dug his nails beneath the constricted web only to have them bend backward in deep, painful creases.

Samantha looked around the bow of the trawler. She ran to the crane mast and unhooked a wire that had been used for hanging laundry. She fell next to Jack and used the wire to tug at the knot. Jack got his index finger within the widened ring. He pulled viciously. Finally the knot relaxed and fell free.

"Hurry!" he said.

They undid the other tie. This time the knot came loose more quickly. Jack let the rope whip through the deck hoop. A gust of wind lifted the tarp back and folded it onto itself on the other side of the crate.

Jack retrieved an iron winch handle hanging on the crane mast. Slipping its neck between the slats near the corner of the crate, he pried back the small nails, Samantha helping with leverage. The last corner gave way, and the side of the crate fell onto the deck.

Jack and Samantha paused.

Lights flashed all over the device—seemingly in sequence. The machine throbbed with a deep pulse that sent shivers through Jack's body. He felt heat rise from the bottom of the cylinder, but the temperature seemed too cold compared to the massive amounts of energy building inside it. In fact, he saw that the rounded cone top was glazed with ice.

Fire and ice, Jack thought.

He knelt next to *The Source*. A wave of desperation rolled through him. The outline of the top three modules still showed clearly, but the bottom module had become a seamless part of the device. A vinyl strap was wound tightly across the spot where the fourth module would have shown if it hadn't already been incorporated into the machine's surface.

"It's the fourth module!" Jack shouted. The belt must have instigated the process. The doomsday module they feared most had been activated.

Samantha looked in panic. "What do we do?"

"You stand right there and raise your hands up!" a voice shouted behind them.

# IMPEDIMENT

Lieutenant Dekansky's F-14 was supersonic. The wings had folded back toward the tail, creating a streamlined aircraft in the shape of a delta. The jet cut through the air at 1,462 miles per hour. The voice of Dekansky's rear navigator crackled over his helmet intercom: "330 contact." His navigator, sitting behind a priceless radar system, reconfirmed the location of the target on the teal screen.

"Stand by affirmative," Dekansky said.

"Head 035. Over."

"Heading 035." Dekansky banked the plane toward

the target and began the attack flight path. They would be in range within eighty seconds.

The Tomahawk skimmed across the Atlantic barely a hundred feet above the surface. It closed on the trawler at a shade slower than 430 miles per hour, leaving a long vapor trail in its wake. No one noticed how beautiful the guided missile appeared in flight. Or how cameras inside the nose kept it close to the water and safe from radar. Slower than sound, the missile whistled merrily to itself—its steady whine preceding the blur.

The Tomahawk had but one purpose for its short life: track down the object moving forty-six miles northwest of its current position.

Then kill it.

The captain of the trawler held a shotgun on Jack and Samantha. Two other crew members shied away from the humming fusion device.

"Get away from that cargo," the captain said. Jack could see the fear in the man's eyes as he looked at the machine inside the crate. Jack looked at the device, then back at the captain.

"This is going to explode," Jack said. "Any second!"

The crew members behind the captain shifted nervously.

"What are you doing on board?" The shotgun visibly shook in the confused captain's hands.

"If you're going to shoot us," Jack said, "then do it. But I suggest after you do—you get the hell off this ship. Because unless you know how to stop this thing I doubt if there'll be one!"

The two crew members bolted for a red rubber dinghy suspended from wires at the side of the trawler. Jack redirected his attention to the device. If the captain wanted to shoot him he could. If he and Samantha didn't stop the chain reaction the result would be the same. Ice atop the cone broke off in chunks, falling onto the deck.

Condensed moisture beaded over the lower portions of
the extraterrestrial equipment. A puddle formed beneath
the machine. Jack's hands slipped off the cold alloy as
he tried to pry out or deactivate the vanished module.
Samantha joined him, steadying herself on the swaying
deck.

"It won't come loose," she yelled.

The captain hadn't fired, Jack realized. He turned in
time to see him join the two other crew members and
what looked like the chef as they prepared the red Zodiac raft.

Jack pushed at the panels on the module. Nothing
worked. A sequence of large, square lights began activating from left to right across the collar of the machine.
Jack counted nine. Two of them had already been lit.

"What's that?" Samantha screamed.

"I think it means we're running out of time," Jack
said. "Let's see if the device will accept another module!"

Samantha's heart sped. "How?"

Jack positioned himself beside the top drawer of the
device which housed the Mali artifact. "See if we can't
push it in or trigger it to accept the top module instead
of the fourth one. We have to disrupt the process. We
have to get it to change functions!"

Samantha placed her hands on the other side of the
homing module's drawer.

"Steady and slow. We'll only get one shot. Are you
ready?"

Samantha nodded.

"On three," Jack took a deep breath. "One. Two." His
fingers reached out. "Three—"

Their move had been motivated by nothing but desperation. But Jack and Samantha watched in awe as the
seams on the top module morphed into the smooth
curves of the device and disappeared.

The light sequencing paused.

The machine shut down. It grew quiet. *The Source* had been silenced.

Samantha whispered, "Oh my God . . ."

Jack couldn't speak. He waited for the bottom module to re-form. It didn't.

Instead—startling both of them—the device lit up like a Christmas tree. The sequencing had begun again. This time more furiously than before.

In the confusion of the next seconds, Jack realized the device was charging even faster.

# IGNITION

Samantha screamed. The sensation that followed raised the hairs along the nape of her neck. "What's happening?"

Jack's watch slammed into the device, pinning his wrist against the metal. "It's getting magnetized!"

Jack struggled with the clasp and slipped off his watch. Two more square lights on the collar panel illuminated. An energy vortex swirled about him, demanding control of his body. Jack clawed in vain at the top module, but it had disappeared just like the fourth one. Both pieces had integrated into the larger device.

The second-to-last panel light ignited.

At the same time Jack felt a tingling on his scalp. He looked over at Samantha, whose hair had begun to rise on her head. Every follicle along Jack's arms stood up at the command of the electromagnetic tempest that surrounded them.

The last panel light illuminated.

Samantha looked up at Jack. For the briefest moment time seemed frozen—a half second that refused to die. Her eyes conveyed more information in that indelible juncture than she could have spoken in an hour.

The moment shattered like a mirror.

The loose winch handle bounced along the deck and struck the device, remaining suspended on the system's module. The machine had become a giant magnet. Metal objects not securely fastened to the ship began hurtling toward the device. Jack dodged a steel tray as it smacked into the bottom of the generator, followed by the sub-machine gun. Samantha screamed; there was pain in her fillings. She fought the invisible pull. Jack pushed her down. A toolbox flew over Samantha's head.

The anchor chain began to rattle.

Then it happened. A loud crack—like the snap of a massive bull-whip—exploded through the air!

It was followed by a brief, blinding light—a saber of charged particles that burned into space. The brilliant column disappeared almost instantly, transferring the energy back to the ship in the form of an unseen wave, which catapulted Jack and Samantha from the device.

The energy pulse. The burst of color. The twenty yards he traveled airborne above the deck of the ship. They would be the last memories, Jack thought, before he died.


The glare blinded Lieutenant Dekansky a moment before the panel in front of him exploded. The F-14 shuddered. "What the hell was that?" his copilot yelled.

For a millisecond Dekansky thought he had seen the whole sky ignite in a wispy neon palette as an intense beam stabbed through the stratosphere. He fought for control of his aircraft. They had been within twenty seconds of dropping their ordnance and completing their mission. Now klaxons blared throughout the cockpit.

"Complete systems failure!" Dekansky shouted.

"Electromagnetic pulse!" the copilot screamed. "I've lost everything!"

The plane became a metal leaf at the mercy of gravity. Dekansky struggled with the stick but couldn't control the spin. His hand swiped for the ejection handle. Confusion consumed him. He couldn't see. *Where was it?*

A quarter mile to the east, Lieutenant Hinkel's plane fell from the sky like a rock.

Dekansky's navigator screamed, "Eject! Eject!"

Blow the canopy or die, Dekansky thought. In the next instant, the canopy blew in a cascade of sparks. Then the booster rockets beneath his seat shot him to freedom.

A Brazilian fisherman suddenly awoke from a sangría-induced siesta. He thought he heard thunder. The man climbed the ancient wood steps from the cabin. He reached the teak deck just as a silver object exploded into the ocean, just a hundred yards away. A plane. He shouted for his second cousin, who was working on the engine beneath the floor panels.

They cursed and talked. Mainly cursed. Three times the fisherman explained to his skeptical cousin exactly what he had seen. The cousin didn't buy it.

A minute later they watched four white parachutes float down toward the ocean.

# ARRAY

It's been said the controllers at the S.E.T.I (Search for Extraterrestrial Intelligence) research program are some of the top poker players in the country. The heated games played beneath the twenty-seven massive receiving dishes that make up the Very Large Array had become legendary. The plains of San Augustin, just west of Socorro, New Mexico, was a hotbed of casual gaming action.

Half the team still slept—though the late-morning sun had long since finished its conquest of the clear skies. The other half practiced for the annual Pro-Am Poker Tournament, which would be held in two weeks in Reno. Life could get boring at S.E.T.I.—the small VLA science wing that searched for extraterrestrial intelligence—which is why no one even twitched when the rookie radioastronomer ran into the room screaming.

The rookie shouted that he just received a signal.

"Save it."

"Screw you."

A few players flipped him the bird. The joke had gotten beyond old.

Back in the receiving room at the VLA, a controller, who had just thrown off his earphones because of a piercing signal, ran to various monitoring computers. The commotion inside drew a few sleepy scientists and the program director to his side.

"Computer's showing it's definitely a code! This isn't random!"

Another radioastronomer read a spectrum analyzer. "Nothing on Earth generates a signal in this bandwidth. It's nearly off the scale!"

A foreign exchange student from Tokyo said, "I'm getting similar readings."

The director of the program hunched over the monitors. She yelled into the room behind her, "Who has a pinpoint on a quadrant? I wanna know where the signal originated. Which system?"

The entire lab reverberated energy.

Two radioastronomers stood in front of a supercomputer and stared at a readout that spit from a laser printer. One looked speechless. The other said, "You're not going to believe this . . ."

The director ran toward them. "Where the hell did it come from?"

The astronomer swallowed. "It . . . It came from here."

The wave of energy pushed Jack onto a steel vent, which he glanced off before skidding across the deck. His sore ribs took the brunt of the impact. Samantha fell mercifully in a pile of cargo netting. The scientists didn't move. For a few moments they lay where they fell, in shock. A ghostly silence swept over the trawler in the wake of the mercurial event. Jack slowly picked himself up, shaking out the confusion. Eventually his eyes focused. Samantha sat at the base of a pile of nets. He could hear only the muted sounds of the sea now.

The device sat silent. The top of the crate had vaporized in a ring of charcoaled wood that opened to the sky around the generator like a giant portal. Samantha crawled off the pile of net. "What just happened?" she asked.

The bewildered pair walked toward the device. Condensation from the top of the machine meandered onto the deck in small rivulets that Jack's boots spread into thin, watery footsteps. He didn't answer, though he had thought of a possible explanation that made him shiver.

Samantha said, "We did it. The top module must have activated instead of the fourth."

Jack nodded. The power generation must have been incredible, he thought; the steel of the ship's deck had melded onto the bottom of the device. The seams around all four modules were now easily discernible—all deactivated, all waiting. Jack traced the strange, engraved laser script above the top module, which had directed the burst of energy apparently into space. "The Dogons were right . . ."

Samantha looked puzzled. "What do you mean?"

"The chief. He said his people needed the artifact to talk to the Fathers of Knowledge."

"Yeah?"

Jack remembered the fields of Mali—the dry heat, the cooking fires, the enigmatic tribe, the conversation with the Dogon chief. "The Dogons believe they needed the artifact to talk to the Shining Ones," he said.

"Right."

"And they *did* need it, Samantha."

"What do you mean?"

Jack held both of Samantha's hands. "Don't you see? The top module must have served as a homing beacon—a communicator. I think that blast sent some kind of energy pulse into space."

"I remember the sky," she said. "It changed colors . . ."

"Maybe over the course of thousands of years the purpose of the artifact was forgotten but not the basic theme. The Dogons must have integrated the artifact into their religion. That module *was* needed to speak to the Fathers of Knowledge, but not as a sacred symbol of authority for the chief. It wasn't some supernatural gateway to the gods."

"It was an actual piece of communication equipment," Samantha said.

"I think the original humans with the extraterrestrial crew member we found in Mali were told what the device was for . . . and the legend—though slightly mis-construed—was passed down to the present day."

"My god," Samantha said. "A beacon?"

"I think we just sent some kind of *message* . . ."

"An SOS?"

"I don't know."

The two pondered the implications: What was just sent? And to whom?

"We found both pieces of the top module in Mali—thousands of miles from Tiahuanaco. Remember the viewing cube—in one scene a Shining One had left with that module and obviously never returned."

"Killed in the eruption," Samantha said.

"What if they sent someone to collect beryllium be-cause the extraterrestrials needed the isotope for this homing signal or beacon?"

Samantha stared at the device. "And their crew mem-ber never returned . . ."

"They wouldn't have been able to send an SOS," Jack said. "Unable to leave or relay their coordinates, they all eventually died from the virus."

"But not before giving great technological gifts to the local inhabitants," Samantha murmured. "Not before leaving behind the gift of civilization . . ."

Wind whistled through the hoisting crane's steel lines.

Jack smiled. "And not before leaving a piece of them behind—in us," he said. "They molded *sapiens* into ex-istence."

"Jack," Samantha said. "It's perfect."

The War Room in Virginia swarmed with activity. An-alysts in contact with the USS *Vicksburg* fed facts to Kirby, who sat beside Wright in the communication al-cove. McFadden cracked his knuckles and stared at the overhead display. The last remote-sensing image of the area showed only a ghost of the electromagnetic field. The weapon had somehow stopped. They were just receiving the update reports from the mission commanders in the South American theater.

"We're not getting any signs that the device reached detonation. Our people in Brazil report nothing out of the ordinary," Kirby said. He listened to a voice in his earpiece. "The device has shut down, sir."

Relief washed over Wright's face. McFadden whispered, "Thank God . . ."

A sense of deliverance permeated the room. A few people laughed. Others sat silent, blankly staring at the display screens in front of them.

"From what we can figure, the device generated an electromagnetic pulse," Kirby said.

"An EMP?" McFadden slid his chair over.

Kirby cupped a hand over his ear. "The F-14s are down."

"The pilots?" Wright asked.

"Safely ejected, sir."

Vitality pulsed through Wright's veins. He'd be able to appropriate the mysterious device after all. "Detonate the Tomahawk," he said. "I want a Navy retrieval team in the area in thirty minutes. Let's bring this damn thing in."

Kirby relayed the commands to the bridge of the USS *Vicksburg*. He stopped midsentence.

Wright and McFadden hovered over the pasty analyst, concerned.

"What is it?" Wright demanded.

"The Tomahawk, sir," Kirby turned. "The pulse must have taken out its override system."

"What?"

Kirby turned. "The missile's not responding, sir."

Wright slid into a leather chair, his facial expression resigned.

"Ninety seconds to impact."

Wright stared at the overhead display and took off his glasses—a beaten man with no options. "Well, whatever that thing was," he said, "it won't be much longer."

*    *    *

As Jack inspected the melted steel beneath the device he realized why mica had been used on the floors of the temple. The warped steel fused completely around the underside of the fusion generator.

"It's welded onto the ship," Samantha said.

The whistling of the wind had increased dramatically. Jack wondered about a storm, but the sky was cloudless as far as he could see. Looking out over the horizon he saw something low to the water—a jagged trail that rose into the sky on the crosswinds.

Samantha noticed too. "Is that a plane?" she said.

"Too low," Jack responded.

The whistling got louder.

"Oh, God. No," Jack said.

"What is it?"

"A missile."

Samantha looked panicked. "The fossil—the extraterrestrials! Everything's on board!"

Jack tried frantically to free the device from the deck of the ship. The exhaust plume closed in fast. "Leave it!" Samantha screamed. She grabbed his arm. Jack's instincts took over. He ran toward the stern. Samantha kept pace. The two reached the back of the trawler. Jack passed over a chain-link barrier between protective rails. He looked at Samantha and took her hand.

Then they leaped over the stern.


Dorn's chin adhered to the causeway in his own drying blood. Finally, he managed to lift his head. His neck ached. His palm made a perfect imprint in the sanguine puddle as he pushed himself off the deck.

A swell made him falter. Dorn grabbed the rail to steady himself and stumbled forward toward the bow. He had only a disjointed recollection of prior events. A struggle. He was on his ship now, that he knew. But his sixth sense troubled him, panicked him. He reached the edge of the superstructure that looked out over the bow of the trawler. To his delight he saw the precious machine. *But who had uncovered it?*

Sunlight attacked his eyes and made him wince. His ears rang. Or rather, he thought, whistled . . .

The frothy white foam from the props rushed toward them.

Jack hit the water first. Bubbles surrounded him. His ears exploded with pain. The cold tore through his system; his body demanded air. He kicked toward a gleam somewhere above him. His wet clothes felt like anchors. Jack broke the surface and gasped, spitting salty water from his mouth and nose. A second later, Samantha surfaced behind him, in the roiling propwash.

Jack kicked over to her and wrapped her shivering body with his arm. She pressed herself close to his chest. The trawler continued forward.

An instant later, the whistle grew to a whine.

Dorn saw the missile a fraction of a second before impact. He watched the bow of the ship rupture in a maelstrom of fire. A twelve-yard piece of the starboard side blew free from the hull and skipped across the ocean. The shock wave lifted Dorn off his feet.

Then killed him.

Fifty yards away the ship disappeared in a brilliant white flash.

The cacophony reached them a half second later. Jack buried Samantha's head into his chest and submerged them both. Debris rained over the sea. The pair surfaced just as a black cloud followed the dissipating fireball into the sky. Flaming pieces of material parachuted down to the water, the fragments raising tiny geysers in a wide circle around the ship, which was now ablaze.

Samantha shook in Jack's embrace. "Oh no. Oh no," she breathed.

Treading water in the rise and fall of the south Atlan-

tic, the scientists held each other and watched the broken
ship start to slip beneath the surface. A flaming oil slick
seemed to summon the craft into the depths of perdition.
Dorn's trawler heeded the command. The stern began to
raise out of the water. The bow disappeared in the
bubbling cauldron. The two huge props—still turning—
chopped at the surface of the water before spinning
uselessly in the air. In minutes, the stern stood straight
out of the sea. The scientists watched, trembling with
cold, as the broken ship, the fusion device, all the incredible technology, the proof of the origins of the human race . . . slipped into the fiery slick and disappeared
into the Atlantic.

# OCEAN

The ship had vanished into the sea forty minutes ago.
Jack and Samantha clung to a wooden cabinet that had
floated by them along with a multitude of other debris.
Jack lost sight of the bubbles that had marked the spot
of the trawler's grave.

Everything they hoped to reveal to the world had just
disappeared.

"Why?" Samantha asked.

Jack comforted her, trying to conceal his own feelings
of despair. "At least we know where the ship went down.
Maybe, we'll be able to salvage the fusion device from
the wreck."

"But the bones . . . the extraterrestrials . . ." she said.

"Those cases were airtight, so you never know." Jack

looked into her eyes and felt oddly disconnected from the pain of the loss. He held her shivering body close to his and kissed her as if nothing else in the world mattered.

A thumping echoed from somewhere near the horizon. Appearing from the glare of the afternoon sun, Jack glimpsed two helicopters. One seemed to circle in the approximate place where the ship went down. Another made long runs back and forth above the ocean—as if scanning for possible survivors. Both looked like military aircraft. Within minutes the closest helicopter spotted them. The craft hovered a few hundred feet above them and dropped a bright orange signal flare into the water. The stenciling on the nose of the Sea King helicopter read USN 72. The USS *Carl Vinson*, Jack read on a buoy affixed to the side.

"It's U.S. Navy," Jack said.

"Do you think it was their missile?"

"Had to be," he said. "No one in South America uses ordnance like that."

In the spray of rotorwash two rubber-suited divers dropped into the ocean wearing masks and fins. Within seconds they had paddled over to Jack and Samantha. A large mesh basket appeared out of the open door of the helicopter, and the men on board lowered the rescue harness to the water. The frogmen helped Samantha and Jack into the basket, on either side of the central support bracket. Once inside the helicopter, they were met with warm blankets and two IVs, which a medic applied into veins in their forearms.

"Are you folks all right?" one of the flight crew asked.

Jack nodded, his teeth still chattering. "There was the captain—some crew—in a lifeboat . . ."

"Already picked them up," the airman said.

Neither of them knew of any other survivors.

As the helicopter continued searching the debris field,

Jack and Samantha drank warm coffee from the airman's thermos.

The copilot stepped into the cabin from the cockpit. "I'm glad to see you folks are okay," he said over the howl of the rotors. "Do you think you're up to answering a few questions?"

Jack and Samantha looked at each other.

"Whatever you got mixed up in is pretty important. The captain wants to speak with you as soon as possible. He says there's a friend of yours in sick bay who refuses to talk," he said. "Only repeats his name and his E-mail address."

Jack grinned. "Ricardo."

"That's him," the copilot said. "The man won't say anything until he sees and speaks with both of you. Can I put him through?"

Jack and Samantha slipped on helmets. Over the com system they heard Ricardo's voice, the sweet Latin lilt never sounding so good. They assured their friend that they were fine, and Ricardo put on the captain of the USS *Carl Vinson*.

"Who wants to start?" the captain said into their headphones.

Jack looked at Samantha. Their proof rested on the bottom of the ocean. Jack himself could barely believe the events of the last eight days.

"I'm tired of playing the mad scientist," he finally said to Samantha. "Why don't you give it a shot?"

For a moment, Jack was uncertain whether Samantha would. But she smiled and gripped Jack's cold hand tightly in hers. "You got it," she whispered.

Into the headset she said, "Now I know this might sound crazy. But bear with me."

Jack closed his eyes and listened to her description of a dusty cavern, deep in Mali.

Samantha never once let go of his hand.

# ATLANTIC

Crimson rays fanned the surface of the sea. The radiant dusk illuminated bits of debris like a thousand floating candles. Fish of many shapes and sizes approached the area, drawn by floating scrap and a hundred tons of raw sugar. Beneath a large aluminum case that bobbed defiantly amid the more diminutive bits of flotsam, a school of sardines congregated. Silver streaks darted to and fro beneath the half-submerged trunk, picking at the minutiae that clung to the sides in an oily slick. The fish paid no attention to the stenciled characters on the side of the airtight case that read: PROPERTY OF HELIX CORP. Nor did they give thought to the precious remains within.

Alone on the unending expanse of Atlantic, the container drifted silent and immaterial on the softened notes of a calming sea, beheld by no one, beholden to nothing save the current. Still, with the occasional passing swell—when the sun caught the aluminum case just right—the shiny box bounced brilliant reflections back into space.

# AFTERWORD

The researcher Graham Hancock has said that the human race is a species with amnesia. After eighteen months of research, I would have to agree with him. Scientists from such diverse fields as astronomy, archaeology, engineering, geology, mathematics, paleontology, and mythology have uncovered mountains of new evidence, all suggesting that the history of our species, as we've come to understand it, might be drastically wrong. In fact, a paradigm shift has already begun—one that will forever change the way we see our past. Nothing is more exciting than witnessing the embryonic stages of a scientific revolution before it is borne out by scientists en masse, or accepted by the public at large. Woven through *Link* is a matrix of actual places, peoples, myths, and scientific anomalies that are central to this revolution—anomalies that respected scientists all over the globe have found too compelling to ignore any longer. I sure couldn't.

One has to ask oneself, for instance, how the Dogons, a primitive tribe in Mali, have known for thousands of years that a dense star circled the larger star Sirius every 49.9 years? Western scientists only learned of the second star—Sirius B—when Alvan Clark discovered it with a high-powered telescope near the turn of the century. Furthermore, the Dogons knew the star was much denser than Sirius, making it a white dwarf—a fact only discovered in 1915. The tribe never possessed even the simplest telescope, yet also knew the exact number of Jupiter's moons, and were fully aware—long before modern science—that Saturn has rings. How?

We find enormous megalithic stone blocks all over the globe so heavy—some weighing over six hundred tons—that modern engineers can't figure out how one would move them today in one piece. Yet primitive humans—who supposedly had no access to combustible engines, the power of the atom, electricity, or even the wheel—cut and placed these massive objects with laser precision. How ancient humankind accomplished these engineering feats has yet to be explained.

Nor can we explain the existence of the Piri Reis map. Authenticated by scientists and historians, the map shows parts of the coastline of Antarctica perfectly, which is truly fantastic because the map was drawn in 1513—over three hundred years before Antarctica was even discovered. The maker of the map, a Turkish admiral, said he based his map on source maps collected from even earlier cartography. But where did this information come from? Even more disturbing, the map, and a few others like it, showed parts of the coast that are now buried under almost a mile of ice. Western science confirmed the coastal detail after a seismic survey was performed in 1949, which means that the original map had to have been made when Antarctica was free of ice—a period anywhere from six thousand to thirteen thousand years ago. But civilization wasn't even established back then, right?

And how did our primitive ancestors know that the celestial dome was fixed—and that the planets revolved around the sun? How did they know of a complicated aspect of celestial mechanics called precession—a wobble of the earth's axis that causes our position relative to constellations in space to change slowly over time? Western astronomers discovered this only three hundred years ago. Even more incredible is that this effect takes thousands of years to measure—25,776 years to be exact. Yet our ancestors called one complete cycle of this effect a Great Year. Baffling, because according to today's notions, civilization hasn't been around for even a quarter of one cycle. How did the ancients ever learn to measure it? Who taught them?

Mathematicians have discovered that the units of measurement in many ancient cultures seemed based on the circumference of the planet. But how? We didn't confirm the circumference of the globe until the first satellites in the fifties mapped the irregularities of the earth's shape as they circled it in space.

However one chooses to explain these anomalies—and hundreds of others—one thing is certain: Somehow, mysteriously and overnight, our ancestors acquired miraculous skills and knowledge in engineering, astronomy, agriculture, and mathematics. Civilization appeared from nowhere—and all at once. What was the root of this explosion? And more important, what was the physical link between our species, *Homo sapiens*, and our ancestors *Homo erectus*? That unanswered question is still at the heart of paleoanthropology—something radical must have happened. We are more than a foot taller than our forebears and have pronounced chins. We lack the massive ridges on our foreheads. Our teeth and bones are remarkably delicate for our height—in fact, our skulls are barely five millimeters thick—nothing like those of our thick-skulled ancestors. Then there are the defining characteristics of intelligence, self-awareness, culture, and spirituality—traits our species does not share with any predecessor. Plainly put, an enormous remodeling job has taken place in the equivalent of an evolutionary millisecond.

Perhaps the answer lies in the resonating human myths that scientists are just now starting to fully understand. Identical myths from cultures across the globe all seem to be giving us the same answers—as long as we are willing to listen. And the bulk of these answers might come in the countless legends documenting the existence of a group of mysteriously embodied beings called the "Shining Ones."

No matter what they were called by each culture, their description remained the same. They were considerably taller than the local people, and had strangely shining faces and large, brilliant eyes. Whoever they were, myths from both sides of the Atlantic tell how these godlike creatures performed great acts of magic—were able to levitate stones and heal the sick. They benevolently taught the local inhabitants the cornerstones of civilization—writing, metalworking, agriculture, engineering, and medicine. They were even said to have impregnated the daughters of man in order to create a new kind of conscious being.

Who were they? Where did they go? And did they really leave such an incredible legacy? Someday, if science continues to unravel these mysteries, the truth will be fully known—and it just might be stranger than fiction.

# BIBLIOGRAPHY

Angela, Piero and Alberto. *The Extraordinary Story of Human Origins.* New York: Prometheus Books, 1993.

Atkins, P. W. *The Second Law: Energy, Chaos, and Form.* New York: Scientific American Books, 1994.

Bauval, Robert, and Adrian Gilbert. *The Orion Mystery.* London: Wm. Heinemann, 1994.

Bellamy, H. S. *Built Before the Flood: The Problem of the Tiahuanaco Ruins.* London: Faber & Faber, 1943.

Campbell, Joseph. *The Hero with a Thousand Faces.* London: Paladin Books, 1988.

Chatelain, Maurice. *Our Ancestors Came from Space.* New York: Doubleday, 1978.

Clawson, Patrick L., and Rensselaer W. Lee III. *The Andean Cocaine Industry.* New York: St. Martin's Press, 1996.

Cremo, Michael A., and Richard L. Thompson. *Forbidden Archeology: The Hidden History of the Human Race.* Govardhan Hill Inc., 1993.

Crick, Francis. *Life Itself.* London: Macdonald, 1981.

Darwin, Charles. *The Descent of Man.* London: John Murray, 1901.

Darwin, Charles. *The Origin of Species.* London: Penguin, 1895.

Davis, Kathleen, and Dave Mayes. *Killer Bees*. New York: Dillon Press, 1992.

DeBeer, Gavin. *Homology: An Unsolved Problem*. London: Oxford University Press, 1971.

Denton, Michael. *Evolution: A Theory in Crisis*. London: Burnett Books, 1985.

Eden, Murray. *"The Inadequacy of Neo-Darwinian Evolution as a Scientific Theory."* Massachusetts Institute of Technology conference paper, 1967.

*Encyclopedia of World Mythology and Legend*. New York and Oxford: Facts on File, 1988.

Filby, Frederick A. *The Flood Reconsidered: A Review of the Evidences of Geology, Archaeology, Ancient Literature and the Bible*. London: Pickering and Inglis, 1970.

Godwin, Malcolm. *Angels: An Endangered Species*. New York: Simon & Schuster, 1990.

Hancock, Graham. *Fingerprints of the Gods*. New York: Crown Trade Paperbacks, 1995.

Hapgood, Charles H. *Earth's Shifting Crust: A Key to Some Basic Problems of Earth Science*. New York: Pantheon Books, 1958.

Hapgood, Charles H. *Maps of the Ancient Sea Kings*. Philadelphia and New York: Chilton Books, 1966; London: Turnstone Books, 1979.

Heppenheimer, T. A. *The Man-Made Sun: The Quest For Fusion Power*. Boston: Little, Brown and Company, 1984.

Hoffman, Michael. *Egypt Before the Pharaohs*. London: Michael O'Mara Books, 1991.

Itzkoff, Seymour W. *Triumph of the Intelligent: The Creation of Homo Sapiens Sapiens*. Ashfield, Mass: Paideia Publishers, 1985.

*Jane's Fighting Ships: 1993–94*, ed. Richard Sharpe.

Surrey, England: Jane's Information Group, 1994.

Kuhn, Thomas. *The Structure of Scientific Revolutions.* Chicago: University of Chicago Press, 1962.

Leakey, Richard E. *The Making of Mankind.* London: Michael Joseph, 1981.

Lewin, Roger. *In the Age of Mankind* (A Smithsonian Book of Human Evolution). Washington, D.C.: Smithsonian Books, 1988.

Mallove, Eugene F. *Fire from Ice: Searching for the Truth Behind the Cold Fusion Furor.* New York: John Wiley & Sons, Inc., 1991.

Mayr, Ernst. *Population, Species and Evolution.* Cambridge, Mass: Harvard University Press, 1970.

Mendelssohn, Kurt. *The Riddle of the Pyramids.* London: Thames & Hudson, 1986.

Milton, Richard. *Shattering the Myths of Darwinism.* U.S. ed. Rochester, Vt: Park Street Press, 1997.

Morales, Waltraud Q. *Bolivia: Land of Struggle.* Boulder, Colo: Westview Press, 1992.

Owen, Weldon. *The First Humans.* New York: HarperCollins, 1993.

*Pears Encyclopaedia of Myths and Legends: Oceania, Australia and the Americas,* ed. Sheila Savill. London: Pelham Books, 1978.

Pfeiffer, John E. *The Emergence of Humankind.* New York: Harper & Row, 1985.

Plato. *Timaeus and Critias.* London: Penguin Classics, 1977.

Posnansky, Arthur. *Tiahuanacu: The Cradle of American Man,* 4 vols. New York: J. J. Augustin, 1945.

Prideaux, Tom, and editors of Time-Life Books. *The Emergence of Man: Cro-Magnon Man.* New York: Time-Life Books, 1973.

Sagan, Carl. *Broca's Brain.* New York: Random House, 1979.

Santillana, Giorgio de, and Hertha von Dechend. *Hamlet's Mill.* Boston: David R. Godine, 1992.

Schoch, Robert. Excerpts from AAAS Annual Meeting, 1992, debate: "How Old is the Sphinx?"

Sellers, Jane B. *The Death of Gods in Ancient Egypt.* London: Penguin, 1992.

Sheldrake, Rupert. *Seven Experiments That Could Change the World.* London: Fourth Estate, 1994.

Shulsky, Abram N. *Silent Warfare: Understanding the World of Intelligence.* Brasseys, Inc., 1985.

Smith, Norman F. *Millions and Billions of Years Ago: Dating Our Earth and Its Life* (A Venture Book). New York: Franklin Watts, 1993.

Stanley, Steven M. *Children of the Ice Age: How a Global Catastrophe Allowed Humans to Evolve.* New York: Harmony Books, 1996.

Sullivan, George. *Elite Warriors: The Special Forces of the United States and Its Allies.* New York: Facts on File Books, 1995.

Temple, Robert K. G. *The Sirius Mystery.* Rochester, Vt: Destiny Books, 1987.

West, John Anthony. *Serpent in the Sky.* New York: Harper & Row, 1979.

## OTHER SOURCES

*The Mysterious Origins of Man,* produced by Bill Cote, Carol Cote, and John Cheshire. Broadcast by NBC Network TV in February 1996. New York: BC Video.

# Edgar Award Winner
## STUART WOODS
*New York Times* Bestselling Author of
### *Worst Fears Realized*


### GRASS ROOTS
**71169-/ $6.99 US/ $8.99 Can**


### CHIEFS
**70347-5/ $6.99 US/ $9.99 Can**


### RUN BEFORE THE WIND
**70507-9/ $6.99 US/ $8.99 Can**